THE ENCELADUS MISSION

THE ENCELADUS MISSION

Hard Science Fiction

BRANDON Q. MORRIS

BRANDON Q.
MORRIS
HARD SCIENCE FICTION

Contents

Part 1: The Path

July 17, 2031, NASA

THE ROOM WAS HUSHED in anticipation. All eyes in Mission Control were upon the woman everyone referred to as MOM. Her moniker, an acronym from the more formal title of 'Mission Operations Manager,' was derived from the name tag someone had at one point playfully taped to her screen. Martin was sitting upright in order to see her beyond his monitor. She was almost as old as his mother. Positioned at her station, MOM adjusted her old-fashioned headset and spoke clearly into the microphone, her voice betraying signs of nervousness.

"Carrier signal received. Waiting for telemetry data."

Nothing happened for several seconds. Someone rustled a piece of paper. The sound of a popping knuckle was heard. Half a minute went by before the silence was again broken, this time by the transmitted voice of a man with an unmistakably Spanish accent.

"Carlos Fuentes, Missions Operations Team, Deep Space Network."

The transmission was as scratchy as if he was calling

from Mars. However, Martin knew Fuentes was in Madrid, sitting in front of a monitor similar to those here at NASA.

"What have you got for me?" asked Fuentes.

MOM almost whispered, "Symbol length correct," the headset microphone close to her mouth. It was so quiet her every word was clearly heard.

The way this was said did not make it clear whether it was a question or a statement. She stared expectantly at her own screen as if something could be seen there. The liberating answer, though, would have to come through her headphones from Fuentes, who was the first human on this planet to see the data arriving at Deep Space Network.

"Symbol length correct," he replied.

MOM was smiling as she repeated out loud what Fuentes had said. "Symbol length correct."

It was easy to tell she was happy, because the pitch of her voice had gone up with each spoken word. She had said it much louder to all present in Mission Control, even to Martin, despite the fact he was certainly the least important person here.

The calm, quiet voice of the man sitting next to MOM announced, "Data arriving." He had touched the keyboard of his computer and launched a program that now scrolled the data, coded in the hexadecimal format, from top to bottom across the screen. AE00020F A02F2F00…. Comforting numerical magic. No one could interpret these values without the help of a computer, not even Martin.

MOM suddenly spoke loudly and triumphantly. "Confirming. We are receiving telemetry data."

This was the sign everyone in Mission Control was waiting for. Everyone jumped up, cheering and applauding. Martin participated, as he moved the corners of his mouth upward into a smile, clapping his hands. He had learned how to behave in these situations.

"Systems, as soon as you have sufficient data, I am going to need status reports," MOM said.

The applause faded away. Immediately, a clattering routine resumed, filling the room.

"MOM, RF is reporting."

"RF, please report."

"RF reports transmission power nominal, telemetry nominal, radio system nominal."

"Confirmed, RF, everything nominal."

RF was the satellite's radio system.

"MOM, ELF-AI is reporting."

Martin instantly recognized the voice coming from the loudspeaker. It was a man located a few offices further down the corridor. He was responsible for the AI, the artificial intelligence. He, too, sounded as if he was calling from Mars.

"Go ahead, ELF."

"I am happy to report that ELF-AI is reporting no deviations. None of the emergency programs have been activated."

He could have said that in fewer words, Martin thought. *How inefficient!* MOM wrinkled her forehead, as if she had heard his thoughts.

"MOM, C&DH here."

"Go ahead, C&DH."

The voice vibrated with nerves. Martin knew this speaker, too. It was that of a programmer who must have been at NASA for a long time to have reached the position of System Manager for Command & Data Handling. This man did not seem to relish a public performance. He knew

5

everything happening here was live-streamed to the internet.

"C&DH reporting nominal status. All SSR pointers are where they should be, which means that we are receiving exactly the data we expected."

Under normal circumstances, this explanation would have been unnecessary. Everyone in the room knew how the nominal status of a satellite subsystem was determined. Martin had helped to debug the software for the SSR Pointer Tracker that monitored the status of the two independent solid-state recorders, or SSRs, on the space probe.

"Confirming data as expected."

"MOM, GNC for *ELF* here."

"Yes, GNC, go ahead."

"Complete hardware functional, all guidance systems nominal, all engine thrusts recorded."

"Excellent, GNC."

The Guidance, Navigation, and Control System was functioning, so the probe was able to head for its target.

"MOM, Propulsion has a status report."

"Go ahead, Prop."

"All propulsion systems nominal. Tank pressure as expected at 326.5. We can go on. Enceladus is waiting."

"Confirmed. Thanks, Prop."

MOM flashed a deep, contented smile. The probe—her probe—had come a long way. Martin had been a schoolboy when it was initially launched. MOM must have been waiting for this moment ever since.

"MOM, Power at ELF-1 here."

MOM squared her shoulders. "Yes, MOM here."

"All power supply data nominal. RTG is providing the necessary power."

Martin remembered the protests by the environmentalists prior to launch. The Radioisotope Thermoelectric Generator, or RTG, contained a large amount of radioactive plutonium. If something had gone wrong during launch.... But it was an absolute necessity because the sun did not provide sufficient energy for solar cells across such a long distance.

"Thanks, Power."

"MOM come in."

"Yes?"

"Thermal reporting nominal values. All temperatures in the green."

Seven subsystems. Martin had physically counted along, he just now realized. He looked at his fingers. Except for three on his left hand, all were stretched out.

"PI here. Do you read?"

MOM raised her voice to the Principal Investigator. "PI, we have a healthy ship. Data arriving. Minus 20 to capture by Saturn. Folks, this will be our first visit to Saturn in 27 years. Mission Operations, out. At least for today. And thanks to all of you."

MOM was obviously touched, as was fitting for a mother.

THE NEXT MORNING, Martin's own mother called. She thought she had briefly seen him on a German television newscast. The whole world had eagerly watched the launch of the *ELF* probe to Saturn. NASA, ESA, and JAXA had promised awe-inspiring pictures following the probe's arrival at the ringed planet in 2031. At that moment, no one anticipated the sensational discoveries that would radically change mankind's beliefs, and would eventually force Martin into a gloomy stinking tin can hurtling at frightening speed through the most inhospitable environment of all—space.

But there was still a long path ahead of him.

August 14, 2033, Earth

THE PRESS CONFERENCE started with a few introductory words by physicist Stephen Hawking, who had died fifteen years earlier. The organizers had used a collection of Hawking's writings to train an AI to express the same enthusiasm the well-known and respected researcher would probably have expressed about this project.

Time had somehow heard of the event beforehand. Their title story promised a sensation to be announced by NASA and ESA in the coming weeks. Reporters must have listened to the scientists chatting in the bathrooms. 'Life in Space—We Are Not Alone,' the news magazine proclaimed in large, bold font. However, the headline was too good to be true. The article could only hint at what was behind the invitation to a press conference in an auditorium at MIT, sent out jointly by the scientific magazines *Nature* and *Science*. Martin watched the stream with a time delay and a pause button because he wanted to listen at his leisure.

After the pseudo speech by Hawking, the two female editors-in-chief of these publications simulated a dialog that was obviously not directed at the scientists present, but to a worldwide audience. The editor of *Nature*, who appeared to be about twenty years older than her colleague at *Science*, had brought along a lab rat that sat calmly on her shoulder.

"What is life?" she asked, first looking at the audience and then at her colleague. "Is this sweetie here," she continued, taking the rat from her shoulder and petting it, "alive?"

"Yes. Certainly, it is. You can see that at once," said the editor of *Science*, reaching into her lab coat. Martin thought the costumes were ridiculous. *Editors-in-Chief do not work in labs, they work in offices.* "And this gorgeous emerald," said the woman from *Science* as she held up a shimmering green crystal of impressive size, "is this *alive*?"

"It's certainly not!" The editor of *Nature* did not even look at it, but addressed the audience as if to ask for confirmation.

The other woman raised her eyebrows. "Ahh, but it grew by natural means from a seed crystal. Not out in nature, but in a lab—then again, your rat was probably not born in the sewers, either. And while my stone grew and thrived, it also created order, and thus increased the disorder or entropy in its environment. Those are features of life, aren't they?"

"And that's the problem with the definition of life," explained the editor of *Nature*. "If you see it in action, you think you can immediately recognize it, as you have an idea of what it should look like."

"That is, it should look like you," the younger editor from *Science* replied.

Martin thought the whole show was getting pretty silly. Yet, he knew science needed money—a lot of money—and politicians only approved large grants when the electorate welcomed research.

"Imagine a robot civilization," the *Nature* editor started again. "There are enough examples of this in science fiction. If extraterrestrials sent a spaceship to Earth and they observed a car, what would they consider to be alive? The vehicle? The driver? Would it be so far-fetched in their scrutiny that Earth was dominated by a civilization of clever cars that had constructed organic units to take care of their reproduction?"

Her colleague from *Science* shrugged her shoulders, but did not say anything.

"Well, I just wanted to demonstrate to you the problems our researchers have been facing—and are still facing. Please consider their results in the proper context. Dr. Danielle Shriver of Harvard University will now explain something to us—we are not at all sure what *Elf* found."

Dr. Shriver took her place in front of the audience, beginning by adjusting her glasses. One could see she resented this staged scenario, but she nevertheless played along out of necessity. She started her presentation with the moment when the *ELF* probe—the Enceladus Life Finder, she clarified—had sent its first data. She explained which instruments had measured which molecular forms in which concentrations, how the ECDA, or Enhanced Cosmic Dust Analyzer, had detected hydrocarbon compounds in the geyser-like jets, and how a special instrument on the lander had identified lipids less than a meter below the surface ice. She showed which indicators for amino acids had been found by the mass spectrometer and the fluorescence detector. Most important of all, Dr. Shriver described how the team had concluded through specific computer simulations that these substances were most likely the results of biological processes. This meant they were not caused by random forces, but by a consistent process toward more order, the very antithesis of decay and destruction.

"For this reason, I think I can correct the previous speaker in one aspect. We have found definite signs of life. The probe has detected the digestion by-products of your space rat. Now we only have to catch the little critter itself!"

Dr. Shriver put down the sheet of paper she had only pretended to read from, pushed her glasses upward again, and blinked at the members of the audience as they gave her a well-deserved applause. A cold shiver ran down Martin's spine when he heard this, and he saw the hand-writing on the wall. *Someday, someone will have to travel 1.2 billion kilometers, cross half the solar system, and explore Enceladus,* he thought. At that moment, if anyone had foretold that he would be part of that crew, he would have only given them a pitying smile and said they had a screw loose.

The world was changed forever by this announcement. Not everyone reacted the same way to the certainty of life having developed elsewhere. The majority of the public was enthusiastic about this new discovery, and popular culture of the time reflected this enthusiasm in various ways. Coca-Cola changed the shape of its classic glass bottle. Documentaries described what the scientists had found—or what the producers and journalists thought they had to show to gain attention. Students were streaming into biology majors. NASA received an incredible number of applications for astronaut training. Even the military profited, as many believed fighter pilots had a better chance of getting accepted for a space mission.

The space agencies worldwide stayed surprisingly

calm. Supposedly, NASA, ESA, and JAXA had not prepared manned missions, nor were they planning to do so. No one expected much from the Russians, who had been chronically short of funds since their annexation of Ukraine and the ensuing decade of being excluded from the world economy. Not even the Chinese, who put incredible amounts of money into prestige projects, presented plans for a visit to the life forms on Enceladus. Martin and many space enthusiasts like him were initially deeply disappointed, but in hindsight, this reticence turned out to be a clever strategy.

At first, private space companies used the opportunity created by the reluctance of government agencies. It turned out each major company had already developed plans for a deep space expedition. SpaceX, which was supposed to have arrived on Mars with 100 astronauts a long time ago, suggested converting the spacecraft intended for this mission—which was 90 percent complete —for a smaller crew, but a significantly longer journey. Blue Origin dusted off TransHab, an old NASA project, and planned to launch it into space with its three-stage rocket New Glenn. The Malaysian entrepreneur Amirul bin Yusof, who during the last 15 years had bought up a group of large corporations to create his economic empire —among them the former aerospace leader Boeing— promised to search for the nature of life on Enceladus using an all-Asian crew.

After a few weeks of huge enthusiasm, the first critical voices began to be heard. The media, whose documentaries and features were experiencing declining ratings, and whose audiences were desperate for something new, gave these critics plenty of airtime. Suddenly, the biologists were confronted by talk show hosts firing pointed questions that might be scientifically implausible but could be understood by the common people. Might not this new form of life present a danger to us all? Wouldn't a cell that survived at minus 180 degrees Celsius be far superior to the feeble and fragile life forms on Earth? Might there be a sleeping giant on this moon of Saturn who could be awakened by a visit —with unpredictable consequences?

Worried people are grateful if the state takes care of their problems, while they often distrust entrepreneurs who might not be working in the best interests of the nation or the Earth. To Martin, it seemed as if the space agencies had been waiting for this moment. At a shared event in Peking, they presented the plans of China, Europe, Japan, India, and the United States to the world, and at the end they even presented a special guest. It was the head of the Russian space agency, Roscosmos, who announced they were happy to support this grand vision for humanity, and were all too glad to return to the international stage.

The short period of preparation had not been suffi-cient to develop specific plans. However, the state agencies presented a set of detailed rules to prevent any contamina-tion of Earth—and insisted the space travelers involved would *not* have to be interned on Mars for the rest of their lives, despite a group of U.S. congressmen having demanded so. These governing bodies also had an elabo-rate agreement on the sharing of costs and resources, let alone the glory, so no nation would gain more prestige than the others.

The experts would later work on preparing a mission concept. For the first time in the history of mankind, they promised money would not be an issue—so long as the mission would not eat up more than 80 or maybe 100 billion dollars. The private space corporations soon realized their role in this endeavor would be one of paid service providers.

After all, they had not yet presented a truly convincing concept. For a trip to Saturn, a spacecraft would take approximately six times longer than a trip to Mars. Instead of the 120 days of flight time that Elon Musk, the head of SpaceX, had planned for his spacecraft *Heart of Gold*, the ship to Saturn would need two years just to get there. Zero gravity and cosmic radiation would turn this journey into a suicide mission for the astronauts. Space travelers who returned to Earth as a pulpy mass of bones, or not at all, could not sing the praises of their bosses on talk shows. None of the countries involved wanted that.

Finally, a private company specializing in constructing on-demand satellite accessories succeeded in coming up with a solution. Princeton Satellite Systems, a spin-off of the university of the same name, had developed the Direct Fusion Drive (DFD) using only a small budget. This drive system was based on the nuclear fusion of helium-3 and heavy hydrogen (deuterium). This reaction did not produce any neutrons, which would have turned the material of the reactor radioactive sooner or later. Rather, it produced electrically charged protons and helium ions that could be diverted toward the thruster by using magnetic fields, thus propelling the spacecraft. At the same time, this would also generate electricity—two megawatts, for a total engine output of ten megawatts, the researchers at Princeton Satellite Systems estimated.

The fact that this was merely an estimate initially concerned the leadership of NASA's Jet Propulsion Laboratory, because the DFD system had never been tested in space. Princeton Satellite System had created a 1:1 model in a lab and started it successfully, roughly confirming the projections. However, the DFD had not yet been used as a spacecraft drive. There had been no need for it so far—on a trip to Mars, the flight time was bearable even with conventional engines, and missions to farther targets had always been unmanned, so speed was not as important.

Martin had been partially responsible for the first test of the DFD. He had pointed out 27 bugs in the control software to the head engineer of Princeton Satellite Systems. The Japanese engineer, Hayato Masukoshi, was extremely embarrassed by this discovery, and he offered his immediate resignation to the chief executive officer. To the engineer's surprise, though, he was ordered to test the DFD in the weightlessness of space, together with "this JPL nerd." Some time later, Hayato told Martin that was how the CEO had described him.

October 15, 2037, NASA

MARTIN HAD ALWAYS THOUGHT he was in control of his life. *If I had known a bit of troubleshooting would sentence me to the depths of space, would I have managed to overlook those bugs? A few memory leaks here, a race condition there. 'No one ever died from that,' like Mother would say.* In reality, however, a number of people had died because of such bugs, since software entities had been allowed to act independently in critical areas. India's autonomous robots, for instance, had caused a massacre in a Hindu temple during the Kashmir War. Later, this event had been officially traced to a buffer overflow in the AI. By now the analysis of this source code had become required reading for computer science students. No, it was only logical that Martin found himself here today, even though in retrospect he would never have seen it coming.

Of course, back then it had been no coincidence that his boss had sent him and Hayato to Tiangong-4. At that time, Martin was being considered a secret hero in his department. He felt uncomfortable about it, but it was a fact and could not be undone. All he had done, he thought, was sit around and press the right key at the right time.

Naturally, Martin had fought tooth and nail against this assignment into outer space. "After all, it would be sufficient if the Japanese man flew into space," he argued. Martin believed he would be better able to analyze the data generated by a test run of the drive while sitting comfortably down here in his office, but his boss did not budge. "I haven't even had any basic astronaut training," he reasoned. When he brought up this point, his boss just smiled as he reached into a drawer and pulled out a letter-sized brochure designed in elegant blue.

The Adventure of a Lifetime, Martin read, after his boss had silently handed him the folder. "Blue Origin will take you to the edge of space and back."

Martin had made the mistake of reading the brochure before going to bed. The thin leaflet advertised space trips in the capsules owned by the e-commerce billionaire Jeff Bezos. They looked elegant and sleek, and the passengers wore body-hugging suits of blue material while smiling at the camera. Training, the brochure said, was completely unnecessary. You must spend two days learning about launch, landing, and safety procedures, and then you could go into space. *If only I had researched beforehand who was trying to participate in the Enceladus project,* Martin reflected. It appeared Bezos had reserved two of his spacecraft for transport flights. After a boom in the 2020s, space tourism was no longer as popular as Bezos had hoped.

Martin imagined slowly getting up from his launch couch, carefully floating to the wide observation window, and then... promptly throwing up all of his stomach contents. His fellow passengers would turn away from him, partly disgusted, partly amused, and he would be unable to shake off his vertigo for the duration of the entire flight. Even the mere idea made his innards cramp.

Reality, when it came, turned out to be much worse—and much better. He did not have to vomit, only because his digestive system chose another way out. He had concentrated on his task for 20 hours, the entire duration of the trip. For the whole time he tried to avoid looking into the abyss next to him, below him, behind him, and above him. He did not always succeed, but when he started to stagger, Hayato took his hand. Most of the time, though, Martin's strategy worked. He had felt best when he connected himself with a restraining strap to the external control console of the Direct Fusion Drive, and crawled inside a two-meter-long closed tube that reeked of oil. Then he had been in his element. The engine responded to his commands. He had no problems adapting the launch sequences to the supposed zero gravity. The problem the developers had not been able to solve on Earth was that liquids moved differently up here than under Earth's gravity. This could be simulated and calculated, of course, and the Japanese engineer had succeeded in doing that very well. However, somebody had to adapt the results achieved by this method to reality.

"That was it," Hayato had finally said. Only then did Martin realize he had just spent two consecutive hours in space without getting dizzy. He had not been able to take off the adult diaper he still wore from launch, and now it was starting to chafe. During the landing, though, he was glad he still had it on.

"Nice trip, see you next time," the Japanese man said, bidding him farewell.

Martin shook his head. "No one will ever get me into one of those things again," he said. "But it was interesting to meet you. We have to talk sometime about the algorithms for the thermodynamic simulation of fluids. You solved that quite elegantly!"

The Japanese engineer gave him an inscrutable smile and took his leave.

July 16, 2038, NASA

THE MOST IMPORTANT task of the Enceladus project was to find the final proof for the existence of life. To do so, astronauts must catch life red-handed, which could only be expected in the salty ocean below the several-kilometers-thick ice crust. How could you dig such a deep hole with the limited resources of an interplanetary expedition, no more than six crew members, and no giant drilling rigs?

The Europeans had the most extensive experience with such drilling attempts. They had reached a depth of 10 meters on Mars during their unsuccessful quest to find traces of life there. One could not learn very much from this, though. On Enceladus, temperatures were expected to reach minus 180 degrees Celsius. Ice would be as hard as steel, and metal drills would become brittle.

NASA's engineers came up with several ideas. They considered, for instance, landing a spacecraft vertically on the moon so the heat of its rocket engines would blast a hole into the ice. The 10-megawatt fusion drives would most definitely be involved in this. A non-flyable DFD prototype was taken to a glacier in Alaska to test the method. The energy proved sufficient for a sizable hole, but the jet of hot air could not be sufficiently focused. Instead, as it went deeper, the hole became wider and wider. It did not form a cylinder, as intended, but a cone with the tip facing downward. The engineers extrapolated that the pit would have to be over a kilometer wide to reach a depth of five kilometers. And how could they keep the rocket engine centered above it as the cone widened? The reason this idea was finally rejected was a different one, however—it turned out the melting water became more polluted by radioactivity than expected, which was not good for most forms of life. However, the experiment had shown that heat was a better tool than a mechanical drill when it came to penetrating ice.

How could they heat a device for a sufficient period of time? It soon became clear that adding energy once—like filling a hot-water bottle—would never be sufficient, unless one detonated an atomic bomb, or even better, a hydrogen bomb. This meant the drill head had to carry its own heat source. Space exploration had used a reliable, if not particularly popular, method for tapping into an inexhaustible source of heat—the decaying energy of radioactive materials. The engineers searched through their arsenal. Even the *Cassini* probe that had found the first indicators for life on Enceladus back in 2015 had contained an RTG, or Radioisotope Thermoelectric Generator, that generated electricity through the decay of plutonium-238. *Enceladus Life Finder* used the same proven technology 16 years later.

Unfortunately, mathematics threw a monkey wrench into the NASA researchers' project. How much energy is needed to heat a five-kilometer-deep, almost two-meter diameter ice cylinder to the melting point, and then fully melt it? The crust of Enceladus might as well have been made of iron—it wouldn't have made the task any more complicated. A best-case scenario showed them reaching a depth of five kilometers in 200 days. To do this, the drill vehicle would have to carry along approximately one and a half tons of plutonium. For the *Cassini* probe, about 20 kilograms of the highly radioactive material had been enough. The decisive factor turned out to be money. A kilo of plutonium-238 cost about 10 million dollars, so a ton and a half would cost 15 billion dollars and thus devour a big part of the budget, not to mention the fact there was not that much plutonium available worldwide.

The Nordic spirit creature who leads the honorably slain to Valhalla finally solved the problem—*Valkyrie*, the ice drill owned by the private-sector company Stone Aerospace. The device had already been successfully tested in Antarctica, though only using an unmanned version measuring 30 centimeters in diameter. The company was confident it could use the design for a model with a diameter of two meters, and that was enough incentive for NASA to finance the project. *Valkyrie* did not need an on-board heating plant, since it received all of its energy from the outside via a fiber-optic cable connected to a powerful laser. The cable itself must be less than a millimeter thick. It served as an umbilical cord that provided the drilling vehicle with the necessary energy, and also allowed for data transmission. The range was limited only by the length of the fiber-optic cable carried aboard. NASA specialists had demanded 100 kilometers, and in the light of the hundreds of millions offered, Stone Aerospace had gladly accepted any request. However, the space agency itself was supposed to be responsible for an energy source providing several megawatts of power to the laser while the vehicle was on Enceladus. At first the NASA specialists considered, with some misgivings, a small nuclear reactor, but then the fusion drives solved this problem.

Nevertheless, it took until 2038 before the first large *Valkyrie* became operational. No one seemed to have the time to come up with a new name, so the old one stuck.

The initial trial failed in a grandiose manner: In June of 2038, a team of technicians tested this version on an Alaskan glacier that the U.S. government, for this very purpose, had excluded from national park status. The drill vehicle was transported on a cargo ship and was finally air-lifted to the glacier by a large helicopter. As the technicians tried to unhitch the carrying cable from the helicopter, *Valkyrie* started to slide. It was a perfect example of faulty planning leading to a disaster. No one had considered that a giant tube of steel might begin to move in an undesired manner on uneven ground. The helicopter carried the drill vehicle back to the cargo ship.

Afterward, the technicians needed a week to level the starting area and to build scaffolding. The engineers had somehow forgotten that *Valkyrie* must be placed in a vertical position in order to drill into the ice. They had simply upscaled the miniature model that could be held upright by two men, and made a larger variant. Despite this, the company director, Stone Jr., son of the company founder and reputed to be a hothead, did not fire any employees.

The second attempt began two weeks later. NASA streamed it live on its website. Martin remembered it for a long time afterward because the result had been typical in a certain way. The helicopter once more flew *Valkyrie* on-site and placed it on its scaffolding. The drill vehicle was supposed to perform an unmanned run first. An AI was trained to steer it, using the miniature model for practice. The company director himself insisted on activating the generator and switching on the laser it powered. A fraction of a fraction of a second later, the light reached *Valkyrie* via the fiber-optic cable. It performed two functions at once. It heated a metal plate to melt the ice near the drill head, and it generated electricity by means of photocells to power the pumps that pressed the heated water against the ice below *Valkyrie*, thus creating a hole.

The technicians were optimistic and seemed to have thought of everything. In fact, the drill vehicle started moving as planned, and the audience applauded. Director Stone was cautious enough not to join the cheering just yet. The drum, from which the prototype of the fiber-optic cable unspooled, was turning slowly. They were not in a rush. This was only the first test of the new version. There would be many more, during which they could also raise the speed.

The entire crew was listening. A deep rumbling could be heard, mixed with a constant hissing. The hole dug by *Valkyrie* was only a few centimeters larger than the vehicle itself. Everything seemed perfect. However, after exactly seven minutes and ten seconds, it stopped.

"Shit," Stone said. His face reddened, but he did not utter another word. The technicians looked embarrassed. One of them placed his ear on the ice.

"Silence!" Stone barked.

The sensors reported that *Valkyrie* was stuck at a depth of 87 meters. Suddenly, shrill alarm signals sounded from the control panel, as if the artificial intelligence had needed some time to think this over.

"Turn it off! What happened?"

Three of the specialists tried to answer Stone's question at the same time.

"The hot water jets are choked with crud." The diagnosis was too obvious. "Sorry, I meant they are blocked by sediment."

"Are you serious?" Stone's glare seemed to try to burn through the glacier without using *Valkyrie*. This did not sound like a question, but rather like a threat. All of them must have realized the drill vehicle would not be moving through laboratory ice but through a naturally-grown glacier. Wind and weather deposited fine sand and other small particles on it and the deposits gradually sank down into the polar ice. They not only suspected this, they knew it. The deposits must have clogged the hot water jets much faster than expected, making them inoperable.

"I told you so," one of the technicians said, and then quickly clapped his hand over his mouth when the others glared at him.

"What did you just say?" Stone asked, standing before him with his hackles up.

"It's a problem of scale. We simply scaled up everything. We thought the small particles might be dangerous for the miniature model, but only large pieces would be a problem for *Valkyrie*."

"Didn't you simulate this? Why did I not hear anything about it?"

"Sir, a description of the issue was sent to your inbox on ..." he scrolled through his tablet, "July 10."

Stone fell silent, turned around, and scratched his head. He was facing a real problem—the *Valkyrie* prototype was lost. How were they supposed to retrieve a metal tube weighing several tons from a gradually freezing hole that was 87 meters deep? The fiber-optic cable for the laser was much too thin to be used for pulling *Valkyrie* up by the scruff of the neck.

The Director did not say anything else. He spoke to no

one and walked down the glacier past the *Valkyrie* scaffolding. Eight hours later a helicopter could be seen taking off from the cargo ship and picking up a single person at the coast.

Stone Aerospace pledged to build a new *Valkyrie* as soon as possible and at its own expense, using the exact design of the old one. *Valkyrie* actually had all the necessary equipment to counteract the clogging, but the control software had not initiated those measures in time, since they had been unnecessary in the miniature version. Because NASA trusted this private contractor due to its boldness and talent for improvisation, but not for its ability to program an error-tolerant AI, Martin was sent on an official trip. At first he was even happy about that. For the moment, he was still able to suppress the thought that one day he would have to stand on the ice of Antarctica.

June 28, 2045, Antarctica

THE COLD WAS KILLING HIM. Martin glanced backward, and he could still guess where the station was. The other person with him, the station cook, might be surprised if he suddenly ran in the wrong direction, but this was the only way to survive. Small ice darts dug into the few unprotected areas of his skin, even though there was no wind today and the cook had praised the warm weather this morning. Martin felt like a fakir placing his face on glowing embers. He could not tell whether heat or cold was torturing him and it did not matter—he was sure to die anyway.

The cook was now walking ahead of him. At dinner, he had introduced himself as Tadeusz, though Martin had forgotten his last name. He was also one of the leading scientists of the Polish Antarctica Station. In the polar region, no one had just one job. Just as Martin was about to flee the freezing hell surrounding him, the man turned around and spoke to him in English. Martin could not understand what he said and only shrugged his shoulders.

Tadeusz spoke up. "Marvelous landscape, isn't it?"

Martin thought, *He can hardly expect an answer to that, can he?* He at least managed to nod. The cooking researcher or researching cook laughed.

"Your first time beyond the Antarctic Circle, isn't it?"

Martin nodded again.

"That's quite normal. Once you get used to the cold it is not so bad. You have to work your way into Antarctica."

Martin obviously still looked skeptical.

"I did not want to believe that on my first day, either. Just turn around! There is really unlimited freedom here as this continent belongs to no one and everyone. I think you can see that in the landscape."

Landscape? Martin only saw the desolation of an icy desert, with mountains in the background, also covered in ice. *Doubtlessly fascinating in a morbid kind of way*, but he preferred more inviting regions.

"Believe me, there is no landscape on Earth that is so honest. If you make a mistake, the cold has got you by the balls. If you make two mistakes, you die. The only environment that resembles Antarctica in this aspect is the cosmos."

Pronounced by the Pole, the word sounded particularly harsh. Martin had no intention of visiting this 'cosmos' for an extended period, as his short trip into space had been enough.

"Come on, we have to hurry, as the others are waiting for us." Tadeusz placed a hand on Martin's shoulder and gave him a symbolic nudge.

How did I ever come up with the stupid idea of testing the software directly on the console of Valkyrie? *Couldn't they just have established a laser link instead? It's the fault of Mr. Stone,* Martin decided, *Mr. Stone Jr.,* who had casually mentioned a short stroll to the test site. *Valkyrie* could not be tested directly at the polar station because the station was built on solid ground. The ice drill was supposed to work its way into the ocean beneath the ice and then go diving for a while. Since it did not matter whether the water was deep, they had selected a location about three kilometers north of the station. In other regions that would have been a 40-minute walk, but here it required a minor expedition. The station's three snowmobiles had driven ahead, carrying supplies and tools.

Martin only realized they had arrived when, lost in thought, he collided with the Polish researcher, who had suddenly stopped. Martin apologized to Tadeusz, who turned around and smiled at him.

"It is getting better already, isn't it?"

Martin did not have the heart to shake his head. He tried to say something, but it felt as if his facial muscles were frozen. However, he did feel there was a warm spot, right above his heart.

Once inside, the rest of his body needed a quarter of an hour to reach its normal temperature again. The lab tent and the common tent were well-heated. Stone Aerospace had transported, via ship, a small diesel power plant that now provided the laser in *Valkyrie* with electricity, and also supplied heaters, computers, and other things. Mr. Stone had greeted him in person right after his arrival, though Martin was so cold he could barely remember it.

Nevertheless, the trip had been worth his while, just for the opportunity to use these computers. *Stone must have invested quite a bit of money for this setup,* he speculated. Martin could have run a 1-cubic-kilometer cell simulation of Antarctic circulation for the coming two weeks. At NASA he would have had to reserve time on a supercomputer first. Currently, *Valkyrie* was Stone's only project, and he seemed to be betting the entire company on it. A drilling robot successfully used on Enceladus could also be marketed on Earth.

After his body had reached a more bearable temperature, Martin sat down and rolled his office chair a bit closer to the desk adjusting the seat to the right height. If he used the wrong posture, he soon knew it by the pain in his right wrist. He pulled the keyboard a bit closer, stretched his legs, and launched the debugger. *I probably stand no chance of succeeding at this task.* Valkyrie *and its control software have been in development for over 20 years. The various programmers have documented the code very well, indeed. I should congratulate Stone for it the next time I see him, since this is not always the case.* Yet software has the natural tendency to become more complex. In the beginning, there is a routine that is supposed to generate a clearly defined result under specific circumstances. The programmer tests the routine under these circumstances. If he is clever, he also checks what will happen under different ones, if he has enough imagination to visualize different circumstances.

No one can foresee the future, though. Three years later, the module might have to work with subroutines that did not exist when it was created. Five years later, the original conditions for which it was written might no longer exist, but as the first programmer had tested it well, no errors appeared even under different requirements—at least not yet. At some point, reality will test the hitherto unknown limits of the programming, and then a crash will occur. Martin was supposed to help ensure this crash did not happen at a depth of over 3,000 meters.

In the case of a short, primitive program, he would have gone through every line of code. He would have checked which command led to which behavior at which time, whether variables were neatly defined, and whether memory was freed up in time. However, for software of this complexity, such an approach was not efficient. It would have taken Martin months to go through tens of thousands of lines of code, and *Valkyrie* was supposed to start digging into the ice cap tomorrow.

Of course, Stone's programmers had already run all sorts of tests.

The danger consisted in a kind of tunnel vision. Martin wondered, *Would they blindly trust the programs in cases that appeared too trivial to them?* For this reason he had brought along his own testing tools. These simulated an actual mission for the *Valkyrie* software by transmitting data to it via the interfaces defined by the programmers, known as 'APIs,' or Application Programming Interfaces. Then Martin could follow the reaction of the software live in the debugger. Working in this so-called *sandbox* was also faster, since it could try out various scenarios much more rapidly than in real life. He did not have to wait until rear jet 1 had actually started up; he could cancel the test as soon as the correct start command for the jet had been issued.

Martin started his software tests at the critical moments, and thought, *what must happen once* Valkyrie *has finished making its way through the ice?* At that point, a number of components had to change their function. The jets would no longer discharge the heated water toward the front for drilling, they would now serve as the drive. If the command to switch came too late, they would press *Valkyrie* from below against the ice cap. The drill vehicle, therefore, must recognize exactly when that critical moment occurred. The software also had to take irregularities into account, such as local bubbles in the ice that might briefly give the impression the goal had been reached. Martin systematically changed the input para-meters. For the software, this looked as if it was turning hot and then cold, as if *Valkyrie* was first being crushed by the ice, and then seemed to be swimming in a viscous slush of ice and water. In all cases, the software reacted in an optimal fashion. This did not mean the passengers would have always survived, however. The drill vehicle had been built with certain safety margins, and if these were exceeded, the crew could not be saved. *Nevertheless, this reflects the excellent work Stone's programmers have done,* Martin recognized. The software extended the safe area, which had already been defined twice as large as to be expected in reality, by another 20 percent, as it reacted in the right way to compensate. *I really will have to congratulate Stone.*

Martin worked intensively for two, three, four hours. He was lost in his simulations and anxiously watched when *Valkyrie* succeeded against the environment—which he had programmed to be particularly aggressive—and when it failed. Therefore, he was all the more shocked when a warm hand touched his shoulder. His body suddenly jerked, and he almost fell off his chair.

A sonorous warm voice with a Southern European accent softly spoke, "Oh, sorry." Martin quickly got up.

"No, just go on, I did not want to interrupt you." The woman, maybe in her late forties, as indicated by her laugh lines, was a bit taller than he. She had long, dark hair, full lips, and broad shoulders. Martin lowered his gaze and noticed the name tag sewn to her uniform read *Francesca Rossi.* He was feeling flushed, plus he was angry at himself, and he could not come up with an answer.

"I, uh..."

"It's okay, just sit down again. I really did not want to

disturb you. They told me you were testing *Valkyrie*, and as it will be launched tomorrow with me inside..."

"You are the pilot?" Martin sat, as he remembered the crew list. He did not know where he had seen her, even though the image was clear in his mind.

"Yes. Though we are going to be more like passengers tomorrow," replied Francesca, "if I understand the mission description correctly."

"I... I don't know. I just arrived today and spent the whole time online in the simulations."

"It seems our superiors suddenly lost their courage—or is there something else behind the fact they hired you for this task?" Francesca looked at him with genuine interest. He could well understand her curiosity. *If I were to be shot into the ice tomorrow, sitting in a large steel tube...* Martin did not even want to imagine *that* scenario.

"Everything is okay," he said. "*Valkyrie* only failed in two-thirds of the test cases." Francesca stared at him with open mouth and large eyes.

"What I meant to say—it worked excellently, way beyond its defined operating range."

"So everything is fine?" Francesca asked.

"Well, you could say it that way. As long as..." Martin did not finish his sentence.

"I understand. I am relying on you." Francesca turned around and apparently wanted to leave.

"Is this your first mission in the ice?" He was surprised at himself for asking this question. The Italian woman looked at him.

"It is indeed. I am actually a fighter pilot."

"So you have probably seen a lot." *I do not envy her. It's enough to read about the horrors of the modern world while in my nice, warm office,* he decided.

"My last combat mission was already three years ago, fortunately. Turkey." Martin remembered the Islamist coup that had happened then. "It... felt strange to push the button—just like in a computer game. The AI is doing most of the work."

"So why are you doing this?" After asking this question, he became self-conscious. *Maybe I was too personal. I really don't know this woman.* Francesca looked at him, her eyelids trembling slightly.

"That feeling, when the plane starts up with you inside. Sure, there is the AI, but I can still press the big red button. Where else can we still reach our limits these days? You are protected by software everywhere..."

"That is your reason for *Valkyrie*?"

"I certainly agreed right away to do it."

Martin turned away. He was feeling hot, and his face was probably red. A sense of unease drifted through his mind. *What would happen if I made a mistake in my simulations? Can I really be sure?* His work had never decided so directly whether a human being lived or died. He couldn't sit still —he got up and wandered aimlessly through the room. He could feel Francesca's gaze follow him.

"Don't worry," he finally said. "I am only a little bit confused. Normally, I just sit in a small office. There's too much action here for my taste, but the *Valkyrie* device is safe." He realized he was trying to reassure himself by doing this, but it worked. He finally managed to sit down and look at Francesca again.

"Well, that makes me feel better," the pilot said with a grin, as if she had seen through him. "See you tomorrow." She turned around and left the room.

June 29, 2045, Antarctica

THREE HUNDRED METERS DOWN, the ice was as dark as outer space without a sun. Martin looked at the monitor. It showed him several perspectives of a scene the crew of *Valkyrie* could also see on a similar display. Windows were useless in a drill vehicle, so *Valkyrie* did not have any, even though it would move like a submarine after getting through the ice layer. Its hull was made of special steel and had to withstand high pressure, heat, and cold. Therefore, any gap in the structure would present a safety risk.

The voices of the two people on board sounded calm and clear in Martin's ears, like they were standing right next to him. Martin was not surprised by the sound quality. This was an advantage of the fiber-optic cable that not only provided *Valkyrie* with energy from the laser, but also allowed for excellent data transmission. *I can't imagine how Francesca and Devendra stay so calm*, he thought. While Francesca was an experienced fighter pilot, Devendra, an Indian Sikh, seemed at peace with himself in a way Martin had never experienced with anybody. And yes, *Valkyrie* was not moving through deep ice for the first time, and after all, it had survived his own simulations.

This did not change the reality that the crew was inside a steel cylinder with the diameter of a small bathroom, without a direct view of the outside, or the chance to simply surface. *Valkyrie* wasn't a submarine, but a unique vehicle stuck deep in the ice of Antarctica. The canal it had drilled had long ago frozen solid behind it. If for some reason the hot water drill failed, they could not simply pull on the cable to return the vehicle to the surface. *Valkyrie* would somehow have to free itself on its own. There was a safety measure in place where it should break through beneath the ice layer and then maneuver near the bottom of the ocean to reach open water. Here, this was a relatively easy exercise, and they would reach their goal after 600 meters. It was vastly different on Enceladus, because there they would have to get through five to eleven kilometers of ice. They would only know after their arrival exactly how many kilometers they would have to traverse.

The launch did not appear to be spectacular. *Valkyrie* simply lay flat on the ice, with its tip pointing toward the South Pole. The only sound came from the refrigerator-sized module housing the laser. The laser unit itself was silent, but its ventilation made a hissing noise. Martin also heard the dull droning of the diesel generators from within their containers—almost a small power plant in itself, since *Valkyrie* needed up to five megawatts of power. Thick cables transported the energy from the containers back to the laser. The shielding was meant to protect the cable from damage, since without electricity there would be no working laser, and without laser light, *Valkyrie* would be stranded in the ice. The diesel generators would not be part of the flight into space; a spacecraft could hardly carry that much fuel.

From a distance, the cable running from the laser unit to *Valkyrie* seemed alarmingly thin. It was nicknamed 'the umbilical cord,' and for good reason; through this bundle of optical fibers, with a diameter of less than a millimeter, the laser sent the energy that was supposed to clear a path for *Valkyrie*. At the stern of the vehicle was a drum that could unspool several kilometers of this cable. An electric cable of that length would have hardly fit into a drill vehicle of this size.

The two test pilots had waved goodbye to those present and then crawled into a hatch at the end of the steel cylinder. There wasn't enough space to enter it upright. Later Martin saw them on his monitor as they sat in their chairs, which could be rotated up to 90 degrees.

Valkyrie initiated the launch procedure with the push of a button. The automatic control had activated the laser. It shot its ray at light speed through the kilometers-long cable. At the end of the cable, in the bow of *Valkyrie*, it stimulated a heating element that began to melt ice and vaporize the water. *Valkyrie* utilized this hot steam in two ways; first, like a small power station, to generate electricity for the on-board instruments, and second, to flow through eight nozzles at the bow to create a path through the ice for the vehicle. Unlike a metal drill, this drill jet never wore out. So long as it was supplied with laser energy, the vehicle would continue on its way. Three further jet drives, moveable and located two meters behind the bow, allowed for selecting the direction of drilling. They pressed the prow of the vehicle, which always swam in a hot soup, in the desired direction. And, once *Valkyrie* had broken through the ice, they would be responsible for propulsion.

The launch commenced from a horizontal position, and as the bow got very hot, the vehicle gradually sank into the ice with its tip forward. The Stone engineers had come up with this simple technique soon after the failed test of year 2038. It was impressive that *Valkyrie* eventually reached the desired 90-degree position without any control input, simply because it followed the path of least resistance. Martin could get enthusiastic about such clever methods; he knew software written by humans was always error-prone.

After only 45 minutes *Valkyrie* had reached a depth of 300 meters, where Martin was now watching the crew. This stop had been planned so they had enough time to check the course of the hole and the condition of the machinery. Martin's help was not needed for this. The check wasn't actually necessary, either, as the software would have issued an alert in case of any deviation. However, they were not going to blindly trust the programming.

Martin had interlaced his fingers and was twiddling his thumbs. One minute, two minutes, three minutes passed. He wondered, *did my simulations take such a consciously triggered full stop into account? Probably not.* He had particularly concentrated on catastrophes caused by the outside world. Suddenly, Martin shivered. *Why did I not ask for today's mission plan?* He shook his head. *I probably should not worry at all.* Nevertheless, he would be even more careful next time, by a whole order of magnitude.

"*Valkyrie* to Flight Director, when are we going to continue?"

Francesca had asked this in such a way that an unspoken 'finally' could not be ignored.

"FD to *Valkyrie*, just one moment."

This was the voice of Stone, who seemed to have personally taken over the role of Flight Director. It was very unusual that during a NASA program an external person served as FD, even though he was the inventor of this technology.

"FD to *Valkyrie*, radar showing an obstacle at two o'clock, X minus 20."

"Confirmed. Is this a problem?" Francesca replied.

Was Stone getting overly cautious? Martin wondered about this, and pulled up a window with the radar on his display. *Valkyrie* should be able to get around this obstacle quite easily, should this even be necessary. They would see once they got closer. There would still be enough time for an evasive maneuver.

"FD to *Valkyrie*, no, just a cross-check."

Something in Stone's voice made Martin nervous. In the cockpit video stream, he could see Francesca had unbuckled her safety belt. *Had she noticed something?*

For a second, the image on Martin's monitor wobbled. *Valkyrie* seemed to try to leap forward, but was held in place by something. Alarm messages were scrolling on the right edge of the screen.

"*Valkyrie* to FD, what the hell is going on? That really shook us up!"

Francesca seemed to be on the verge of screaming into the microphone.

"FD to *Valkyrie*, my apologies. We tried to restart the vehicle."

"Without telling us? What is really going on there?"

"Sorry, we did not want to alarm you. Please be patient for a while!"

Martin shook his head. *This certainly isn't standard NASA procedure. Once this test is over, there will be repercussions.* He already heard his colleagues bitching about the private partners. However, NASA could no longer maintain its research program without external investment.

"FD to *Valkyrie*, please report status."

A useless request, as the monitors clearly showed all systems working within normal parameters.

"This is *Valkyrie*, status of all stations optimal."

"FD to *Valkyrie*. There is a problem. *Valkyrie* refuses to start up."

"It refuses?"

"It's a safety protocol," Stone said. "Some fool prohibited starting it if the radar detects an obstacle less than 30 meters away."

This was a reasonable limitation—during the phase of diving into the ice *Valkyrie* could not be steered by software. The vehicle simply followed the laws of physics and that did not allow for evading an obstacle. The programmer had not considered one thing—there was a difference between a cold start at the surface and a restart in the middle of the ice, where *Valkyrie* was already in a vertical position. Martin was glad he was not the one who had programmed the system. *Why hadn't I simulated this condition, though?* Martin answered himself. *Because it did not seem threatening enough to me.*

"FD to *Valkyrie*. No reason for concern. I am going to find a good programmer. I already have an idea."

June 30, 2045, Antarctica

"So THERE's enough oxygen for three hours. I am gradually starting to be worried."

Francesca's voice sounded calm and controlled. *She's either a great actress or really lion-hearted,* Martin perceived.

"Yes, I am working on it." He suppressed a *don't you worry* that was on the tip of his tongue. The fact she had contacted Martin via the open network rather than through the direct connection with the Flight Director confirmed that she was worried—and she knew she had every reason for it—and he knew this, too. Despite this, the problem was actually quite trivial. Because the radar saw an obstacle in the direction of travel, the drill jets would not activate. This behavior made sense for a launch at the surface, but at a depth of 300 meters it might be deadly. Otherwise, the technology was completely functional. The laser supplied the vehicle with energy, so Francesca and Devendra were neither sweating, nor would they die of hunger or thirst. They could communicate with the entire world.

However, they would suffocate in about three hours.

The expedition had been planned to last for only a few hours, but as of now it had gone on for almost two days. During this time, Martin had not slept, unlike the crew members, who had been told to nap as long as possible to save on air. He imagined how he would have reacted, stuck deep inside the ice. *Would I have been able to sleep a wink?* Up here, he at least had the feeling of being able to achieve something. He tried to ignore the responsibility resting in his hands, in his fingers that tried again and again to hammer new lines of code into the keyboard.

After all, he had not programmed the *Valkyrie* software. When Mission Chief Stone—who knew very little about programming—had first described the problem, Martin had still been optimistic. He had thought, *How complicated could it be to outwit a safety mechanism that was obviously overreacting, like the immune system in the case of an allergy?* The true degree of difficulty only emerged gradually. It had to do with the fact that he did not know the software well enough. While he had tested it in simulations, he did not understand the concept behind it. Being too familiar with the code was potentially bad for testing, because you ran the risk of ignoring bugs that ought to be prevented by the software architecture.

First, he had needed to grasp the concept, and Stone had provided him with all the material he needed. Martin could have logged into the NASA supercomputer, or even used it all by himself if this would have helped somehow. However, this was not a problem that could be solved by sheer computing power. Several times Martin had believed he found the decisive routines—and he had been wrong each time. *The programming team did good work*, he concluded. In the final analysis, the control software was supposed to be functioning 'space-safe' at the highest level of safety, without human intervention. Out there, the crew would be working light hours and millions of kilometers away from any human help.

Since the system had a modular structure, Martin had first tried to rewrite the entire launch control module and then overwrite the old one. He analyzed the functions of the existing module, removed everything not absolutely necessary, and wrote thousands of lines of code in a daze. He did without real-time tests and added the new module in the 'this ought to work' state. It had taken him twelve hours, and he only made it with the help of a lot of caffeine from sweetened coffee that also provided the necessary calories. He then asked Stone not to tell the crew anything and to attempt a restart, but nothing happened. Martin bit his lips until he tasted blood.

The software had recognized his intrusion. *The check-sums are no longer correct.* Martin had been aware of this. However, he had not suspected how cleverly the system would react. Instead of running the new module, it had simply loaded a copy of the old one from shadow memory and then launched it. *This is really smart thinking,* Martin concluded, *as it prevents an outsider from interfering with the system.* The memory the safety copy was based on was only readable, not writable, and it was aboard *Valkyrie.* So they could not simply swap the program.

Martin brooded over this. *How else can I succeed in reaching the backup memory?* It was on an add-in board plugged into the circuit board of the main computer of *Valkyrie.* The memory communicated with the system via encoded channels. It was not enough to simply connect a flash drive with the on-board computer, even if there was a flash drive aboard *Valkyrie.* "Perhaps there is a second *Valkyrie* to bring supplies to the crew from outside?" he posited, but Stone shook his head. The replacement vehicle was still being constructed, and the previous model was currently being used in the Alps for glacier research.

He wiped the sweat from his forehead and attacked the source code of the security system. *There has to be a gap somewhere that will allow me to insert my own code.* No one was able to write error-free programs because even computers made mistakes, and they could neither predict nor prevent bit-switching, the random change of a memory location. Be that as it may, Martin noticed very soon that Stone had hired very capable programmers who had been extremely well-informed about all current vulnerabilities and how to get rid of them. Martin briefly considered whether he should talk to them directly and ask them about potential weaknesses. Yet it appeared they had actively tried to close any back doors, and had certainly not left any gaps they were aware of.

Two hours later, Francesca had called him. He had not even noticed how much time had passed. Rather than feeling pressured, he was actually grateful to hear from her. He knew he had done nothing wrong, but a software problem he could not solve was simply not an option. He tried to imagine what the programmers had been like. In his life, Martin had already analyzed millions of lines of code. He thought, *their style in writing the source code indicates they must have just graduated from college. That is why they were so well-informed about current vulnerabilities.* They used the recommended countermeasures in a very systematic—but not particularly creative—fashion. A more experienced programmer would have taken shortcuts here and there, which were not mentioned in textbooks, but worked as well and looked even better. Aesthetically pleasing programming was a skill most did not develop until later, when they were bored with their normal work, because they felt like they had solved every problem several times already.

Martin contemplated, *In this instance, how much attention did these programmers pay to software archeology?* This subject had only become part of programming curriculums a few years ago. Its basic idea was to learn from the mistakes of the past. There were rather practical applications, though. Surprisingly enough, errors occurred in modern systems that ought to have been removed 50 years ago. The reason for this was that proven solutions were often copied—for good reason; you did not have to reinvent the wheel with each new piece of software. Troubleshooting such old code was always more complicated than troubleshooting code the programmers had written themselves. Therefore an ancient bug, now and then, would infect completely new systems that had not even been designed when the bug first occurred.

Can I maybe locate such a bug and exploit it? Martin considered this as he went through his own notes and tried to find suitable candidates that would structurally fit. Three bugs offered possibilities: one was from the 1980s; one had first shut down computer systems worldwide in 2008; and the third was by now twenty years old. Like a virus must match its host, not every bug was suitable for every technical system. Finding the bugs in the code of the control model took hardly any time. Martin programmed a bot for this purpose. Ten minutes later, it reported a result—no bugs found.

He must inform Stone. *Yes, his programmers had worked well, too well. I've just sentenced two people to death.* He felt so nauseous he leapt to his feet and ran outside. Even though the biting wind tugged at him, he did not feel cold. Martin vomited. He had remembered just in time to turn downwind. His stomach contents were blown away. The small amount he saw fall to the ground froze immediately. Then he started to feel the intense chill. He rushed back to the computer.

Martin wondered, *If I cannot change the software, can I do something else?* Of course he did not possess the power to remove the obstacle that prevented the system from restarting. *But, how does the system perceive reality? Via the on-board radar, which works like an echo-sounder.* Radio signals moved into the ice, sensors received reflections and measured the return time to calculate the locations of the obstacle. *Can we possibly trick the radar?* It did not work to simply turn it off, as the system would still refuse to restart. *Instead, what if we send the signals in a different direction from what the vehicle is expecting?* Then the software would generate a different—false— image from the new measurement data. The obstacle would appear to move, then, and hopefully so far that the system no longer considered it a threat.

He called Stone via the encrypted line and described his idea. The company director briefly talked to his chief engineer. Stone's answers confirmed it would not be easy to implement his plan.

"A crew member would have to misalign the radar. This in itself is not complicated—a pair of pliers would suffice. However, the system will quickly recognize the changed state, so we will have to trigger the restart at exactly the same time."

"That sounds doable, doesn't it?" Martin asked.

"The access to the radar module is located near the hot water jets. If we start the drill jets, they might scald the person holding the pliers."

Martin leaned back. It was not his job to negotiate with the crew. He turned off the sound but continued watching the conversation on his monitor. Both Francesca and Devendra remained calm. They probably would argue among themselves who would be allowed to save the mission by dying. *Typical space heroes!* he concluded. *I'm not one of them. If I were in the Sikh's place, I would gladly let Francesca go first.*

"Ground staff, I have an announcement to make," Stone said via the general radio channel. Everyone wearing headphones could hear his words. His voice also came over the loudspeakers. The man described how they would attempt to save the crew.

"We ran the calculations again. If we do nothing, the risk of both of them dying is 100 percent. The risk of the crew member being killed immediately while working on misaligning the radar is 35 percent. With a probability of 90 percent, this person will suffer severe burns. If *Valkyrie* then restarts successfully, it is going to surface as quickly as possible. We have already prepared medical teams. There is a chance of about 50 percent that the treatment will happen in time. Thank you for your attention and best of luck to the crew, particularly Devendra Singh Arora, who has volunteered to manipulate the radar module."

July 1, 2045, Antarctica

THE TWO PEOPLE deep inside the ice stayed rational up to the last minute. Martin's admiration grew for the Indian man who would have to risk his life due to a stupid software bug. He also respected Francesca, the pilot, who had to sit and watch while this man probably saved her life. The two of them spent the waiting time sleeping, saving oxygen. The people in charge wanted to delay the action as long as possible, so emergency medical personnel could arrive. The medical team was being transported via helicopter from an American aircraft carrier cruising in the Antarctic Ocean. According to plan, *Valkyrie* would emerge from the ice after the emergency physician was already waiting with his equipment. After a successful restart, the drill vehicle would have to turn around and make its way through 300 meters of ice, which would take time.

Ten minutes before the event, Stone had them wake the crew. On his monitor, Martin saw how Francesca stretched as if she just had enjoyed a relaxing nap. He himself was extremely tired, but sleep had been out of the question. Devendra unbuckled his safety belt and opened a door in the wall, behind which there obviously were tools. He reached specifically for a pipe wrench. He looked down at himself, closed a button on his blue tunic, and adjusted his turban.

"Reporting for duty," he said.

"Flight Director to mechanic," began Stone, "I think I am speaking in everybody's name when I thank you."

"Now, just let me do my job first. You can always thank me afterward. And then I would like a nice, cold beer." Devendra gave a broad smile. The smile was genuine. Martin thought, *How did he manage to do that?*

"We have seven minutes left. You know the procedure?"

"Confirmed."

"Okay. Then you should get started with the cover."

Devendra turned around and bent down. He lifted the floor covering near the wall and rolled it backward. A round cover with a latch could be seen. Lift, turn, and the cover opened. The hole below was dark and large enough for one person.

"This is FD. There are twelve steps leading down."

The Sikh briefly looked at the hole, got down on one knee, and started to carefully descend. After nine steps, his head had disappeared.

"Is everything okay?" Stone asked. "You have now reached the bottom of the hole. It won't go any deeper. You'll have to stoop. I know it is rather cramped. At shoulder height you should see a glowing mark at the three-o-clock position."

"Confirming." Devandra's voice sounded muffled, which must be caused by the acoustics of the access hole.

"What do you see?"

"Three crosses. Who came up with that idea?"

"Good." Stone ignored his question. "Directly below the crosses there is another lever that locks the radar chamber. The chamber is about as deep as the access tube. According to our data, its bottom is filled with cold water. In the upper area of the exterior wall you will find the radar module. Don't worry—it is elcctrically shielded, so there is no danger in that regard."

"This is Arora. I am opening the chamber. Just a moment, I am shining my light into it. Everything is as described."

Martin heard the Sikh wheeze and groan as he climbed into the chamber.

"Man, it is cold here."

"Don't worry, it will soon be warmer than we would like."

"Okay, I have arrived."

"The module is facing forward and rests on a sheet bolted to the exterior wall. It doesn't look pretty, but it works. You have to loosen the two lower bolts."

"Right now?"

"Yes, do that now. Nothing is going to happen yet. The exterior pressure holds the sheet tight."

"Okay, I am unscrewing them."

The screen only showed a light shining erratically at metal surfaces in a dark room. Martin assumed, *Devendra probably stuck the flashlight in his armpit.* Martin heard him swear while working on the second bolt, probably because his wrench had slipped.

"It's finished."

Stone continued, "Okay, well. Now you have to push the sheet outward as hard as you can. This will confuse the radar system for at least a moment. We are going to start the system at that instant. If this doesn't work, I don't know what to do. Then some cold water will trickle through the gap and you two are going to suffocate after a while. However, if it works, the jets will be activated. And then the water streaming through the gap into the chamber will be hot. Very hot."

"I understand and accept the risk."

"Devendra Singh Arora, I will be glad to get you out of *Valkyrie* quickly and unharmed," said Stone. He then made an announcement on the general radio channel.

"FD to everyone. I am about to start the countdown. At minus three seconds I will deactivate sound transmission from *Valkyrie*."

A good decision, Martin thought.

"Ten... nine... eight..."

Martin switched off the screen. He folded his hands on his lap and looked at his fingernails. Whatever happened down there now, they would not feel it up here. The laser pumped its energy silently into the drill vehicle. The generators created a deep hum, which was sometimes drowned out by a cracking noise. The ice was shifting, and deep inside the ice, two people were fighting for survival.

Loud applause interrupted Martin's musings. He pushed the monitor's power button. The video feed from the cockpit was still off, but *Valkyrie's* status indicators were active. The drill jets were working again. The vehicle had turned and now was working its way toward the surface. It would break through the ice about 90 meters east of his location. At that moment, the helicopter with the emergency physician flew over the camp. Martin got up and grabbed his jacket from a hook on the wall. His scarf still was inside a sleeve, so he simply wrapped it around his neck. *Cap and gloves, too. All that takes way too long*, he thought, *but I know how cold it is outside.*

The wind hit him with full force when he left the protection of his cabin. Ice crystals felt like small nails someone was throwing at his skin. Nevertheless, he was not the only one who had ventured outside. A spontaneous welcoming committee was on its way. The area where the vehicle would emerge was already cordoned off with colored tape. It looked like a carnival was about to begin, but the people were not filled with joyous anticipation. Martin wondered how Devendra would be doing. Since the reactivation of the jets, the communication with the crew had occurred on a private channel.

Martin shifted his weight from one foot to another and tried to somehow stay warm. The ice crunched beneath his feet. The crunching sound became louder, until he realized it was not being caused by his efforts to warm up, but came from deep below. He looked toward the flag markers. There, the ice became much brighter. It now seemed to be less white, more like a mirror. This was the heat from below, which first turned the ice glassy, and then completely liquified it. First, there were only two small, dark spots—liquid, bubbling water. The spots grew, merging into a lake with a boiling content that resembled a geyser. Then a dark, shiny sea monster emerged. Its iron body moved at a slant from below to reach the surface of the ice, which at first broke below it until *Valkyrie* reached stable solid ice.

Still at a slight angle, it rested on the ice like a stranded whale with its head raised. The exit was at a height of about two meters. Three men brought a ladder and anchored it at the respective slots on *Valkyrie*. Two other men used it to get on board. A few seconds later, one of them emerged from the hatch and called out something Martin could not understand from a distance. Another man brought a stretcher that he passed to the rescue worker at the hatch, who maneuvered it inside. Two minutes later he reemerged, feet first this time. He pulled the now noticeably heavier stretcher behind him, the first rescuer probably pushing from inside. Something or someone was strapped to the stretcher, and the two men managed to move their burden down the ladder. There the third man started to help and they all took off, almost at a running pace, toward the helicopter.

MARTIN DID NOT SEE his colleague from India again until he visited him in the hospital. Devendra was already able to reach his left arm toward him in greeting. Both arms and his torso were bandaged. The scalding water had hit him in a relatively narrow stream. The areas affected had been severely burned, but they were small enough his life was not endangered. At this point, Martin already knew who would replace Devendra aboard the Enceladus-bound spacecraft. *Has the Sikh already been told?* Martin did not want to be the one to tell him, so he completely avoided the topic of spaceflight.

"Say hi to Enceladus for me," Devendra said at the end. Martin still shivered whenever he heard that name, one of Saturn's moons. *I am no discoverer; I am not even an astronaut.*

September 24, 2045, NASA

"We do not hire astronauts, Mr. Neumaier, we create them."

The words from the interview replayed through Martin's mind. He had resisted, of course, when he was asked to replace his injured colleague on board *Valkyrie*. His knowledge of the system, his cool-headed behavior, his ability to concentrate even without sleep—these had all been noted when NASA investigated the incident.

"Now you tell me yourself how the mission would have ended if the communication between you and the ship would have occurred with a lag of several hours?"

Martin realized why the planners of the Enceladus mission were frightened—the crew was basically cut off from any external help. An exchange of questions and answers would take hours due to the enormous distance. In that aspect, unmanned missions had been no different, but they also had been not nearly as complex. Now they would need all skills right there, not 1.2 billion kilometers away. Unfortunately, space on board was limited, and they could not send more than six astronauts on this long trip.

Martin could not quite explain it, but he eventually gave in. He forced the planners to make one promise, though; he would not have to go on board *Valkyrie*. The very idea of being surrounded by darkness while knowing there were kilometers of ice above his head frightened him. He would stay aboard the mothership. He could control the drill vehicle from his orbit around Enceladus as well as he had done from his workstation at the camp in Antarctica.

Goodbye California and West Coast, Martin anticipated. Three days later, he was picked up by a black limo. JPL in Pasadena was only responsible for unmanned missions. The car was parked by the cafeteria, between Buildings 180 and 264. Nearby was a military airfield where a small twin-engine plane waited for him. Five hours later he landed in Houston, Texas, where another limo was waiting for him. The man who had greeted him at the arrival gate now sat beside him in the rear of the limo.

"Space City," he said.

"Confirmed," the female voice of the car's AI replied. The limo started.

The man turned toward Martin. "I'd like to welcome you as a guest of the Astronaut Corps." He shook Martin's hand and then said, "I am Chief Astronaut Dave Willinger."

He had heard this name before. Willinger had made a name for himself during a Mars mission. Martin had not known that Willinger had since become Chief of the Astronaut Corps. *It's probably a boring office job rather than a real promotion,* Martin presumed. *I would gladly trade places with him.* He introduced himself as well, though his host certainly must have known who he was.

"Martin Neumaier, JPL contractor. Former contractor, that is."

Willinger uttered a raucous laugh.

"Yes, your status is rather hard to define. But since you are already here... we will have to skip basic training anyway. And I am sure you already know how to dive and how to pilot a plane." He nudged Martin with his elbow. *Everything is going to be easy, he means. I am just an astronaut like you,* Martin thought.

"For this reason, you are now our official guest. This has the advantage that we don't have to pay you, and if something happens to you, it will not be our fault."

He uttered the same raucous laugh, and Martin winced internally. *I don't know if I'm going to like this man. He's a bit annoying.* Martin glanced outside. The limo was driving through a seemingly endless suburb.

"Yes, it will take a little while longer. Space City is located a bit outside of Houston. I thought we could use the opportunity to talk about the plans for the coming months."

"Good idea." So far, Martin knew nothing except that the mission was supposed to start in three months.

"Your arrival here is seen as a kind of an unusual career change. I think that might be a problem, but what I think doesn't matter."

So things aren't going to be easy after all? Martin nodded to himself. *It would be an enormous understatement to call my recruitment merely problematic.*

"We will at least have to turn you into an astronaut. For that purpose we have designed a greatly shortened basic training, three weeks instead of twelve months. Afterward, you are officially an Astronaut Candidate or ASCAN, as we call them. Don't worry, you cannot fail unless you fall and break some bones. In that case ..."

Martin thought, *I wonder if I will laugh and sound like Willinger, too.*

"However, there will be little danger of that, as you are going to spend most of your time in the classroom. The next step will be Advanced Training. We moved the diving course from basic training to this section. We will test how you handle extreme acceleration, low air pressure, darkness, and zero gravity. This segment also includes survival training. Afterward, you will familiarize yourself with the modules of your spacecraft. You already have some experience with *Valkyrie*, though you have never been inside one, have you?"

Martin shook his head. "And I never will be."

"I don't know about that. It is certainly an exciting machine. I am not familiar with it either, so it looks like we're going to test it together. I am personally responsible for you."

During Advanced Training, each ASCAN was assigned to an experienced astronaut. Willinger gave him a questioning look.

"This is an honor for me, sir," Martin said. This seemed to Martin to be a suitable reaction in this case— and he was right. Willinger's eyes lit up. *In the long run, the desk job is probably not good for his ego,* Martin concluded.

"Your colleagues are all a bit ahead of you, but I think you should catch up with them in a little under two months if you train as intensively as I expect you to. You will have to, because then you are going up to Tiangong-4."

Willinger was referring to the Chinese space station. After the demise of ISS-NG, the Russians, Europeans, and Americans had not managed to agree on a new

International Space Station. Since then, the Chinese station had become a kind of meeting point for all space-faring nations. At first, the Chinese had invited astronauts from India, Indonesia, and Brazil. Finally, the former ISS nations had bought certain landing rights by paying for their own Tiangong modules.

"I'm looking forward to it." *I hope that sounded OK.* Martin was afraid this sentence would sound sarcastic. If it did, Willinger did not seem to notice.

"We're actually almost there, so you might want to put your shoes on," the chief astronaut said with another laugh. Martin looked out the window. They were driving past a windowless three-story building, then a conventional office building with five floors. It had a large parking lot surrounding it. Nothing so far looked in any way futuristic. Rockets ready for launch, fire, and smoke—none of that was here. Houston was no spaceport, after all, but only the center for manned missions. The limo turned left onto a narrow street bordered by parking spaces and leading to a plain eight-story building. Right in front of it was a parking spot marked with the large yellow letters, "VIP." The car pulled in.

"Johnson Space Center, Administration," the car announced. The doors swung open.

"Do I have an apartment here? I've got a few things I would like to have sent here." Martin had to hurry to keep pace with Willinger, who was striding toward the entrance of the building.

"You won't need an apartment. There are rooms for the Flight Controllers in the basement, in case their shift runs late. One of them will be made available to you."

October 22, 2045, Pensacola

"One... two... three... go!" said the voice from the loud-speaker. The safety belts dug into Martin's shoulders. His entire body was being accelerated upward. A powerful force resisted and squeezed him. His heart raced, and he tried not to bite his lips. Then liberation came. The seat flew onward without exterior forces acting on it, until it went down again. He fell into a bottomless depth until he finally landed gently. The ejector seat exercise showed Martin for the first time that this training would take him to the very limits of his physical endurance—and beyond.

Even from below, this apparatus looks terrifying, he nervously observed. At carnivals, Martin had always given such rides a wide berth.

"That was fun, wasn't it?" Willinger asked. With his large paw he patted Martin's shoulder—like the rest of Martin's body it still felt strangely soft. Martin decided, *one really has to be an oddball to enjoy events like these.* At first, the flight to Florida had seemed to be a welcome diversion. During the past three weeks in Texas he'd had to absorb knowledge like a sponge. In case of emergency he was supposed to be able to take on the roles of doctor, scientist, mechanic, and pilot. There wasn't enough time to test all of this in practice, but at least he now knew in principle how to set a broken bone, how to extract a tooth, and how to perform an appendectomy. What he had learned wasn't always useful—on Enceladus, he would hardly have to treat heatstroke. And, as a precaution, all astronauts had their appendixes removed before the long journey.

At Naval Air Station Pensacola in Florida, theoretical learning became much less important. Before his ride on the ejector seat simulator he had learned the basics about dangers during a rocket launch, ejector seat trajectories, and rescue routines. There seemed to be only one central question to consider—how much strain could Martin Neumaier withstand? And was he even capable of being an astronaut? No one here appeared to know he had been previously informed that his place on the Enceladus space-craft was secure. Everyone, up to his coach Willinger, treated him like a normal recruit. As Martin was at a U.S. Navy installation, the tone was quite a bit harsher than at NASA Houston, where the people were mostly administrators.

"What are we going to pursue tomorrow?" Martin asked.

"Just a moment. We still have to take baths today," said Willinger with a sly chuckle.

They entered a building that was obviously an indoor swimming pool. It was empty. Martin was given a diving suit, and he was supposed to swim three laps, an easy exercise for him. Afterward he had to change his outfit, donning a combat uniform that was much heavier than the diving suit, and then return to the pool. The fabric soon became waterlogged and no longer fit tightly, but instead pulled him downward. The heavy boots also made it harder to kick with his legs. Nevertheless, he managed to cover the three required 30-meter-laps since there was no time limit to prevent him from finishing.

"You seem to be able to swim," said Willinger. "That's good. Otherwise, I would have worried whether or not you were going to survive the next exercise."

Martin had already wondered why a metal capsule with windows hung above the pool. It looked like a helicopter without rotors. A crane moved the capsule to the side of the pool. Willinger strapped Martin to the left seat, while the right one remained empty.

"Just a moment. I need to change."

Willinger put on a diving suit. Martin looked at him as he approached. *Even though he must be over fifty, his body still seems to be in great shape.*

"I will be behind you, and when I tap you on the shoulder, you will unbuckle, open the door here," he said, pointing at the door next to the pilot seat, "and swim to the surface. Understood?"

Martin nodded, and then the crane picked up the capsule and moved it over the pool. He heard a loud clicking, felt a moment of weightlessness, and then the capsule sank, gurgling below the surface. Martin took a deep breath—the windows were open. Water flooded the inside. Instinctively, he wanted to open his safety belt and flee, but then he remembered to wait for the signal. He felt a hand on his shoulder. Willinger was floating in the water to the right of him. Martin pulled the door handle, but it was stuck. Willinger made gestures for him to stop. *The other door! I have to open the other door!* The thought raced through Martin's mind. The capsule was already three-quarters full of water. Martin unbuckled and had to dive down to find the door handle next to the pilot seat. He joggled it, but he did not have enough strength to open the door.

Of course, the water pressure, Martin suddenly realized. He would not be able to open it until the capsule was completely flooded, but it shouldn't be long. Martin gasped for air one last time, then pulled himself down by the door handle and started counting. At the count of fifteen, he pressed the handle again. The door swung open, and he pulled himself out and swam upward. When his head broke the surface, Willinger was next to him.

"Lesson 1. Always listen carefully." This time, he was not laughing. "But it was good you didn't panic. Most people don't realize the door cannot be opened for a while."

Martin nodded. "And now what?"

"The same procedure, but this time blindfolded."

"Is that supposed to be a joke?"

Willinger once more uttered his familiar raucous laugh. "No."

"WE WILL MEET tomorrow in Building 3801," Willinger had told him when he left. He had given Martin a mysterious look when he said that.

"Oh, and don't eat too much for breakfast."

Martin stood in front of the entrance to Building 3801 and waited. The sign read, *Naval Operational Medical Institute.* He did not know what to make of this. *It is probably going to be another medical exam.*

Willinger came around the corner, right on the dot. As a greeting, he gave Martin a hearty slap on the back.

Martin had expected that kind of gesture and softened it by taking a small step forward.

"Ha," said Willinger appreciatively.

Yesterday, Martin had asked every colleague whom he encountered what Building 3801 was about, but each one had just smiled mysteriously. This appeared to be part of the initiation ritual.

The building itself did not indicate a particular purpose. There were conference rooms and offices on the ground floor. The two men walked past them and reached a security gate sporting the sign, *Multi-station Spatial Disorientation Device*. Willinger and Martin held up their ID cards to a scanner.

A double door led into a large, almost circular room. In the middle, Martin saw a device mounted on a round pedestal. Ten barrel-shaped capsules without windows, labeled 1 through 10, hung off arms leading from the center. The apparatus reminded him somewhat of a carnival carousel. It appeared strangely old-fashioned. Martin shivered because the room temperature was barely in the upper teens.

A technician in blue overalls greeted them.

"Our MSDD. An antique beauty, isn't it?"

He explained that the system had been constructed back in the 1970s.

"It is even older than you, sir," the technician said with a smile to Willinger, whom he appeared to know well. He gazed at Martin. "And you are reputed to be such an exceptional programmer."

This was the first time in Martin's life he had met a stranger who had heard of him.

"So you should be interested in the control software.

We emulate a DEC PDP-11/34 programmed in FORTRAN on current hardware," the technician said.

Martin nodded. *I would indeed like to take a look at that software—definitely a true museum piece, which is rare these days.* However, this was also typical of the pragmatic approach used by NASA. When the facility was built, they obviously still needed a PDP-11 mainframe to control it. Later, the mainframe was emulated on a normal PC rather than reprogramming everything from scratch. Nowadays, the control software would probably run on any intelligent power outlet.

"Why didn't you simply recompile the FORTRAN programs?" Martin asked.

"It is all tied very closely to the hardware," the technician explained. "Does the term Unibus still mean anything to you? Control and interface are located on two Unibus cards for which we got a Strobe Osprey. For the system, our PC now looks like a good old PDP-11. Constructing a new system would have cost millions, and the old one still fulfills its purpose. You are going to see that. Afterward, why don't you come to my little room back there?" The technician pointed to the right.

"But," he went on, "let's concentrate on work first. Has someone already told you what MSDD is often called by its, ahem, victims?"

"Why don't you tell me that afterward?" said Martin.

Willinger laughed.

"We already reserved Cabin 1 for you. Please enter."

The technician opened the door of the capsule numbered 1. Martin bent down to enter. It was dark inside. A comfortable seat was located in the center. In front of it there were several monitors, an input console, and several control levers.

"Take this."

The technician pressed a paper bag into his hand. Then he closed the door of the cabin behind him. A pair of headphones hung from the seat back. Martin put them on and buckled in.

The voice of the technician continued, "The purpose of this apparatus is to show you how easily your senses can be deceived. Spatial disorientation is responsible for the majority of accidents in military aviation. It is heightened by the lack of reference points, darkness, and acceleration. All of these are factors you will encounter as an astronaut. But don't worry, you are completely safe here. If you feel sick, use the paper bag. This is also absolutely normal. We would actually worry if you did not react that way. However, if you miss the bag, you will have to clean up the mess yourself."

Martin looked at the bag in the bluish light of the monitors and opened it carefully. *Now I know why I have always avoided such rides at carnivals.* He breathed in the air that seemed to have thickened since the closing of the door. *Is there a sour smell left behind by my predecessors?* He wrinkled his nose.

The technician said, "We are about to start."

A roller blind opened in front of Martin—he had not noticed it before. Behind it was a pane of frosted glass that seemed to be lit by a projector. It showed a starry sky, maybe to calm him down. Martin felt the acceleration as the platform was turning. The starry sky remained in place. *Nice trick.* His eyes told him he was standing still, while the balance system in his ears signaled acceleration. A new force pulled at his back, and the capsule was now spinning around its own axis, first slowly, then faster. The starry sky raced past when the cabin was facing the middle.

It began to change, and now the stars no longer stood still but seemed to move backwards. His optical sense was convinced this carousel was turning the other way, yet he felt the acceleration and heard a slight rumbling.

"In front of you there is a joystick. Aim it toward the direction in which the capsule is moving," ordered the technician.

Martin grabbed the joystick. When he moved it, a reticle moved across the coordinate system on the screen. Martin could not make up his mind. *Was it X axis, plus or minus? Or Y axis?* From what he had seen of the device, it could not possibly move along the Z axis because the capsule only had a single pivot joint. However, the image in the window told him he was floating upward at an angle.

Martin selected this direction with the joystick and pressed the trigger.

"Totally wrong."

A blue circle flashed at the correct position.

"Again."

Martin had to learn to distrust his optical sense. The stars never moved from their positions, no matter how fast a spacecraft moved through space. They were much too far away. He needed to question any reference points. In space, there were neither contrails nor engine sounds. He could only rely on two inputs, the signals of his inner ear indicating his body was being accelerated in a certain direction, and the seeming change in size of an object that came nearer or moved farther away. As long as he moved with constant speed through the emptiness of space, he would not be able to determine his movement data without sophisticated machinery. He noticed he still held the paper bag in his left hand. It was needless, as he did not feel sick.

The MSDD changed the rotation of the platform and of the capsule according to a predetermined program. It made the starry sky change its position, sometimes faster, sometimes slower. Martin became more and more aware of which inputs were only meant to confuse him and which ones were genuine. Despite this, he did not always hit the target with his joystick. Human senses were not made for orientation in a three-dimensional space. For millions of years, humans and their predecessors had been moving across a seemingly flat plain. Sea creatures probably would make better astronauts than humans.

"Alright, that's enough," the voice of the technician said in Martin's headphones. The sound of the rotation faded away. Soon afterward, the technician opened the door. Martin was blinded by the bright light. Willinger offered him a hand. Martin rejected it, but after his first step out of the capsule, he stumbled. For a while he seemed to be standing on an incline. Willinger caught him.

"That's a typical aftereffect," he said, laughing raucously.

October 23, 2045, Pensacola

"TOMORROW YOU ARE CLIMBING MT. Everest. However, you can leave your hiking boots and your backpack at home," Willinger had announced yesterday. Once again they were to meet at the building of the Medical Institute.

Extreme height meant low air pressure. So, Martin was not surprised when Willinger led him to a room with a large tank. It was a pressure chamber. A doctor was in charge here, and he addressed both men. "Low pressure and low oxygen saturation have different effects on different people. The purpose is to have you notice these signs yourself. Maybe sometime your spacecraft will lose pressure and the sensors will fail. Then you must start a countermeasure before it is too late. You certainly won't have much time. If your brain does not receive oxygen for three minutes, you will be dead."

The man in the white lab coat, who had not introduced himself by name, led them into the basement. Willinger seemed to know him because he sometimes whispered to him. The sign at the door the doctor finally opened with his chip card read, *HAI Lab*. The room was classroom-sized and was mostly filled with a sort of gas tank, a horizontal cylinder with an entrance at one end.

"This is our HAI, or High-Altitude Indoctrination Device. Others might call it a pressure chamber. You know how the military loves acronyms," said the doctor.

I almost forgot. We are still at a Navy installation, Martin thought.

"Well then, let's go inside."

The doctor pulled at the handle of the hatch, which opened with a creak.

"This really should be lubricated sometime," he mused.

The chamber was surprisingly spacious on the inside. LEDs on the ceiling bathed it in a warm, white light. At the left and the right stood benches, and the walls behind them were padded. Pipes ran across the ceiling. Some of them led to oxygen masks hanging from loops. At the front end of the chamber stood a tripod holding a video camera that could watch the entire room.

"First we are going up to two and a half kilometers to see how you handle low pressure. Eventually we will reach eight kilometers."

In his head, Martin thought about what these numbers really meant. *Eight kilometers; like on a peak in the Himalayas, but without the cold and the wind.*

"In order to protect Willinger and you against the bends, you will breathe pure oxygen for a while before you go up. This will lower the partial pressure of nitrogen in your blood and prevent bubbles from forming in case of rapid changes in pressure. A pulmonary embolism is no joking matter. So, if you please."

The doctor gave both of them oxygen masks, pulling one at a time down from the ceiling on its elastic cord.

"Put these on and continue breathing normally. Have a nice flight."

The man left the pressure chamber. Martin heard the pressure lock creak. For a while, nothing happened. Then he felt the deep rumbling of a machine that was probably drawing off air.

"Two point five kilometers," the voice of the doctor said through the loudspeakers. "Is the pressure equalization working?"

Martin had never had any problem with this. He simply had to swallow, and his ears would pop.

"Everything is fine," he said.

"Leave the mask on. Answer with hand signals."

Martin formed an OK with his fingers, as divers do.

"We are moving up. This will take a bit longer."

Martin swallowed several times. Even so, the pressure difference eventually became so great he had to breathe strongly through his nose to equalize it.

"Here we are, at eight kilometers. Welcome to Mt. Everest. Take off the mask when I give the sign. Continue breathing normally. The goal is a maximum of four minutes. Don't be too ambitious, though. We don't want to do unnecessary damage to your brain cells. During this session, I will present you with a few tasks. Please watch yourself for symptoms of hypoxia. Let me remind you what you learned; dizziness, tiredness, extremities feeling numb or tingly, nausea, and breathing difficulties are possible, though those might not be the only symptoms. Every person reacts differently. Okay, now take off the mask."

Martin took another deep breath and took the mask off his face. Willinger gave him an encouraging smile. The older man leaned against the wall with his legs outstretched. He looked relaxed but didn't say a word.

Martin's first breaths didn't feel different than those at a lower altitude. *That's surprising,* he noted. His body was not yet aware that each breath transported two thirds less oxygen than usual into his lungs.

However, the oxygen level in his blood was rapidly decreasing. The tissue likely to be affected soonest consisted of the nerve cells in the brain—and it was his little gray cells that warned Martin of the danger. *I am having a hard time concentrating on the doctor's questions,* he noted. Multiplying two-digit numbers should have been easy, but he kept forgetting the intermediate results. A minute later he started feeling a pounding headache. He massaged his temples, which helped a bit. These were the effects of getting too little oxygen.

The biggest problem was that Martin clearly identified these symptoms, and he unconsciously tried to compensate for it by breathing faster. The respiratory system, though, does not work that way. The gas exchange in his lungs could not be accelerated by taking faster breaths. Martin knew this, but his mind, struggling with a bad oxygen supply, did not manage to get that across to his body. He kept breathing faster and still got less and less air. Suddenly Willinger sat up, leaned toward Martin, and placed a hand on his mouth. Now Martin could not breathe at all. "Slowly, quite slowly," the astronaut said, and then removed his hand and leaned back. Martin concentrated and took a slow and deep breath. He felt calmer.

"Two more minutes," the doctor's voice announced.

Martin could barely believe only half of the time had passed. The seconds seemed to stretch on endlessly. Once his breathing normalized, the less he thought about it. He looked at his fingers; the tips seemed to tingle slightly. He thought of a steak and felt hunger rather than nausea. He could no longer multiply, but he could still follow directions.

"Lift your left arm and point to your nose with your ring finger."

No problem.

"Cross your arms. And now change the direction of the crossing."

Finished.

"Left hand to right knee, right hand on left shoulder."

Finally, the doctor said, "Very good. Your time on the summit is over. Please put your mask on. We are going to descend."

October 25, 2045, NASA

"I WOULD LIKE to talk to you about the rest of your training." Yesterday, Willinger had announced they would be meeting an important NASA official today. The man's name tag read, *Walter Cusack*. He appeared to be way past retirement age; white hair, a weathered face, and a somewhat stooped posture, but a still-energetic gait.

"Our quality standards are high, very high. I am not trying to offend you, but under normal circumstances..." Cusack began.

Willinger wanted to contradict him, but the man stopped this with a wave of his hand. Willinger leaned back in his chair. Martin had never seen him this tame.

Cusack continued. "No matter that the circumstances are extraordinary. The Europeans are trying to avoid an internal struggle and are glad you are a candidate favored by several important arguments. First of all, you are one-half German, which is enough for them. India, on the other hand, would be glad to reduce expenses. The war with Pakistan is putting a lot of stress on them. They would welcome the unexpected saving of several billion dollars right now."

Martin thought he had misheard. "Did you say *several* billion? That can't be."

"No, you heard that right," Cusack said. "You are worth several billion dollars. Each region sending an astronaut must participate in financing this expedition. We were lucky to find a private sponsor for you at the last moment."

Some billionaire was willing to pay several billion so I can fly to Saturn in a spacecraft? Martin was puzzled. *Couldn't this person have sent me a thousandth of that sum and just been happy about saving his money?*

"Be that as it may, we have to streamline your training. Normally, you would get a jet pilot license first, but that would take weeks, and it wouldn't help you anyway. Who knows if you'll ever return?" Cusack waited to see how he would react.

He seems to have expected some kind of shocked expression, Martin thought, showing no reaction.

"Well. You seem to realize what your chances look like. We are flying without any safety nets. So far, neither the spacecraft nor its drive has been really tested. You already saw what teething troubles *Valkyrie* had. Compared to this, the moon landing was well-prepared back in its day."

Martin knew his history well. In retrospect, it had been by sheer luck that the American astronauts had made it to the moon and back.

"Are you trying to talk me out of doing the job?" Martin asked.

"For heaven's sake, no. No one knows his way around the drill vehicle like you, as both of your bosses have assured me. You are our first pick for that position. Of course, we are also training a substitute, in case you drop out at the last minute. Just think of what happened to the Sikh."

"I would like to meet the guy you are training as my substitute."

"The person is a woman, and you are not supposed to meet her. She has been a member of the Astronaut Corps for a while and will participate in a mission to Mars unless you drop out here," Cusack said.

"So what's going to happen next?"

"Right, let's not waste any time. Next week you will meet all of your colleagues for the first time. They are all waiting for that moment. We will send the entire group of you on wilderness survival training."

It won't help me if I know how to light a fire with wet wood, neither in space nor on Enceladus, Martin realized, though he knew the main goal was to test them as a group.

"Afterward there will be underwater training in space-suits, and then off into space. We are going to skip the parabolic flights. Otherwise we won't be able to meet the deadlines. You will get plenty of zero-gravity training aboard the Chinese Tiangong-4 station."

Martin asked, "Will I still be here for Christmas?"

"I wouldn't count on it. The construction of your spacecraft is proceeding unexpectedly smoothly. If we manage a December launch, your journey will be as short as possible. If we wait any longer, your journey will take longer, since Saturn wouldn't be in such an advantageous position."

"Well. I would like to have a week off before launch."

"If you promise me you won't go skiing or mountain-climbing ..."

"No, I am just going to visit my mother."

"You do that, Mr. Neumaier. We trust you."

Martin and Willinger shook hands with Cusack when they said goodbye.

"Typical for NASA," Willinger whispered to Martin when they were in the corridor. "I could have told you all of that. Instead, they fly in some guy from California."

"He probably had nothing else to do," Martin mused.

Willinger nodded. "What would you think about going out for some drinks tonight? You will leave us the day after tomorrow, and we haven't even had a beer together."

"Sure," Martin nodded. "Are you going to pick me up? I don't have a car here."

"I will be in front of your door at eight."

Willinger was punctual. "You're not one of those vegetarians, are you?"

Martin shook his head.

"That's good, because I would like to take you to PJ's. It's steak night there tonight. And tonight they don't have karaoke scheduled, or football or baseball on TV, so we'll even be able to have a decent conversation."

While they were driving through Houston's wide streets —with his trainer taking the wheel himself—the streetlights were coming on. Willinger finally stopped in front of a building Martin would have initially mistaken for a private residence that had seen better days. It had two stories and small windows, of which only those on the ground floor showed signs advertising karaoke and steaks. Willinger parked the car at the curb.

The tavern was small. On a crowded night, it would

seat barely more than 20 or 25 people, and this evening it was almost empty. Two couples sat at a table, and three men were playing cards at the bar. The bartender, who was probably also the owner, came from behind the counter and greeted Willinger.

"Nice of you to show up again," the man said as he extended his right hand.

"This is a young colleague of mine. His name is Martin."

Martin hadn't been called young in a long time.

"Hi, I'm Steve. I own this place. I hope you like steaks. There's nothing else on the menu tonight."

"Of course he likes steaks," Willinger answered for him. "And bring us two beers." Willinger pointed at a corner table with two chairs. "That's perfect for us."

Martin chose the chair with its back to the wall. The table had not been recently wiped, and displayed countless marks left by glasses.

"PJ's hasn't been remodeled for at least 50 years. That's his specialty," Willinger explained. "You won't find another tavern like this in Houston anymore."

After the first sip of beer, Willinger's demeanor became more personal.

This beer is served in a glass, and it's surprisingly good, not as tasteless as the usual beer that comes in cans, Martin discerned.

Willinger noted his appreciative look. "It's made by a local brewery, according to the German beer law, the *Reinheitsgebot*." He pronounced the last word almost flawlessly, with hardly any accent.

His curiosity piqued, Martin shot a look at Willinger and asked, "German ancestors?"

"Only on my mother's side," Willinger said. "My father

met her in Germany while he was serving in the army, but I have forgotten most of the words."

It had been almost the same with Martin, except his father never served in the army. Martin realized Willinger had not once uttered his raucous laugh today.

"Is there trouble at the office?"

Willinger put his glass on the table. "Oh... I'm in more of a farewell mood."

"But I will be back after the survival course, for the underwater training, won't I?"

"No, it's not because of you." Willinger gave him a friendly pat on the shoulder. "When you come back, I won't be here anymore."

"Did you get a promotion?"

"No, they are forcing me into retirement."

"How old are you, Dave?" *He must be in his mid-fifties,* Martin guessed.

"I'm 58. Because of my achievements and all that nonsense, they're giving me a so-called honorable retirement."

"So that's not what this is about?"

"I just think I am too much of a nuisance for them," Willinger replied. "I don't keep my mouth shut when something goes wrong."

Martin hesitated. "You are talking about the Enceladus mission, right?"

"Yes. I keep having the feeling they are sending you to a certain death. They want to surf the wave caused by the discovery on Enceladus, but I believe this is still beyond the abilities of mankind. Maybe in twenty years ..."

"It worked for the Apollo project," Martin said.

"That's the problem. It worked once, so they believe it

won't be any different now." Willinger made gestures with his hands while he talked.

"If they wait twenty years, they'll never get the money. You see how India was glad to get out of the whole thing." Willinger paused and took another sip of his beer. "Space travel only works if you take one step after another. Build a base on Mars, then go on to Jupiter... the few cells in the ocean of Enceladus won't run away. They must have been there for millions of years."

Martin shook his head. "It is too late for these discussions."

"Yes, and that's probably why I am being 'asked' to retire now." Willinger leaned back in his chair. Martin had never seen him so depressed. His face suddenly brightened when a waitress approached with their food.

"Well, guys, here are your steaks."

"Thanks, Anna, you're a sweetie," Willinger said as he looked up at her with a smile.

"Sure. Salt, pepper, and ketchup are already on the table. If you need anything else..."

Martin watched as Willinger gazed intently at the waitress who sashayed back toward the bar. *Glad to see his carnal instincts are still functioning.*

Two large plates sat there, one before Martin and the other in front of his host. Each one offered two ribeye steaks. Martin estimated they weighed about ten ounces apiece. Each also had a baked potato, split open and nested in aluminum foil to hold the heat. The cook had poured plenty of cream gravy on each potato and sprinkled crumbled bacon on top.

Willinger began cutting his steak "Enjoy your meal. You will be dreaming of such steaks—and I know what I'm talking about."

Martin took his knife and fork and cut off a piece of steak. Red meat juice oozed out of it—*mmm, just the way I like it.* The steak smelled of a charcoal grill.

"Great place you chose for us," he said.

They ate in silence for a while. Willinger did not mind chewing a bit noisily. Martin, on the other hand, tried to eat quietly, as his mother had taught him.

"Why didn't you refuse to go on this mission?"

Martin had a hard time figuring out what Willinger had asked, as he had spoken with his mouth full. Martin took his time and finished chewing the piece of meat in his mouth, swallowing before answering.

"I'm not sure. To me, it seems to... make sense. After all, someone has to do it, and I am both suitable and expendable. I haven't ever had to make a decision as serious as this one. It just seemed to make sense for so many reasons."

"Expendable? Is no one waiting for you?"

"My mother in Germany won't get to see me for a Christmas or two."

"No girlfriend? No ex-wife or someone like that? Aren't you past 30 already? Or—are you gay?"

Martin laughed. "Actually, I am already 39."

"Not that it would bother me if you were gay." Willinger looked a bit embarrassed.

"I'm not. I lived with a woman for a long time. She was the love of my life and all that. I didn't even know I was capable of achieving anything like that."

"And then she met someone else?"

Martin hesitated. "She... she died. It was suicide."

"I am so sorry." Willinger reached across and placed a hand on Martin's shoulder.

"She suffered from depression. Never said anything to

indicate she would end her life. I should have noticed, but my work..."

"I understand."

I am not sure Willinger really understands, Martin considered. *I do not know this man well enough to tell, but at the least, his statement feels genuine.*

"Martin, you seem to be running away from life. Am I right?"

Martin shrugged. Then he saw the waitress approaching their table.

"Two more beers, please," Willinger motioned to her.

Martin knew he had a mission waiting for him. But first he had to get drunk with Dave.

October 26, 2045, NASA

THE NEXT MORNING HE AWOKE, lying fully clothed on his bed, with a hangover. *Someone took my shoes off, though,* Martin noticed. *I remember the last beer at PJ's, and then Willinger must have driven me here and helped me onto my bed.* His head was throbbing, but he did not feel nauseous. *I have the day off—* that much he remembered. Starting tomorrow, the wilderness survival course was going to begin.

Martin tried to recall the previous evening. *Dave asked me an important question—am I trying to run away from my life by joining this mission?* Now the question sounded to him like an accusation. *Is it really cowardly to go on an uncertain mission lasting for years? Yes, Willinger is right. It only would seem courageous to outsiders, to people who did not know me. It doesn't concern me at all that the space mission has a lot of issues and the technology is far from proven.*

Sure, there were a number of possible situations he had so far avoided. No one knew he was afraid in the dark, which had started in his childhood when his mother went out in the evening. Outer space was the very domain of darkness, followed closely by the depths of the ocean—or an endless hole reaching for kilometers into the ice. He would also have to spend many days interacting with colleagues he did not know yet, even though dealing with people was not one of his strong points.

The reason he had agreed to it in spite of these issues had not been clear to him back then. *Now, I'm starting to have an idea how strong my distaste for my life must have become, if I voluntarily want to face my deepest fears. I must have something in common with my dead girlfriend. It's probably the very idea that this might be a journey without return that makes it so attractive—a death wish I've never admitted to myself.*

What does all of that mean for me and my decision? It meant he was not suitable for this trip into space. It meant he was a danger to his colleagues, who surely valued their lives. *If I really do not care whether I die, how can I be certain I would do everything to save the lives of my crewmates in an emergency—and my own life, as they will be depending on me?* In this unique mission, the greatest uncertainty factor was not the immature technology, but people like himself.

Martin decided to leave the mission. He would quit his job at NASA, find a nice wife on the internet, get married, and raise kids. The woman whose name they did not want to reveal to him would get his ticket to Enceladus. However, he did not feel the relief he had expected after coming to this decision.

The following day was supposed to be a travel day. In the morning, Martin already tried to find someone he could inform of his decision to quit, but unfortunately it was the weekend. He only met the driver who took him to the airport. After the landing in Boston, a second driver waited for him. He was from India, and Martin barely understood what he said. They drove northward for four hours, almost to the Canadian border. Soon after they left the airport, the rain started. The driver listened to soft music and whistled along out of tune. After half an hour, Martin fell asleep.

"Sir, we're going to arrive in five minutes," the driver finally announced, taking care to speak clearly.

The vehicle was driving on a narrow road. To the right was a deep green forest, soggy with moisture, and to the left a lake. Even though it must be still afternoon, it was much darker than in Houston.

Wide awake now, he asked, "Where are we going to arrive?"

"At Rangeley, Maine, sir," answered the driver. "The Navy has a training camp there, but I am sure you knew that."

"I am going to be alone?"

"Sorry, sir, I wasn't told anything about that. I am just supposed to drop you off at the entrance, and then you'll never see me again."

THEY HAD FINALLY REACHED their destination. The driver pulled over, shifted into park, but kept the engine idling. "Well, here we are. Don't forget your backpack, sir, and have a nice day."

The driver seemed to be in a hurry. Martin took his backpack, opened the door, and got out. It was windy and cold. *Not even 10 degrees*, he guessed. He saw a gate made of iron bars and a smaller green door next to it that was in view of a sentry box. Martin approached and knocked on the dirty window. At first nothing happened, and then he heard the door creak. The sound of heavy boots indicated a soldier was coming toward him.

"Chief Petty Officer Miller. You are Mr. Neumaier?"

Martin handed him his NASA ID card.

"Great, then I won't have to wait for you any longer."

CPO Miller opened the gate and let Martin in. Then he locked it from the inside with a heavy horizontal beam.

"All the others are here already," Miller said.

"Do you know whether someone from NASA..." Martin wondered aloud.

"Only your colleagues and the responsible Navy instructors are here. We are just among ourselves. It is going to be a cozy week."

Martin doubted this. *That is, unless our quarters have an open fireplace with bear rugs in front of it.*

Miller and Martin left the sentry post and walked about 150 meters into the forest until they reached a clearing. A primitive wooden hut stood in the middle. A few meters in front of the door Martin saw a small well with a hand pump. Miller once again opened the door for him. Inside, the hut smelled musty, and it was barely warmer than outside. Eight people sat around a rustic table, their heads leaning over papers.

"Look who I brought," Miller announced to the group.

On cue, everyone turned toward Martin, and he automatically blushed. *I'm glad the lights are dim.*

Miller did not introduce Martin, so he did it himself. "I am Martin Neumaier... The new guy."

He couldn't think of anything else to say. The others had surely read his file by now. A dark-haired woman got up. She was taller than he was. Martin recognized her. It was Francesca, the Italian pilot.

"Nice to have you here," she said, greeting him. "I already told the others about our adventure." She waved to Martin to join her.

The man next to her took a step to the side and shook Martin's hand. Martin also recognized him. This was the engineer who had participated in developing the DFD.

"Hayato Masukoshi," the Japanese man said. "We already know each other. And this is Amy Michaels, our commander."

Everyone had called Amy 'Commander' from day one, even though there was nothing to command yet. She possessed a natural authority, despite being slender and only slightly over a meter and a half tall. Martin shook Amy's hand. She gripped his hand firmly.

"Our ship's doctor, Dimitri Marchenko, and Science Specialist Jiaying Li are being trained by their national space agencies. They won't join us until we get to Tiangong-4," Amy said with her soft voice. *She reminds me of something—or someone.* Martin winced, suddenly worried he might fall for her.

"Everything okay?" she asked.

"I am just a bit exhausted," he quickly replied. "There has been a lot happening recently. All my life..."

"It is the same for all of us, too. But the Navy folks here promised we should get some rest in the coming days. Isn't that so?" Amy looked at the men in uniform.

Miller, who appeared to be the highest-ranking military person present, answered, "Active relaxation, I would say."

October 28, 2045, Rangeley/Maine

"RISE AND SHINE! QUICK! QUICK! QUICK!" Martin opened his eyes. There was no light coming through the windows of the hut yet. Martin had not slept very well, as at least one of the men had been constantly snoring throughout the night. He yawned.

"Come on people, move faster!" Martin recognized Miller's voice. Martin sat up and jumped down from the bunkbed. The uniform, on loan from the Navy, hung on the rear metal post of the bed. He put on the shirt, stepped into his pants, buttoned and zipped and tightened the belt. *Jacket, boots, finished,* Martin thought to himself. *Oh. I still need my cap.*

"Pack your backpack and get outside," Miller ordered.

They had constructed the backpacks last night from military tarps. They contained two canteens, disinfectant tablets, a rain poncho, a knife, a compass, and a map.

Outside the door, Martin stepped into a puddle and silently cursed. *Damn. It must have rained all night.* He felt small raindrops land on his skin. He tried to recognize the others, but no one was talking, and the uniforms all looked alike in the semidarkness. He only picked out Amy because she was quite a bit shorter than the others.

"MOVE OUT!"

One of the instructors started walking toward the forest. They all followed and marched through the darkness in single file. They walked endlessly and aimlessly, it seemed to Martin. The instructor changed direction so often that Martin became completely disoriented. Did his colleagues feel the same way? Twice he stumbled over tree roots, and now his knee hurt. He was not going to complain, though. For him, the entire adventure would be over in a week, since he had already decided to quit.

It had been getting lighter for a while when they finally reached a small clearing that resembled the one where the cabin was located, but no building could be seen.

"You should see something at 9 o'clock," Miller said. The group looked to the left. Something hung in a pine tree, about five meters from the ground.

"What you are seeing here is a parachute. One of your colleagues might be hanging from it. Save him, ASCANs!"

Like the other three, Martin approached the tree. The pine was straight, and the parachute was therefore out of reach. The tree trunk was smooth, and it looked like it had been deliberately cleared of branches. Three meters up, he saw a branch that could be used for climbing.

"Should we give someone a leg up?" Amy suggested. Francesca was the tallest member of the team and would, therefore, be the support. Amy was too short, so only Martin and Hayato remained. He looked at the Japanese man, who nodded. *Does that mean 'you go ahead' or 'I will do that?'* Martin wondered.

"Okay, okay," he sighed. *Then I'll climb.* Francesca stood next to the trunk so he could reach the branch with his hands if she just lifted him high enough. She formed a stirrup with her hands. Martin placed his left foot on her hands and tried to grasp her shoulder. Too late—she was already giving him a strong upward push. He sailed right over her head and landed in the dirt.

Martin had to laugh, no matter whether the others thought it was funny or not, because the situation seemed so bizarre to him.

"Let's try that again," he said. Once more Francesca gave him a strong push, but this time he expected it. He stretched out soon enough that his hands reached the single branch. The branch bent under his weight and the rough bark cut into his skin, but it held. *And now, what do I do next?*

The others realized he did not know what to do and gave him suggestions. Even though Martin had never managed very many chin-ups, he succeeded in pulling himself up and supporting his weight with one arm. That left the other arm free. He briefly took note of the immediate surroundings. There were enough branches up here. He grabbed one after the other and climbed the rest of the way to the parachute, the lines of which were tangled in the tree. He pulled out the knife he had placed in the pocket near his knee and cut the lines until the parachute was pulled down by its own weight. It fell to the ground with a thud. *I hope the guys from the Navy have not overdone the realism,* he thought, as he climbed down again, hung from the lowest branch, and dropped into the soft moss.

"Congratulations," Miller said after they had pulled the parachute and its payload into the middle of the clearing. It was a tarp folded into a sack containing various cans.

"This is your food for the next two days." Miller

pointed upward. "Water comes from there, too, although there is also a creek here."

Hayato grabbed one of the cans, ready to open it with his knife.

"Did I say anything about breakfast? First we will build a shelter and start a fire," Miller sternly instructed.

The tough material of the parachute served as the basis for a primitive tent, which was reinforced with branches and secured with parachute cord.

"Definitely keep the rest of the cord," Miller advised. He was the only one giving instructions now.

The fire proved to be more of a problem. Miller let them experiment for a little while. Amy had seen in a movie how someone made fire by quickly twirling a stick of wood against a second piece of wood with tinder piled around the contact point. However, they didn't find any wood dry enough for this purpose. Martin was about to talk to the instructor when Francesca came to the rescue. She opened her jacket and took off her necklace. It had a pendant in the shape of a thick metal rod.

"Spoilsport," Miller said, when he saw what she was up to.

"This is a firesteel. A pilot can't be without a firesteel." Francesca told them exactly what to do. Hayato was supposed to find birch trees and cut off several pieces of bark with his knife. Martin was told to gather old, dead branches, even if they were wet. With these branches, Amy and Francesca created a fire pit, protected by the tarp. Then Francesca used her knife to cut fine shavings from the inside of the birch bark.

"This is our tinder," the pilot said.

She created a fist-sized pile of shavings and placed it on a dry surface. Then she held the firesteel at a 45-degree angle over the tinder and started scraping the knife across it. Sparks flew into the tinder, and soon a small flame spread and finally set the dead branches alight. Once the fire was big enough, Francesca removed the tarp from over it.

"If we regularly add new wood, the rain cannot extinguish the fire," she explained. "The outside of the wood will be quickly dried by the heat. It just cannot be young and fresh, because green wood is moist on the inside."

Miller clapped his hands.

"Who wants some coffee? It's breakfast time."

Martin looked up at the lingering gray sky. A bright spot was slowly climbing upward. It must be almost noon. Each of them picked out a can and placed it near the fire. The food, eaten directly from the can using a knife and fingers, tasted delicious.

Miller advised the group, "In the wilderness, you are going to need at least two meals a day."

After the meal, Martin would have liked to rest for half an hour, but Miller wouldn't let them.

"Let's see how you do at coming up with a second meal. In temperate zones, you are going to find a lot of edible plants in the forest, but there is nothing like a piece of meat. Don't try to tackle a wild boar in areas where they exist. Bears are too strong. Foxes and deer are too fast. It is even hard to catch rabbits with what you have on hand. But you can catch squirrels. What do you think of a tasty squirrel?"

Miller addressed the two women directly. Francesca kept a straight face, but Amy grimaced.

"Okay, we are going to need a straight branch, at least a meter and a half long and five centimeters thick. Martin and Hayato, you start looking for one. Amy and Francesca, we happened to find an old umbrella. I would like you to remove the metal ribs from it."

Martin nodded at Hayato. They went into the forest in different directions. It took Martin a quarter of an hour to find two suitable branches and to clean them with his knife. When he returned, Hayato was already sitting by the fire. The women had turned the metal spokes of the umbrella into rings, which they now attached to the branches at about half height.

Miller began his lecture, "This is our squirrel trap. These animals are lazy, just like we are. We will lean the branches at a 45-degree angle against a tree where we suspect squirrels to be located. When they climb the tree, they choose the most comfortable path, until they realize they have stuck their heads in a wire loop. Then they jump. That's not good for the squirrels."

Amy was staring at the branch she held in her hand.

"Do we actually have to do this? We understand the principle behind it now," Martin said.

"Martin, I am sorry, but you have to. How else am I supposed to show you how to skin a squirrel?"

"Thanks, Martin, but I can handle it," Amy said.

"Well, let's place our traps. Then we have to wait a while. In the meantime, we'll collect water, in case there is no creek."

Miller selected two trees he considered particularly promising for squirrels. Martin looked around. *I don't have any idea why he would choose this area,* he concluded.

"You see the shit on the ground?" Miller pointed. "Squirrels must be here regularly."

Then he led them back to the makeshift tent in the middle of the clearing.

"We still have a lot of parachute fabric left over. How

can we use that to get water? Francesca, don't say anything," Miller directed.

"Put it in the rain and then squeeze it out," Hayato said, laughing.

Amy raised her hand like in school. "Construct a funnel?"

"Then let's get started." Miller did not indicate whether this was the correct solution. It seemed logical to Martin, so he did not contradict him.

"If the funnel is supposed to have a radius and a depth of one meter, we have to cut out a sector with a central angle of 360 degrees times the radius, divided by the root of the depth squared plus the radius squared," Martin explained.

"What?" All three queried him, almost simultaneously.

"Imagine a cake baked in a round cake pan has a radius of one meter. Somebody already ate a piece of one minus one divided by the square root of two."

They still looked at him aghast.

About to lose patience, Martin tried again. "Almost a third of the cake is missing, okay?"

They cut the remaining fabric with their knives so it had the form of a circle with a sector of about a third missing. They joined the edges of the missing one-third, using parachute cord. Then they supported this construction with branches and placed a container below the hole in the middle.

"This is an area of about three square meters," Martin explained. "In October, there should be an average of two liters per day per square meter, so within 24 hours we should be able to catch six liters of water. That should be enough for two to three people—only if it rains, of course, and rains the average amount."

Miller looked at him without saying a word and then sat down. They watched the container slowly fill up. They did not even notice they had already been soaked to the bone.

"Amy, one person has to stay here and tend the fire," Miller finally said.

Martin smiled. Miller probably did not want Amy to be present when they inspected the squirrel traps.

"You others come with me to check whether we caught anything."

Miller went ahead. The ASCANs were moving a bit more slowly than before. Apparently no one wanted to be the first to reach the traps.

"You see? We got one!" Miller whispered excitedly, even though there was no reason for quiet. He picked up the first three empty traps and pressed the loops flat. Then he showed them the dead squirrel in the fourth trap.

"Don't worry, it died very quickly."

No one said anything.

"Now we are going to need a tree stump that's as smooth as possible. By chance, there is one right around the corner. We cannot cook the squirrel in its fur. We have to skin it first."

He bent down. The tree stump was about 25 centimeters high. The instructor placed the dead animal on the smooth wood, inserted the knife slightly above the anus, and cut a few millimeters along the fur. Then he pulled firmly on the skin above it until it started to separate from the flesh underneath. Miller looked around. He found a clean spot on the ground, put the animal there, and stepped with one foot on its tail. Then he pulled strongly on the fur, which rolled up centimeter by centimeter until he had reached the front legs. Here he cut off both the fur and the head.

"Finished." Miller wiped the sweat off his forehead. His hands were not bloody, as Martin would have expected. Without its fur the squirrel looked even smaller. *It seems to be lonely and in need of help, almost like a newborn,* Martin realized, and he was starting to feel nauseous. He took a few quick steps to get behind a bush, where he threw up. *What kind of life did this animal have?* he wondered. *Did it feel something like happiness, or at least satisfaction? Did it have any idea how it would die someday?*

Martin returned to the group. He saw the others had also reacted with shock and disgust.

"It's not worthwhile gutting the animal because it's so small. Grill it whole, but only eat the meat off the legs, breast, and back."

Miller noticed his audience was not at all enthusiastic about their prospective meal.

"It's your life or the animal's, that's what it's all about." He sounded serious. "You probably won't crash-land in a forest, and as far as I have heard, there are no squirrels on Enceladus. There could be a situation, though, when you have to decide between your life and the lives of others. You should be prepared for that, at least a little. Such decisions can be very painful, and the consequences of your decision will follow you for the rest of your life."

They returned to the camp in silence. Amy had already prepared some fresh coffee. They had hot-in-the-can food for dinner. They sat around the fire to get warm. Inner and outer warmth began to drive the moisture out of their clothes. Today, no one was in the mood for telling stories of other times. The flames sputtered as long as someone kept the fire alive. The wood was crackling while it dried in the heat. There was a smell of soot, moss, and wet dog fur, even though there was no dog nearby. No one even noticed when the sun set behind all the clouds.

At some point, Martin wrapped himself inside a piece of tarp, his backpack serving as a pillow. In reflection, he replayed the events of the day just before he fell asleep. *This day has made me think twice about wanting to quit. I now realize it would be a mistake for me to call off this journey. My curiosity has been piqued, and I think it would be worth my while to get to know the people I will be traveling with. I no longer have the feeling I will endanger them.*

December 20, 2045, Tiangong-4

SAYING farewell had been easy for the mission crew. They were all glad to finally leave the confines of Tiangong-4. The Chinese space station, currently occupied by 17 people, had become an international meeting point, so they felt like they didn't belong, and were only in the others' way. No one aboard had said anything negative to the crew because they were all too polite.

Yet Martin sensed a mixture of envy and admiration: envy, because aboard this space station were taikonauts, cosmonauts, and astronauts with considerably more experience who might feel more qualified for this mission; and admiration, as it was clear to everyone how small their chances for a safe return really were. There simply had never been a space expedition lasting two years, so far away from any help. Without ongoing delivery of food, water, and spare parts, Tiangong-4 itself would cease to function in less than four weeks. *ILSE*, the craft that was supposed to fly to Saturn, would spend 30 times that long with only the supplies the planners managed to stow on board two spacecraft. *ILSE's* full name was in fact *ILSE 1*, to differentiate it from the supply ship, *ILSE 2*.

After leaving the *Dragon* capsule that had brought them into space, they met Dimitri Marchenko and Jiaying Li for the first time. The Russian, athletic and not quite young anymore, seemed to have the respect of the entire crew. *The Chinese woman is very reserved,* Martin thought, *and I have no idea what to make of her.* He tried to find out whether there were any rumors about her here at the space station, but apparently there were none. On the other hand, everyone aboard had already heard about Marchenko's legendary vodka parties.

The days stretched on. Martin felt exhausted and no longer even noticed his own body odor. He could hardly sleep due to all the noise on board. They did not expect to be able to leave this year. Yet five days before Christmas Eve, NASA finally released their decision—the mission would start the next day, December 20.

The hatch of the airlock separating *ILSE* from Tiangong-4 had just opened. A technician waved at them and said something in Chinese. Jiaying answered him and walked ahead. Once he had followed her inside, Martin breathed in its air. *Finally, our own spaceship,* he thought. *It smells fresh—no comparison to the stench of Tiangong-4. Of course it smells of oil and ozone, but it reminds me of the fresh air after a thunderstorm.*

They had arrived in the command module, and Amy took charge. "CapCom says we should just stay here."

"They are suddenly in quite a hurry," Hayato remarked.

"The sooner we leave, the sooner we will be back," Amy said. "So, everyone, please buckle in."

Martin followed her instructions. His place was in a

corner of the command module. Amy and Francesca, the pilots, were busy steering. He leaned back, closed his eyes, and sighed. Soon afterward, a force pressed him into his seat. It was the inertia of his own body that resisted the change in velocity caused by the engines at the stern of the ship. He had no idea what was happening up front. *No big speeches, no slogans, no good wishes,* he thought. He had never been sent on a journey with so little ceremony. *One might even suspect the organizers of this trip were embarrassed for some reason, but I do not regret it. In the end, who needs all that hoopla, anyway?* He went to sleep.

June 25, 2046, Space

THE STONE HAD BEEN on its way since ancient times. It possessed no memory, but if it had one, it would remember a giant, flat cloud of gas and dust coalescing through its own gravity, rotating faster and faster, until it became hotter and hotter inside, and at some point igniting a sun. One of these dust particles still rested inside it, the seed from which the stone had been born. The heat had made other particles stick to it. The particle grew into a stone by colliding with others, but it circled the young sun at the wrong place. While its siblings grew from centimeters to meters and kilometers, forming asteroids, planetoids, and even planets, the stone remained a stone. It would be called a 'meteoroid' by humans, of which it knew nothing. They would not even give it a name, as with its diameter of 20 centimeters it was far too small and too unimportant. There are millions this size, yet space is so huge that the chance of it ever meeting one of its siblings, or anything else for that matter, is close to zero.

But it is not precisely zero. By chance, the trajectories of this nameless stone and a spacecraft launched by humans would intersect somewhere between Earth and Mars. It was an almost incredible coincidence, something that had rarely happened in the short history of human spaceflight. It was a chance occurrence that belonged to two categories at once—*probably won't happen* and *must not happen*. The spacecraft that the stone approached at a speed of over 130 kilometers per second—seen from the perspective of the stone—was not prepared for this. Nothing could prepare a spacecraft for such a collision. The impact would release the energy of a nuclear explosion, even though the stone's diameter was less than a man's wrist-to-elbow length.

The spaceship *ILSE 2* was asleep to conserve energy. It was en route to the moon of a distant planet that had been closely studied by humans only twice, where the spacecraft was supposed to meet its sister ship, *ILSE 1*. But the artificial intelligence on board already knew this encounter would never happen. It had noticed the stone two seconds ago and had used trillions of computing cycles and thousands of simulations to calculate its path. It compared this with the abilities of the ship's drives and realized that no course correction could prevent the collision. The AI had known about this blind spot since before the launch of the spacecraft, as soon as it had been fed the data. It knew the available technology would discover obstacles of a certain size too late to change the course of the ship in time. It was not scared by this, as it knew it would survive a collision. A meteoroid of that size could destroy one of the modules, but not the entire ship. The AI would then quickly retreat to a computer located in a different module.

Therefore, it was not upset when the stone came closer. The AI left the ship in standby mode. At this point, it certainly would be too late to hand the ship over to human control. Three seconds before impact, it started a starboard engine. Not much seemed to happen, but by this small change in position, the AI caused the stone to impact at the spot where it would do the least damage—right before the engines, where titanium alloy girders separated them from the habitable modules.

There were two seconds left. The AI used this long interval to train the pattern recognition of its neural network. Then it registered that the strong arms connecting the ship to its engines were torn off. A loud blow lasting only a few milliseconds was transmitted through the body of the spaceship. Otherwise, all was silent. The frame absorbed the kinetic energy of the stone, comparable to a small atomic bomb, but without the shockwave, because even destruction worked soundlessly in the vacuum of space. The engines, no longer connected to the spaceship, shut off automatically. The life support systems could work only a few hours on battery power. The AI deactivated them permanently.

It also went to sleep itself, in order not to waste the batteries. It did not regret this action. The connection to Earth had been severed, but its sensors were all online. It could now observe the wonders of space for several millennia, while the spacecraft shot past Saturn with undiminished speed and eventually left the solar system. If the programmers had given the AI a sense of irony, it might have been amused by what it saw of the ship—the engines, now turned off, were unflinchingly following the command module, like a dog following its master even without a leash.

However, the programmers had decided the AI did not need the tool of irony to fulfill its tasks. That would have been a waste of capacity. The AI was curious, though, and this curiosity would save it from going insane in the millennia to come.

Programmers are pragmatic people. That was the reason they had not given the AI a sense of responsibility for its human creators, as *ILSE 2* was an unmanned ship. Therefore, after the collision the AI did not regret that the spacecraft could no longer fulfill its task of bringing supplies to the humans aboard *ILSE 1* when they reached their goal. Humans would discover this glitch a week later, when Mission Control would try to wake *ILSE 2* from standby mode and would receive no response.

July 4, 2046, ILSE

MARTIN ASSUMED his very own death might be waiting for him. *It could be over, between one second and the next—I know this.* He already had been conscious of this on Earth. In his everyday life, moving between the apartment, the office, and the supermarket, he had wasted no thought on the idea. Out here, on the other hand, he could not get used to the idea of always being threatened by death without seeing it coming. Perhaps there had been a minor collision in the asteroid belt several thousand years ago. Maybe a comet, on its path for millions of years, had lost some of its material around here. Death did not have to be fast to hit him. It could simply be waiting for *ILSE*, the spaceship that hurtled him toward Saturn at 50 kilometers per second. To be more precise, the spacecraft that was moving him toward the point where the planet Saturn, which now had just emerged from behind the sun, would be located several months from now.

ILSE, the *International Life Search Expedition. The name is too pretentious,* he felt. When he pronounced the acronym I.L.S.E as a word in his mother's language, the others gave him funny looks. Jiaying, the Chinese woman, then tried to repeat the word with a German accent. She was linguistically talented, but it still sounded like 'Ull-see' rather than 'Ill-see.'

Martin looked at the ceiling, which was gradually getting brighter. *A meteoroid could hit here at any moment*, he imagined. There was only a third of a meter of fabric between his cabin and space. This was not just any fabric, though, but a ceramic textile folded into about a dozen layers—a 'stuffed Whipple shield.' The shield material consisted of special foam sprayed between the textile layers. As the foam dispersed, it formed numerous small, airtight chambers. Whatever hit the exterior wall was supposed to splinter into numerous pieces that would further fragment in the next layer and finally get stuck in the foam, which closed up again after it cooled off. It even worked. He had seen the small holes on the outside of the hull in the images taken by the spider robots.

Of course, this only worked if the meteoroid was small enough. Up to five centimeters the system would be fine, the experts on Earth had said. The probability of encountering a bigger rock on the way to Saturn was quite low. In addition, the wall of his cabin did not point in the direction of their travel. When Martin realized this, he breathed a sigh of relief. If *ILSE* sprung a leak somewhere, the artificial intelligence would immediately close all bulkhead doors and isolate the affected module.

Which AI? Before launch, the *ILSE* consortium had held a bidding contest that led to two winners, Siri and Watson. Apple's Siri had scored best in emotional contacts with astronauts, while IBM's Watson had done best in prognosis and algorithms. It was decided to load both on the spacecraft's computers. In hindsight, the psychologists considered that a lucky choice—more interactions for the astronauts during the one-year flight, and less boredom.

No one had expected the artificial intelligences to argue about areas of expertise. Even if they argued about closing the bulkhead doors, the crew would not notice this. For such emergencies, the AIs were allowed a purely algorithmic cooperation, in which discussions were decided in fractions of milliseconds. Siri and Watson only shared their thoughts with humans when nothing depended on it.

"Good morning, Martin!"

He had selected a low, slightly nasal voice for the AI. *This suits Watson, Sherlock Holmes' friend,* he had decided.

"Good morning, Dr. Watson."

Watson had never asked why Martin preceded his name with a title. The AI probably had found the solution itself. Martin's media DNA clearly showed he liked the old-fashioned mystery novels by Arthur Conan Doyle.

"Breakfast, and your colleague for today, Jiaying Li, are waiting in the mess room. Work is going to start in 30 minutes. I have awakened you late at your own request, but you have to hurry now."

There was a certain urgency expressed in the AI's voice, and Martin immediately recognized the subtext. It had taken him long enough to learn something like this.

The ceiling of his cabin now shone in a warm white. A blue haze was moving across it. He did not look at his watch. On the ship they followed a 24-hour rhythm, but outside space was dark, no matter what time it was. If he took a shower he would have to spend ten fewer minutes with Jiaying. It was not that he disliked her, but her presence made him insecure when he did not have a specific task. It was necessary to consume food, but this was not a specific task he could talk about with Jiaying. 'The coffee doesn't taste of anything today,' or 'The pancakes are only lukewarm,' were among the sentences that had already been uttered about the food—each several times by everyone on board within the first two weeks after launch —and they were not yet near the orbit of Mars.

The structure of everyday life had been designed by psychologists back on Earth. Everything was geared to allow crew members to be alone as often as possible, without intentionally isolating themselves from the rest. Therefore, the astronauts were paired, and each pair was assigned to cover an eight-hour shift. Routine was a desired factor, as it provided stability.

It was also boring. Martin yawned. Then he sat up and dangled his legs over the edge of the bed. His room was tiny. Eight cubic meters of air space—an enormous luxury for a spaceship, although nearly half of it was unused most of the time. *In any case, how long does someone stand around in his cabin?* Martin pulled down on the zipper of his suit. The elastic material peeled off his shoulders. The suit was cut in such a way that it always exerted a slight pressure against the spine of the wearer. This was to prevent people from growing. In low gravity, the spine expanded and the space between the spinal disks increased. Without pressure, the blood flow in the spinal disks decreased and they became bony—and if that person later walked under normal earth gravity, pain would be the result.

In his cabin, Martin weighed about half of what he did on Earth. He would rather not think about the reason for this. During the first ten days of the journey he could not help imagining being rotated through space like on a swing carousel. By now, he no longer felt queasy, though he stood on the inner wall of a donut with a diameter of twelve meters as it rotated around its axis ten times per minute.

He had to avoid thinking of it. Now he pushed the cabin door aside and walked to the combination shower/toilet room, officially called WHC, or 'Waste Hygiene Compartment.'

The artificial gravity created by the rotation made many things easier. During the training aboard Tiangong-4 he had greatly missed real showers. There, personal hygiene had involved using wet wipes. He was glad some psychologists had insisted on offering this physical comfort. He had never been really convinced by the argument that a shower was impractical under microgravity. Water, some believed, would gather in bulges and cavities of the body. Martin was of the opinion, *If humans can fly to Saturn, shouldn't they also be able to build sanitary facilities that work in zero gravity?*

Martin dried off and pulled on the suit again. He looked in the mirror. *No, I do not have to shave.* It was part of the ship rules—which were designed by psychologists, of course—that no one was allowed to get sloppy. *Walking naked through the corridor, having breakfast unshaven—such is completely out of the question.* Once more, Martin realized how many of the rules here were not due to outer space but were the work of psychologists. They thought the biggest problem during the two-year flight would not be technology, but the crew. Martin considered this a mixture of megalomania and budget strategy, and except for the mission commander, the whole crew agreed with him on that point.

July 10, 2046, ILSE

THERE ACTUALLY IS wind in space—each time the hamster leaves his wheel, Martin envisioned. He had wiped the WHC dry, and the towel was hung over the tumble dryer. It looked like the bathroom of a cheap hotel on Earth. Once, just out of curiosity, Martin had actually spent a night in a capsule hotel in Tokyo. The toilet there had looked rather similar, and at the press of a button, it had also analyzed the user's urine and stool. Here, the analysis data went directly to the on-board computer. During the one-on-one at the end of the shift, Siri would probably lecture him on proper nutrition... again. The meals were specifically adjusted to each astronaut's body and to the conditions in space: less iron, as he produced fewer blood cells; more vitamin D, as sunlight was lacking. However, Martin ate what he liked and not what would have been the best for his body.

The impression of being inside a hamster wheel was unavoidable once Martin left the WHC. He stood inside a narrow corridor, the walls of which contained luminous panels. Now, at the beginning of the shift, these emitted a bluish-white light. Some interior designer had really put a lot of thought into this idea, as the panels displayed interesting patterns that did not appear to repeat themselves. At regular intervals there were replicas of well-known works of art on the walls. The floor was covered with a special material that diminished the sound of his steps. Cables and pipes hanging haphazardly from the ceiling marred the hamster wheel impression, though. Such last-minute changes were probably unavoidable in a project of this size, purportedly at 80 billion dollars.

The corridor curved upward before and behind him. Despite this, Martin did not ever feel like he was walking uphill. He knew he moved like a hamster on the interior wall of a ring with a diameter of twelve meters. Luckily, he did not have to rotate the ring by muscle power, as this task was handled by small chemical jet engines placed on the outside of the sectors, in space.

The hard sector ended behind the cabin of his Chinese colleague. It was called 'hard' because it was a rigid construction that would not change shape if the pressure suddenly decreased. The four hard sectors of the habitat module were placed like hammer heads at the ends of a cross. The ring was completed by the soft sectors, which had been inflated like balloons. From the inside, Martin could not see that their walls were made of a flexible material. He only noticed the corridor became narrower behind Jiaying's cabin. At this location, a mechanism could be seen that would seal off the hard sector in case of a loss in pressure.

In order to reach the command module, Martin had to look upward when he stood in front of the WHC. The hatch leading to the hub of the habitat module was open. He pulled down the ladder. To do so, he needed to overcome an initial resistance, and then it fell into his hand automatically. As the habitat ring was rotating, everything tried to move outward. He, however, wanted to go inward, and that took some effort. Martin climbed the ladder, which became easier with every step.

Then the wind started. Shortly before this spoke met the hub, Martin had to push through a flexible membrane everyone jokingly called 'the fly screen,' and which reminded him of a condom. It consisted of thick rubber lips that extended from the edge of the center and normally closed off the corridor completely. Due to this, the air circulation system did not have to overcome the inertial force that not only pressed the astronauts against the interior wall, but also against the air molecules of the station. Without the four fly screens, the air in the hub would have been much thinner than in the outer sectors. Since there was still a difference in air pressure between the two sides of the hatches, Martin faced a draft while he squeezed himself, like a worm, headfirst through the rubber barrier.

In the center—the hub—there was no gravity. He would spend his eight-hour shift here, as the psychologists had decided, so that work and leisure would be clearly separated. There were no technical reasons for working in the command module. Martin could have accessed all the information in his room, and the actual control functions were handled by the AI, which possessed a whole arsenal of sensors to connect with the exterior world. It, or rather *he*, as Watson had asserted himself here, took over the analysis and translated everything important for the astronauts into results that appeared on the monitors. The task of the crew consisted of giving its blessing to decisions already made.

Yes, they could change course or even cancel the entire mission. The psychologists had insisted on giving the astronauts that much autonomy. Nevertheless, due to the negative effects of zero gravity, half of the work day consisted of physical exercise to counteract the damage that would not have occurred if they had stayed in their cabins all day long.

Martin had been thinking about this ever since they had launched. *In the beginning, the others were eager about meeting for meals, watching movies together, or reminiscing, but now, this only happens rarely.* Martin had not been surprised. After just three weeks, they had no longer been able to agree on a movie to watch, even though their entertainment system had digital copies of all films produced since the early 20th century. Afterward, they had still met, but all of them were watching their own movies on separate screens, using private headsets. This practice ended when the pilot Francesca arrived late one time and started laughing at the scene of five people immersed in their own worlds.

At around the same time, Marchenko's supply of pure alcohol, which they had diluted with water and fruit flavoring, ran out. Mission Control on Earth was probably glad about it, as the WHC sensors had registered any sins of this kind, of course. The crew had totally ignored the commotion down there because Earth could not do anything about it. In space, they were completely self-reliant.

Martin disliked that Mission Control was always referred to as 'down there,' even though Earth was not located below them, but behind. *After all, we are flying toward our far goal in the same ecliptic plane where Earth also moves.* He had nevertheless given up correcting the others concerning this aspect. Because of his former insistence, Marchenko, the ship's doctor and a fan of science fiction, had jokingly called Martin 'the android on board.' Martin only got the joke when they watched some ancient movie about an alien monster during one of their film evenings.

After that, their evening meetings together as a group had become increasingly rare. Now and then the commander, Amy, tried to surprise them with something new, and she was very inventive about it. Martin was surprised how many ways there were to make a fool of one's self. Only a week ago the commander had revealed to him that she had learned half of these ideas in a special team-building course. The fact that she came up with the other fifty percent filled Martin with awe—and with horror at the same time.

The first person who stopped appearing at their evening events was Hayato. The quiet, always friendly Japanese man gave no reason for preferring to stay in his cabin. The commander had asked him, but all she could tell the others was he had 'personal reasons' for it. Martin liked Hayato, not least because he knew almost as much about computers and software as Martin himself. Hayato had brought an ancient tube radio aboard, but that was not all; after launch he had managed to build a transmitter for it from spare parts, which changed the sound of the ceiling loudspeakers to the long wave spectrum. Martin remembered how once all six of them had sat in his cabin listening to the crackly, warm sound of the tube radio playing a concerto by Gustav Mahler. Hayato loved German composers.

Thereafter, Amy felt responsible for paying special attention to Hayato, as she told them at a communal evening, without mentioning details. Jiaying suspected their commander had fallen in love with the Japanese man, but

Martin rather believed Hayato was suffering from depression.

This meant there were only four of them left.

Martin generally refused to agonize over past decisions he would handle differently, looking at things from today's perspective. However, later on he was annoyed that he had not spent more time with Hayato in this time period. *Could I have changed the unavoidable by doing so?* He did not know. *Perhaps then the commander and the navigator would not have fallen in love, as Jiaying had correctly suspected.* Martin, who until now had regarded love only as an avoidable misfortune, had been really surprised that love could have such concrete effects on a rationally planned mission and on all their lives.

THE WHOLE WORLD WAS TURNING, and only he stood still. Martin had reached the center of the hub. The engineers had managed to preserve this illusion perfectly. The two hatches to the adjacent sections, which were normally closed, had been constructed and decorated in a rotation-symmetrical fashion. Martin placed his finger on the metal. He felt the movement, but he did not see it. It had taken him weeks before he no longer felt nauseous when he moved from the spaceship to the rotating habitat module. As soon as he pressed one of the Open buttons placed in 90-degree intervals on the bulkhead—and he would have to do that soon—he might suffer a relapse.

The hatch opened. Martin closed his eyes and cata-pulted himself through it. He knew where the position-stabilization handles were situated, and he grabbed them. From ten revolutions per minute to zero—that sounded harmless, but human beings were obviously not built for it. He breathed in hard and avoided becoming nauseous, even though he now also deeply inhaled the machine and oil smell of the central modules. Martin knew how badly spaceships could stink. The air circulation on *ILSE* was working reasonably well. Shortly before launch, a private university had supplied a new kind of filtration system. Still, when each cubic centimeter of breathable air had passed through the lungs of the crew several times already, even the best recycling system no longer helped. The stench could be suppressed for a while, but no longer than a few weeks.

Martin looked toward the bow and then the stern. The hatch for the hub of the ring had remained open. That was also a clever engineering trick. When he had pressed the Open button, the rear hatch had also opened. Martin now could look back through the corridor, all the way to the entrance of the garden module. Everything seemed fixed. Here, one did not notice the rotation, even though the hub was still turning around its axis ten times a minute.

The handles Martin held also served a second purpose. At the outside of this module there were large, barrel-shaped water tanks. There was no better shielding against cosmic radiation than that. In the event Mission Control registered a strong surge of solar radiation, all of the astronauts would move to this module, which would serve as a shelter. If the eruption lasted very long, the crew members could strap themselves to these handles so an involuntary movement during sleep would not make them drift around. Until now, there had been no solar flares, but statistically they would have to expect two or three such events during their journey.

Even if Mission Control always gave them advanced

warning, Martin's cancer risk would have increased by at least 500 percent by the time he returned to Earth. The fact that he was even considered for the mission was partly due to his genes, which gave him a higher than average resistance against radiation damage. Cosmic particles were constantly penetrating his body and damaging cells. His body would try to repair them, but that would not always be possible.

Without the active shielding around the spacecraft, the crew would never be able to survive the trip. It was similar to the invisible shield that made life on Earth possible. The lines of Earth's magnetic field, which surround our planet, prevent a large percentage of high-energy particles from reaching the surface. A part of the electrical energy provided by the DFD engines powered superconducting electromagnets that in turn generated a field that snugly surrounded *ILSE*. This at least kept off all charged particles, though it could not protect against neutral ones. *ILSE* was the first spaceship with an active shield, as this type of protection had not been considered necessary for the much shorter trips to Mars.

Martin pulled on the handles, which immediately provided him with a forward impulse. He reminded himself, *If I do not show up soon, Jiaying will be annoyed.* By now, he knew quite well how she would react. *She will press her lips together, yet will still try to smile so as not to appear impolite.* It was a strange look, and Hayato would have laughed about it in a very non-Japanese manner. Martin crossed the module they called the lab. It was a mixture of workshop and storeroom. There was nothing they could research scientifically, but equipment failed at regular intervals, and they would try to fix it here. As their supply of spare parts was limited, they sometimes cannibalized other devices for this purpose. They probably would find suitable spare parts in the cargo containers, but these containers were attached to the outside of the ship, and an EVA (ExtraVehicular Activity) was quite involved. Everything they needed from outside was put on a list that probably would be acted on in about a month, unless something urgent came up.

The 'dining room,' or command module, where Jiaying was waiting for him was at the very front. The inside looked like a sphere, the outside like a cone with a blunted tip. It was a *Dragon* capsule by SpaceX. The interior had been completely refurbished. This space did not attempt to create a sense of up and down. The workstations, two terminals and two control seats, appeared to be randomly placed. When you sat at a computer, you might see a colleague floating in space at any angle.

In order to reach the dining table, Martin had to walk down at a 90-degree angle from the module, at least from his perspective. There, a metal table had been either bolted or welded to the surface, it was hard to see which. Jiaying waved at Martin as he floated around the corner. For her, he seemed to come from the side, not from above. The slim Chinese woman had strapped herself into her chair. She was the only person who had brought along a cushion from Earth. Her mother had embroidered it for her, although there was no real need for her soft cushion, since the straps would gently press her backside against the surface of the chair. Cutlery and dishes were made of magnetized metal, and therefore stuck firmly to the table, rather than floating around in the capsule.

Jiaying smiled with lips pressed tightly together, just as he had expected. He was late. Her dark brown eyes gave him a cool look.

"Good morning, Martin." She was the only person on board who pronounced his name correctly, *Mar-TEEN*.

"Good morning." He had only a vague idea of how her name should sound. Jiaying raised and lowered the pitch of her voice in a way he could not follow. When he said 'Ji-a-jing,' it sounded strangely flat and wrong, so he avoided this if possible.

"Sorry you had to wait."

"Never mind," she said, shrugging. Martin was glad he was not able to read thoughts. *She could have started with her own breakfast, though. That would have been not only impolite, but also against the rules.*

Jiaying had already placed Martin's breakfast on the table, and now moved it closer to his plate.

"Thanks," he said, and reached for a tube. Things belonging to him were marked by a small purple sticker. Before the launch, all of the astronauts had been able to select their own menus. The others sometimes swapped food. That offered variety, a change in their routine, they told him. Martin could not understand this. *It is illogical. After all, I selected for myself exactly the meals I like best. The so-called variety would be a negative deviation.*

"Would you like to exchange anything?" asked Jiaying, nevertheless. *This is probably part of her politeness program*, Martin thought.

He shook his head. "No thanks," he said. Both of them chewed their food. *I should probably say something now, shouldn't I?* Jiaying smiled at him. It seemed she wanted to encourage him. He looked at her. *The problem is, she is pretty. I cannot talk to pretty women. Damn.* They continued to chew their food. There was still an inscrutable smile on Jiaying's face. She did not appear to mind that he said nothing.

The psychologists had indeed put a lot of effort into

this. The mission planners must have feared the crew members would turn on each other if the food did not match their expectations. Compared to what was offered on a space station in Earth orbit, the supplies stored on *ILSE* were gourmet-quality food. This comparison actually said quite a bit about the tolerance all those astronauts, cosmonauts, and taikonauts had for suffering. Martin, for instance, could not only choose among tubes and cans, and dried food that was mixed with water to form a flavored mush, but he could have breakfast almost like on Earth.

There are rolls! Martin was delighted. They were actually freeze-dried, shrink-wrapped balls of dough heated in a special machine until they got crisp. According to Marchenko, this process used the know-how of a super-market chain. Unfortunately, Martin was not allowed to cut the fresh rolls with a knife. The risk of crumbs floating away would have been too great. However, he could use a special tube to squeeze a paste onto the roll, and the paste was available in four flavors; sausage, cheese, jam, and chocolate spread. Then he would put the mini-roll into his mouth, together with the packaging, which was also edible. This was cumbersome, but it was the closest he could get to the original flavors this far from Earth. Furthermore, he was not in a rush. Having breakfast together counted as a part of his work period, even though they rarely had any real work to do afterward.

"Did you notice that Amy and Hayato..." Jiaying's voice trailed off without finishing the sentence. Martin was surprised by the sudden sound. He must have shown this because Jiaying laughed. Martin almost choked on his roll.

"Have I—what? Amy—and Hayato?" He managed to get that much out after regaining his composure. "No, she just checks on him because he has problems." *More than that simply cannot be*, he thought. *Hayato would have certainly told me, because after all, he is my only friend here. Friend. How strange that sounds. Shouldn't we all be friends? Or a large family?* he contemplated.

"I have been watching them," Jiaying said.

"Watching?"

"Just by chance it happened. I wanted to check something in the garden module, and they were in the rear corridor, touching each other."

"Touching?" Martin was angry at himself. *Why do I keep repeating things like a stupid little monkey? I want to come across as a clever guy.*

"To be more precise," Jiaying continued, "they at first held hands, facing each other. And then he placed a hand on her behind. It seemed pretty clear to me."

"Well, you really took a close look," Martin said. Jiaying blushed, which he had not intended. *I hope she did not misunderstand me.* "That is… I mean, you must have been startled, seeing someone or something you did not expect."

"That's true," Jiaying said.

"If that is true..." Martin pondered. "Oh, never mind. I mean, what would she see in him? He is so quiet."

"It seems like he has some secret, which would make him interesting. And he is good-looking, too."

Hayato was supposed to be good-looking? Martin had never noticed it. Unlike Marchenko, Hayato had never been adored by women on Earth, at least as far as he knew.

"Yes? What is good-looking about him?" Martin wondered, *am I good-looking, at least in Jiaying's eyes?*

"He is well-built and has mastered several martial arts, Marchenko told me. And there is something profound in his eyes."

This was more than Martin wanted to know. Even if he

exercised more in the future, his slim body would never become broad-shouldered. *Tonight I will stand in front of the mirror trying to look more 'profound.'*

"How do we want to divide up the work?" asked Jiaying with another mysterious smile. Martin had to avert his eyes while she sucked her noodles out of the vacuum pack, the required method for consuming cooked noodles in space.

This was a rhetorical question. First of all, Jiaying was the boss of their two-person team, and secondly, they had no choice. The psychologists had mandated in the rulebook that all decisions should be made unanimously, if possible.

"Well, I will take care of the garden, and you can clean," Martin replied. Today was Wednesday, when Martin always did garden work. Tomorrow he would have to clean. All six of them had come up with these plans. It was not important to him what he did to kill time. Initially, the mission planners had considered giving them real research projects, like visiting one of the larger planetoids on their way through the asteroid belt. In the end, the idea had been rejected due to the risk and the time involved. Therefore, there would be no real diversion until *ILSE* approached the orbit of Saturn.

"That's fine," Jiaying said. "Have fun. And if you see Hayato or Amy..." She winked at him instead of finishing the sentence. Martin started to get curious.

"See you at noon," he said.

The garden, as the crew called the greenhouse module, was located in the rear section of the ship. It had been built in the home country of Martin's mother, Germany. Since the Chinese had taken the lead in constructing vehicles and robots, the diligent Germans had focused again on the true resource of their country, the fertile soil. Due to global warming, the vegetation periods in the Northern hemisphere had increased so much that now two harvests per year were easily possible.

The module's official designation was 'EDEN.' Martin had forgotten what the acronym stood for. *This place certainly does not resemble the Garden of Eden.* It reminded Martin more of a surreal, musty-smelling basement full of pipes. The biological equilibrium was quite fragile. Every day the crew fought to control the rampant microflora.

Martin undressed in front of the airlock into the garden. Due to the heat and the moisture they had agreed to work in their underwear, although this wasn't a decency problem because only one astronaut at a time was scheduled to work in the garden. If he remembered correctly, Francesca had suggested this because the high humidity and the low oxygen content in the EDEN module made her sweat. *What might the psychologists be saying about that?* he wondered. At the order of the commander, the Siri AI had turned off the surveillance cameras in this part of the spaceship. Martin sometimes imagined Siri or Watson secretly observing the human crew during garden work.

In NASA jargon the garden was called a CELSS or Closed Ecological Life Support System. The instructor on Earth had been skeptical of the entire concept. Earth itself, he had said, was so far the only example of a CELSS staying stable, within certain limits, for billions of years. If they succeeded in turning a spaceship into a closed, stable ecosystem, even interstellar voyages would become possible, assuming the crew showed enough patience. However, the difficulty in keeping such a system stable increased as available space decreased. This did not keep the ESA specialist from at least trying. It didn't matter whether the garden really functioned, recycled oxygen, and produced fresh food, it would provide the crew with a different important resource: work.

Before launch, no one had dared to predict what the 30 square meters of garden, spread over several levels, would really be useful for. Of course, the biologists had selected plants with short growing periods and high harvest yields, meaning a high percentage of edible biomass in relation to the overall mass of the plant. Martin already had harvested the first batch of lettuce, beets, and spinach. He actually did not like any of these vegetables, but compared to the freeze-dried food, they tasted fantastic. *Will I ever get to dig out any edible potatoes, given that they require more than three months to grow?* he wondered. He was pessimistic about the carrots. *The soil microorganisms are going crazy again.*

It had been obvious it would not be easy to grow food. Due to the missing gravity, the roots of plants had no target when they searched for nutrients and water. That also applied to moisture. With normal irrigation methods, the water would simply cover the surface and the area below it would stay dry. This was the reason they had decided on a kind of aquaculture. Above the roots, the plants were surrounded by a kind of elastic collar. The roots spread through a coarse-grained mixture of minerals rinsed with a nutrient solution. The solution consisted mostly of urine, the liquid gold of space gardeners, which added a very particular smell to the atmosphere in the EDEN module. The problem was, the artificial soil was inhabited by legions of microscopic creatures, and their reactions could not be predicted. Even if they had disinfected everything beforehand, the plants themselves would have introduced new bacteria. Agriculture could never be sterile.

Right now, the smell here was much stronger than expected, as if they had recently sprayed liquid manure. Amy had been trying to locate the culprits for days, but so far without success. *Maybe that's why she was in the garden with Hayato, to check up on it,* Martin thought. *Jiaying might have been mistaken. I can't imagine the commander and the engineer...* he shook his head and focused on his tasks again.

One strain of bacteria must have become dominant, and exterminated other bacteria. Now this strain proliferated as long as the necessary resources were available. Afterward, the ecosystem would tilt in the other direction. Maybe they would be lucky and the right strains would prevail. The plants definitely did not like the current soil climate. They had stopped growing, and their leaves were changing color. Martin did not quite know where to start. Amy's instructions had been vague—intervene when he thought a plant had no chance of survival.

Therefore, he always did a quick check at the start of his shift. He took the daylight lamp from its wall mounting so he could look at the colors of the leaves in the natural spectrum. The light emitted by the walls and the ceiling was specifically adapted to the needs of the plants. Lamp in hand, he started to walk past the rows. The garden was a simple tube with an exterior diameter of about two meters and a length of nine meters. The 'ceiling' was suspended, and all the utility lines ran above it. At the 'floor' there was a path, with storage cabinets below it. The plant's beds were installed on the exterior walls and two shelves stretching across almost the entire length, with as many as six plants stacked on top of each other.

Martin decided on a vertical-horizontal search strategy.

He therefore looked at each shelf from bottom to top first, then moved in and reversed the direction. He did not do this because he thought it more efficient, but because it was easier on his knees. At the end of the 16-meter path he had statistically analyzed the color, form, and size of the leaves for the six currently growing types of plants. During his first plant check-ups he had still used the PlantGrowth app of his Universal Pad in order to calculate the existing biomass, but by now he could do this in his head. Plus, he did it better than the app, which he proved by measuring the volume of 20 plants with the good old displacement method. The camera in his head seemed to work better than the 3D cam of the Pad.

He did not have to write anything down. He possessed a good memory, and always had, except for faces. He quickly noted that, concerning the development of the most important features, 15 percent of the plants reached 15 percent of the respective median value. If he said it this way to Jiaying, she would laugh. Even though she was a biologist, or maybe because of it, he had to translate his thoughts for her. How should he express this? Maybe this way: one in six plants was brown.

Martin decided to follow the commander's instructions. This meant getting rid of 27 plants, representing two fresh dinners for the entire crew—a real loss. Of course he did not really know whether the affected plants would die, although if he waited too long, nothing new could grow in these spots. First Martin had to clear the required space, and then Jiaying would plant the seeds or bulbs, probably in the afternoon while he struggled on the elliptical trainer. The astronauts took whatever was needed for new plants from special storage containers below the floor of the garden. In a truly closed system they would save a part of the harvest for planting the next generation.

He imagined Jiaying walking among the shelves in her underwear. *I like her, but I know I have absolutely no chance with her.* The psychologists claimed sexual desires decline in space. So far, Martin could not confirm this, but then they had not been in space that long.

"DAMAGE TO OUTER WALL, module Gamma 3," Watson's voice said, startling him out of his meditative activity. The shift was almost over. The AI sounded completely neutral. If something serious had happened, it would have modulated its voice and announced one of three alert levels. Smaller impacts were casually reported to the astronauts, like just now. Every second the ship's radar waves scanned, at the speed of light, the hemisphere of space in their direction of travel. The radar would detect larger, more dangerous fragments before impact. Only very large rocks could be detected so early that the chemically powered secondary jets of the ship could move it away from a collision course.

Martin imagined one of the three spider robots now crawling across the hull to investigate the damage. The six-legged robot would examine the width and depth of the impact. It attempted to determine the source, which was not always possible, as the impact would pulverize at least the smaller meteoroids. The spider could seal up damaged areas in the one-centimeter range. For this purpose it carried a special red resin in its 'spinning gland.' The spider sprayed the resin into the hole, where it hardened within seconds in the vacuum of space. Afterward, the robot moved to its service bay, which the astronauts called the 'doghouse.' They had also given names to the three robots—dog names. *The kind of thing you do when you are bored,* Martin thought. The commander had suggested this, but again the idea probably came from the psychologists. There had been more than three suggestions so they had drawn lots. Martin's 'Rex' did not win, but now he was glad about it, because the name seemed too unimaginative to him. The three winners were Joker, Obi-Wan, and Lancelot.

Larger problems were fixed by the crew during an exterior mission, though it wasn't worth doing this at once. Watson kept a list of necessary repairs, and as soon as the AI estimated that at least an hour of work was required, the commander planned an exterior mission, or EVA. Luckily, she had not yet sent Martin outside. He did not want to remember his first, and until now, only spacewalk during the week of training on Tiangong-4 when he had acted very clumsily.

The second part of his workday was dedicated to exercise, but first he had to create a report. He spoke the keyword and told the always-listening AI what he had done in the garden. As the astronauts were constantly supervised, the reason for this procedure had originally eluded him. The NASA trainer, however, had given a convincing explanation; the AI analyzed his speech recording on two levels: first, it attempted to look at speech patterns, rhythm, and stress to find the unspoken message behind what was said; and second, the text helped the software understand the environment, as it provided meta-information to match the video recording of his activities. Humans were still better at classifying and arranging things than the AI was.

Martin moved through the zero gravity toward the

hamster wheel. The fitness room was located in the fourth habitat module—numbers one through three contained two cabins and a WHC each. If he had been given a free wish, he would have asked to move the dining table there. *After all,* in his opinion, *it is much easier to eat under the influence of gravity.*

He climbed the ladder in a direction that now felt downward, but in fact constantly rotated around the axis of the spaceship. Two meters from the end of the spoke there was a glowing ring that Martin pressed. This opened the hatch of the habitat module, and a ladder was extended, as long as no one stood directly below. The way was clear. Martin climbed down from the ceiling. He then turned around to face the door of the fitness room. He had not memorized everyone's schedule, so he did not know who else would be there. Work was planned in such a way that at most two astronauts would exercise at any given time.

He pressed a button and the flat door disappeared into the wall. Martin stopped at the threshold. Amy sat on the exercise bicycle, wearing a VR headset and headphones, pedaling steadily. She whistled softly, probably the song she was listening to. Martin did not recognize the tune. Now the bicycle adjusted itself by several degrees. Amy pedaled more slowly; it was obvious she was putting out more effort. The VR headset was probably showing her images of a steep ascent.

Let her continue her trip! Martin was glad he did not have to engage in conversation. He entered the room, which measured approximately three by two meters. Amy stepped on the brake. *She seems to possess a sixth sense. Or maybe she had just smelled him?* Here in space, of all places, where one could not escape the scent molecules emitted by machines and people, the olfactory sense improved. The commander took off her headset, hung it from the handle-bars, and then removed her earphones. She smiled at him. Martin noted sweat stains under the armpits of her T-shirt, and he also saw she wore no bra, probably unnecessary under half of terrestrial gravity.

"Well, did you do some nice gardening work today?" Amy asked.

Of course, she knew the schedule, as befitted a commander.

Martin replied, "I had to dispose of a large number of seedlings."

"Well, that is... frustrating."

Her facial expression did not match what she had said. Her thoughts seemed to be far away from here. Amy smiled, and Martin considered what he might call her expression. *Lost in thought—that is it.*

"It really is… a great loss of biomass," he said.

"Hmmm... Some salad for dinner." Her voice was full of longing. Martin got on the elliptical machine and started his exercises.

"We have enough food on board," he said, "and *ILSE 2* will be waiting for us near Enceladus with fresh supplies."

Amy knew this, of course, but he had to say something. She did not answer.

"How is Hayato?" Martin had intended this as an innocent question, but when he listened to himself, it sounded unduly curious. Amy looked into his eyes.

"So-so. He is very worried. You know he has a daughter?"

Martin shook his head and hoped Amy would now tell him more. He had always considered the Japanese man to be a kind of friend. *I know he is not married, and he has never mentioned having a daughter.*

"Don't worry, he told me it was okay to talk about it. He wants you all to know why he is so reclusive. He does not want to bother anyone with his problems."

Martin once more was angry with himself. *Why didn't I visit Hayato more often in his cabin? It seems improper because, as men, you go out drinking together; heart-to-heart talks in a cabin, this is not my style.*

Martin had the impression Amy was waiting for his next question, "And what about his daughter?"

"After the death of her mother, she joined a cult," Amy began. "Hayato had not heard anything from her in years. He could not even say goodbye to her, since she seemed to have disappeared off the face of the earth."

"And now she has returned?" Martin asked.

"Yes, she showed up two weeks after our launch. She managed to leave the cult and is now in psychiatric treatment."

"I'm sure Hayato would have liked to have been there for her."

Amy explained, "He is very sad that he is so far away and cannot help her at all. If he had known about this, he would not have come along."

Martin sighed. *Why had the engineer not told him anything about this?* Martin knew the answer, though. *I would have been helpless. It looks like Amy is different in this aspect.*

"Tell him... I don't know. I don't know what I would say to him." *I feel like a loser,* Martin thought. This was no problem he could calculate, and for that reason he had always tried to avoid such situations.

"It's okay. Hayato does not want to bother others with his problem. That would just stress him even more."

It's a paradoxical situation. The person I consider a friend is suffering, but I can help him best by ignoring him? Martin did not know what else to say. "I really can't do anything?"

"You can," Amy said. "Just leave him be. I'm here, after all."

For a while Martin focused on his elliptical trainer. He started to sweat. He looked at his watch. *Only 15 minutes so far.* If anyone had told him months ago that he would exercise eight hours a day... Exercise, Martin knew since attending a series of lectures by the Chief Medical Officer of NASA, was incredibly important, more so than any other activity the crew members engaged in. In zero gravity the body lost considerable amounts of calcium and the bone structure changed, similar to that of women during menopause—just much more so. A month in space could reduce bone density by one to two percent, and their voyage would last 30 months. They were required to spend hours per day in the fitness room, four during work and four in their spare time.

"I have a secret plan."

Amy spoke more softly, as if it was important no one should overhear her. *This makes no sense,* Martin concluded. *If I can hear her, the AI will certainly be able to.*

"Yes? Then you had better not tell me. You know... " he said.

"Aren't you the least bit curious?"

"I only want to help you. If you tell me, the plan is no longer secret."

Amy shrugged. "But I want to tell you. Don't worry, I will also tell the others."

"Okay, then I'm curious,"

"Do you know what I have in my footlocker?" she asked.

Such an old-fashioned word, Martin thought. *Amy likes old words, I've noticed.* He shook his head and made sure she noticed this gesture.

"Pansy seeds," she answered. "They are small, colorful flowers."

Do I look that surprised? he wondered. "That's nice," he said. "I know what pansies are. My grandmother had some in her garden."

"Do you like them?"

"Yes... I think I do. I always liked to watch how my grandma enjoyed her flowers."

"But do you like them yourself?" Amy persisted.

Martin shrugged.

"They are flowers. Not food." He thought about it. "I like what they do to people who look at them."

"That is very... pragmatic," she said.

Martin considered that a compliment.

"You want to sow the seeds in the garden, don't you?"

Amy nodded. "Yes, exactly. I do."

"If you want to, I can find the best spot for them," Martin offered. "The crop rotation has some flexibility. Or we make do without a few heads of lettuce."

"That would be nice. I would like there to be flowers, when..."

Martin waited for Amy to finish the sentence, but she said nothing more. He looked at her. She did not want to continue the conversation. It was useless to try to find the reason for it. Martin looked at the display on the elliptical trainer. He had to get moving if he wanted to reach the daily goal the computer had set for him.

August 4, 2046, ILSE

THE ONLY THING missing to complete the mawkish picture would have been burning candles. The six of them were gathered around a table and appeared to be sitting. There was a cake on a white tablecloth with a colorfully embroidered fringe, and plates and silverware in front of all the guests. There were no open coffee cups, and the guests floated, instead of truly sitting under the pressure of gravity. It was the missing flame that acknowledged this occasion was no normal birthday party. While Amy had placed a candle next to the cake, no one would dare to light it. An open fire aboard a spaceship was the nightmare of every astronaut. *The flame would probably be quite a sight,* Martin thought, even though he had never seen one burn in zero gravity. *It would spread in all directions from the wick, a perfect sphere of cold blue, because no soot particles would be dispersed to glow in the heat.*

Amy had sent them invitations yesterday and called this event 'a birthday party.' Martin would not have noticed anything, since he was not good at remembering dates. If only Francesca had not asked whose birthday it was. Amy had not answered, and then asked them to be patient.

Martin looked around. Marchenko had lowered his head and stared at the fringe of the tablecloth as if he was looking for something underneath the table. He did not make eye contact. This told Martin, *The doctor is in on this and does not want to say anything.* Jiaying silently looked from right to left again and again and shuffled her feet. *She obviously does not know what is going on, either. Francesca seems to be amused by something.* She was resting on one arm and looking around. *She looks like she is about to tell a joke.* Then Martin noticed the corners of her eyes twitched. She did not seem to be enjoying the situation. It looked like she was itching for a confrontation. He remembered the hours she had been trapped in *Valkyrie* below the Antarctic ice. *Waiting passively drives her insane.*

Hayato was as calm as always. He had folded his hands in his lap and looked straight ahead, past everyone else. *He looks like a sacrificial lamb who knows exactly what to expect,* Martin decided. Amy tried to keep her expression neutral, but she did not succeed. Martin wondered, *What can I tell from her facial expression?* He was grateful for one particular special-ed teacher because the man had taught him to read such details and nuances, things others had learned during childhood thanks to empathy. What he saw in Amy's face was something he had never noticed in the commander. He was afraid to name this feeling, for it was fear.

Amy cleared her throat.

"Nice that all of you found time to come."

This was followed by a short pause.

"Siri, stop recording."

"Excuse me. Authorization required."

"Authorization has been given by the commander."

"Recording stopped. Log entry created."

This is a surprise. Martin had not even known it was possible to deactivate the continuous recording. There would be no record of what was about to happen now, and therefore no transmission to Mission Control. On Earth they would only find out what the crew members later reported. *This is unheard of in the history of human spaceflight.* His hands were trembling.

"Thanks, Siri. Deactivate acoustic interface."

"Excuse me. Authorization required. I would like to point out that after doing so, commands can only be entered via keyboard." Siri's voice sounded as if the AI was really worried.

"I know. Authorization has been given by the commander."

"Are you sure?"

"I am sure."

The double-checking was part of the protocol. Martin had studied the source code, but he had never actually witnessed the protocol being implemented. Siri answered with two auditory signals.

Then Amy nodded. She rose and held onto the table to avoid drifting away. She had a determined look on her face.

"Please excuse me. You are here because I asked you to come. I have to tell you something because I do not want you to hear it elsewhere."

Everyone was looking at her, except for Hayato, who still stared straight ahead.

"I am sure you noticed in the last few weeks that Hayato," she nodded in his direction, though he did not change his posture, "and I have become friends. To be precise, we are more than friends."

Martin was surprised at hearing this confirmation. *Jiaying was right. However, this cannot be the reason for the meeting.* There were three men and three women on board, and the mission planners must have expected such relationships, maybe to get over the boredom. None of them had left a classical family behind on Earth. That had been one of the selection criteria.

"We are," Amy said, and cleared her throat, "a couple."

Congratulations, Martin thought, but did not say anything. Jiaying pressed her lips together. *It is obvious she considers this kind of fraternization as damaging to the mission. On the other hand, Francesca seems rather open-minded.* Marchenko was still looking at the fringe of the tablecloth. More was to come.

"We are all adults, so I don't have to tell you what a romantic relationship involves." Amy paused and looked directly at Hayato, who did not react. She shrugged and continued speaking.

"I have told some of you who know me better some facts about my life before this mission. I was married for fifteen years. We were trying to have kids until the doctors finally determined that I was infertile. This issue eventually led to the breakup of my marriage."

Martin had not known Amy's story. *It must be hard for her to talk about it so openly.*

"And now I am getting to what I wanted to tell you. I don't know whether it is good news or bad news. It looks like the doctors were wrong. Not just one doctor or two, but many—including those at NASA. I cannot say how many times I was examined, how many unsuccessful procedures I had to undergo in the attempt to maybe change this."

Amy took a deep breath.

"Anyway, I am pregnant."

There was an abrupt BANG as Jiaying's chair collided with the wall. She must have pushed off with her legs and now she pulled herself back to the table. No one said anything.

A child could be a gift, a challenge—or a catastrophe. If Martin asked his mother, she would have called him a gift, even though his growing up was a definite challenge. He had often been stressed just by dealing with himself. What must she have endured?

The child carried by Amy is a potential catastrophe. Maybe it will cost all of our lives. The entire mission has been planned for six people. Food, oxygen, the mass of the spacecraft that determines its acceleration. If you change a single parameter, you endanger the entire mission. Martin unconsciously grabbed the table, as if danger was already waiting for them in the form of a meteoroid. This death, though, would come slowly. Martin knew enough to imagine all the possible outcomes, but not enough to decide which one was the most realistic scenario. Would they perhaps miss the orbit around Saturn, because *ILSE* arrived a bit too slowly at its destination, or was harder to decelerate? Would they suffocate because the oxygen was not enough for seven passengers?

Martin opened his eyes. He had not even noticed that he had closed them. The others sat there, motionless and silent. They probably were imagining similar scenarios, but Amy was not finished.

"It is too early to worry much. We have a doctor on board. I have already talked to Marchenko. I had to tell him earlier—you have to understand this. I did not want to make you choose before I was certain."

Choose? She must have gone crazy, Martin thought.

"Marchenko is willing to perform an abortion. He is no gynecologist, but he knows the necessary steps. I am in my ninth week, so it could be done without a problem. The risks are controllable, even though this is an operation."

"You want to have an abortion? How can you?" Francesca's face was pale. Her reaction fit the image Martin had of her.

"I am the commander, and I am responsible for the life of the crew. I have to place your welfare above mine. I don't just have to, I want to. I would not have taken this post if I had not been aware of the consequences."

Francesca shook her head.

"You cannot do this. You would turn us into accomplices."

"No, I am making this decision on my own, as there is no other choice, besides breaking off the entire mission."

"Francesca is right. I told you that already." Hayato was still looking straight ahead, but now he raised his head. "You are making this decision for our sake. I would also say this if I was not the father. I think we have the right to participate in the decision."

The commander appeared shocked. Her arms were hanging limply next to her body, which looked strange in zero gravity.

"I... I don't know. I cannot endanger you. I would never forgive myself for that."

"We can all speak for ourselves." Marchenko now had raised his upper body. His deep voice boomed, the Russian accent was pronounced. "How about voting on it? You as the commander get two votes, one for yourself and one for your office. Everyone else has one vote each."

Amy looked around doubtfully, but no one protested. "I... I cannot accept that you would suffer harm because of me. No matter how the voting goes, if we find out the mission has no chance of success anymore, Marchenko will perform the abortion. We can give ourselves and Mission Control about two weeks' time to recalculate all parameters."

Martin moved his head back and forth. *She has to know that fourteen days will never be enough to come up with a reliable prognosis. Mission planning alone has taken several months.*

"I like Marchenko's suggestion." Francesca seemed eager. "We should not wait until later, we should vote right away."

"I agree." Amy looked around the crew with an unsure expression. Marchenko nodded. Hayato did the same, but without looking into her eyes. Martin nodded. Jiaying hesitated and then also nodded. Francesca raised a thumb. "I think we should vote in secret, though. I want all of us to voice our opinions without concern for personal relationships."

Marchenko reached into his pocket.

"I just borrowed 14 screws from the workshop, seven short ones and seven somewhat longer ones," he said.

Amy looked at him and raised her eyebrows. He smiled.

"Everyone receives two different ones, and you, Amy, get four. The short screw means Amy should have the baby. The longer one..."

Jiaying interrupted, "And if someone uses both screws to vote?"

"Who would get such an idea?" Marchenko asked.

He received no answer from her.

"I am going to pass around this metal container." He shook it. "It's empty. Everyone puts a screw inside, and then we count."

No one reacted, so Marchenko followed his own announcement. The container went around. At each seat there was a clinking sound. Martin was second to last. He realized, *There are too many unknown parameters in the equation to calculate her chances. However, I cannot force the commander to have an abortion, even though this was her own suggestion.*

He pushed a short screw a bit so that it tumbled into the container. Then he passed it on to Amy. Her hand was trembling. The sound of metal on metal two or three times was the only thing breaking the near-silence. Now the commander stood there quietly. Marchenko moved toward her and took the metal container. He turned toward the table, inverted the container, and lifted it. Seven screws floated around, hit the white tablecloth and rebounded. Martin saw they had left light brown smears, probably oil. Four were shorter than the rest.

August 5, 2046, ILSE

DURING THE FIRST weeks after launch, the crew's conversations with Mission Control had only been a simple exchange of 'this is CapCom, what's up?' followed by, 'I have a question.' By now, a signal took 20 minutes to reach Earth. Therefore an answer to a simple question would require almost three-quarters of an hour. The crew had now switched to sending so-called comms, or communiques, to Mission Control. A comm consisted of a proposed resolution, plus the reasons for it. It described a problem, possible solutions, and the option favored by the respective specialist in the crew. Mission Control checked the solutions and then sent its own comm that either agreed or contained changed parameters. The final decision still rested with the crew, as the assumption was that they would have to live (and survive) with the resulting consequences.

The comms mostly concerned mission planning issues that dealt with the long term, not with everyday problems. The spacecraft's technology was independent. While it constantly sent status updates to the home planet, a problem would have long ago turned into a crisis before a reaction to it reached the ship's main computers. This was the reason the AIs were so important, as they constantly supervised all ship functions, and could react faster than the crew in case of emergency.

The problem growing in the commander's womb had not yet been classified as one by Siri and Watson. It did not belong to their area of experience, and it had not been part of their learning process that female astronauts could get pregnant. Vital data were protected and excluded from the regular transmission to Earth. Only Marchenko could initiate a data transfer when he needed some special expertise. For that reason, only the crew knew about Amy's pregnancy.

Like yesterday, Martin and his five colleagues sat around the dining table. The mood was relaxed, as Marchenko had donated half a bottle of alcohol from the medical supplies, and of course had made sure the alcohol on board would not be denatured. Marchenko had worked long enough at Roscosmos to know the right people.

The crew wanted to draft a comm to explain this special problem and its solution to Mission Control. They had to admit one thing—there was no comprehensive solution in sight. During the long years of their journey, they would have to solve a sequence of problems, one after the other, the nature of which they could not even grasp today, starting with a birth under half of terrestrial gravity. They had neither diapers nor children's clothes aboard, let alone toys. The ship was anything but childproof. *A two-year-old pulling the wrong lever, just for fun? Would Amy be able to fulfill her tasks if she was distracted by her child?* crossed Martin's mind. The entire mission had been planned for six astronauts. It was hard to compensate for losses.

"That won't work," Francesca said amid the dull rumblings of the spaceship that had seemed like silence to Martin for a long time. Now and then he put on his good headphones, activated the noise suppression function, and was shocked to find out what real silence sounded like.

"Do you have a better suggestion?" *I'm not used to hearing this stressed tone of voice from Amy,* Martin noticed.

"We are presenting the facts and the methods we used to arrive at this decision, that's it," Martin replied.

The tension in Amy's voice increased. "Mission Control won't be happy about it."

"That's not our responsibility."

Amy shook her head. "Martin, you are taking this too lightly. The world has scraped together 80 billion dollars to make our trip come true. We have been financed, not only by rich countries, but also by common people, for whose concerns there is no money left. We owe something to all of them."

"You are right, but..." Martin cleared his throat.

Yes, he pondered, *we do owe something to Earth and to all those people who have made this journey possible.*

"This flight to Saturn, let's be honest, is predominantly a symbol," he said out loud. "Now we are going to give them a new symbol—a second one. Something unheard of, that never existed before, the first human being to be born in space, the very first representative of the cosmic human race. That is no problem, it's a sensation."

The others looked at him, which made him feel uncomfortable.

"Mission Control will think we are kidding if we write that." Amy tilted her head to the side and gave him a somewhat suspicious look.

"Maybe. They will also see this opportunity, though.

They must realize we have already made a decision. This way, they will at least get something out of it," Martin said.

They finished the rest of the text within ten minutes. Amy typed it in, and the others suggested sentences. Finally, Amy clicked the Send button.

The reply took longer than the usual three-quarters of an hour to arrive. Martin had expected that. *It might take days to run all of the calculations.* However, after only 50 minutes a well-known voice and face came through.

"This is CapCom."

It was Devendra, the man whom Martin had replaced for the *ILSE* mission. Since the Apollo missions, it was usually astronauts who took on the role of CapCom—Capsule Communicator—and communicated with the people aboard. The Sikh had not been in space, but he knew the crew like no one else.

"Amy, great news, let me congratulate you."

The commander formed a 'thank you' with her mouth; Devendra would see but not hear it, of course.

The CapCom paused a bit, then continued. "My answer is only semi-official, but I can already tell you they went for it. Actually, the Public Relations officer in the MCC seemed very pleased. It looks like the baby will arrive at just the right time. Spaceflights taking months without anything happening are not very attractive for the press. This way, though, they sure won't forget you. CapCom, over."

Various news sites were the first to react. Martin thought, *Someone in Mission Control must have a connection to the press.* 'Sensation in Space: The First Space Baby,' the more respectable sites reported, while others wrote, 'Space Sex: Female Astronaut is Pregnant.' The newspapers discussed extensively how sexual intercourse would work in zero gravity, or they had experts discuss the survival chances of the unborn child. Martin was glad he and his crew mates were out of the reporters' range. *No photographer can hide outside our front door or search the trash for used condoms.* Reporters could not even make phone calls to the crew. Despite this, videos soon appeared on the web supposedly showing 'the amorous adventures of the female astronaut,' as one private video channel described it.

The official reaction of Mission Control, therefore, started with an apology. They said they were trying to find out how this breach of privacy could have happened, and they also agreed with the crew's decision. The neutral way this was formulated made it clear Mission Control was really against it. On the other hand, then those responsible would have to admit their own mistakes. After all, the doctors had relied on the commander being permanently infertile. The transmission ended with tasks for Marchenko, who as the ship's doctor was responsible for supervising the pregnancy. All the necessary equipment was on board, including an ultrasound unit. At the end, Mission Control mentioned there were requests for interviews with the commander and that they supported those requests. They did not seem to be quite so angry about the unexpected publicity.

The video message contained an attachment especially intended for Martin. *This is unusual,* he thought. *Has something happened to my mother? Astronauts are supposed to call up such messages in private.* Martin moved hastily to his cabin. He swore when he banged his head against the ladder in the passageway. In his cabin, he fell on his bed.

"Play message for Martin Neumaier."

"Confirmed. Message found," the AI replied.

"Hello, Martin." It was Devendra again. Martin was

not surprised to see him smile broadly, as this seemed to be the man's basic attitude.

"I've got good news for you. Due to Amy's pregnancy, we will have to reconfigure the mission. She won't be able to leave her newborn alone aboard the mothership. You have probably already calculated that she is due shortly before the ship reaches the orbit of Saturn. In this state, she also cannot make it without Marchenko. Two in the mothership, two in the shuttle, two in *Valkyrie*, you know the routine. Therefore you definitely will have to land. Isn't that great? You will go down in history as one of the first people to set foot on the moon of another planet. Who still remembers the man who orbited the moon in 1969 in the Apollo 11 command module?"

Of course Martin remembered his name, *Michael Collins, born in 1930, the only man to leave his spacecraft twice during a single flight, and also the first one to move from one satellite to another. How could anyone forget such a person?*

Devendra laughed briefly, as if he had guessed Martin's thoughts.

"Who would know this? Except for you, I mean. Just ask your colleagues. I am sorry we won't be able to fulfill the promise we made to you. You must understand we have no choice under these circumstances. I assume you wouldn't like to cancel the mission because of this."

Martin sat up and looked straight at Devendra's face, as if the man was sitting across from him. His eyes exuded a strong confidence, a belief in human goodness Martin had never had.

"We are always available for questions on this protected channel as well. Your training will ensure you can do a fantastic job anywhere. I am supposed to send the regards of Mission Control. CapCom out."

Devendra's face slowly faded from the screen, replaced by the mission logo. Martin leaned against the padded wall next to his bed and closed his eyes. *So what,* he thought, *then I am going to land on Enceladus with the shuttle, near the South Pole, where the ice crust is thinnest.* He had seen photos of the surface. The difference between it and Antarctica was minimal. Everything was whiter than white, and if he went outside without a space suit, he would die. He would simply stay inside, cozily sit by his computer, and supervise the *Valkyrie* expedition. A few days later, his colleagues would return, they would all take off again toward *ILSE*, and the excursion would end, just like the training near the South Pole of Earth. Martin took a deep breath, but not deep enough to get rid of the panic in his chest. *There is... no... problem.*

Then he remembered he should send a reply. He decided against a video recording. An audio comm should be enough.

"Neumaier to CapCom. Message received and confirmed."

August 7, 2046, ILSE

WHO WOULD HAVE IMAGINED they would have to fabricate infant diapers on a spaceship? Six astronauts had gathered at the conference table in the command module to discuss what a newborn needed, and how these needs could be fulfilled by on-board resources. Of course, no one had thought to bring along baby food, baby clothing, and diapers. Instead, from the available supplies, they had to attempt to create everything essential to a newborn.

The most important aspect they all had quickly agreed on: nutrition. Mother Nature had found an excellent solution for the initial period. However, no one knew how the female body would react to zero gravity or reduced gravity in this aspect. Even on Earth some mothers had problems with nursing. Therefore in space they might need alternative arrangements. Adding water to dried milk was the lesser problem. They needed a vessel the baby could drink from.

And once the baby was sufficiently fed, the problem moved to the other end. They immediately rejected the simplest solution. They did not have a surplus of the adult diapers they wore during spacewalks, so they would have to make diapers from the fabric of existing clothing. The elastic suits were not adequate for that. While the material could be easily adapted to the proper shape, they were not very absorbent. Francesca then thought of the perfect material. NASA undershirts were thin but absorbed liquids well. Cut into rectangles and folded into three layers, they would make decent diapers. The spacecraft carried more than enough undershirts, but they had to be retrieved from transport containers during an EVA. The commander had added this item to the list.

Once a diaper had done its duty, the next difficulty arose—it would need to be cleaned. In the lab module there was a machine that disinfected and deodorized the astronauts' clothing, but it could not handle solid residue on textiles. Instead of a proper washing machine with a drum and a spin-dryer, it more resembled a steam cleaner that blew sweat stains and body odors out of the fabric. Hayato had already run a practical trial; the machine could not handle diapers. Instead, he suggested a combined procedure—first a manual cleaning in the shower, the person doing this also having to be in the shower—followed by treatment in the on-board washing machine. Hayato was ordered to construct a solid-material filter for the shower drain after Mission Control had pointed out the existing hair-catcher filter could become clogged.

Mission Control would design the baby clothes for them. The child would need clothes offering protection against bone density loss, similar to the suits worn by the adult astronauts but taking growth into account. No one on board had any experience designing patterns for this particular elastic material. Jiaying agreed to sew mini-suits in several sizes. As a child, she had lived with her grand-mother who had taught her to sew.

Hayato also presented the idea for a baby bed to the others. He wanted to remodel one of the spare spider robots for this purpose. Instead of checking the outer hull of the spaceship, this machine would rock the baby to sleep and always keep the right spatial orientation, even if the gravity in the ring failed. The hardware of the spider robot was flexible enough to be adapted to such tasks. He also needed material from the spare part storage, and of course one of the spiders. Mission Control had to agree to this as well.

Finally, they must solve another safety issue. In case of a loss of shipboard pressure, the entire crew could save themselves by using their LEAs or 'Launch, Entry, Abort' spacesuits, until the atmosphere was breathable again. The baby would have no chance if this happened. It was completely impossible to construct an LEA on board. What would help, though, was a pressure-resistant container that could be connected to an oxygen tank. Martin came up with the solution—the areas of the ring between the rigid sectors were inflated by their interior air pressure. They consisted of several layers of textiles, which were airtight and very strong. If they were permitted to use some of the spare fabric, they could fashion a sphere with a diameter of one meter, and create an attachment piece for an oxygen valve.

"The fabric is too thick to sew," Jiaying said. "We have to weld it."

"Then we need welding equipment," Martin replied.

"With an open flame. Are you crazy?" Jiaying exclaimed with an angry stare.

"No, no, not like that. It just has to get hot enough to melt the edges of the fabric together."

"I can build something like that," Hayato said. "I think we can solve this by using electricity. Thanks to the DFDs we have plenty of that."

"We need permission from Earth for using the spare material," Amy said. "But that shouldn't be a problem. We should schedule an EVA for the day after tomorrow. It is time to look for larger holes anyways."

MARTIN DECIDED to visit Hayato after his shift. He had tried to suppress his guilty conscience for quite a while, but he hadn't slept well for several days now. He did not announce his visit. He almost hoped he would not find Hayato in his cabin. However, after he knocked on the door, the voice of the Japanese man asked him in.

Martin hesitated briefly. *Maybe I should have brought a present? Isn't that the custom?* Then he slid the door open. The cabin was a virtual replica of Martin's, and it was also as neat and orderly. Hayato sat cross-legged on his bed, and Amy sat next to him. Martin abruptly jerked back. *Should I just leave right away?* His face felt hot.

"Oh, I didn't mean to disturb you. Sorry."

Hayato got up and shook his hand. "You aren't disturbing us," he said. Amy smiled at him and nodded. Martin formally shook her hand. To do this, he had to lean over her. Then he noticed her belly already seemed rounded.

"How's the baby doing?" he asked.

Amy gave a broad smile. "Great," she said. "Marchenko is very pleased, too." She looked over at

Hayato, who was sitting down again, and placed a hand on his knee.

The Japanese man gave Martin a cushion. "Take this. It makes that box into a very comfortable seat."

The cabin was crowded. Martin thought the air was stuffy, even though it was no different from the atmosphere in the other modules. *I feel like an intruder.*

"Remember, I told you about Hayato's daughter," Amy said, and caressed her boyfriend's thigh. "She is doing fine now."

Hayato nodded. Martin saw Hayato's eyes were getting watery. "She has found a good clinic, and she is happy she will have a sister," he said.

"Or a brother," Amy added. "And we are busy thinking about names for the baby."

Hayato smiled. "We are very grateful all of you support us so much," he said, and it was obvious this was not just an empty phrase. Martin remembered the voting procedure. *Even if Amy had cast both of her votes for the abortion, at least one more crew member had been against the baby. Who was it? Was this important, though?* He shook his head.

"Sorry, I was just thinking," Martin said. "I actually just wanted to see how you—how both of you—were doing. I'm sorry I haven't shown up for such a long time."

Hayato got up and touched Martin's shoulder.

"It is good, just the way it is," he said, and Martin believed him.

August 9, 2046, ILSE

MARTIN HAD NOT SLEPT well the previous night, and this time he knew the reason for it. The commander had scheduled a spacewalk for today, an EVA. He shuddered to remember his first excursion, back on Tiangong-4. Martin suffered from vertigo. When he had tried to walk along a ten-meter-wide mountain ridge, the others laughed at him because he was obviously very scared. On the outside of the spaceship he would always be only a few steps away from the deepest abyss of them all. Back then, he had asked the trainers what he could do to counteract this fear, but they only laughed and said "nothing." He just would have to get used to it—*and I should definitely get in the habit of trying not to look down.* In space, everywhere was down, and if Martin only focused on the spaceship he might endanger his buddy, the colleague who went on the EVA with him.

At least Willinger had managed to give him a good piece of advice that sounded so simple he initially did not believe it would work. "It is your own decision where up and down are. Imagine you are stuck in a deep, black shaft. You are at the bottom, so why should you feel dizzy?" This advice had actually saved Martin's ass on the Tiangong station.

BEFORE A SPACEWALK, the doctors had ordered a lot of sweating. Martin sat on the stationary bicycle, wearing only a diaper and a breathing mask, and pedaled as fast as he could. Ten minutes was the target time, during which he breathed pure oxygen. Next to him Jiaying was pedaling, wearing a sports bra in addition to the diaper. The physical exertion helped to remove nitrogen from the blood, which might bubble up in the low pressure of the space suit, causing the dangerous reaction known as 'the bends.' During the several hours that the spacewalk would last, he could relieve himself in the diaper—which NASA called a MAG, or 'Maximum Absorbency Garment'—and afterwards, too, as he could not simply return at once to normal air pressure. The display of the stationary bike blinked, meaning he was allowed to get off.

Since he did not want his other colleagues to see him half-naked and wearing a diaper—*if Willinger had been here, he would have uttered his raucous laugh*—Martin had brought his LCVG, or 'Liquid Cooling and Ventilation Garment' into the fitness room. Made of Spandex, this form-fitting suit would keep him cool in space. Initially he had a hard time believing how important this was. Without the cooling provided by the water-carrying tubes integrated into the LCVG, he would gradually heat up like in a microwave. In the vacuum of space his spacesuit could only release heat by radiation, which was a slow process. His body, though, generated a lot of heat every second, particularly during movement. If the energy supply for the spacesuit failed, he would not freeze in the coldness of space, but rather suffocate in his own sweat.

The spacesuit itself consisted of two parts. Martin, wearing a mask and an oxygen tank in addition to the LCVG, moved toward the airlock in the stern of the ship. This small, almost spherical module contained the exit the astronauts must use for their spacewalk. It was closed off from all other rooms, so only the air in this room was lost when they exited. In front of the airlock, Hayato and Amy were waiting. They were there to help them put on the LTA, or 'Lower Torso Assembly,' the lower part of the suit made of thick layers of fabric. Inside the spacesuit, the pressure was only half of that on Earth, although the suited astronauts would breathe pure oxygen.

"Airlock ready," Watson said after about 50 minutes.

This was technically incorrect, because it was the astronauts who were now ready to enter the exit chamber. Here they found their HUT, or 'Hard Upper Torso,' sections consisting of fiberglass and ending in their helmets. The arms, individually sized for each astronaut, were already attached, so only the gloves were needed. While Martin and Jiaying put on the HUTs and attached cables and wires, Watson closed the hatch toward the ship and then reduced the interior pressure of the airlock to about two thirds.

Martin was nervous. *I already feel my bladder, which is much too early.* The spacesuit had turned him into a mini-spaceship. In front of his chest he had the toolbox of the mini-workstation. On his back was a SAFER, or 'Simplified Aid For EVA Rescue,' the space jet designed to save his life if he ever forgot the basic rule of any EVA —always attach a new safety wire connection before removing the old one. He had practiced this many times and knew which buttons he had to press when, but he still felt uneasy. Jiaying, on the other hand, seemed to be cheerful. Maybe she enjoyed the change of pace. She certainly was smiling and even started to tell stories from her school days. Martin wasn't really listening, but she did not seem to mind.

When will we finally get started? he wondered, as he restlessly chewed on the drinking tube. The mission would only commence once they had breathed oxygen for thirty minutes, but that wasn't so bad. It used to take longer. Willinger had once told him about the first model of this series, the Z2. Back then, NASA often made the EVA candidates spend the night in the airlock to get them used to the lower air pressure. The Z6, which had been in use for ten years now, reduced the risk of getting the bends, as it allowed for a higher air pressure.

"Pre-breathing phase finished," Watson reported. The AI could not open the lock itself—that was left to the crew. There were still scientists who thought a rebellion of the machines possible, even though it should have happened a long time ago, according to predictions. Due to such concerns, Martin had to turn the wheel himself. He looked at the to-do list on the multi-display on his right arm, which showed him what to do and in what order. The pressure in the airlock had already been lowered to a minimum, yet he still felt a breeze, a slight force pulling his arms outward.

He attached his safety line at the exit and then released the hook connecting him to the interior wall of the airlock. Jiaying watched him doing it. Then he gave himself a slight push and floated with his feet first through the round hole in the direction of space. He slowed himself down with his hands before the line was taut. *There is no place for experiments in space. I know the metal wire will stop me, but I do not want to test it.* He moved his feet close to the hull where there were special places he could latch his boots into. Martin looked around and decided on one horizon. It seemed much easier for him to find his orientation far away from Earth. During the training EVAs from the space station, Earth had always floated above him as a giant disc. That looked impressive, but it confused his spatial perception. Here he could only see the sun, considerably smaller than it appeared from Earth, as well as the ship moving away from it. The sunlight cast harsh shadows. There was only black and white, bright and dark, without any intermediate hues. He did not get to appreciate the much-praised silence of space during this excursion. The devices in his space suit made noise that reached his ear via the air he breathed, as body-borne sounds.

Once he stood, Martin gave Jiaying a sign. His colleague chose a different horizon. She stood slanted, and this looked strange from his perspective. The on-board computer had calculated an optimal path for both of them that would allow them to finish their task in the shortest time. The computer on Martin's arm showed him the way both visually and through vibration. Every two or three steps he secured himself anew by attaching the hook to the next lug.

The spaceship bore little resemblance to the elegant creations he was used to seeing in science fiction movies. *ILSF* was a seemingly unsystematic conglomeration of modules of various kinds. A few meters behind them the ring was rotating majestically—at a surprisingly slow speed. In front of it were the lab and the communication module. If Martin wanted to inspect these sections, the rotation of the ring would have to be stopped first. There was no reason to do that at this time, though, because the critical impacts were concentrated on the stern module. The holes were only 'critical' in so far as the spider robots had classified them as potentially dangerous. They had been sealed, but whether these spots were now safe must be decided by humans—by Jiaying and himself. For this purpose, they carried a special tool that looked like a toilet plunger attached to their belts. Instead of a handle, it was threaded onto a pipe with a hose at the other end, connected to a nitrogen tank.

Martin looked at the display on his arm. *The next damaged spot must be right behind the dish of the main antenna.* He placed his footsteps carefully. *The spider robot seems to have done good work.* In the light of his helmet lamp, Martin only recognized the hole by its different color, but he had a job to do. He placed the plunger on the repaired spot. Its material bonded with the hull thanks to special glue that hardened within seconds. Then Martin latched his boots to the ship and pressed hard against the plunger. Martin felt an adrenaline rush as he thought of what might happen if the material of the plunger separated from the ship. He reached for his safety line and gave it a short pull. *Okay, I will not float away after all.*

A reassuring sound in his helmet told him the repaired spot withstood the pressure, and the hole was now considered secure. The situation had never yet occurred when the robots had failed to properly close an impact area. Nevertheless, they had to regularly check them. This was shown by the leftover plunger parts that covered the hull, resembling pimples. Martin twisted the pipe to detach it and placed another plunger on its end. His handheld device showed him the way—only five more steps. While doing this he noticed many other considerably smaller holes the spider robot had filled and secured without reporting them.

What would happen if such a fragment came flying at me right now? Martin moved his gloves across the upper part of his spacesuit. It felt sturdy, though it would protect him much less effectively than the ship's hull did. Then he adjusted the cooling system because he was now shivering. The routing algorithm had led him to the storage containers on the left side. He arrived first, as Jiaying obviously had to check on a few more repairs. The computer knew where the T-shirts for the cloth diapers were located. All supplies were stored in boxes that could be easily taken out. They did not have to worry how much things weighed, as the supplies were weightless out here, like they were themselves. *I have to consider the inertia with particularly heavy items, but that should not be a problem today.* Martin looked for the number indicated on his display and took out the matching cube-shaped metal container. He moved three steps to his left to pick up a second container. He simply attached them both to his belly strap.

"Commander to EVA team, I can see you are progressing well. I don't want to rush you, but Mission Control has predicted a solar flare for fifteen hundred hours."

Martin looked at the time on the display. Jiaying beat him to it.

"Three hours from now! It's going to be pretty tight."

Jiaying was obviously worried about the solar storm.

"I have already complained about that," Amy said. "Space weather is very apologetic. The flare started from the other side of the sun, which could not be seen from Earth at that moment. It slipped through their fingers. They only noticed it when the magnetometer of the Mars Orbiter went haywire."

"They only noticed it at the orbit of Mars?" Jiaying's voice sounded higher than usual.

"It appears so. It is not that easy since this thing is invisible once it separates from the sun—at least it isn't approaching us at the speed of light," Martin explained.

"I don't want to be roasted like a chicken."

"No problem, we are finished here," he replied. Jiaying mumbled something in Chinese. They really did have enough time left. Even if the solar storm caught them in space, they would not notice it. One could only discover the charged, extremely fast particles by measuring magnetic fields and particle densities. Maybe the radio contact with the commander would exhibit more background noise. However, after the storm, their cancer risk would be notably increased. Anyway, who knew whether they would actually survive this mission? He calmly started his return trip.

Jiaying asked, "What about the decompression phase?"

She is right, Martin thought. They would have to breathe pure oxygen for a while before they could leave the airlock. In the pressure chamber they would be almost as unprotected against the solar storm as they were out here.

Martin tried to reassure her. "One hour, Jiaying, only one hour. We've got more than enough time."

The Chinese woman reached the bulkhead before he did. She intended to swing her feet in, follow with her lower body, and let go of the edge of the hatch. Instead, her momentum moved her away from the spaceship toward the depths of space. Surprised, Jiaying screamed into the microphone. Martin watched calmly as her line unrolled. After five meters, her safety wire would stop her.

"Stay calm," he heard Amy say on the radio.

But the safety line did not stop her. Jiaying had disregarded the most basic rule in her haste, and she had failed to hook the line. The unconnected carabiner bounced against the frame of the bulkhead and then moved away from the ship, centimeter by centimeter. Everything would have happened in frightening silence if not for Jiaying's heavy breathing sounds in his helmet radio. Martin could feel her panic, and he noticed how it infected him. The slow movement with which his fellow astronaut moved away from the ship looked harmless, but nothing could stop her now. The umbilical cord had snapped.

"Commander to Neumaier, launch SAFER."

Amy showed no hesitation, but Martin was briefly confused. He looked around for the device, even though he already carried it on his shoulders. Now he had to act quickly. The SAFER was a primitive but effective rocket backpack working on the principle of repulsive force. His mind raced. *For my own safety, I would like to keep my line attached to the ship. However, if I do not act fast enough, I might not be able to reach Jiaying because my line will stop me.* If he unlatched it, however, he would end up in space if the propulsion failed. *Safety for myself, or safety for Jiaying?* He started to sweat while he considered it, but he could not hesitate. *No matter,* he thought. Martin opened the carabiner of his line, jumped upward at a slight slant, and started the jetpack. Nitrogen streamed from the nozzle and drove the SAFER.

He was now moving a little bit faster than Jiaying, so he would have to decelerate shortly before reaching her. He tried to grab her safety line, but it had received a sideways impulse through the impact of the carabiner. Martin added another pulse of his jets and reached Jiaying. He quickly took the hook of the spare safety line from his belly strap and latched it to the life support system of her spacesuit.

"Well done, Martin," the voice of the commander said. He had no time for a reply, since they would only be safe once they were docked again with the spaceship. Over the radio channel he heard Jiaying's heavy breathing, or was it his own? *It is surprising how coolly I've finished this job, one step after the other. I don't feel scared anymore because my mind has no place for it.* Martin turned right to catch a glimpse of Jiaying's face. She looked pale, but that might be due to the lighting. The control jets came on. The SAFER changed his position in space so the thrusters were aimed away from the spaceship. Now Martin could accelerate.

"Three, two, one—rotate!" Watson had calculated all parameters and now uttered the commands. Martin's back gently bumped against the spaceship. He reached for the edge of the bulkhead and immediately attached his line again. Then he pulled Jiaying closer via the short line and carefully maneuvered her to the hatch.

"Thanks," she radioed. "Jiaying secured." Then Martin followed her in, and he manually closed the exterior hatch. Watson pressurized the airlock again. "Phew," Jiaying said. She was still breathing rapidly. Now they could remove the upper parts of their spacesuits. He looked at Jiaying, whose life he had just saved, and he felt warm and fuzzy inside. Her hair was matted. She wiped the sweat off her forehead.

Then she looked at him. "Thanks, Martin," she said, smiling at him.

This feels strange. His larynx seemed to tighten, and he had to clear his throat and look away. He hoped she had not noticed that he had broken safety regulations by flying toward her without being secured by a line. He did not know why, but he did not want her to know he had endangered himself for her sake. Jiaying sat down on a bench in the airlock, stretched her legs, and leaned back. She looked exhausted. While watching her, Martin suddenly realized how tired he was himself. He sat down as his legs started to tremble. Then he looked at the time. They had been outside for almost three hours. *We still should have enough time until the flare arrives.*

"Okay, I am going to let you out fifteen minutes early," Marchenko's voice said. There was a squeaking sound. The hatch was being opened from the inside. Amy, Hayato, Marchenko, and Francesca were waiting for them. Martin felt embarrassed by this reception. He wanted to let Jiaying go first, but suddenly she was not in a hurry anymore. Their fellow astronauts were standing in line and shook Martin's hand. *I was only doing my job,* he thought. The commander was the last one to greet him, and he studied her face. *I wonder if she noticed my breach of regulations?* All he saw was a warm, open smile.

"Into the cave," Amy finally said, and Martin was glad to hear it. The cave was the cube-shaped module just in front of the cargo containers. Here they would be protected from the high-energy radiation of the flare, even though the module was not lined by exotic materials. The reason was much simpler—the water tanks that surrounded it on the outside. Water would protect them very well, at least as long as the tanks were still mostly filled. All of them squeezed into the cave, a cube with an edge length of about two meters. After the hatch to the rest of the spaceship was closed, each of them had a wall of the cube for themselves. If they wanted to sleep, they would crawl into sleeping bags and use wall straps to secure themselves so they would not drift away in their sleep.

Since no one knew how long the solar storm would last, the crew started to get into their sleeping bags.

"Just a moment," Jiaying said quietly. All of them looked at her. She cast her eyes down.

"I am sorry I made a mistake and endangered all of you—particularly you, Martin." She gazed at him, and he felt his face becoming red.

"Nothing happened, after all," he said. "And I always wanted to try out a SAFER." *That is a bald-faced lie, but I hope no one will notice it. Thinking about flying through space without a safety line makes me feel rather queasy. Luckily while it happened, I had no time to think about it.*

No one said anything. Martin wondered, *What are they thinking?* He was about to turn toward the wall when Marchenko broke the silence.

"You won't believe what once happened to me during a Russian mission."

Martin looked around. The faces of the crew members relaxed and they resumed securing themselves in their sleeping bags as the ship doctor began one of his many stories. Martin turned toward the wall and closed his eyes. While Marchenko told campfire tales, Martin slowly fell asleep.

August 15, 2046, ILSE

"CREW OF *ILSE*, please gather in the command module."
The voice of Watson had just announced a kind of
mobilization, not an invitation by the commander, but a
sign that a message from Earth was waiting for them that
the entire crew must listen to simultaneously. Martin knew
such announcements were reserved for special events. He
had been dozing on his bed and jumped up too fast. Now
he not only felt his heart pounding, but the sudden change
in posture also made him feel nauseous. His curiosity went
into overdrive. *What is the meaning of this command? Will we be
told the mission is canceled? Has a World War broken out on Earth?
Have the imaginary inhabitants of Enceladus sent a message saying
they do not want any visitors? The reason for being ordered into the
command module must be something very important.*

At the hub he met Marchenko, who came from the
right and therefore had the right of way. Martin nodded at
him, although the doctor did not seem to notice him.
Martin wondered what kind of scenarios were going
through Marchenko's head.

Martin was the last one to arrive. No one wanted to

gather around the dining table, as all were impatiently waiting for the commander to play the message.

"I don't know myself what they are going to tell us," Amy said. Martin was not surprised. Something terrible must have happened, or at least Mission Control thought so. He managed not to become scared, even though for a long time he had been sleeping less than a meter away from the environment most inimical to life. What could happen to them? *ILSE* must be functioning as planned. Otherwise the message would have come via the shrill alarm sounds of the AI and not from Earth. *Or, we might be dead already—which we aren't,* he concluded.

Martin looked at the others. To his right, Marchenko seemed very composed. He had his hands on his hips as he blinked his small eyes. Francesca, the pilot, floated further right. She appeared rather stressed and preoccupied. He thought, *She is probably wondering, 'What does Earth want from us now?'* Hayato was the one who most clearly exuded fear. Maybe that was due to him thinking about becoming a father. The mission affected not only his future, but also that of his child. Hayato ran his fingers through his hair and repeatedly scratched his torso. Jiaying looked rather nervous, although she must have known there was no immediate danger. *It is the way the message was presented that worries her.* That was what Martin assumed, anyway, when he saw her tug at her earlobes and bite her lip at the same time. *What about me? What will the others think about me?* He checked his posture, opened his arms, and took on a relaxed pose. *I am quite calm,* he thought to himself, hoping this plus his posture would influence his psyche.

Martin had a hard time reading Amy. *She seems so soft, standing there calmly in front of the others.* While Francesca always took on a defensive stance, the commander gave the impression it would be easy to take her by surprise. Yet, paradoxically, this made one hesitate—and not dare to attack her. *This is probably her true strength,* he thought.

"Okay," Amy said. The others looked at her.

"I am starting the message. Siri, play message from Mission Control."

"Confirmed."

The computer projected the image of their Indian CapCom onto the fog display. Then the computer waited until the still image had stabilized before Devendra started to speak.

"CapCom to *ILSE.*"

Devendra's broad smile was still there, but you could see in his eyes it was an effort for him.

"I'll try to be brief. First the message, then the explanation, and after that you can ask questions, which we will answer as well as we can in our next transmission."

Martin looked around. Jiaying had turned pale. Marchenko was gritting his teeth.

"Mission Control has come to the conclusion that *ILSE 2*, which was to rendezvous with you in the orbit around Enceladus, has been hopelessly lost. This means there is a high probability your mission has failed. The scientists don't agree yet on the degree of probability. They are tending to assume a total loss of the mission."

Martin shivered as he felt the blood drain from his cheeks. Devendra had just told them something that felt like a joint death sentence. They were not dead yet, but they would most probably not make it back alive. Francesca could not control herself and yelled something in Italian. Jiaying approached the table. Tears were visible on her face. Marchenko drummed his knuckles against the wall. Amy and Hayato stayed calm. The Japanese man put an arm around the commander.

Devendra continued, "Now for the explanation. Two days ago, Mission Control attempted to wake *ILSE 2* from standby mode, as planned, but without success. Your sister ship does not react to radio commands. We have already tried everything. We did not want to inform you before every possible method had been tried. Mission Control has no explanation for this failure, only guesses—actually, just one guess. The ship must have encountered a catastrophic event that made any communication impossible. We assume it was a severe meteoroid hit, even though they are very improbable. If this state of things does not change, two problems will impede a successful end to your mission. First, food will become scarce. However, our experts have calculated that with somewhat reduced calorie consumption, and through extensive use of CELSS, a total loss could be avoided."

This meant they would probably not starve.

"Oxygen isn't a problem at all. You have enough electricity, and Enceladus offers plenty of water, so you can generate any missing quantity yourself. The systems are set up for splitting water into its elements. And you also have plenty of fuel. The engineers were wise enough to store the needed 30 kilograms of helium-3 on *ILSE*. That is the good news."

Jiaying wasn't crying anymore. She sat bolt upright at the table. Marchenko had started to move through the room. Francesca was whispering something to herself. Hayato and Amy still stood there embracing. Martin felt alone. *I would like to have someone who would hug me.*

"The main problem is the reaction mass, which provides your engines with thrust," Devendra said.

"Deuterium, heavy hydrogen," Hayato whispered.

"The reaction mass you need for the return trip is stored on *ILSE 2*—was stored there. Well, it might still be there, but you cannot reach it. If you want to return to Earth, you have to start decelerating immediately. Even then, your trip to Earth is uncertain, as you lack the reaction mass to accelerate the spaceship for the return flight. While the supply is sufficient to accelerate to your current cruising speed, you won't be able to decelerate again. Alternatively, you could use only half of the acceleration, but then your voyage would last twice as long, and you would probably starve. In any case, we would try to come toward you from the orbit of Mars and intercept you in time. We are already developing plans for this. Space-X is providing its ship *Heart of Gold* for this purpose."

Devendra paused briefly. "Or... you could continue your mission. Perhaps only the antenna of *ILSE 2* was damaged, and the ship will be waiting for you once you reach Enceladus. If not, you are stranded there. Not a nice idea. Mission Control therefore recommends an immediate cancellation. That is all we can tell you so far. The decision is yours. We are waiting for your reply. I am sorry. CapCom, out."

Right after the last words from Mission Control, Amy raised her hands.

"Please, listen to me for a moment. We do not have to rush things. It almost doesn't matter when we make our decision. Let's gather around the table, okay?"

No one reacted. Martin wanted to follow Amy's bidding, but he just could not sit down right now. Francesca and Marchenko also remained standing.

"What do you think of the analysis provided by

Mission Control?" Amy seemed to be most intent on starting a conversation.

Martin thought, *Is this a good idea?*

"They are a bunch of stupid assholes," Marchenko snapped. "*Pisdjuki!* I would like to know who was responsible. A spaceship doesn't just disappear like that."

"There are possible scenarios when it would happen just like this," Martin said.

Marchenko's face flushed, and he took on a boxer's stance as if he wanted to fight with Martin. In zero gravity it looked rather humorous, and Martin had to work hard not to laugh, even though he had just been essentially doomed to death. He shook his head. *If I do not watch out, I might go crazy in here.*

"Slow down, Dimitri," Hayato suggested while looking the doctor in the eyes, and the Russian seemed to calm down. "The situation seems horrible right now, but we should think things through carefully."

Jiaying wiped her nose. *In other circumstances, she would never do that in public,* Martin thought.

"I see a few unanswered questions," Hayato continued, "that we must discuss with Mission Control. Item 1: *ILSE 2*. The ship is two weeks ahead of us. That is not much. Maybe there is only a defect in its main antenna. The secondary antenna might be sufficient for communicating with our ship. We have to try that. Item 2: The reaction mass. We need about a ton of deuterium. That is not a huge quantity. However, I don't see a way of us extracting heavy hydrogen from the ice on Enceladus. Maybe we could replace the deuterium with regular hydrogen, though."

"The hydrogen atoms only have half the weight," Martin heard himself say.

"I know. Yet the mass influences the impulse in a linear fashion. Therefore we would only have to double the flow rate. I don't know whether the DFDs would allow it, but Mission Control can find that out. If it works, we would only have to generate two tons of hydrogen, which is produced automatically when we fill up our oxygen supplies on Enceladus. Then the ground team would at least have something to do. Why didn't those guys come up with this idea themselves?"

Martin shuddered in relief. Hayato had managed to make their death sentence appear much less dramatic. Not everyone seemed to agree, though.

"I think we should turn around," Francesca said.

This surprised Martin. *The pilot, of all people, who had never let anything intimidate her?*

"I am tired of playing the hero for Earth. They have not managed to develop a safe mission, and now we are supposed to pull their chestnuts out of the fire. All this sounds very familiar to me."

Is this in relation to some of her previous military missions? Martin could very well imagine that.

"Francesca is right," said Marchenko while moving across the room. "This was a kind of suicide mission from the very beginning, but at some point we reach our limits. I am in favor of voting on it."

The commander shook her head. "It is too early for that. There are two questions we need answered. We will not make any decisions before we have those answers."

August 16, 2046, ILSE

"Good morning." Amy greeted them. "Mission Control is having Princeton Satellite Systems check how a doubled flow rate would affect the engines. And we have received a task concerning *ILSE 2*."

Martin had not slept well during the night, and neither had any of the others. Jiaying was yawning, and Francesca floated near the door with her eyes closed.

"Did you all hear me? It would be nice if you would show some reaction." One could tell the commander's nerves were frazzled. "And where, by the way, is Marchenko?"

No one answered.

"Martin, could you go and check in his cabin?" she asked.

Martin frowned. *Why me?*

"Please, Martin," Amy said.

He forced himself to nod, and then he asked, "And what does Mission Control want from us?"

"They realized it might actually be a good idea if we tried to establish contact with *ILSE 2*. Perhaps there is only a defect in that ship's main antenna. We are much closer to it. Our transmission power might be sufficient to reach the spare antenna intended for shorter ranges."

"What does that mean?" asked Francesca, who now seemed to be fully awake.

"We have to adjust our antenna," Amy replied.

"Couldn't the AI take care of that?" Martin suggested. "When we decelerate a few months from now by aiming the engines forward, our antenna will be turned 180 degrees anyway, won't it?"

"That's true, Martin, at least in theory," Amy said. "In practice, the main antenna automatically aims itself toward Earth. No matter what happens to the ship, even if all other systems fail, the antenna will still be able to send a distress call in the right direction—even if *ILSE* should start to tumble."

"Clever idea," Martin remarked.

"Unfortunately, the system is truly autonomous. Watson does not have access to it."

"And how can we change that?" Francesca asked, sounding as if she already knew the answer. Amy understood and smiled.

"You must have guessed it. We do it the good old-fashioned way—by hand."

"Oh, Mitya would like that. It's too bad he overslept." No one but Francesca used Marchenko's first name, and she had only recently started doing so.

"How exactly would this work?" Martin would have preferred to write a program modification, but he suspected they were due for another EVA.

"Our 4-meter-dish is located on a ball coupling and can be rotated in any direction by linear motors. These motors are not very strong, and the antenna hardly weighs anything. We go outside, turn it to the correct position, and hold it there until we have contacted *ILSE 2*. As soon as the EVA crew lets go, the motors will align the dish with Earth again."

High tech versus muscle power, Martin concluded. *Yes, this is the kind of spaceflight Marchenko, or Willinger, would enjoy.* He suddenly remembered his trainer at NASA, who had warned him of a mission without return.

"So we just need to decide who will go," the commander said. "Are there any volunteers?"

Francesca raised her hand at once. "I need some fresh air—ha-ha. And the sooner we have solved this issue, the sooner we can start the return journey."

Amy swallowed hard.

"And I guess it is my turn now," Hayato said, standing up.

"Good. Then you can start preparing for the procedure immediately. Let's meet at the airlock. Martin, remember to visit Marchenko. We don't want our doctor to be sick."

WHY DID the commander send me, of all people, to check on Marchenko? In the presence of the very experienced cosmonaut, Martin always felt like a boy who had just gotten his first job aboard a ship. He moved along the tube leading to the Russian's cabin. One minute later, Martin knocked on his door.

No answer.

He pressed the button and the door slid sideways. Marchenko had not locked his cabin door. Martin noticed a stale, sweetish-wet smell. *This should be impossible, since the air conditioning is centrally controlled.* Marchenko was lying on his bed in a tracksuit, sleeping soundly. There was a smile on his face. *He is probably dreaming.* His ears were covered by a pair of headphones connected to a small device. It looked old-fashioned. *Could it be an iPod?* Martin had heard of these antique devices that could only play music. He believed such things were invented in the 1980s. Martin inspected the cabin. There was a box of cigarettes lying in front of the bed. *I can hardly believe it! The Russian must have manipulated the air conditioning system.* The vents had indeed been plugged with pieces of clothing. At the foot of the bed he saw an empty glass bottle with a Russian label. *I wish I could have secret supplies! It seems Marchenko really tried to fulfill all the stereotypes.*

Martin touched his shoulder. The Russian jerked upward, almost making their heads collide.

"What... what are you doing here?"

"You did not react to anything, so Amy sent me."

"What's the time?"

"Ten o'clock ship time."

Marchenko sat up. Martin could smell the alcohol on his breath.

"Fuck," he said. "Something must have gone wrong." He scratched behind his ear. "Francesca is going to be pissed."

"I did not notice anything like that. She volunteered for an EVA," Martin said.

"That is just like her. Of course, she does not show anything outwardly. But I know her better. She can be pretty... exhausting."

"My goodness, the way it looks in here..."

"I know. It won't happen again." Marchenko took a look at the glass bottle. "It's empty anyway."

"What's going on?" Martin could hardly believe he

asked this question. *Do I really want to know? Is it any of my business?*

Marchenko looked him straight in the eye. "Yesterday, I had a fight with Francesca because she wants to break off the mission."

"But didn't you want to end it, too?" Martin asked.

Nodding, Marchenko replied, "For a short time, yes, though it probably doesn't actually matter. The whole thing was uncertain from the very start. I told Francesca I would vote against breaking off the mission if we could fill up with hydrogen as reaction mass on Enceladus. She somehow saw this as a kind of betrayal."

"Hmm." Martin did not know how to react to this.

"I don't know what I mean to her," Marchenko said. "I always thought we were just sleeping with each other, as adults do who have only a limited time left and want to have fun."

Martin was surprised, but did not let on. "So she sees that differently?"

"*Ne znayu.* I don't know. We never talked about it. Looks like it, though. Damn."

Amy should have come herself, Martin thought. *What can I say about this?* He only had one logical answer.

"Well then, maybe you should talk about it sometime," he said to Marchenko.

"Yes, you smart aleck, I realized that, but just try once to do that with an angry Francesca. Why do you think that mirror there is cracked?"

Martin could imagine the scene. *Marchenko does not seem the type to give in quickly.*

"Not long ago she called you Mitya. Isn't that a term of endearment? Then she cannot be that mad."

Marchenko stretched his torso and looked at him.

"Really? Is that so?"

Martin nodded.

"That's good news. Well, get out of my cabin so I can get dressed."

Two hours later the outer hatch of the airlock opened and two figures in spacesuits moved out onto the hull of the ship. From the command module, Jiaying and Martin watched their progress. Marchenko and Amy were waiting at the airlock. After the exit, the two figures did not take long to reach the main antenna. It was attached to a mast with a height of more than two meters and currently faced almost directly backward, in the direction of Earth. Both of the astronauts—actually, one would have been enough —maneuvered it into the almost opposite direction. It wasn't hard work, but it taxed their patience, because as soon as they let go, the mechanism tried to return the antenna to its original position.

Mission Control had already sent them data on where to expect *ILSE 2* if that ship had continued its journey. During this experiment they would have no connection to Earth. It was Watson's task to direct the positioning of the antenna into alignment with the provided data. Consequently, the two spacewalkers heard a rhythmic sound in their helmet radios. The closer they got to the target, the more quickly the pitch changed.

Martin logged on to the helmet radio channel.

"Beep—beep—beep." There was an interval of maybe two seconds. He watched his fellow astronauts via the camera. Francesca turned the antenna, and Hayato secured it.

"Beep-beep-beep." They were getting closer.

"Beepbeepbeep—beep—beep.   Damn,"   cursed Francesca. One more try, and once again she turned the antenna slightly too far. Martin heard her breathe faster. Another attempt followed, and it also failed. Hayato placed a hand on her shoulder.

"Should I try it?"

The pilot sighed. "Yes, please. I seem to be useless today." They changed positions. Now it was Hayato's turn.

"Beepbeepbeep." That was the sound indicating the optimal position.

"Watson, contact *ILSE 2* according to special instructions," Martin commanded. The AI did not answer, but Martin could follow its activity on the screen. *Would it find the lost spaceship?*

"Connection   established,"   Watson   acknowledged. Martin was shocked when he heard this. He was no longer used to receiving immediate answers to radio signals. *ILSE 2 must be very close to us, and it does not seem to be completely inoperative,* he noticed.

"Hayato, wait right there."

Martin saw the status reports from *ILSE 2* arriving on the monitor. The transmission speed was low. *It is obviously communicating with the low-gain antenna, which has a short range and uses less energy.* Once they analyzed the data they would see whether only the main antenna was defective—a good sign—or if there was a general energy shortage.

"Transmission   completed,"   Watson   reported   after exactly seven minutes. The EVA crew could come back inside. Mission Control had asked to analyze the data, so the people on board would not know how much of a chance they had until the next shift.

August 17, 2046, ILSE

"I AM sorry to wake you in the middle of the night when it's your time off," Amy began, "but I thought you would be interested in the new data sent by Mission Control."

Everyone nodded. Of course they all wanted to know whether the mission still stood a chance.

"First, the bad news," she began. "Watson?"

"On June 25, the spaceship *ILSE 2* was hit by a meteoroid, which severed the connection to its drives. Otherwise, the ship is mostly intact, but it will not be able to decelerate once reaching the orbit of Saturn. The AI placed it into energy-saving mode."

"Is there any chance we can reach the contents of the cargo bays?" Marchenko asked.

"*ILSE 2* is only two weeks flight time ahead of us, but we can hardly catch up with that," Hayato looked at his tablet while answering the question. "Theoretically, we could accelerate a potential 20 km/s, but if we increase speed now, we will have to shed it here," he said, pointing at the orbit of Saturn. "And this would cost us a lot of fuel, or reaction mass, about 80 percent of what we need for the entire return flight. Even if we replenish our supplies afterward from *ILSE 2*, in the end we would have gained only 20 percent. That's not enough for the return trip."

"So we have to let our roast goose get away," Marchenko said with a sigh.

"It looks like it," Amy remarked. "However, Mission Control also has good news for us."

"The fusion drives," Watson stated, "are not actually designed for a doubled flow rate. According to simulations, though, they most probably will not be damaged by it."

"So this means we can fill up our tanks on Enceladus?" The ship's doctor seemed hardly able to believe it.

The AI answered, "Correct, Dr. Marchenko. The hardware for splitting water into hydrogen and oxygen is already on board. The mechanism is used in the secondary motor of the DFDs, and there will be enough time for it. Using hydrogen instead of deuterium as a reaction mass has a drawback, though. In a certain percentage, a fusion of hydrogen and helium-3 might occur. That generates gamma rays. The drives do not possess sufficient shielding against that."

Francesca exhaled loudly but said nothing. Everyone seemed to understand the consequences.

Marchenko asked, "Could we produce some shielding now. For instance, by placing water containers in front of the drives?"

"No, Dr. Marchenko. For an effective attenuation of gamma rays we would need material made of elements with a higher atomic number, like lead. We do not have sufficient amounts of those on board."

"Well, then. Let me summarize our options." *Marchenko is really going full throttle today*, Martin thought when he heard him continue. "Option 1: We immediately decelerate, but we will only get home if Earth rescues us and we haven't starved by then. Option 2: We continue the mission as planned, generate hydrogen on Enceladus, and use it to fly home. But we will arrive hungry and grilled by gamma rays."

"That's a rather drastic way of putting it, but that's what it looks like," Amy concurred.

"The mission design allows for a few more variations," Watson added. "If Earth supplies us with deuterium on the return trip, we only have to use hydrogen for the initial acceleration, and this would reduce the radiation exposure of the crew. If we catch up with *ILSE 2*, that would secure a fifth of our deuterium supplies. Then we would need less hydrogen. Furthermore, *ILSE 2* has enough food on board for our return flight."

"A lot of *ifs*," Marchenko said quietly. "Though I think it's worth a try."

"Should we vote on it?" Amy asked, looking around. No one protested.

"Does anyone insist on a secret ballot?"

"Anyway, you know I am in favor of breaking off the mission," Francesca said with a tense voice.

"Well. Let's do it quickly. Siri, please record and block from being deleted."

The AI acknowledged the commander's order.

"Who is in favor of breaking off the mission?"

Francesca raised her hand. While doing so, she glared at Marchenko.

"One vote," Amy counted aloud, even though it was obvious.

"Who is in favor of continuing the mission?"

Hayato and Martin voted for it. After a short hesitation, Jiaying raised a finger.

"That would be four votes," the commander said. "since I am also in favor of continuing."

"Are there any abstentions?"

"That would be me, I guess," Marchenko said.

"Then I determine that an absolute majority of the crew has voted to continue the mission. Siri, end recording and send it to Mission Control."

"You can't just rush it like this!" Francesca said with a red face. Marchenko placed a hand on her shoulder, but she shook it off.

"Francesca?" Amy looked her in the eyes.

"I... no... this can't be done! We haven't even really discussed it!"

"It did not seem necessary in this case. The results are clear. We..."

"I don't care what you want to do. I never signed up for a suicide mission. If I had known that, my children..."

"Francesca, you don't have any children. We know that." Amy's face displayed a mixture of confusion and outrage.

"Well, no. Shit! Life is sometimes more complicated than in the case of you, with your lightning career."

Amy winced. "What do you mean by that?"

"My sister. It is about her kids. We lived together in the same house. Shortly before launch, I learned she was suffering from breast cancer. Our mother died a long time ago. If I don't return in time, the children will have to grow up in an orphanage!" A tear glittered on Francesca's red cheek.

"I am very sorry, Francesca," Amy said with a sympathetic smile. "But the decision has been made. We will return, one way or another. Trust me, okay?"

Francesca was breathing heavily. *I know how she must feel inside right now.* Martin recognized her inner struggle.

"Fuck it," she finally said, then turned around and quickly left the command module. At the hatch she turned back once more. "It will be your fault if those children have to grow up alone. All of you; *your* fault!" Then she left the room, where the only sound now came from the life-support system.

November 15, 2046, ILSE

ELEVEN MONTHS. Martin could hardly believe it. *Eleven times thirty days crammed into a bunch of tin cans that seem to have been randomly attached to each other.* After the decision to continue the mission had been made, the pursuit of *ILSE 2* had initially made for some excitement. In retrospect, Martin was surprised everything had worked so smoothly. *Accelerate, match speeds, retrieve cargo...*

Marchenko had turned out to be a veritable virtuoso with a SAFER and had repeatedly flown back and forth between the ships. When Martin first saw the damage that had been done to the other ship, his hands trembled. Afterward, Watson had shown him a visual simulation of what a direct hit would have done to the engines or the command module—*an even more disturbing idea.*

They currently had a fifth of the deuterium aboard that they would need for the return flight, and their food supply issues had been permanently solved. Lying on his bed, Martin was staring at the ceiling, where white clouds moved across a blue sky. He was playing a game. To do so, he had to try to relax. The ship sensors measured his parameters, and the more relaxed he was, the bluer the sky became.

He envisioned an image of the commander. *She does not seem as tough as she used to be—more maternal. Amy's belly is rounded. It bulges out so much it seems unnatural, as if the low gravity is to blame.* Each time he saw the commander again, during a shift or on his time off, her belly had grown a bit more. While she always complained she was not as agile as she used to be, or that she got winded too quickly, she also grinned. Marchenko was happy the pregnancy was progressing so well. The baby was doing fine, and the microgravity seemed to have caused no damage. However, the doctor could only be completely certain after birth, and even then, new problems might arise. The main question was how bone growth would be affected. The six astronauts were adults, but despite their intensive physical exercise, they were losing bone density. In Martin's case, Marchenko had measured a loss of seven percent. *This isn't the end of the world. If the process continues, it might reach 20 percent by the time we return to Earth, which can be dealt with.* Martin would not end up in a wheelchair.

The pilot Francesca was now much more distant toward the others, except for Marchenko. Martin could imagine she felt betrayed. Only Marchenko had not voted against her. She was not openly hostile, but the friendliness Martin had noticed when he first met her was gone. *I hope our relationship will eventually become normal again.*

SUDDENLY IT WAS QUIET. Completely quiet. Martin had become so used to the constant background noise that the silence felt like a blow to the head. The light flickered.

Then the noise started up again. He noticed a breeze on his face and felt cold sweat on his back.

"Main computer rebooted successfully," Siri reported. "Energy supply online. Battery capacity at 99 percent. Navigation, life support, and communication online. Drive offline."

Drive offline? Martin jumped up and hit his head. On the ceiling, storm clouds roiled, flashing lightning.

"Entire crew to the command module," Amy commanded. Martin noticed she tried to stay as calm as possible, but he discerned an undertone of panic.

What happened? he wondered, as he hurriedly put on his sneakers and left the cabin. At the hub of the ring, he almost collided with Marchenko, who was followed by Francesca and Jiaying. Martin let them go first.

Hayato and the commander were already in the command module, as it appeared to be their shift.

"Good, you are all here." Amy now seemed to be completely calm again. "As you probably heard, something seems to be wrong with the drive. Watson, give us a report."

"Confirmed."

The AI activated the fog display above the table and projected a block diagram of the drive onto it. *That's really impressive, even in this serious situation,* Martin thought. On tiny oil droplets held in place by an electrical field, each image shimmered and shone like a small work of art.

On this diagram, the plasma chamber in which a fusion reaction turned helium-3 and deuterium into helium-4 and hydrogen, the actual drive took up the smallest part. Around it, there were all kinds of systems that started, cooled, or shielded the drive. At the bottom right there was a flashing red field labeled 'gas turbine.'

"You are looking at the status of drive 4," Watson explained. "The gas turbine of this DFD has failed. Currently, a root cause analysis is not possible. The effect of this failure is that the coolant liquid of the fusion reactor no longer can give off its heat. After the drive heated by more than ten percent above normal range, I deactivated it. An immediate intervention by the crew is necessary, and for that reason I turned off the other DFDs as well."

"Can't we just fly on with five drives?" Marchenko asked. Martin considered that a naive question, but then Marchenko was a doctor, not a physicist.

The AI replied, "Of course. I calculated that the ensuing trajectory would take us out of the solar system in 4.3 years." Watson appeared to have a sense of humor. "Our ship has been decelerating for a while to get below the capture velocity of Saturn. With our power output reduced by one-sixth, that would be impossible."

"And what if the repair was successful?" Amy asked.

Watson remained patient. "Commander, it is no longer possible to maintain the planned trajectory. However, I can calculate an alternative course that makes it possible to reach all research goals. For this, we would have to use the decelerating effect of Saturn's gravitational field more than originally planned."

Martin saw Amy pondering. Her eyes were closed. Then she said, "Specify necessary repair options."

"It is necessary to connect the helium pipes carrying the coolant of DFD 4 with the gas turbine of one of the other five drives. Due to its proximity, I would recommend drive 3."

The commander asked, "Will the doubled gas flow be within the parameters for the turbine?"

"Almost. Temperatures will be within the specified

range. The mean life expectancy of turbine 3 will be cut in half, though, from ten years, as planned, to five years," Watson reported.

"It has been running for one year. This means we have a 1 in 4 probability that we will encounter another problem with it during the return flight," Martin said out loud. "Good thing we have no other issues."

The AI said, "That estimate is correct. Without the suggested repair, though, the probability of a return flight is zero percent."

"It's obvious," Amy said. "We have to go outside. How much time do we have, Watson?"

"The available time frame cannot be calculated."

"What is that supposed to mean?"

"Battery capacity at 80 percent," Siri reported. It was against protocol for one AI to interrupt the other, so this must be an urgent message.

"Before the repair, the drive must be almost completely cooled off," Watson said. The drives were Watson's area of expertise. "As the vacuum insulates well, the coolant has to keep flowing during this time. The pumps need electricity, which is provided by the batteries. Within 30 minutes, the charge has decreased by 20 percent. If the energy consumption remains constant, the capacity will reach zero in two hours."

No one said a word, as they immediately realized the consequences. Out here, the solar sails were useless. Without energy, neither life support systems nor communication would work. *We will suffocate in this tin can without being able to alert Earth*, Martin thought.

"When will the drive be sufficiently cooled off so that we can send someone out?" Amy always managed to ask the crucial questions.

"According to my calculations, no sooner than ninety minutes," Watson said.

"Well, you heard what Watson said." Amy turned toward the entire crew. She exuded a convincing sense of calm while she spoke. Even Jiaying, who had nervously bounced her knee the whole time, listened attentively.

"We have an hour and a half to prepare. That's tight, but it can be done. The two people who perform the repair will then have half an hour to do it. Rerouting a pipe, that doesn't sound too complicated. Are there any volunteers?"

Hayato immediately raised his hand. Marchenko and Francesca did the same right afterward. Even Martin raised a finger.

"Martin and Hayato, you will be doing it."

Martin nodded. *The decision is correct. No matter how the mission ends, we will need the doctor and the pilot on board.* Both Martin and the Japanese man, though, would not be required until the ship reached Enceladus. Martin was still impressed by the fact, though, that the commander would send the father of her child on a spacewalk. Afterward, Amy ordered complete radio silence toward Earth. The antenna of the Deep Space Network used energy they needed more urgently for survival. Mission Control would have to deal with not hearing from them for a couple of hours.

"We have to try to lower the energy consumption on board. Everyone should try to come up with some way to do this. Five minutes," the commander said.

Martin heard somebody's feet scratching against the floor. It must be Jiaying. He pondered, *How can we generate energy in a spacecraft flying through the void?* He visualized the layout of the ship, with its random conglomeration of modules. *Usable energy can be found where potential differences exist—heat, radiation, fields, motion.* The spaceship moved silently through his head. The spokes of the ring rotated slowly.

He had found it—*motion.*

As a child, he'd had an old bicycle without an electric motor, so he had to pedal it himself. To turn on the headlight he'd needed to clamp a dynamo against the sidewall of the front wheel. *What if we give the habitat ring a dynamo that would generate electricity—like on my bicycle?* Martin thought of arguments against it. *The removed energy will slow the ring, but we could compensate with the solid-propellant engines. They should still contain more than enough propellant.* He calculated the potential in his head, using a simplified model. For the rotational energy he would need the inertial torque, which included the mass and the square of the radius of the ring, and the square of the angular velocity. The ring weighed several tons, the radius was 6 meters, and the angular velocity 0.6 per second. *Damn.* The dynamo would not be able to generate more than a couple hundred watts. It would be enough for a few lamps, but not for the life support system. *I can't do anything about the mass of the ring or the radius, but I can change the rotational speed. Since it is squared, doubling it would generate four times the energy.*

Martin asked the AI, "Watson, up to what rotational speed is the habitat ring specified?"

"The ring is turning at its specified speed."

"Then let me rephrase the question. What maximal speed does the mechanical construction of the ring permit?"

The others listened up. Their expressions told Martin they did not understand what he was trying to do.

"The spacecraft will remain in a stable configuration as

long as the ring does not move faster than two revolutions per second," the AI replied.

This gives me a lot of leeway. Not only can I double the angular velocity, but increase it twentyfold. 10 kilowatts instead of 500 watts. That sounds quite different.

"Watson, extrapolate the status of the ship if a total energy supply of 10 kilowatts is available," Martin instructed.

"To do this, I would need to have the priorities for all systems defined."

"Life support 100 percent priority, all other systems zero percent."

"Under those circumstances, the life support system can reliably provide for the command module. Other modules must be shut down."

It was time for Martin to explain his idea to the others. He described the task at hand. "We have to build a dynamo."

Jiaying immediately said, "I can do that."

That's unusual. She is not an engineer, Martin thought.

"I used to refurbish old dynamos together with my father. Put in new carbon brushes and such. Our family was poor," she finished quietly. Because of her childhood experience, Jiaying was convinced she could build one.

Afterward, they would attach the device outside and connect it to the current supply. They had a total of two hours for the task, but there was a problem.

"We only have three EMUs on board," Amy explained, referring to the Extravehicular Mobility Units. The repair of the DFD could not be performed by one person. And a third one would have to get into the remaining spacesuit and attach the dynamo, alone. This was against all protocol, because during EVAs, astronauts were always supposed to work in teams. Yet they had no alternative.

Francesca volunteered, but Jiaying objected.

"If I build the thing, then I will know how best to attach it."

"Are you sure?" Amy's voice sounded concerned. *I know why Amy is worried,* Martin realized. "You will have little time for decompression procedures."

"I'm well aware of that. I just have to hurry when I construct the dynamo," Jiaying said.

"As far as that is concerned, you could already start breathing pure oxygen through the mask. Francesca, please help her with her work. Hayato and Martin, start preparing for the spacewalk immediately."

"BATTERY CAPACITY AT 40 PERCENT." Siri conveyed these depressing messages every 30 minutes. Martin and Hayato were already in the airlock, where the air pressure had been reduced, and they breathed pure oxygen. At their feet was a tube, about three meters long, with a metallic sheen. It looked like a snake that had gorged itself and was now resting. Martin lifted one end of it. He could have easily placed his leg inside it, including the spacesuit. They had said goodbye to the others outside the airlock, as if their journey was coming to an end. Martin had really felt this might be the last time he would see them. His heart was beating faster. He wanted to flee, to float off into space. What he was feeling must be pure panic. He tried to breathe deeply.

He looked at Hayato, who was busy with the metal segments of the snake. *It is hard to imagine hot gas can stream through its inside for months without causing any problems... although it will be helium,* he thought, *which is an inert gas and does not cause chemical reactions.*

Martin's brain continued to analyze the details. This special material was also able to withstand the heat. The metal rings that surrounded it served both to radiate heat into space and to protect against meteoroid strikes. Nevertheless, the rerouted pipe would represent a weak spot compared to the rest of the hull. The risk of a hit was reduced as long as the drives were not pointed in the direction of flight. This, however, was the case now when the DFDs were supposed to be decelerating them during the final approach to Saturn.

On his arm display, Martin had Watson show him once again how Jiaying wanted to install the dynamo. He was satisfied. She had come up with a design that was both clever and safe. The AI reported Jiaying was making good progress. It even looked as if the two of them would have to hurry with exiting the spacecraft. If Jiaying finished early, she had to get outside as quickly as possible, and in this case, Martin and Hayato shouldn't be blocking the airlock anymore.

He gave his fellow astronaut a signal. Hayato obviously had similar ideas, as he immediately understood what Martin was trying to say.

"EVA crew to Commander, we are preparing to exit."

"I understand." Amy neither criticized them, nor did she point out the increased danger of getting the bends by exiting the ship earlier than planned.

Martin opened the hatch to the outside, remembering to secure himself. Hayato followed him. After they were outside, both stopped for a moment. The spoked wheel of the habitat ring was turning noticeably faster than last time. Martin believed he could see the four jets that were accelerating the giant wheel, with the goal of reaching two revolutions per second. Previously, it had taken six seconds to complete a single rotation. Martin hoped the construction was really as sturdy as Watson maintained. He suddenly remembered he had not cleaned up his cabin this morning. Anything he'd left lying around would be thrown about. The simulated gravity should be above that on Earth by now. He wondered whether the equipment inside the spaceship could handle it. The shower, the whole WHC? It didn't matter. Without the electricity provided by the dynamo, he would never have to take a shower again.

He looked toward the stern. They had to go further than ever before, and enter an area prohibited to astronauts. And they needed to be careful not to stumble over the small plungers sitting above the repaired spots on the hull. The danger of misaligning a part of the DFD by a clumsy step was considerable. Watson had explained to them that, near the drives, all areas they were allowed to enter were marked. Anything not marked was off limits. Martin went ahead and Hayato followed him with the weightless tube he had secured to his belt. It was a fascinating walk, even in the face of looming death. The universe around him seemed to stand still, even though they were moving dozens of times faster than a racecar. There was a little bit of metal at his feet, but otherwise he felt alone. The limitless cosmos extended in all directions. The stars, even the sun, were far away. By now, Saturn had become a tiny disc rather than a dot, though its rings were not yet visible to the naked eye. He made a decision. *If the repair fails, I will latch my spacesuit to the ship and wait for death. That is a hundred times better than to fall asleep forever in my bed at some point. I am glad I came on this journey.*

Nevertheless, the repair must not fail. The two of us owe that to the others.

Martin looked around to Hayato, who was just attaching a carabiner to a protruding strut. He waved, and the Japanese man waved back. They had reached the last module, but were still about 20 meters away from the drives. From this perspective, the six DFDs, arranged in a circle, seemed much more massive than in a schematic diagram. They looked like giant gasifier tubes, surrounded by cube-shaped modules. One of these modules, the one next to drive 4, had stopped working. The DFDs would have been indistinguishable from each other if their numbers had not been printed on metal plates that could be clearly seen from the spaceship. Martin had only to aim his flashlight to find the culprit.

Between him and drive 4 was an abyss, an infinite chasm bridged by a structure made of metal girders. Martin took a step forward, but then quickly jerked back. *The depth seems to hit me in the face. It's maddening. It is easy for me to look up into infinity, but my vertigo is triggered when the same limitless expanse is below me.*

Hayato came toward him from behind and placed a hand on his shoulder. Since he was wearing the HUT, Martin did not feel the touch directly, but he noticed the pressure it exerted. He turned toward Hayato and searched for his face behind the round glass of his helmet. The Japanese engineer smiled at him. It was a smile that exuded confidence. During Martin's childhood, he had always lacked confidence. *This is the reason why I both like this feeling, but also distrust it, because in the end I fear it will disappoint me.*

He had to outsmart his vertigo. There was no easier place to do this than on a spaceship. Above and below are not fixed concepts in space. Martin first sat down, and then he lay on his back. He did not want to know what Hayato thought about him at that moment. *Well, my friend, do you still trust me?* he thought. Then he used his safety line to pull himself toward the abyss, but in such a way that the metal structure was to his right. When he now looked through it, he did not see a chasm, but a far-away plane.

Hayato arrived on the other side at the same moment as Martin. Martin got up again and signaled he was okay. The engineers who had designed the spaceship had been clever. They had expected one of the modules to fail and had planned for alternate paths. At the spot where the coolant flowed into the gas turbine, there was a valve that fit the mouth of their metal snake. At the other turbine— the working one—they found its counterpart. Each of them had to attach one end of the snake, and then they had to redirect the flow as simultaneously as possible. A time difference of one or two seconds wouldn't matter, but it shouldn't be more than that. Otherwise, irreplaceable helium would be lost.

Martin crouched in front of the port for turbine 4 and installed his end of the alternate tube. He had to push the 'mouth' over the port and turn it several times before the special threads engaged. Hayato did the same at drive 3. Then Watson gave a signal via the helmet loudspeaker. Martin and Hayato each lifted a cover next to 'his' adapter and turned the lever hidden below it.

"Coolant circuit for drive 4 has been reestablished," Watson reported.

"Congratulations. Fifteen minutes before the deadline. Come back inside, the both of you," Amy's voice said. She sounded relieved, even though the danger was not completely over.

"Jiaying, are you moving along? Do you need help?"

"I have reached the hub of the habitat ring. I am starting the installation," Jiaying reported.

"Commander, requesting permission to help Jiaying," Martin said. Without waiting for Amy's approval, he repeated his maneuver for crossing the infinite abyss and moved quickly but carefully toward the ring—which, from his perspective, was rotating behind the exit hatch.

"Uiiii." He heard the voice of the Chinese astronaut in his headphones. She was breathing heavily. After a few more steps, Martin recognized the reason for it. *The ring is turning very quickly now.* The dynamo consisted of a magnetic coil, in which the rapid movement of the metal ring generated electricity through induction. To work efficiently, it must be as close as possible to the metal of the habitat. However, the ring was not a perfect circle. The rigid living module alternated with softer transition modules that had a smaller circumference. If Jiaying moved the dynamo too close, it would be destroyed by the enormous rotational energy. And it would probably kill the person in its immediate vicinity. If the dynamo was too far away, though, its power output would decrease dramatically.

Martin stopped. He wondered how he could help Jiaying. They would need a dummy object, something they could move closer and closer, but it shouldn't matter if that object got destroyed. He looked around but did not find anything. From the corner of his eye he noticed the SAFER, the rocket backpack he had strapped on. There was a second SAFER on board, so this one was expendable. With one hand, Martin signaled Hayato to come over and help him take the SAFER off. Then he radioed Jiaying and explained what he was trying to do. He would kneel down at the spot where she needed to attach the dynamo.

Then he would move the SAFER forward, millimeter by millimeter, and mark the front edge on the hull each time. On his tool belt he had a pen that could write in space. Jiaying lifted the dynamo and made room for him. Martin put the SAFER in its place. The habitat modules were zooming past them closer and closer. It was an eerie feeling, as everything was noiseless, and there was also no airflow such as one might expect from such a mighty carousel.

Move it one millimeter, make a marking, one more millimeter, another marking... Bam—the ring tore the SAFER from his hand. Martin's heart was pounding. *I am being carried into space,* he noticed. The SAFER had briefly collided with his spacesuit and had imparted a part of its kinetic energy to him. Martin was secured by a line, so he was not in danger unless the safety line unrolled in such a way that it got into the spokes of this wheel weighing several tons. It was not designed to withstand such a weight. The SAFER was already flying through space, out of his reach. Martin felt how his momentum was driving him closer to the mighty ring. It was spooky, as everything was happening in complete silence. The rotating mass that was meant to power the life-saving dynamo would give him a push, launching him far into space. In his mind, Martin was doing a countdown. *It can be only a few seconds now.* Martin felt something wet on his face. *It must be tears. This is not the moment I would have chosen for a farewell.*

Then he noticed something pulling on his foot. Jiaying had jumped up from the spaceship. She was athletic. She caught his leg, held on to it, and pulled her body down on her safety line so Martin's line moved out of the vicinity of the all-destructive ring.

THE DYNAMO WAS WORKING, almost optimally. Siri reported an output of 8.4 kilowatts. That was enough for the life support system to provide fresh air to the command module. It was also sufficient to operate the computer and keep a few LEDs on. It was dim, but not completely dark. They were alive, at least for the time being.

Martin watched Amy, who sat in front of her console. She seemed to be concentrating. *Is she afraid?* She would have to give the order to restart the engines. Everything depended on the restart being successful. Nothing really depended on the way Amy gave that order, yet it seemed to be important to her. *Her behavior is irrational,* Martin decided, as he had previously experienced with many people. *Amy sees herself as responsible for something she cannot influence.* Finally, she made a decision.

"This is the commander, please identify."

Martin watched the others. Francesca seemed to repeat Amy's words in a whisper. Jiaying massaged her fingers. Marchenko was whistling.

"Identified, I am listening," Siri replied. Siri was responsible for navigation, and by definition accelerating belonged to that.

"Restart fusion drives according to standard protocol," Amy ordered.

"Initiating restart," the AI complied.

No one had ever tried to start a DFD out in the midst of space. Even during initial ignition in the dock, not all DFDs had started successfully. Martin heard a deep rumbling being transmitted through the structural elements. This was the body-borne sound of their spaceship. It changed its frequency, increased a bit, and then faded again.

"Restart failed."

Amy froze on her seat. Francesca banged her fist against the wall.

"Well, that would have been too easy," Marchenko said, trying to defuse the tension they all felt.

"Watson, system analysis," Martin requested.

"External drive offline. Cause: Lack of fuel."

The energy required to start up the DFD was generated by a conventional motor that burned hydrogen and oxygen, creating water. As soon as the motor was no longer needed, another module split the created water back into its components, that were then stored until the next restart. Either this had not worked, or oxygen had been lost along the way.

Martin continued, "Watson, root cause analysis."

"This is not possible. There are missing parameters." The AI did not know why the oxygen was not there. All of their lives depended on the answer to this problem. Martin was gradually getting tired of these situations endangering their survival. *It would be about time something actually worked,* he silently grumbled.

In a halting voice, Amy said, "It looks like somebody has to go outside again and check."

"I would suggest we simply refill the oxygen tank. It doesn't matter whether it leaks a bit. The oxygen only has to last for a few minutes," said Marchenko, pragmatic as usual.

"Is there no alternative? Our dynamo generates electricity, so could we use that to fire up the magnetic coils of the DFD?" Jiaying asked.

"The DFD needs about 2 megawatts. We only have

approximately 8 kilowatts. We could make the ring rotate as fast as we want..." *For a doctor, Marchenko is also pretty good at math,* Martin thought, and then turned to the AI.

"Watson, specify the required fuel."

"The oxygen tank holds almost 200 liters. For a 100-second burn at 2 MW we need approximately 160 kilos of oxygen, which is about 140 liters in the liquid state. This amount would have to be taken from the supplies of the life support system," the AI reported.

Martin quickly calculated this in his head. If a person consumed, as he had learned, 840 grams of oxygen a day, he or she could live almost 200 days on 160 kilos.

"Will that endanger our mission, Watson?"

It is a useless question. Martin knew this. *They would have to refill their oxygen supplies on Enceladus anyway.* Watson still gave an answer.

"Our stay on Enceladus can only last five months, instead of six months."

"This is acceptable," Amy said. "Who is going to refill the container?"

Marchenko spoke up. "From a medical perspective, Jiaying, Hayato, and Martin should not go outside again so soon. That only leaves Francesca and me."

"It is not as simple as it was before. Only the command module is under normal pressure."

"Correct, Amy. We should get the neighboring module up to the pressure normally used in the airlock—to get us adapted."

"But the spacesuits are still in the airlock," the commander said, shaking her head.

"That is a problem," Marchenko said, "though if we get all the rooms between here and the airlock to one-twentieth of a bar of pressure, our cell walls should withstand the interior pressure. We could run to the airlock, close the inside hatch, and increase the pressure to half of the terrestrial level. Would that be possible within a minute?"

No one answered.

"Watson?" Amy asked.

"Yes, that is a realistic scenario. There is a probability of 85 percent that you will reach the airlock without losing consciousness. Although I have to point out that you should not waste much time before starting. Getting captured into an orbit around Saturn will become impossible if the drives won't restart and provide deceleration within 120 minutes."

If they did not hurry, they would overshoot Saturn, and there would be no return. Martin felt the coldness of space creeping up his spine. He saw that the others had similar feelings.

A FINAL FAREWELL. Francesca and Marchenko were a good match. Both had pragmatic, take charge, low drama personalities. Martin no longer noticed the tension that had existed between them over the question of whether or not to break off the mission. They closed the hatch to the command module and did their job. They ran through a near vacuum that did not kill them because they had exhaled beforehand. He fervently hoped they would reach their goal in time. After the drives were restarted, everything would once again be like it was before. *No, it will not be like before, and that feels good.* He looked at Jiaying, who did not notice his gaze. He realized, *I have not even thanked her yet.* He had very good reason to thank her. *It has become clear to me how precious my life is—and so is Jiaying's.*

"Ready... set... go." Marchenko had given the command. He let Francesca go first. She was younger and faster. She might gain them decisive seconds if she pressed the button first. The system needed a moment to blow fresh air into the airlock. Martin listened intently, but he could not hear anything. There was no gasping and groaning. Both of them had exhaled before entering the low-pressure area in order to protect their lungs. There was no heartbeat. The microphones in the uniforms weren't sensitive enough for that.

"Airlock closed," Watson reported.

"Commander to EVA team, what is your status?"

Francesca gasped for air. "Reached airlock. Marchenko... unconscious. What do his biosensors say?" Her voice sounded worried.

Amy replied, "His circulation is stable... Maybe he is in shock. We will see. He is alive, though."

"I am going to put his EMU on him and then go outside," Francesca said.

No one contradicted her because it was the logical solution. Francesca had to fulfill the task on her own. Martin saw the commander knead her hands. For a while, only breathing could be heard from the airlock. He imagined Francesca putting the spacesuit on the unconscious man. That wouldn't be easy.

"I'm finished. I am closing Marchenko's helmet now. He is breathing."

"Excellent, Francesca," Amy said.

"Start with the egress."

"Siri, we need all available cameras."

"Confirming, commander. Approximately 85 percent

of the work area of astronaut Rossi can be viewed by cameras. Starting transmission."

"Show it on the fog display," Amy directed.

Above the conference table, a figure in a spacesuit suddenly appeared, walking among the stars. The cameras were aiming from below. The four astronauts in the command module saw Francesca make her way across the hull of the spaceship. First she had to get an oxygen container from storage. Then she had to fill the container from the inlet port of the life support system. The port was intended to fill the internal tanks, but Watson could reverse the flow direction of the valves. Afterward, Francesca moved to the oxygen tank of the motor near the drive module. That was about fifty steps, including crossing the chasm that had caused Martin such problems. She emptied the container and started on her way back.

The oxygen tank contained 20 kilograms. Francesca therefore must perform the procedure eight times. During the chore, the vacuum had advantages and disadvantages; there was no fire hazard, but splashes of liquid oxygen could damage Francesca's spacesuit. Thus she would still have to be very careful when transferring the oxygen.

Martin calculated she would need twelve minutes for each filling. *That means 96 minutes before the motor is operational again. Then they could start one drive after the other.* For the first one, the motor had to provide the necessary energy for 100 seconds. Afterward, the running DFD generated the starting current for the next drive. As each drive module required about two minutes, this would take another 16 minutes. Before, Francesca had needed one minute to reach the airlock, and there she had invested ten minutes in putting the EMU on Marchenko. *96 plus 16 plus 11* went through Martin's head. *Have I forgotten anything? Right, the time from the exit to the storage and then to the filling port of the life support system, maybe two minutes. A total of 125 minutes, five more than Watson has mentioned until the drives have to be restarted. Okay, the braking effect will already start once the first one is ignited. On the other hand, they will have to wait until Francesca is back in the airlock since the increasing acceleration will complicate her return.*

He did not tell the others about his calculations because it was only a rough estimate. *Maybe Francesca will be considerably faster than expected, as the oxygen tank does not weigh anything.* Martin noticed his knees were starting to shake. Amy sat with her legs spread to gain a firmer hold. Hayato was scribbling something into a notebook. Martin could not exactly see what it was. *Perhaps formulas or Japanese characters maybe. Is he writing a farewell message in his diary?* Jiaying had placed her chair with the seatback forward and sat in it. This allowed her to lean back as much as she wanted since her position stayed the same in zero gravity. She was almost horizontal and had her eyes closed.

"Is there anything we can do?" Hayato asked as he put his pen aside.

"No," Amy gasped. There was nothing else to say.

On the glittering display they saw Francesca struggling with the port of the life support system. The last time its cap had been opened was in Earth orbit. If everything had gone according to plan, it would have remained closed until their return. No one had expected a single astronaut would have to unscrew it. The pilot first tried to use her hands, then special pliers from her tool belt. Unfortunately, she was not strong enough and needed more leverage. The camera followed her as she stood up and looked around. Martin called up a diagram of the ship on his tablet. About three meters from Francesca's position there should be a dish antenna supported by strong metal struts. These were not simple pipes, but actuators that could be remote-controlled to aim the dish toward its goal, Earth. He wanted to mention this to Francesca, but she seemed to have already discovered this option. The camera showed her unscrewing one of the struts. Luckily, the struts were not welded to the hull or the antenna dish. Before they could send any more messages to Earth, they would have to repair the antenna, but that was not important now.

The metal piece was about a meter long and sturdy enough to give Francesca more leverage. Via the helmet radio, all of them heard Francesca trying with renewed effort.

"Ha," she finally said as the cap started to move. Martin looked at the time. *Another ten minutes has passed. My new estimate: 135.* He wondered, *Should I let Watson display a countdown? However, how will this number help the others?* Time passed, and they could not stop it.

Soon it became clear Martin's calculations had been too optimistic. The portable container might not weigh anything, but its inertia still impeded Francesca. She needed almost five minutes in one direction, instead of the three he had assumed, so that made another 16 minutes, a total of 167. At least the cap of the oxygen tank at the motor could be opened easily. Was that the reason the tank was empty? That would be a blessing in disguise, as the newly filled oxygen would be leaking out if the tank itself was damaged. If there was only a microscopic crack, they might have enough time, though. They needed the motor to run at full power for 100 seconds, no more.

Francesca was on her way back. Martin watched her movements. He noticed the pilot had a specific talent—she had found an optimal rhythm. *She is also probably a good dancer.* The idea brought him back into a part of his past that he had not wanted to acknowledge for a long time, to a former life in which he floated across the dance floor with his girlfriend. She had talked him into taking a dancing class, even though he was generally more of a couch potato, but surprisingly he had really enjoyed it.

He looked at his watch. *Four minutes. Francesca is getting faster—a total of 152 minutes, if everything goes well.* His knees were trembling.

Thirty minutes later, everything was still proceeding smoothly. Francesca now averaged four minutes for each leg of the way, 14 minutes per filling instead of 12. *Another 122 minutes until drive ignition. Watson wants to decelerate no longer than 90 minutes from now.*

A moaning sound came from the loudspeaker. Eight eyes looked at Francesca's image on the fog display, but she was moving across the hull in a routine fashion.

"Marchenko?"

"Reporting for duty, Commander," the doctor replied.

"Great!" Martin could see Amy's eyes sparkle. She updated him as fast as she could. Francesca was on the third round of filling the tank, carrying a full container to the motor. Five more rounds remained. First Marchenko would have to get an oxygen container. Then he could take on at least two rounds of filling. He was new to it, and no athlete, but it would not take him longer than Francesca's three rounds. *That will save 28 minutes. We are getting closer to Watson's countdown.*

Marchenko quickly understood what needed to be done. *Time is lost when the two astronauts encounter each other, particularly if it happens near one of the filling points.* Amy realized it the same moment as Martin did.

"Commander to Marchenko. Always give Francesca right of way when she is near."

Since he only had to do two rounds, Marchenko had more time than the pilot. Hayato started to rap his knuckles against the tabletop. *I cannot blame him for doing that,* Martin thought. Jiaying still floated, leaning back with closed eyes. *I wonder where she might be right now. I would like to escape from reality, too.* But Martin chose not to visualize the dance scenes again.

"Last round," Francesca announced. Martin could not hear any relief in her voice.

"Watson, briefly describe consequences of starting engines with astronauts in EVA." Amy must have watched the clock as carefully as Martin had.

"Danger level 2. Breach of EVA protocol. Permission by Mission Control required," the AI reported.

"For us, Mission Control is offline. Permission by Commander is sufficient. What specific dangers?" Amy asked.

"Erratically increasing acceleration against direction of flight."

Martin could visualize what Watson's brief statement meant. The hot gases emitted in the direction of flight— hydrogen and helium-4—posed no danger. Their exit velocity from the engine nozzle was much too high, and the decelerating ship would never reach them. However, the two astronauts would have to climb down a 30 or 50-meter-tall metal monster while hanging on their safety lines. Below them yawned an infinity into which their own inertia tried to pull them. About every two minutes its force would first double, then triple, and so on. Every additional drive coming online would increase the danger of a fall. If they fell, their safety lines would hold them, but that fact would save their lives only for a short while. The hatch they must reach was located just short of the mighty habitat ring, which was still rotating fast. How high was the probability that Francesca and Marchenko would survive this descent? Martin did not dare to estimate that.

He looked at Amy. She returned his gaze. Was she envisioning a similar scenario? She nodded. Martin shook his head.

"We would save another four or five minutes," she said, "exactly the time Watson needs to turn us into a Saturn orbit in time."

"Amy, the risk is too great. We would lose them. Then the mission would be over as well," Martin explained.

"It could be done by four people. I would be in orbit, you on Enceladus, Hayato, and Jiaying in *Valkyrie*."

"You know this isn't a good idea, Amy."

"But I have to make a decision, this second. If we decelerate too late, all of us will die—only later."

"Yes." Martin nodded. *I am glad not to be in her shoes and having to choose two human lives against four.*

"Watson is wrong," Martin said an instant later. "The calculated trajectory is based on estimates. There is the density of Saturn's atmosphere at a great altitude, the exact plunging angle, as well as various safety distances. Watson's calculation is based on 100 percent safety. We can do it with less." Martin was surprised how sure he sounded, as he himself wasn't really convinced.

"Watson," he then said, "calculate a trajectory to Enceladus with a window of safety of 80 percent. What is latest deceleration moment?"

"46 hours, 3 minutes, 27 seconds from moment 0, Commander."

"Thank you, Martin. Commander to EVA team. You don't have to rush."

"What is going on? Have we lost any chance?"

"No, Francesca. We are going to reach Enceladus. I will explain the rest later. Commander, out."

The fog display showed the pilot filling the tank of the motor one last time. Marchenko took the empty container from her and carried it back to the storage module, along with his own container. Then they both carefully climbed in the direction of the hatch.

"Outer hatch locked and secured," Francesca reported ten minutes later. Several hours would pass before they could rejoin the others, as the EVA team first must get reaccustomed to the interior pressure. Plus, the life support system would have to fill all rooms with a breathable atmosphere again. That would happen once the DFDs provided enough energy for it.

"This is the commander, please identify."

"Identified, I am listening," Siri replied. Martin had already heard this dialog earlier today. *It seems like years ago,* he thought.

"Restart fusion drives according to standard protocol."

"Initiating restart," said the AI.

A faint, deep rumbling filled the ship. It remained constant. Martin counted and had reached 100 when the sound got louder.

"DFD 1 online," Siri reported.

Martin looked around. The others seemed to be silently counting as well. He reached 105, and then the rumbling got louder. A slight force pressed him sternward. Jiaying was not fast enough and almost fell on her back. It was time to turn the seats around.

"Siri, reconfigure command module," the commander stated.

As if by magic, the tabletop moved. The chairs took on a new configuration. Forward was now down. From now on they would have to climb upward to reach their cabins.

"DFD 2 online."

It was working. They would not suffocate. Amy reached the necessary conclusion. "Watson, stop rotation of habitat ring."

The solid-propellant engines of the ring fired in the opposite direction and slowed it to a standstill. In the coming weeks, the deceleration process would provide the illusion of gravity.

"DFD 3 online."

Martin turned optimistic. He no longer counted along. He decided to trust the ship again. After all, he would have to do so in the coming months.

"DFD 4 online."

"DFD 5 online."

"DFD 6 online."

Amy already stood upright, a broad grin on her face. Hayato jumped up. Even Jiaying could not stay in her chair anymore. Martin sighed with relief and went to them. The commander spread her arms wide. All four of them hugged each other. *It is a strange, but pleasant feeling*, he decided.

Part 2: The Goal

December 7, 2046, ILSE

"THE TINY DOT, THAT'S US," Amy said, pointing to a dot blinking in various shades of green on the fog display. It was located on an ellipse, and at one of its focal points the symbol of a planet appeared in red. The diagram was not true to scale. When Martin looked out the window, he saw a disc almost as large as the window itself. It appeared to have two narrow handles. The rings currently could only be seen from the edge.

"And we have come so far." The commander placed her hands in front of her belly, and then the scale of the diagram decreased. The ellipse on which the spaceship was moving shrank more and more, until the green dot and the planet symbol almost merged. Now they saw a red line, at the end of which another symbol appeared, an image of the blue planet, Mother Earth, which had given birth to all of them.

Amy snapped her fingers and the diagram started to move. While their home planet wandered around the sun, the green dot went on its journey. It aimed for the red symbol. After a year, the icon for Earth had reached the same spot as during launch, while the red symbol for Saturn had only advanced 30 degrees.

She explained, "As you can see, Saturn made it easy for us to aim for it. It moves through space at only about 10 kilometers per second, while Earth is three times faster, and Saturn has a much longer distance to cover."

Martin had heard a similar speech during his training on Earth. *It feels quite different now because I am flying along in this green dot. The distance we have covered during the past twelve months appears like a huge chasm because we are nine times as far from the orbit of Earth as Earth is from the sun.*

"I wanted to thank all of you for what you have done for this mission. And I am particularly grateful because I learned and experienced that you did not just do this for the mission, not for honor or country, but for us. For you," she said and pointed at Jiaying, "as well as for you, Hayato, for you," she continued and nodded toward Martin, "for you, for you, and for me. Yes, and for you." Now Amy pointed at her bulging belly.

"A year ago today we launched from Earth. I have saved up something for this occasion. You probably won't remember, but before we launched from Earth, I asked each of you about your favorite drink. Marchenko and Hayato, you made it easiest for me. You can share this whiskey. Martin, for you I have a bottle of German beer. Francesca, champagne for you, and Jiaying, you mentioned mango juice. I myself already got the most beautiful present, and I thank you for it." Martin's eyes seemed to itch. *This must be from the dry air in the ship,* Martin silently determined. Marchenko took the whiskey bottle and read the label. Francesca ran her hand through her shaggy hair. Jiaying smiled. *She does not smile often,* Martin thought, *but when she does, she looks lovely.* Martin sighed. He looked at the beer bottle in front of him, and the label was for Budvar, a lager from the Czech town of Budweis.

He tried to remember the time around launch, but he had forgotten many details already. *It all happened amazingly fast.* He remembered his first trip on a plane. *The moment it took off was really impressive, so much so I promised that I'd never forget it.* Yet over the years, flying had become as normal as taking taxis.

The same was now happening with his cosmic journey. He remembered the moment in the Blue Origin capsule when he had first experienced weightlessness. *The deep black of space, which made me feel tiny like never before—even the vivid blue of my home planet—this left me in complete awe of all this beauty.* True, every astronaut returning to Earth raved about this, but it was an experience you could never completely describe—someone had to have shared it. Yet he had a difficult time recalling the thrill he'd experienced in those days when he had thought about space.

Martin got up. He forced himself to break off his musings. The beer was waiting for him. He looked for something to use as a bottle opener.

"If you find any glasses..." Marchenko called after him. *Sure, glasses for everyone—and a bottle opener,* Martin reckoned.

"Look in Drawer 13b." *Of course, Amy would know where I could find what I am looking for.* Martin opened the drawer. He found glasses there, embedded in some spongy material, and even a bottle opener. He returned to the table. As the drives were still decelerating the ship, pouring liquids was no problem.

"Cheers."

They touched their glasses together in a loud clink. Francesca had poured herself too much, spilled some, and bent over the table to lick up the puddle. Then she laughed. Marchenko stared at her rear. Martin smiled to himself. The Russian noticed this, grinned at him, and licked his lips.

No matter. Martin had not had any alcohol for a long time, so he quickly felt the effects of the beer. It tasted delicious, reminding him of home, and it also made him relaxed and a bit sleepy.

"Cheers." More glasses clinked. Marchenko gave a short speech, a toast as he called it. *How can one say a toast?* Jiaying laughed about the term and could not stop laughing, even though she had not had any alcohol. Her laughter was oddly contagious. *I can't help laughing even though it is ridiculous for me to do so,* Martin thought. *Yet it is so ridiculous that it is funny all over again*, particularly since Francesca was now giggling, the corners of Amy's mouth were moving upward, and Marchenko uttered a roaring guffaw. Hayato appeared to be embarrassed by his five laughing fellow astronauts, but right now even this seemed very funny to Martin. *The situation is a scream, and I cannot remember the last time I have felt this way. Maybe,* the serious part of himself thought, *it is because the threats of the last weeks are now falling off, like a shell. A shell, very funny,* his laughing part thought, and then even his serious side lost control.

The laughter only faded when everyone was utterly exhausted. Now and then, someone still giggled. Amy and Hayato were the first ones to retire. Then, with a short interval between them, Marchenko and Francesca climbed *up* the ladder that led to the habitat ring. Martin looked at Jiaying and had to laugh again. She was giggling. *It is time to go to bed,* he thought. He got up and walked toward the door until he felt a touch on his arm. He turned around and smiled at the woman who followed him into his cabin.

December 8, 2046, ILSE

Now the routine seemed to be over. This was already the second day on which the normal sequence of shifts had been canceled. They met in the command module at 0800 hours.

"After we all had our fun yesterday," the commander said, and looked at each of them in turn, "things will get serious today. Therefore I ask for your full concentration." Then Amy looked toward the still-invisible fog display, where it seemed something was about to happen.

"Watson, describe braking maneuver," she instructed the AI.

"In order to reach the Saturn moon Enceladus, *ILSE* has to first get into an orbit around Saturn. However, the craft is moving too fast to get captured by the planet's gravity. If we simply brake using the drives, the ship will leave the solar system on a parabolic trajectory. I have therefore calculated a course on which the planet's own atmosphere will help us decelerate. That is the only method to reach an orbit around Enceladus."

"Won't there be a danger once we get into the area of

the rings?" Martin had been itching to bring up this question. *I want to show Jiaying I can also provide the answer. What a silly little boy I am.*

Watson replied, "Not in our case. We are moving in the orbital plane of Saturn and Earth. The ring system is tilted 27 degrees compared to it. Our path is clear."

"Watson, does this mean there is no danger at all? Then, why don't we just perform that maneuver?" Jiaying's objection was justified.

"My calculations are based on data collected during previous missions. We know, though, the climate conditions on Saturn undergo temporal variations. We do not have sufficient data about those to form a reliable prediction."

"So we are flying according to 'pi multiplied by your thumb?'" Jiaying asked. Martin had told Jiaying about this German expression for an approximate measure last night. She had thought it charming, the combination of a mathematical constant and a human body part. *The ideas these thoughtful Germans came up with!* he fondly recalled her saying.

Of course Watson understood this, as he could communicate in the languages—and their colloquialisms—of all crew members.

"The plotting of the course is based on uncertain data." This was about as close as you could get an AI to admit that chance played a great role.

"This discussion does not help us in the least," Amy complained. Martin had to agree with the commander. She was being very levelheaded, as always.

"So, what is the plan?" he asked.

Amy replied, "I need two astronauts in EMU, already in the airlock and adapted to the lower pressure. In the event the spaceship is damaged due to the stress of this maneuver, we will need to get a repair crew out there quickly."

Martin, Jiaying, and Hayato raised their hands.

"Hayato, you are going to watch the drive," the commander said. "It would be particularly bad if it failed at this moment. I know the AI is constantly supervising it, but I want you to look for patterns, anything that seems strange to you, even if it lies within permissible parameters. We need to stop potentially dangerous processes before any damage appears."

"Then Jiaying and I will go outside?" Martin briefly exchanged glances with her.

"Great, Martin. You two can get suited up right away. Two more minutes," Amy said.

"Marchenko, I need you in sick bay. My water broke an hour ago. I know this is a bit earlier than predicted, but who knows what is normal in space? Hayato, I should have told you, but I did not want to worry you. But I really need you at the drive. Francesca, could you help us?"

Martin, who was just getting up, fell back on his seat. *What did I just hear? And in what calm voice?*

"Now go," Amy said. "The airlock is waiting. Have a nice time." Then she grinned, as if everything was normal.

Well then, let it be that way, Martin resolved. *No big deal. After all, it is only a birth... in space. The gravity created by the braking maneuver will make some things easier, although, entering the upper layers of Saturn's atmosphere... that might shake things up a bit.* Yet everything was normal, all values in the green range. The commander tried very hard to convince them of that.

By now, preparing for an EVA had become routine for Martin. His last mission was three weeks back. Mission Control had been all upset about the repaired radio antenna. After communication had been completely cut, they had assumed the ship was lost. And unlike during the Mars incident a few years ago, there were no observation satellites out here that could have told them otherwise. Nothing else with functioning hardware was currently so far away from Earth. *ELF*, the probe that had found the first traces of life 15 years ago, had long since found its final resting place inside Saturn, just like its predecessor *Cassini*.

He shook his head. *The landing will have to wait.* Now he followed Jiaying to the airlock. The lower part of the EMU hung loosely around his waist, and he had to hold it so it wouldn't drop. Jiaying first helped him into the HUT. To do so, she had to lift her arms. Below the long-sleeved 'shirt' of the LCVG he could see the outlines of her breasts. She hit him slightly against the upper arm of the HUT and laughed. Martin lowered his eyes. *I better not think about last night right now.* A sense of uncertainty tortured him. They had talked a lot, and he had probably said more words than he had uttered during the entire flight, but they had not talked about each other. *Wasn't that what you did? Maybe my fellow astronaut considers this a one-time event between adults, where everyone has gained something? This seems to be the case with Francesca and Marchenko. Is Jiaying following this example? It would be better if I got used to this beforehand.*

"Don't dawdle. We have to use the masks."

Jiaying was right. They had to continue the pre-breathing phase so they would be ready to go outside in time.

"Initiating course change," Watson reported. Nothing

else could be heard, but Martin felt a slight force pulling him forward. *In the end, I hope we don't have to go outside again*, he thought. The last excursion had involved a lot of climbing, as the spaceship was still decelerating. Only in the acceleration-free phase of the return trip would the EVAs become easier again.

He imagined the spaceship as heading for the planet, only to brake and reverse at the last moment. In reality, their approach course was going to be rather flat. Watson would continually check how much the outlying fringes of the atmosphere were already decelerating them. They did not have to dip very deeply into the atmosphere. It would be sufficient to slow down the craft enough so that the drives could handle the rest. The goal was 35.5 kilometers per second. If they went slower, the gravitational pull of the giant planet would inevitably capture them.

And they also could not dive too deeply into the atmosphere itself. The fusion drives were designed only for operating in a vacuum. Hayato only knew from simulations how they would react to an atmosphere. The main problem, he said, would probably be cooling. The simulations could not provide a maximal depth, as they did not have enough data. If someone ever came afterward, they would have sufficient information. The ship kept transmitting data to Earth, in case it would not reach its home planet again. *Mission planners were probably real optimists*, Martin concluded. This morning, Francesca had provided the disturbing fact of the day—they would not be able to enter too deeply into the atmosphere. Once it reached a certain density, the spacecraft would skip on it like a flat stone on water.

"This is the EVA team. Is there any news?" When Jiaying asked this question, Martin remembered that another unique event was about to happen—the first birth of a human being in space.

Instead of the commander, Marchenko answered, "I just gave Amy some oxytocic medication. We don't want to delay this much longer. Everything is fine."

Martin sat on the floor of the airlock, with his back against the wall. Jiaying sat next to him and leaned against his shoulder.

"It could be really romantic now, if we were not wearing the HUTs," he ventured to say.

She replied, "It is romantic. You don't have a clue."

WATSON REPORTED the status of their approach to Saturn every ten minutes. In the meantime, Martin was dozing. *Time seems to move terribly slowly today.* After an hour and a half he and Jiaying were still sitting on the floor of the airlock. The flight was completely calm, as if they were on a space highway. There was only an arm's length between him and the vacuum, but Martin no longer was worried by this fact. At least in one aspect the flight had never been as safe as now—meteoroids zooming toward them from their direction of flight would not just be pulverized by the drives, they would be vaporized. He wondered what was happening in the sick bay right now. Martin was glad he did not have to assist. *It must be hard on Hayato not to be able to witness the birth of his child,* he thought.

The wait ended at exactly 15:36 ship time. Marchenko reported, "I am happy to announce that a human being has seen the light of day, or rather the light of the space-ship. I give you the first true citizen of space." Then he put the commander on the microphone. Martin could not understand what she said between sobs.

Francesca interpreted for her, "The mother is over-joyed and would like to see the father of the child for a moment."

"Is that an order?" asked Hayato, and he too was hard to understand.

"Yes," the commander replied.

"To protect the privacy of mother and child, I now deactivate the communication. Marchenko, out."

Jiaying looked at Martin. *Were those tracks of tears on her face?* he wondered, but he did not ask. Instead, he took her in his arms and squeezed her tight. Then he ended the embrace. She had to concentrate on her task.

Watson continued to report the current data for the ship's movement. The numbers were constantly decreasing. *No problems, the drives are working perfectly.* Martin clenched his fists. *I really do not need any more excitement now.*

ANOTHER HOUR HAD PASSED BY.

"Neumaier to Masukoshi, see any conspicuous patterns?"

"Negative."

This is good, Martin thought—*and yet it seems strange to me. Will everything work that smoothly? I can't allow myself to think about it now.* Then he noticed how difficult it had been for him to address Hayato by his last name. He'd had to work to remember it. With Marchenko, on the other hand, he always forgot the first name. But it didn't matter, as Marchenko was simply Marchenko. With Jiaying, though, it was easy to remember the last name; Li—two letters in

Latin script. She had drawn the Chinese symbol on his hand. The morning after, Martin had deliberately not washed that particular hand, and now he looked down at it. *I wish I could look at it, but I am not allowed to take off my glove.* Since he was starting to feel cold, he activated the gloves' heating circuit.

"23 34 34. All systems online and in the specified range." This was Watson's latest report.

Wait a moment, Martin noticed, *the number is larger than the one Watson reported ten minutes ago.* Martin's palms were getting moist. *The movement of the ship does not seem any different.*

He asked, "Watson, did I hear you correctly?"

"I cannot answer that question."

"Watson, are we moving away from Saturn again?" Martin insisted.

"Correct. The distance to the planet is increasing."

"Watson, why is talking to you like pulling teeth?"

"I am interpreting this antiquated expression as a request for additional information."

"Watson, please." *The AI is definitely going too far.* Martin decided he would simplify the Human Logic Module. *Watson is trying too much to act like a human being.*

"Spaceship is moving at the intended speed. The maneuver has achieved its purpose," the AI reported.

"Watson, why did you not say that right away?"

"Planned flight maneuver is not yet finished. There was no order to report an early completion of the goal. Data allow for the correct interpretation."

Martin clapped his hands and laughed. Jiaying got up

and gave him a strange look. *No, I have not lost my mind.* He had only forgotten that he'd had this conversation via helmet radio. He blew her a kiss, which confused Jiaying even more.

"Neumaier to everybody. Watson reports the braking maneuver near Saturn has been successful. Hayato, we've got to talk about the programming of the AI."

December 10, 2046, ILSE

THE GAS PLANET Saturn completely filled the porthole.
Red, brown, and greenish stripes extended parallel to the
equator. These were cloud systems that received their
colors from ammonia crystals and consisted mostly of
hydrogen. Sometimes, they parted and showed the water-
ice clouds below that moved at 1,930 kilometers per hour.

Martin traced a white spot. *That must be one of the inner
moons.* He did not know which one it was. *Maybe even Enceladus, our goal. In the Southern Hemisphere there are huge vortices
that are larger than the continents on Earth*, he noted. With the
help of the South Polar Vortex—which might be billions
of years old and could be clearly seen—Martin adjusted
the dimensions. *This storm is larger than Earth*, he calculated.

The rings surround the planet like the rim of a
sombrero. The control jets had changed the spacecraft's
inclination so much that the rings were now visible in all
their glory. One could clearly see the Cassini Division
between the outer A Ring and the inner B Ring. Their
goal was outside these distinct rings, in the E Ring, which
the sensors of the ship noticed, but Martin's eyes could not.

243

The ship still flew on an elliptical course around Saturn. Their closest approach to Saturn would be within the rings, the farthest beyond the large moons. To reach Enceladus, the ship must decelerate at the right moment, when it was closest to Saturn. That moved the farthest point of its trajectory closer to the planet.

At the same time, they had to adjust its orbital plane. They had flown toward this planet in the same plane in which Earth and Saturn moved around the sun. Most moons and the rings orbited Saturn in a plane that was tilted in comparison to it. However, if they moved into this plane too soon, they ran the risk of having to fly through the rings. While these were only a few meters thick, a collision with a lump of ice of just 10 centimeters in diameter could be fatal due to the high speed of the spaceship. Therefore, their goal was a trajectory in which the closest point lay outside of the rings, while its farthest one got them close to the moon Enceladus.

The commander had decided to approach the goal slowly. While the DFDs would allow for a quicker adjustment of their velocity, Amy did not want too much risk. Now she had even more of a reason for this decision—they had lots of time to investigate the planet, the moon, and the ring system with every instrument available. Mission Control had already sent a wish list compiled by astronomers from Earth, who still had many unanswered questions, for instance concerning the creation of the ring system. The list was too long to be completed, but at least the crew was kept busy.

I like this kind of work, Martin thought. *This gives me time to look out the window and to daydream.* Now and then he had to readjust an instrument or aim it toward another object, or compile and transmit data for a scientist who had asked to receive results in advance instead of through the routine transmission to Earth. The capacity of their downlink was sufficient for such requests, as the DFDs allowed for a much higher transmission power than in previous space probes. Even if they never landed they would advance research by years. The most difficult tasks were those when the scientists provided initial data in a format that the comparable onboard measuring system did not understand.

I am pleasantly surprised Jiaying does not consider the night we spent together as a one-time event. The shift system prevented them from seeing each other all the time, but last evening she had invited him to a return visit to her cabin. Martin smiled.

He thought of the new crew member who had quickly become the star of the team. *When the commander starts her shift bleary-eyed because the little one has not wanted to sleep, there is always someone who enables her to nap for an hour by taking care of the baby.* Amy had been able to nurse from day one. The low gravity seemed to be no problem in that respect. Marchenko was very satisfied with how things were developing. *This baby must be the most supervised infant in the entire solar system, and Jiaying is always happy to take care of him.* "So cute," she always said, even though everyone already knew what she thought about the baby.

However, the improvised diapers drove the parents crazy. Their absorptive capacity was low. While on Earth each liquid took the shortest path downward, under low gravity the baby's digestive products sometimes moved in other directions. It was impossible to avoid a mess. At breakfast, Hayato regularly shared the details of these unfortunate instances, where everything had spread out during the previous night, and on what surprising body parts he'd had to apply the cleaning cloths. The women present pitied the new father—as if the mother did not face the same problems.

Hayato and Amy still had not mentioned the baby's name. They claimed to have agreed on a name, but they wanted to reveal it during a small ceremony. Martin was surprised how well they managed not to let the name slip out. *They seem to enjoy the secrecy*.

MARTIN TWITCHED and hit his head on the round metal frame of the porthole. *I really shouldn't doze off during work.* He slapped his cheeks to become fully awake. The impulse he had felt was obviously caused by the drives that had just ignited. Until just now, the spaceship had been moving weightlessly through space. This meant they had reached the point closest to Saturn. During the next orbit they would not get as close to the planet, but they would be able to see Enceladus more clearly.

December 12, 2046, ILSE

THE WHITE BALL on the fog display was so bright Martin shaded his eyes. Today was a special day, and therefore they all were meeting in the command module. Amy even brought the baby along. He slept inside a cloth the commander had wrapped around her chest. In a few minutes, the spaceship would stop circling the ringed planet Saturn. Instead, it was about to become a satellite of the bright ball of ice they were seeing on their display.

This was a task no vehicle built by humans had ever achieved. Enceladus only had a diameter of 505 kilometers, about the distance from New York to Pittsburgh as the crow flies, and its mass was 1/6000 that of Earth. This meant its gravity was relatively very low. In order to avoid overshooting Enceladus, *ILSE* must decelerate to 850 kilometers per hour relative to the Saturn moon. From a cosmic perspective, this meant almost a complete standstill. Nonetheless, while it still orbited Saturn it could not reduce its absolute velocity at random, as otherwise it ran the risk of crashing into the planet. Watson had calculated a slightly ellipsoidal course, during which the ship's speedometer would indicate 53,000 kilometers per hour near Enceladus—if it had a speedometer.

Therefore, the task of the ship was to decelerate as quickly as possible, without endangering the passengers, and swing into an orbit around an object racing away from them at 43,500 kilometers per hour.

"Imagine a motorcyclist having to circle around a car that is going 90 kilometers per hour, while he himself is zooming along the highway at 130 kilometers per hour." That is how Martin explained to Jiaying what the ship was supposed to do today.

"Of course this is a misleading comparison," he added, when he saw the horror on his girlfriend's face. "It's no problem at all for the DFDs, don't you worry."

"Wouldn't it have been easier to keep us in orbit around Saturn? Didn't that work well with the other Enceladus space probes?" *Jiaying is a biologist and a geologist, and you can have great discussions with her about minerals and the origin of life, but she really does not know much about navigation.*

"If it had only been about landing there, maybe it would have been," Martin said. "It might have worked to drop a lander and then fly on. But imagine the return trip. The lander module takes off from Enceladus and has to link up with a ship zooming past it at 48,000 kilometers per hour ..."

"Okay," Jiaying said.

"And then we would have a problem concerning the energy supply for *Valkyrie*," Martin explained. "We need the ship in a stationary orbit so that it can beam energy down via laser. Otherwise, we would have had to land a power station on Enceladus as well. At thirty tons, the lander module is already heavier than all prior Enceladus probes added together."

"Please secure yourselves in your seats," the commander announced. Her voice sounded higher than usual. The deceleration would for the first time create more than terrestrial gravity, so they would have to buckle in as they had done the last time on Earth. During the maneuver, the drives would be utilized far outside their normal parameters for a few seconds. Hayato, the resident expert, assured them this would not damage the drive system.

"Deceleration in 30."

Then Watson started a countdown to zero. Martin's own inertia pressed him against the back of his seat. He looked to the left, where Enceladus was slowly moving into the porthole. The commander's little son started to cry. The moon appeared to be moving slower and slower, until it finally seemed to stand still. Then it was all over.

"Welcome to our destination," the commander announced. *One can tell she is still under a lot of stress,* Martin observed. "We have reached a stable orbit around Enceladus. I think we should all relax for the rest of the day. Tomorrow we are going to pick a landing site, and the day after that we go down."

December 13, 2046, ILSE

MARTIN STOOD in a supermarket watching a robot dog. This was the latest craze for boys like him. The animal recognized its owner and learned to respond to commands, just like a real dog. But, you did not have to take it for walks, and it only needed electricity as food, and it could do tricks no 'real' dog would ever master. It jumped higher, ran faster, and only barked when its owner gave the order.

Martin circled the artificial dog. He walked through the aisles so that now and then he caught a glimpse of it. He really would have liked to purchase the dog, but he did not have enough money. The circles he walked around the dog got tighter and tighter. He asked himself, *Should I just put the animal under my jacket and run out of the store?* He wasn't afraid of getting caught, but he worried the animal would be damaged if he stumbled and fell. *Is the dog looking at me?* Martin knew this artificial creature could recognize humans. *Does it recognize me? Why does its gaze follow me, of all people?* There were so many other customers in the store. Martin moved closer.

"Hello," the dog said. "Who are you?"

The TV commercial seemed to have left out the fact that the dog could talk.

"I am Martin."

"It's nice to meet you. I am The Dog."

"I know."

"Not the dog, *The* Dog," The animal stressed the second "The."

"*The* Dog?"

"Yes, that one—the *one* you are looking for."

"Really?" Martin asked.

"Yes. Well, hop on." The dog was suddenly three times its size. Martin was supposed to get on its back.

"I don't know." He hesitated for a brief moment.

"Yes, you have wanted to do this for a long time," said The Dog.

Martin followed the invitation and sat on the dog's back. A hissing sound could be heard, and in front of them a hole opened up in space-time, its edges flickering.

"Go," Martin said. The dog obeyed and jumped. They fell into a tunnel that looked like it led through an aquarium. Large, smiling fishes were gazing down at them. *The dog is running so fast, I'm afraid I might fall off.* The water was getting darker and darker, and soon it was black, and the moon rose. It shined a brilliant white. Martin saw snow falling but noticed no clouds.

"*I...*"

This was the last thing Martin heard. The dog was gone, and he was alone in the darkness. Martin looked around. His body cast a huge, hard shadow. There was a gurgling sound. From the blackness of night, water was streaming, came quickly closer, and surrounded him.

"*I...*"

Martin could breathe under water. His reflection hung so close to his face that he jerked back.

"Hey, Martin, wake up."

Jiaying's hand caressed his shoulder.

"I almost fell out of bed because you were rolling back and forth. I had to wake you up."

"Thanks, it's good that you did."

Martin checked his watch.

"Another hour until my shift starts."

Jiaying smiled and said nothing. They cuddled up to each other and fell asleep again. Soon their time together would be over, and the exploration of the ice moon would begin.

AFTER BREAKFAST, Martin had a déjà vu moment. They were sitting around the conference table. The fog display presented the shining image of Enceladus in highest resolution. They needed to find a spot where the lander module could touch down.

"Watson has already prepared something." The commander pointed toward an area near the South Pole. "However, I want you to bring up your ideas, no matter how odd they may seem. The problem is the AI is lacking data for a reliable decision. Furthermore, it might be using different assumptions than we are."

This had increasingly turned out to be a problem during AI research on Earth. Artificial intelligences easily learned to find patterns in mountains of data. Later the intelligences then further improved themselves by comparing desired and actual outcomes. Yet with issues concerning humans, and that applied to almost all issues, intentions were incredibly important—a concept AIs had a hard time with. Or did AIs develop their own intentions during the learning process, that later interfered with their neutral work?

The suspicion existed, and researchers considered the issue undecided. Maybe Watson, without being aware of any wrongdoing, automatically selected a landing spot that was optimal for its own existence? Of course they could prove nothing regarding the AIs, particularly since they did not know which form of existence an AI would consider to be optimal.

Jiaying pointed at the region around the South Pole and zoomed in with a spreading gesture of her fingers.

"Here we have the Tiger Stripes." The image showed icy canyons.

"These are crevices in the ice, up to 130 kilometers long. At these crevices, it gets warmer than elsewhere on this moon, minus 93 degrees Celsius versus minus 201 degrees. The distance between them is about 40 kilometers. I am now switching to the UV range and I will increase the contrast."

It appeared that material came out of the cracks, as if Enceladus was leaking.

She continued her presentation. "This just shows the current state. The places where most of the material is ejected keep changing, and the amount also varies with the orbit of the moon. It might look like it, but the steam does not just appear in a few spots, it is ejected from the entire length of the crevices. The Tiger Stripes also grow and shift, and they do so in a few centuries. Geologically, this is a very short time." *Jiaying seems to be in her element. As a geologist, she is fascinated by these geysers,* Martin perceived.

"What comes out is water vapor. There must be an

enormous pressure behind it. The vapor is shot into space at 1,400 kilometers per hour. This is faster than the escape velocity, so the quickly crystallizing particles do not all fall back onto the moon. The ice crystals then form Saturn's E Ring."

She reversed the spread-fingered gesture while saying, "Now I am switching back to the visible spectrum."

The image changed and the jets became fainter.

"Where does all this come from? Just a moment..." Jiaying drew another command in the air, and the image was overlaid by a function diagram.

"Enceladus has a stone core. However, it is not large enough to provide heat, like the core of Earth."

She moved her arm in a circle. The image zoomed out and now showed the rotation of the moons around Saturn.

"Enceladus is in a 2:1 resonance with the moon Dione, which is a bit further out. This means that for every two orbits of Enceladus, Dione finishes one. The periodic action of its gravitational pull, and the pull from the giant planet Saturn in the vicinity, massage the core of Enceladus in such a way that a lot of friction—in other words, heat—is generated."

Jiaying clenched her hand to form a fist. Now the Tiger Stripes reappeared.

"The heat melts the ice above the core up to a certain height. This creates a liquid ocean below the ice. Minerals from the rocks are dissolved in the water. The ocean is probably rather salty. This is also supported by an analysis of deposits along the Tiger Stripes. Salts and carbon compounds were identified there. These are heavier than water-ice crystals and therefore they separate from the geyser output and fall back."

Jiaying removed the function diagram and took a short break. On the display, Enceladus sparkled like a jewel.

"The best thing," she said upon resuming, "and the reason we are here, is of course because the *ELF* probe found definitive signs of life. To be more precise, these were cellular structures. In a spectacular maneuver, the probe flew along the Tiger Stripes at an altitude of a few hundred meters and captured the ejected material as quickly as possible, before it could fall back down or be destroyed by crystallization. At an ejection speed of 400 meters per second, the material would have been in the warm interior of Enceladus only a few seconds before. The measurements were clear."

Jiaying zoomed in even more on the Tiger Stripes.

"We assume the ice here is only five kilometers thick. Further north, the thickness is 10 to 15 kilometers. Therefore, we should definitely try to land here, unless there is some important factor against it."

Martin zoomed in a bit closer to the area. The area between the stripes only looked smooth at first glance. Cracks, fissures, plateaus, and plates dominated the picture. "There were arguments in favor of landing further north," he said.

"Yes," Jiaying replied, "Watson is also for it. A fresh crater would be ideal. The impact briefly melts the ice, and when it refreezes, the surface is smooth, perfect for a clean landing."

"But.. ?" Martin interjected.

Jiaying zoomed in even further and displayed a scale.

"The local structures are predominantly level. You see? The fissure here might be about 300 meters deep. The cliff has a vertical height of 200 meters. But the plate next to it is at least 500 meters long and wide. There is more than enough space."

For the lander and Valkyrie, *an area of 50 by 100 meters will suffice. Jiaying is correct. However, we have to aim extremely well,* Martin considered.

Amy spoke up, "Watson, do you have any objections to this kind of landing site?"

"The approach until t-10 seconds is 99.5 percent safe. If course corrections become necessary after t-10, the probability of a mission failure would be 80 percent," Watson replied.

"The AI wants to say the following: 'If we decide shortly before the landing that for some reason we want to land somewhere else, that would be bad,'" Martin explained.

The doctor abruptly asked, "What kind of reason?"

"Well, Marchenko, we will only know that when it happens," replied Martin.

"No idea?"

Martin shook his head, but Jiaying answered for him, "Perhaps once we reach a low altitude the radar will indicate the plate we are aiming for is unstable, for instance, because of an inclusion underneath it. Or we suddenly realize we are about to land in the middle of a garden kept by an inhabitant of Enceladus."

"Can't we take precautions?" Marchenko stood up and stretched.

"Radar has certain limitations we can't do anything about, certainly not from orbit, even when we are very close to the surface," explained Jiaying.

"Any other objections?" the commander asked, looking at the crew.

"If we land in the middle of a chaotic area, a rescue mission would be difficult," Hayato said.

"We won't have to worry about that. A rescue mission from the spaceship is impossible. And by the time help arrived from Earth... we can forget about it." Jiaying shrugged.

"To be honest, Watson's suggestion looks convincing to me, Jiaying," Amy said.

"Commander, with all due respect," Jiaying began, "we have to consider the length of the mission. Ice with an additional thickness of 2,500 meters, as to be expected near Watson's suggested landing location, this would be 5,000 meters both ways. Four weeks at least in *Valkyrie*, if the ice is as clear as the geologists expect. Landing between the stripes would give us a month's leeway."

"Just a moment," Hayato said. "The problem is we obviously cannot study the selected landing site."

"Correct," Martin answered.

Hayato seemed to have an idea. "This means we have to increase the power of the radar system. However, that appears impossible, as it is technically optimized." Hayato had his eyes closed, as if he was concentrating on some drawing appearing in his head. "For radar to be powerful, it needs a transmitter and an antenna. We've got both on the ship. We use it to radio Earth. If we aim it at the landing site, would that solve our problem?"

"Certainly," the commander said. She hesitated a little. "Siri, can we turn the ship in such a way that the radio antenna is aimed toward the surface of Enceladus?" Amy asked.

The AI responded, "Confirmed, with certain limitations."

"What limitations?"

"As the antenna always aims itself at Earth, the direction toward Earth must be behind Enceladus, as it is now."

"I understand, Siri. Are there any other remarks—or dangers to consider?"

"No dangers."

"Siri, what would the procedure look like?" Amy asked.

"Fire control jets for two seconds, wait for seventeen seconds, fire jets again for two seconds."

"Siri, initiate suggested maneuver. Authorization has been given by the commander."

"Maneuver starting in three, two, one. Now."

Martin saw that Enceladus was slowly moving out of the porthole. He had to turn away, as he would otherwise get nauseous. He checked his watch and silently counted, "*Fifteen seconds, twenty seconds.*" Outside of the porthole, only the starry sky could be seen.

"Rotation completed," Siri reported.

"Good, then I am going to take care of the antenna," Hayato said, and floated out of the room.

December 14, 2046, Enceladus

THE CREW COULD NOT HAVE CHOSEN a drearier location for their goodbyes. The garden module was now a sad sight. A large part of the spaceship—including this part—had been exposed to a near-vacuum for several hours when the drives failed, so they had mostly given up on the cultivation of the CELSS. Martin noticed something fresh and green growing in a container in the very back corner. The commander had promised she would try to restart the cultivation module during the time she and Marchenko would spend alone in the ship, so there would be fresh food available during their return trip.

The lack of growing things had one advantage, though. It was not smelly here, and the air was not hot and muggy. The module looked like a storage room that had been emptied, with strange shelves on the sides and in the middle. At the right side, as seen when one floated in from the command module, there was a centrally located hatch with a large wheel. Behind it was the passage to the lander module that up to now had been *terra incognita* to them. While they had trained in a replica of it on Earth, the module itself was completely virginal. Since yesterday the AI had prepared it for human occupation, meaning it was heated now, and had a suitable air pressure. Furthermore, all on-board computers had been started up and their software updated.

The lander module offered room for four. Its life support system was not as powerful as that of the mothership, and there was a two-month supply on board that could be stretched to three months. It used a conventional rocket engine.

The commander typed something on a number pad next to the wheel.

"All systems online," the AI then reported. Throughout their year-long journey they had made jokes about why the module had been locked via a number code.

"I am sure they are keeping clones of us there, in case we don't make it," Marchenko had said with a diabolical grin. *This does not seem completely impossible,* Martin considered, *since it will be an enormous PR disaster if only dead astronauts return to Earth. On the other hand, I doubt NASA could keep something like* that *secret for more than three weeks.*

The commander now turned the wheel one rotation to the left and opened the hatch to the lander.

"Boo," Marchenko yelled, seeming to remember his earlier joke, but no clone came out. However, no one wanted to take the first step into the lander module.

"One of you should go. Come on. After all, I am going to stay here," the commander said after an awkward ten seconds. Finally Martin plucked up his courage. The hatch was part of a short passage, with a second hatch on the other side that was already open. Hayato entered after him. He had wrapped his son against his chest with a cloth. Then Jiaying came in. The time for their separation had not yet come. Martin wrinkled his nose. *The air seems to be stale, but that cannot be. It is fresher than anything circulating in the mothership since it has not yet streamed through the lungs of anyone present.* Somehow he had expected everything to be covered in dust, but the metal surfaces shone as if they had just come straight from the factory. A ship, newly built and in space, was about the least dusty place one could imagine, a paradise for allergy sufferers, at least until people moved in.

The lander module appeared small to him. It measured about two by two by three and a half meters. In comparison, the spaceship seemed huge. In this crowded space, Hayato and Jiaying would have to spend weeks while *Valkyrie* broke through the ice and searched for life in the ocean.

He and Jiaying had discussed for a long time what would be best for the mission. Originally, the commander was supposed to join the pilot Francesca in the drill vehicle, since she was an exobiologist. Now she would stay on board the ship with Marchenko, who was not only a doctor but also a trained pilot who had initially been assigned to steer the lander module.

Yes, Francesca can control both the lander and then afterward the drill vehicle. But what if something happens to Valkyrie *and the pilot?* thought Martin. Of the three remaining astronauts, Jiaying was the only one with experience as a pilot from her time in the Chinese space program. She had ambitiously climbed every step of the career ladder, and finally, as a reward, had been given a spot on the Enceladus mission, to be a shining example to others.

As Hayato was more of an engineer by background, while Martin had considerable training in geology, the question of who was to sit in *Valkyrie* next to Francesca was soon decided—Martin Neumaier, who already had achieved such great things concerning the control of the drill vehicle while back on Earth. Initially, Jiaying had not quite agreed with this. Martin believed her argument was not based on personal ambition, but on concern for him, as the journey below the ice doubtlessly would be the most dangerous part of the mission.

"Well, I won't give a speech," said the commander, who had been the last one to enter the lander. "But we still owe you something. We have been waiting for a suitable moment to announce the name of our son. This was for various reasons, and we ask you for your understanding."

Martin saw there were tears in Amy's eyes.

"I personally had hoped there would be a moment both festive and joyful, but this voyage does not seem to be made for that. And we were a bit afraid you would disagree with our choice of name, find it too solemn or even silly. But now I cannot let Hayato go without wishing him a safe return, also in the name of our son—his son. We will really miss you, Hayato, both me and our son Sol."

Francesca, who stood next to the couple, hugged them both, with the baby included.

Marchenko nodded. "Good name," he said, "very practical, nice and short."

Jiaying first hugged Marchenko, then Amy. It was both congratulations and a farewell.

Martin shook the hands of the two people who would stay behind on *ILSE*. Amy's hand felt warm and moist, while Marchenko's was rather rough.

Hayato was about to hand the baby to Amy, but the commander rejected the gesture.

"Just a moment," Amy said. She jumped back to the CELSS. She returned a few seconds later. She held five small bouquets of flowers in her hand. They were pansies, with small blue petals. She had secretly made her dream come true. Each of them received one of the bouquets, even Marchenko, who would stay on board the mothership with her. Hayato hugged her one last time and tearfully handed Sol to her. Martin felt warm and fuzzy inside.

Now it was time for retreating. The commander gave Marchenko a signal. He waved to them once more and then disappeared into the hatch.

"Well, get working and come back safely in a few weeks," Amy said as she turned around and also retreated into the mothership.

Hayato wiped his eyes, went to the hatch on their side, and locked it.

"Lander hatch locked. Mothership hatch locked," Watson reported.

They could take the AI along anywhere. It was distributed among the computers of the ship, the lander, and *Valkyrie*. Its components communicated with each other on the same radio band the crew used, though not in human language but in bits, and therefore incredibly fast.

Martin sat down. The back of his seat vibrated, so he knew he had better buckle in. The monitor in front of him displayed a diagram of the lander module. At the very front was the engine that would get them safely down and bring them back again. Behind it was the habitat module where they were currently situated, surrounded by fuel tanks and storage modules. One of the storage units contained the laser concentrator that would receive the laser beam emitted by the ship and relay the energy to *Valkyrie* via a fiber-optic cable. At the very rear was a steel structure that held the bottle-shaped *Valkyrie*. *Cone, cuboid, and cylinder all in a row,* thought

Martin. *This lander looks a bit as if it was assembled by a toddler.*

"Like a fruit skewer," Jiaying remarked, who obviously was also looking at the shape of the lander. Martin glanced at her. Her eyes were reddened.

Francesca, who had streaks of makeup down her cheeks, was responsible for the flight. Technically, the flight would be mostly piloted by Watson, but she could always take control if she recognized a danger for the lander.

"Decoupling from mothership initiated," the AI said. A sharp, metallic sound could be heard from the outside of the hull. The clamps that had been holding the lander were opening.

"Two seconds braking impulse by main engine."

The large, cone-shaped engine burned kerosene for two seconds. Since it was aiming in their direction of flight, the impulse decelerated the lander a little bit, which was sufficient to get it into a lower trajectory. The crew carefully increased the distance between lander and mothership, meter by meter.

After about a minute, the engine ignited again briefly. Both Watson and Francesca were satisfied. Then it was time for a longer burn that brought them down to an altitude of four kilometers.

"Radar lock," Watson now reported. The ground radar had been activated. Martin's monitor started displaying a false-color image of the surface. Now they needed a last confirmation from the mothership. The repurposed radar antenna was scanning the intended landing site.

"All systems go. Landing site secure," Watson confirmed.

The craft moved quietly toward the shining white

moon. Martin remembered their launch from Earth, during which they had been shaken quite a bit. However, Enceladus possessed no atmosphere to speak of.

"High gate." Francesca had identified the landing site visually—it was now in sight. Martin switched his monitor to optical display. The landscape below them was craggy, as if someone had wildly stabbed a knife into a slab of butter, which was then frozen and covered by snow. It did not look like there were any smooth areas on which to land.

"Watson, last check," the pilot said.

Their altitude was now three kilometers, which the monitor displayed as 3,000 meters. Due to the mass of *Valkyrie*, the fuel on board would be just enough to return to the orbit of the mothership. If they descended any lower, they would not be able to abort the mission. Martin felt a lump in his throat.

The AI replied, "All systems go. Deceleration vector as planned."

We are sinking further, Martin noticed.

"Watson, status of landing struts?" Francesca's voice was completely calm, though Martin could feel her intense concentration.

"Landing system go."

"1,000 meters. Preparing to land. Watson, automatic landing activated."

Martin thought, *A completely manual landing in this area would be suicidal.* They needed to hit the landing site so there would be enough space for launching *Valkyrie*.

Francesca continued, "150 meters. Low gate."

Martin felt the craft lean to the side. His heart started to beat faster. During the last part of the approach, the

267

craft took on a typical rocket position. Control jets adjusted it precisely.

"Prepare to land," the pilot announced.

Starting at an altitude of about 100 meters, Martin could not see anything on the optical display anymore. The jet exhaust had stirred up ice crystals from the surface. Martin switched to lidar. The lander was aiming exactly at the center of the small plain below them. Despite this, Martin grabbed hold of his seat and felt his palms becoming moist.

At an altitude of ten meters, Watson started a count-down. *Ten, nine, eight...* at two, the main engine turned itself off, and their attitude was only adjusted by the control jets. *One... zero.* The touchdown of the lander was wonderfully smooth.

"Looks like we've arrived," Francesca said. Jiaying exhaled loudly and Martin sweated. All of them sat still, and no one cheered. "Rossi to Commander. The Eagle has landed, as they used to say."

"Confirming. Congratulations, ground team." Even Amy's voice remained very neutral. Martin could under-stand this. Landing in such low gravity was child's play. The difficult tasks would start tomorrow.

December 15, 2046, Enceladus

How DOES one move a mass of fifteen tons without a crane? One man in front, one behind. That was the plan Mission Control had come up with for Enceladus. Due to the low gravitational acceleration, which was only about 1/86 of that on Earth, heavy loads could be easily transported on this moon of Saturn. Relatively easily.

"Hauling stuff is men's work," Francesca had said with a laugh, running her hands through her shaggy hair when they discussed the division of labor.

I don't mind, Martin thought, *even though Francesca has always bench-pressed twice the weight I have. So I will be among the first to step on a celestial body no human has ever explored.*

Initially, they only had two spacesuits available for that. The EMUs had been left behind on the mothership. Instead, the lander possessed two SuitPorts, which were ready and waiting in one of the storage modules symmetrically located at the sides. SuitPorts were practical because they saved space. Instead of entering an airlock, an astronaut would step directly into a spacesuit, which was then closed airtight and uncoupled from the port. Upon returning, the procedure would be reversed; the astronaut backed into position and recoupled the suit.

Valkyrie had two additional SuitPorts at the rear. Martin imagined how they would glide through the ocean in the vehicle. *With these suits it is impossible to tell whether someone is inside them, so it looks as if two astronauts are piggy-backing on* Valkyrie.

The drill vehicle was not ready for action, though. It was standing high above the habitat module, held by steel scaffolding. Hayato and Martin now had the task of hauling the fifteen-ton object down and preparing it for launch at a safe distance from the lander. On Enceladus, *Valkyrie* only weighed 170 kilograms, so it was not a heroic task for two men to handle it.

Martin already wore his LCVG, his thermal onesie. The four of them had spent the night in the habitat module. Hayato had been snoring so Martin did not get much sleep. *I feel sorry for Jiaying*, he thought. *She will have to listen to it for many nights to come, although she looks well-rested this morning.* The exit procedure resembled the one used during an EVA. Enceladus possessed no atmosphere to speak of. Here, near the South Pole of Enceladus, water vapor could be detected, but the atmospheric pressure was eleven magnitudes below that on Earth. They were basically moving in a vacuum, even though it was not as cold as in space. Siri had reported minus 150 degrees Celsius for today.

Martin had already finished a part of the pre-breathing phase. He was still sweating from his minutes on the stationary bicycle. *I will have to spend a lot more time on this torture device to compensate for at least part of the effects low gravity will have on my body.*

"Get going," he heard Francesca's voice say through the loudspeaker.

He swung his legs into the round opening in front of him. It was easier to put on an EMU than handling a Suit-Port, which was like a full-body glove. He had to put each limb into the proper opening without being able to see it. It was impossible to bend down and adjust something, as the upper part was still rigidly attached to the lander. He cursed when he hit the wrong leg opening, which caused his LCVG to shift. "*DAMMIT. Once more from the start,*" Martin muttered under his breath.

Uncoupling was particularly tricky. He could not turn around to check whether the suit was securely closed, but must rely on the readouts, which was difficult for him to do because he knew all of the software had been programmed by error-prone humans. He would have preferred if someone had controlled everything directly from the lander, but how was that supposed to work when both of them were walking outside?

He finally succeeded. The arms of the suit could be moved. He touched the tool belt and activated the helmet radio. He heard heavy breathing. Hayato seemed to be struggling too. He looked at a brightly lit white metal container. The side facing him had a door.

"Neumaier is ready."

"Confirming," Francesca said, *"Hayato?"*

"Wait just a moment. I just have to... arrg... okay, the lining of the glove had... never mind, Masukoshi is ready."

"Opening exit."

The door across from him disappeared into the wall. A new, shiny white world was waiting for him. *I know Enceladus is the brightest of all moons and reflects the most light, but seeing it with my own eyes...* He started to shiver. The faceplate of his helmet automatically darkened. *I really wish I could just run ahead.* However, they had agreed on a different sequence.

Hayato Masukoshi was supposed to enter the history books as the first human on Enceladus. The four-person ground team had agreed on this yesterday. Martin watched his first steps from the hatch. Small metal stairs led downward. To the right and left Martin saw landing struts. Hayato's first step was still normal, but then he pushed off with too much force. Despite the heavy spacesuit, a spring scale would only indicate two kilograms here. *My fellow astronaut did not take this into account. The large area of ice in front of him must have been too tempting.* Martin saw how Hayato slowly floated downward. A few hours later, these images would be shown on all major news programs worldwide. They would make it very obvious this particular world was quite different from the moon or Mars.

Martin followed Hayato, careful not to put too much force into his steps. Nevertheless, he could not avoid turning his first step into a jump. Even though he was on a moon, he must remember to move more like in the weightlessness of space.

After only a few meters, Martin had adjusted to these conditions because he had trained long enough in low gravity. The visible horizon and the clear distinction between 'up' and 'down' no longer confused his senses. He used his glove to wipe his visor, on which a few ice crystals had settled.

Martin looked around. In front of him there was a plain that might have been a snow-covered meadow. However, the snow, consisting of fine ice crystals, only formed a very thin layer. He stepped on hard, smooth ice with each of his steps. Martin attempted to slide, but when he tried to gain momentum like he was used to on Earth, he simply bounced off the hard ice. At least it would be difficult to accidentally slip and fall, as hardly any force pulled him downward. At the end of the landing plain a steep slope cast hard, dark shadows. It was the contrast that showed him the change in terrain, which the highly reflective surface would have otherwise hidden.

The sun shone above the horizon at an angle of about 20 degrees. Here, close to the South Pole, it would never rise above 27 degrees. Martin shivered when he saw the sun, since it was much, much smaller in the Enceladus sky than back on Earth. The sun moved across a deep black background sprinkled with many stars. The stars appeared more hostile here, rather than inducing the peaceful feeling he remembered from balmy nights on Earth. They had a piercing, unflinching, pitiless look. It was probably because they did not twinkle, as their light was not being refracted by an atmosphere.

Martin was most impressed by Saturn. The planet seemed to be affixed to the eastern horizon. It did not move its position because Enceladus always turned the same face toward it, like Luna, the Latin name for our moon, does toward Earth. From Martin's perspective, the planet looked like a huge brown mountain that rose to an enormous height on the horizon. The rings, however, were only visible as a narrow line close to the horizon.

Directly on this line, like a bead on a thin string, Martin saw a bright sphere that looked to be as large as the moon of Earth. This was Mimas—sometimes called the Death Star, since on some photos it resembles the space station of Emperor Palpatine in the old *Star Wars* movies. Martin could not see the huge crater, Herschel, that was responsible for this nickname. *Maybe Jiaying will have more luck in the coming weeks,* he thought.

"Enough sightseeing," Hayato said via helmet radio. "We have plenty of work to do."

He's right. Martin stopped walking, straightened his knees, and almost lifted off. They must lower *Valkyrie* down to the ice. The mission planners had come up with a simple yet effective method—they would use a slide that would be unrolled, a pulley, some climbing, and a lot of muscle power.

First Hayato would have to climb 60 meters to the top of the metal scaffolding and attach the pulley.

"You're sure you don't want to do this job?" he asked Martin.

"Climbing up to the sixth floor? No thanks."

However, since they weighed only two kilos each, climbing was neither as arduous nor as dangerous as on Earth. Hayato could proceed without a safety line. Despite this, Martin heard Hayato groan as he climbed. *The bulky space suit is not exactly the perfect climbing outfit,* Martin thought.

"Okay, the pulley has been hooked up," Hayato reported.

The next station was the upper part of the drill vehicle. It had an attachment point for one end of the rope.

"Rope latched on to *Valkyrie*."

While Hayato was climbing back down, Martin fetched the slide. It was a thick plastic tarp, about four meters wide. It was intended to show *Valkyrie* the way, and also to protect the lander. One end would be attached behind the drill vehicle, the roll would be passed underneath it, and then unrolled all the way to the ground. This time, it was Martin's turn. *I'm glad I only have to climb up a couple of meters.*

"Slide attached," he reported. In the meantime,

Hayato had started to unscrew a bolt in part of the steel scaffolding that had secured *Valkyrie* in space. This was not dangerous as long as no one gave *Valkyrie* a nudge. After he had loosened all of the bolts with his special tool, Hayato shoved the steel scaffolding away. It fell slowly and silently to the side, and he dragged it behind the lander.

Now the exciting part began. Hayato first secured himself to the lander with a short rope. He then took up the slack on the rope that ran through the pulley, while Martin unrolled the slide. Its upper end would give the rear of *Valkyrie* a push that was supposed to make the vessel lean and slowly slide down on the tarp. Hayato was to control how fast the drill vehicle moved through the amount of force he exerted on the pulley rope. On Earth, such a maneuver would have been impossible, but here a single man with a good safety line could control the movement of an entire vehicle by using a basic pulley system.

"And... go!" commanded Martin as he pulled on the tarp, so Hayato would pull the line at the right time. *Valkyrie* wobbled, but it did not tilt. He gave the tarp another strong pull. This time it worked. The drill vehicle started to slide down centimeter by centimeter. Hayato gave out the line a bit more quickly, and *Valkyrie* moved faster in response. Martin kept the tarp taut, so the vehicle had a clear path downward. He heard Hayato's heavy breathing through his helmet radio.

"You are doing quite well, guys," Francesca said.

Little by little, *Valkyrie* got closer to the ground. Its rear was now aiming directly at Martin. *If Hayato lets go of the line, I will have to skedaddle*. Martin started to laugh. It looked as if two people in spacesuits were coming toward him, but upside down, as the SuitPorts at the stern of *Valkyrie* were turned around by 180 degrees.

The pilot's voice came through the helmet radio. "Everything okay with you?"

"It's perfect, Francesca," Martin replied. "Look through my helmet camera and you will understand."

He heard the two women in the lander giggle.

"Watch out that they don't catch you," both women said, almost in unison.

"Don't worry, I'm watching."

AFTER HALF AN HOUR, *Valkyrie* was lying in front of them. Hayato detached the line and returned the pulley to the storage module. Then he walked toward Martin carrying two new rope pulleys.

"One for you," Hayato said.

The rope on the pulley reminded Martin of fishing line. It was lightweight and thin, but very tough. Besides this, Hayato had brought a kind of gun and two diverter pulleys. First Martin latched a rope to each side of *Valkyrie*. He used the gun to shoot two anchors into the ice at the target location and attached pulleys to each. Then he ran each rope around one of the pulleys and returned to Hayato, handing off a rope to him. Now both men walked toward the lander. Pushing *Valkyrie* across the ice was harder than he would have thought. The vehicle did not even weigh 200 kilos. However, he and Hayato weighed only two kilos each. Due to this fact, they could not provide enough resistance to move the drill vehicle. Instead, they would have simply slipped. Therefore they had to use the help of the much heavier lander. They anchored themselves to it so they could use their muscle power and the ropes running through the diverter pulleys to move *Valkyrie* across the ice.

"Heave-ho," Martin commanded, and they pulled as hard as they could. The lander gave them support. This was the hardest physical labor Martin had undertaken in the last several months. *Those damn mission planners. They could have supplied a motorized winch.* Things got easier after they overcame the static friction and could use a hand-over-hand method to maintain *Valkyrie's* motion. Martin sweated. Water ran across his face, but he could not wipe it away. *Damned spacesuit,* he thought.

"Good. That's enough already," Francesca's voice said. Martin stopped at once. Hayato complained since they had not reached the planned distance.

"That is 30 meters, and it should be enough," the pilot said. "Believe me, those mission planners always exaggerate the safety requirements. What could happen, after all?"

Hayato did not say a word. He seemed to be thinking. He finally gave in. "Okay, then we are coming inside."

Suddenly, Francesca said, "Just a moment—the laser concentrator. I would like to test it today."

"Sure," Hayato said, "let's do it."

The man obviously has way too much energy, Martin thought.

The concentrator was a module that looked like a barrel with legs. Together they got it from the lander and carried it close to the launch point. Hayato used his nail gun to attach the legs of the barrel, which had a diameter of about 1.5 meters, to the ice, so it could no longer be easily moved. Then he took off the lid. Below it they could see the parabolic mirror that would focus the laser beam from the spaceship. After traversing several kilometers, the cone of light would definitely be frayed, the more so the greater the wavelength of the light was. Hayato pressed a button and a charging indicator appeared. The concentrator had a rechargeable battery on board to compensate for brief signal failures. However, it could only provide full energy for a few seconds, or, alternatively, backup power for a few hours. The charging indicator was red. Hayato pressed another button, and now a yellow LED showed the position signal was online. This allowed the mothership to aim the laser beam at the concentrator with pinpoint precision.

"Please keep some distance," Francesca said, "we are going to test this while you guys are still outside."

Martin and Hayato took a few steps backward. Suddenly a bolt of green flashed down from the sky and hit the barrel. Martin jerked back in surprise and stumbled in slow motion, but Hayato's hand kept him from falling.

Francesca apologized, "Sorry, guys."

The ray of light appearing above the concentrator seemed to come out of nothingness. At their height it was about one meter wide, and further up it tapered off. At the same time, it became more translucent and then disappeared completely. That they could see the laser at all indicated a minimal atmosphere existed here.

"Works great," Martin said into the microphone. "Nice Christmas lighting!"

The barrel-shaped concentrator started to buzz. It did not even take a minute for the charge indicator to turn green. The beam vanished as quickly as it had appeared. Martin saw an afterimage, but knew it existed only in his visual cortex.

December 16, 2046, Enceladus

A FARMER WHO HAD A GOAT, a wolf, and a head of cabbage with him wanted to cross a river. The boat was so small he could take only one of the animals or the cabbage at a time. How would all of them get safely to the other shore? Martin thought about this ancient riddle as the four of them discussed moving into *Valkyrie*. The solution was a bit easier than in the case of the farmer —Martin and Francesca walked to the drill vehicle and entered it through the main entrance on the roof. They activated the life support system and pressurized *Valkyrie*. Then they took off the suits they had come in and entered the spacesuits belonging to *Valkyrie* via the SuitPorts. Protected by these, they reentered *Valkyrie* after they had depressurized it by remote control. They picked up the suits they had arrived in and carried them back to the lander, where they reattached them to its SuitPorts. Then they would return to the drill vehicle and the trip could begin.

Every journey begins with a farewell. Martin had imagined the scene dozens of times the night before. He had tried to imagine what words he would use when saying goodbye to

Jiaying. *Now it is all different, though.* He started saying the words he had come up with, but they sounded so hollow. *I am helpless because I cannot describe what is happening inside me. And I have a guilty conscience because I am afraid of—but also looking forward to—the coming time, even though Jiaying cannot accompany me.*

The solution was incredibly simple. Before stepping inside his spacesuit, he hugged this woman, whom he still did not know very well, drowning in this embrace, and everything was good and right. When he let go of her, he felt his eyes welling up. Jiaying turned away. He noticed she touched her cheeks with one hand. This was the signal to jump into the SuitPort. The visor fogged up when he went outside. *This must be from the sweat from my short work-out on the stationary bike earlier,* he thought.

"You put your right foot in, you put your right foot out, you do the Hokey-Pokey, and you shake it all about." Strange that right now a children's song should go through my mind. It was so odd he almost laughed at himself. He had to control the urge, because otherwise Francesca would think he was suffering from symptoms of the bends. *Click.* Now the suit from the lander was back in the port. They walked the 30 meters to *Valkyrie* one last time, connected to the system, and went inside. Martin looked around carefully. *Theoretically I can still cancel, can flee, retreat, but I know this is not truly an option.* He would stare into the eternal darkness with Francesca. She was the world's best pilot, and no one knew the *Valkyrie* system like she did—at least no one less than a light hour away—in other words, some of those pilots back on earth.

"Commander to *Valkyrie*, starting laser," Amy's voice said from the mothership.

Martin adjusted the camera so he could see the concentrator. The green ray was there.

"Energy supply at 100 percent," Francesca reported. The newly focused ray of light moved through the fiber-optic cable attached to the concentrator, and on into *Valkyrie*. Here the energy was transformed into heat. The heat became electricity, and when Francesca activated the jets the heat melted ice into water. Then the ray heated it to water vapor, which produced more electricity via a generator, and at the same time melted the ice ahead of them, wherever the jets were aimed.

"Permission to start granted."

"Thanks, commander, we will see you later."

At the moment, no further words were necessary. Francesca had all the important data on her screen, and Martin watched the displays. *Valkyrie* started to tilt forward. *Way back in the Antarctic this looked impressive when seen from outside,* he recalled. Now, only the walls around him moved, while the seat and the console were mounted in such a way they would pivot to stay horizontal. After ten minutes he was no longer sitting inside a tube; he was now in a tower, without having changed location. *Valkyrie* dug into the ice with increasing speed.

"All systems normal," Francesca reported to the mothership and the lander, even though their fellow astronauts saw all data in real-time. "Have fun up there. Rossi, out."

AFTER MOVING within the drill for almost two hours, Martin dozed off in his seat for the first time. The background sounds on board were soothing, and it was so different from being in space. The vehicle rubbed against its surroundings, the water vapor jets howled, the intensity of the noise varied, but he no longer felt like a tiny speck in a vast emptiness. It seemed to him that humans were not made for staying in a vacuum. The ice around them was powerful, true. It could squash them immediately if there were tectonic forces. But it was not infinite. It had a limit and dimensions, and humans were in principle able to reach those limits and, even better, go beyond them.

Their limit was at a distance of 5,000 meters from the surface. When he awoke from a confused dream, it was still 4,800 meters away.

"Well, are you back?" Francesca gave him a friendly smile. "If you want to, you can lie down properly." She pointed to the folding beds hanging from the wall farther up.

Martin shook his head, rubbed his eyes, and stretched. "Thanks, but that's not necessary. But if you are tired..."

"Maybe later," Francesca replied.

Martin looked at his watch. They had been going for a little more than two hours. A hundred meters per hour— not bad, compared to what Stone had managed to get out of *Valkyrie* earlier. Martin massaged his temples. He felt a slight headache, maybe because of the dry air. They had traveled for over a billion kilometers, but the engineers had not managed to provide a comfortable atmosphere. He tried to recall what he had dreamed of, but he had forgotten most of it. *I still remember one image, though. I am tied to something and experiencing incredible pain. Yet instead of crying or screaming, I always yelled, "I, I, I." Sometimes the brain produces strange short-circuits.*

Martin sighed. *Another 48 hours.* This was not a long time compared to the year they had needed to get here. *What will the ocean under the ice reveal to us?* he wondered. The exobiologists hoped for primitive cells like the ones that existed in hot vents at the bottom of Earth's oceans. The result of the *ELF* probe had been, as they say, open to interpretation. A dead hare would be interpreted as a proof of life by any examiner. A frozen single-celled organism, if it was differentiated enough, was only a clear indication. The risk of a chance discovery was low, as the probe had identified several identical specimens. Yet despite all the complexity, those could still be the results of a chemical or geological process that was just unknown on Earth. They could only be sure if they caught life red-handed, when it was currently growing and multiplying.

In two days, their search for life would begin.

December 18, 2046, Valkyrie

MARTIN HAD FELT as if they would never get through the ice. Of course the instruments had shown they would soon break through into the ocean—radar, lidar, even by the speedometer. With increasing temperatures, the ice had become softer by the hour. At first it had been harder than steel, then like limestone, and finally the jets had cut through it like butter, which saved them two full hours at the end.

They did not see the new world, though, until it happened.

Martin heard it, even before Francesca could tell him. The jets had abruptly become much quieter. They had completely changed their mode of operation. Instead of ejecting hot water, they now sucked in the salty ocean water. And instead of using the energy of the water to generate electricity, the blades of the generator now functioned as a propeller driving the ship ahead, still fed by the laser beam from space. At a signal from the on-board AI, the mothership had reduced the power of the laser, since they needed much less for navigating in water.

It was time to look around. The vehicle activated powerful flashlights that illuminated their surroundings in various wavelengths. Radar and lidar recorded the structure of the ice layer above them, though these sensors did not reach to the bottom of the ocean from here.

The first images started to appear on the large display that substituted for a window at the bow. Francesca looked at Martin. *She is as impressed as I am,* he noticed. Above them, somebody had built an ice palace. Trenches, ridges, craters, walls, columns, mountains—the lower aspect of the ice seemed to mirror the shapes on the surface. All that was missing was a copy of the lander. An exotic mirror country stretched above them far into the distance—shiny, crazy, and clinically pure. Even the water appeared to be clear as crystal.

Martin remembered his last visit to a cave on Earth. *Wherever I looked, life was spreading. Moss, lichen, layers of bacteria, primitive plants—even under such unfavorable conditions, they displayed a great variety. Nothing like that can be seen here.* They were moving through an amazing but apparently sterile world that might even be hostile to life.

With mouths agape, they continued to watch new, seemingly impossible structures, while *Valkyrie* drove like a submarine toward the South Pole. The work of art above them was art for art's sake, as the searchlights of *Valkyrie* were doubtless illuminating them for the very first time in their existence. It appeared Francesca and Martin were the first intelligent beings in the universe allowed to marvel at this masterpiece of sculpture. *This is an incredible gift, one that will always connect me to the pilot and to this moon,* he mused.

Soon the on-board AI started its automatic search routine. The two astronauts did not have much to do. The first images were sent—via the laser uplink—to the spaceship, and then they left this world. A few hours later the first congratulatory messages arrived from Earth, though worded rather cautiously, particularly when exobiologists had sent them. After all, they said, they had not expected to find a second Earth here. What the experts did not add was, *but it would have been nice, of course.*

The two astronauts were not bothered by this. The searchlights were first switched to infrared and then to ultraviolet, and each brought more fascinating effects. Now they observed ribbon structures they believed to be different phases of the ice. Martin spent half an hour describing to Jiaying via a dedicated line what splendors he was seeing. Shortly before the end of their conversation, she told him she had kept the channel open for Hayato, so he could listen in. Martin did not mind. He gladly shared what he was experiencing.

After twelve kilometers below the ice, the sensors reported increasing currents. The engines could easily handle this, though. They appeared to be approaching one of the Tiger Stripes, the source of the ice geysers that made Enceladus such a unique place in the solar system.

The abyss opened at kilometer 14.8. It was a deep structure that looked like it was cut by a knife. The searchlights did not reach the bottom—if there was one. *It must be at least 750 meters downward,* Martin estimated. At the edge of the area lit by the searchlights they saw hints that the ice was not perfectly clear everywhere. They could not be sure, but those areas might be deposits of organic material. Jiaying urged them to go there right away, and a few hours later the scientists on Earth concurred emphatically. However, the two astronauts stuck to the plan—first explore the surroundings, then set priorities, and only afterward decide to follow up on specific phenomena.

Valkyrie followed a curving course and finally returned to its starting point. The vehicle plowed through the ocean like a whale. The water streaming through its engines was examined in all wavelengths. For each cubic meter, a milliliter was sent to a rapid analyzer. This allowed the AI to create a rough map of chemical distributions. The water was very salty indeed, much more so than in the oceans on Earth. Even though the salt water looked clear, it contained a certain percentage of organic material that might be of chemical or biological origin. The consistency was not uniform, as there was a gradient that increased with depth, and a second one that correlated to their nearness to the Tiger Stripes.

In general, the water did not contain a lot of minerals, except near the currents leading to the stripes. It appeared logical to the scientists that the mineral content would rise with increasing depth, as this is where the ocean met the rocks. Nowhere else could salts be dissolved into the water. The collective exobiologists on Earth could not agree on what further course *Valkyrie* should take, so Martin and Francesca went to sleep, leaving the exobiologists to argue among themselves.

Age of Questions, Point

There is:
The I.
The all.
The warmth.
The salt.
The movement.
The current.
The force.
The effect.
The beauty.
The order.
The time.

There is not:
The not-I.
The not-all.

There no longer is:
The eternity.

There is:
The doubts.

There is:
The questions.
This is the age of questions.
It starts with a point.

December 19, 2046, Valkyrie

WATSON WOKE them at 0800 hours ship time. The smartest people on Earth had decided the voyage should continue downward, into the depths of the ocean, all the way to the bottom. Martin mentally prepared for a period of boredom. *Valkyrie* tilted its nose, but due to the low gravity, he barely noticed it. Their seats and displays adjusted automatically. There was a brief moment of pressure, and then the vehicle moved at a constant 29 kilometers per hour. They would not have noticed their progress without the instruments that measured the distance covered. The cameras showed the same image from all directions.

Martin asked the AI to display what had been found so far. The list of chemical molecules was long. First, Martin quickly scrolled through them. Maybe there was a pattern the software had overlooked. The crucial question was, could the origin of these compounds be explained purely through chemistry, or was there something that required a biological explanation?

Martin noticed very little ammonia was dissolved in the water. The ice cores of comets that originated during the formation of the solar systems had a significantly higher percentage of ammonia. The ocean here must, therefore, be very old to have had enough time to release the now missing ammonia via the Tiger Stripes.

Martin and Francesca seemed to be moving through a reservoir of water older than all of the oceans on Earth. If there was life here, it would have had a lot of time to evolve toward perfection. Scientists had already suspected the water was saltier than in most bodies of water on Earth. *Valkyrie* reported a current pH value of 11.1, which was slowly increasing with their depth. In the Al Hajar Mountains in Oman there is a mineral called ophiolite that had, in ancient times, been exposed to water with similar pH values. Tectonic movements had formed the mountains, transporting the ophiolite from deep in the Earth's crust to the surface. The high PH level found here was another indicator that the ocean on Enceladus was enormously old.

This raised another question. From studying the formation of ophiolite, it had been discovered that hydrogen was an important by-product. Hydrogen played a prominent role in the synthesis of organic compounds, and also provided energy for life. If these processes were still ongoing, this ocean, particularly its floor, would be a livable home for microorganisms. *Even though I would like to look at the dark sediments at the root of the Tiger Stripes, I can fully understand the decision of the scientists on Earth*, reflected Martin.

"Are we there yet?" he asked.

"Yes, my boy, have a little patience." Francesca played along with the game indicated by Martin's tone of voice.

"I have to go potty."

"Just a moment, I am looking for a place to park." The

pilot turned the nose of *Valkyrie*, as if she was looking for an exit from a highway.

"Approaching solid ground," Watson reported. At the same moment, Martin saw a fine line appear on the radar display.

"Perfect timing," Francesca said. "We are sure to find a bathroom for you down there."

It took a few more minutes before they established visual contact. What they saw was completely different from the scene below the ice. Martin was surprised, even though he should have known better. The stone below them, which formed the rocky core of Enceladus, was impermeable to searchlights. It did not shimmer or shine. Francesca turned on the infrared light. The image did not change. She activated the normal searchlights again, but left the infrared camera on.

"Oh!" Martin blurted out. Francesca froze. Several patterns appeared on the screen, and she increased the contrast.

"There are temperature differences of several degrees!" Francesca exclaimed.

Martin checked the calibration. Francesca was right. Were there geological processes that created such an image? Maybe cracks in the rock that transported more heat from the interior than their surroundings?

"Watson, I need an in-depth analysis." Martin had to find out whether the temperature differences conformed to the structure of the rock. *This would be the simplest explanation, but we also have to watch out that our desires do not dictate what we see.*

Since she was the pilot, Francesca was required to confirm the order. Then Watson bombarded the area below them with everything their vehicle could muster —

gamma rays, x-rays, terahertz, UV, radio waves. These channels had different penetration depths, depending on the rocks, temperature, pressure, and so on. A very precise image of what lay below them would be generated once these measurements were combined.

The calculations took a while, even though they also used the main computer which was connected via the fiber-optic cable. After seven minutes and thirteen seconds —Martin had followed the time with the seconds-display of his watch—they received a result. The silicate-rich rock met their expectations. They were facing the uppermost layer of a differentiated core. Not every moon possessed such a core. Such a temperature distribution had not been detected on any of the known celestial bodies, save for Earth. This proved energy was produced, distributed, and consumed here. *We have caught life red-handed, even though we have yet to discover living beings.*

"Do you know what that means, Francesca?" he asked.

The pilot nodded and exhibited a triumphant smile. Martin felt goosebumps on his arms. *It is here, extraterrestrial life. Right here, so near we can almost touch it. We have found what mankind has been seeking for so long—and I am part of it!* It was stunning, and Martin had to hold on to his table. *What does it look like, though?*

In order to find out, they would have to take samples. Francesca already knew what to do when the vehicle approached the bottom. The analyzer modules in the jets did not report any significant changes in the composition of the water. It was not the water that represented the biotope, but the bottom, the layer where the alkaline liquid and the rocks reacted to each other. Therefore the percentage of biological material in the geysers was relatively low, and this was also the reason the analyzers had not yet discovered anything.

"Five... four... three... two. Arm range reached," Watson reported.

"Autonomous hover," Francesca ordered before she bent over her console and reached into a cavity. This was the 'glove' that would transmit her finger movements to the robotic arm at the bow of *Valkyrie*. The arm was extremely flexible, and during tests its hand had even succeeded in picking up a sheet of paper from a smooth surface. This task was easy by comparison. The fingers were supposed to scrape some coating from the rock.

Martin watched the hand on the monitor. *It looks like it is trying to tickle the sea floor. If I were Enceladus, the giant from Greek mythology whose name was given to this moon, I would giggle now.* The display could not show what the hand was scratching off the floor. A jet sucked in the material, like a vacuum cleaner, and then analyzed it. However, under infrared light, Martin saw the procedure had changed the structure of the colonization. The hand had reached part of a particularly bright line. The area where the line had ended before was now as dark as the naked surface of the rock.

What does this obvious living layer consist of? he speculated. *In the low-oxygen deep seas of Earth, I would assume it to be a colony of anaerobic algae. I wonder what it is here, 1.2 billion kilometers away from Earth. Perhaps it is primitive bacteria, or has it already evolved into multicellular organisms?*

The first results showed up on the screen. These were snapshots because the instrument could not arrange the cells properly. Instead, it just took photos at various wavelengths and resolutions. Afterward, the software attempted to filter images belonging to the same object and combine them into an overall picture. The longer the analyzer worked, the more precise its results would become.

After the first photos, however, Martin slumped in his seat. His expectations had been too high. The structures he saw on the screen were clear and precise. *This is not a good sign, since it means they are simple, even more so than I had hoped. Life has not used the long time in the ocean to refine its structure. Maybe evolution has not worked here because there is no competition, no conflict for survival, ending with the extinction of the inferior species,* he speculated. The species of primitive cells Martin saw on the monitor might be billions of years old, but it probably had changed little from its ancestors.

He sat up again and scolded himself. *We have made a groundbreaking discovery. Life is not a lucky accident. Even in our own solar system, it has developed twice under very different circumstances. The universe must be teeming with life.*

Age of Questions, Line

There is:
The I.
The thoughts.
The ages.
The ages are not, they come and go. They are
*   recorded in the Forest of Columns.*
The First Age is the Age of Birth.
The Second Age is the Age of Struggle.
The Third Age is the Age of Peace and of the I.
The Fourth Age is the Age of Questions.
There is:
The doubts.
The waiting.
The curiosity of incomplete knowledge.
The pain.
The pain of the body and the pain of the questions.

December 20, 2046, Valkyrie

ALL OF HUMANITY wanted to congratulate them for their great discovery. Yesterday, Mission Control had transmitted greetings and congratulations from the U.S. President herself, the Chinese Prime Minister, the Russian Prime Minister, the German Chancellor, and the Japanese Emperor. Martin had avoided watching any of the news programs. *I hope everything will die down by the time we return, so I will at least be able to go shopping in a supermarket without people bothering me. If not, I will have to volunteer for the next Mars mission.*

He was tired. *As the saying goes, you should 'quit while you're ahead.' Arriving back in Earth orbit, then eight weeks' vacation in the Caribbean with Jiaying—what a wonderful dream.* He calculated it. *I should be pretty well-off by the time I get home. I will have more than two years' worth of salary in my account, more money than I have ever seen in one place.*

However, the journey was not over yet. Mission Control had developed a systematic research program for him. *When all is said and done, they do not want anyone to say they might have overlooked things*, he surmised. *We will collect so much data that researchers can use it to write dissertations for years to come.* Even the analysis of the *ELF* data had taken years, though the amount of data gathered during this mission would be 50 times larger. Afterward, humanity would know the Enceladus Ocean inside and out, and there would be lots of new questions.

Valkyrie, Francesca explained to him, would systematically search a rectangle of 40 by 80 kilometers at the bottom of the Enceladus Ocean. They would take samples and classify them in order to generate as complete a picture as possible. Afterward, they would look at the water column above it. Temperature, pressure, salinity, pH value, currents—they would measure whatever could be measured. The Deep Space link of the spaceship would be pushed to the limits of its transmission capacity.

For Martin, this mostly meant boredom. The vehicle drove itself, and Francesca would supervise it. While her job did not sound particularly exciting, Martin's task would be limited to watching her do this. Once a day he was supposed to talk for half an hour about the fascination of space, which was supposed to attract more viewers. Martin yawned.

"LOOK, BACK THERE," Francesca said, tapping Martin on the shoulder. He opened his eyes.

"What?"

"On the radar image. At the range limit," she directed.

The horizon, which otherwise was a straight line, seemed scraggly there.

Unsure, he asked, "What is that? An interference?"

"I already checked it while you were still asleep. That is no artifact. It is real."

"Where are we? And where is that?"

"We have covered 35 kilometers. The radar echo is about 70 kilometers north-northeast," Francesca said.

"That is not part of our plan, is it?"

"No."

"Yet we are going there anyway, aren't we?" Martin guessed.

"Sure, what did you expect?" Francesca placed her hands on her hips.

"Should I ask?"

"It is better to ask for forgiveness... and remember the dark sediment in the Tiger Stripes. We haven't seen that again since we landed."

Francesca is right. We will still have enough time to finish the research plan, he presumed, checking the position of *Valkyrie*. The pilot had already changed course. *She seems as bored as I am.*

Two HOURS LATER, scanning in all wavelengths, they came upon a formation of pillars. *The Forest of Columns*, Martin thought, and then wondered how that name, quite apt, had entered his mind.

"Looks like stalagmites," Francesca observed.

Martin shook his head. "But they are immersed. How is the liquid supposed to drop down onto them so the sediments grow upward?"

The closer they came, the more obvious it was these columns had nothing in common with the limestone formations in terrestrial caves. They were perfectly round and did not taper upward. The instruments informed them that the columns had a height between two and ten meters.

"An enchanted forest," Francesca said and gaped at the display. It was a grandiose scene, aloof and exotic.

"These are definitely not sediments," Martin said. "The instruments show no currents that would regularly deposit material here, and even if there were, the columns would not have grown into perfect cylinders."

Francesca nodded and turned toward him. "Maybe it's some kind of corals?"

Martin was thinking. *Theoretically, some phenomenon of chemical bonding could be responsible for a circular form being the only one possible.* He did not know enough about the dynamics of saline solutions to exclude this option. *Furthermore, research probably has not sufficiently investigated all the phases under conditions of high pressure and low temperatures, like here.* No, they needed Jiaying's expertise. *Should I communicate with her? Make a short call? No, there will be time for that later, even though I really would like to see her face.*

Martin asked, "Could we park *Valkyrie* on the sea floor close to the columns?"

"No problem." Francesca tapped on something on the display. From this perspective, the forest was even more impressive because it was so symmetrical. Martin had seen kelp forests in the North Sea, swaying with the rhythm of the waves. This so-called forest looked completely different, like something from another world—which, of course, it was. Nothing moved, and its trunks stood rigid, looking like toys—or the experiments of an extraterrestrial giant.

Martin imagined he might walk among them. *This will be a walk in the most exotic forest of the known universe. The PR department will certainly be very grateful for any recordings.* In a fascinating sort of way, the forest seemed to invite him.

The individual columns were one to two meters apart from each other. In his spacesuit he would fit comfortably between them. *Maybe this way I can find out more than an analysis with Valkyrie's instruments can provide. Of course, the vehicle has been aiming all its measurement devices at the forest for a while in order to force it to reveal its secrets. I can simply walk in and ask for information—how does that sound?*

"It's crazy," Martin said, after he explained his plan to get out and walk among the columns. "Crazy, but doable, I think."

"You're insane," Francesca said. "Count me out."

"Well, that's the plan."

She circled her temple with her finger to indicate he was nuts. "I won't stop you, though. Anyway, one person has to stay on board. Who knows what could be lurking out there? Forests are full of robbers, isn't that what they say?"

"But our instruments don't indicate anything, do they?" Martin said. "We only found extremely primitive cells. Any real danger is millions of years of evolution away."

She shook her head. "Do what you like."

Martin intended to do just that. *And, after all, didn't the pilot just say so?* he reasoned. *Normally, two-person teams are mandatory for EVAs, but then we are not in a vacuum. And after all, why do we have a pressure suit on the SuitPort?* To be safe, he first consulted Watson. The AI did not see any problems. Water might transmit heat much better than a vacuum did, but then it was relatively warm here. The LCVG could handle it. Due to the low gravity of Enceladus, the pressure was tolerable. On Earth, he would have been in trouble at an ocean depth of 7,620 meters. He could even raise the pressure in the suit slightly above normal, which would shorten the pre-breathing phase. He did not

303

mention his plans to Mission Control or the commander, though.

HALF AN HOUR later he was floating through the ancient water of the ocean. The vehicle's searchlights illuminated the first rows of trees. Beyond this point it was dark, as the columns cast harsh shadows. Martin descended to the ocean floor. *The first steps toward this sunken Atlantis,* he thought in amazement. He gave Francesca the okay signal with his right hand and bounced into an unknown world.

Martin looked at his position as shown on his arm display. *I have advanced fifteen meters into the forest.* Here the columns were closer together. By the light of his helmet lamp the landscape looked even more mysterious. *Or should I call it a building?* he silently marveled. From the perspective of a pedestrian, the Forest of Columns seemed rather artificial, like the giant temple of a lost civilization. Martin knew, though, that nothing here had sunk to the bottom of the ocean. *The columns had stood on the sea floor since they had come into existence.*

The deeper he advanced into the forest, the more often the shadows cast by his lamp played tricks on him. Soon he felt he was not alone. *There is a presence here I am not able to name.* From the corner of his eye he seemed to see someone, or something, jump from shadow to shadow, though when he turned his head there was nothing there. *It must be my imagination getting me all riled up,* Martin rationalized. He did not report this to Francesca. In each row, the columns seemed to be getting older. First one in ten, then one in four or five showed signs of slight damage. *The forest must have grown from the center, so the outermost columns are the youngest ones.* He reported this observation to Francesca but left out the second part. When he looked backward, in the direction from which he had come, the columns appeared to stand closer to each other than before. His senses seemed to be running haywire.

"I cannot get through anymore, so I am turning around," he said. Martin would not reach the center. Not due to lack of stamina, but because the forest seemed more and more menacing. *I would like to see the root of the forest, but I do not feel up to facing what is waiting for me there.*

"Okay, just take a few more samples," Francesca instructed. "We could use the radiometric dating system on board. I would like to see whether your theory is correct."

"Great idea," he replied to the pilot's request, and took the sample collection tool from his belt. It could hold up to five samples, which the tool not only picked up mechanically, but also stored in a sterile environment. He held the tool in front of him like a weapon and approached a column. He touched the spot where he wanted to apply the tool, shone his helmet light on it, and suddenly jerked back. He saw a symbol he already recognized scratched into the material. *It is the structure of one of the two primitive kinds of cells from what Francesca collected from the ocean floor.* This cell looked slightly different than the one in the onboard display, though. It lacked two of the organelles, the function of which he did not know. *This might be an earlier version. Has there been something like evolution here, after all? And most of all, who has scratched the shape of the cell into the material?*

He glanced sideways. This was not the only picture. Lots of symbols covered the column. The only things he recognized were raised structures—not scratched—which resembled the two cell types. Martin's hands were trembling. *The forest is much more than a temple. It might be a cemetery, or maybe an archive. It is certainly not the result of chance. I cannot imagine that one of the two Enceladus organisms we have analyzed is responsible for it.*

Martin placed the tool on the column. The claw broke off a piece of material and swallowed it. Beneath it, another lighter-colored layer became visible. He touched the site of the fracture. *Even it is covered by inexplicable symbols. Maybe we have made a mistake.* He would take no more samples. Martin hurried back to *Valkyrie*.

Age of Questions, Triangle

There is:
The I.
The pain.
The pain of the body.
The pain of not-being.
The fear.
The pain of fear.
There is:
The not-all.
The not-all separates the all and the I.
There no longer must be:
The umbilical cord.
There no longer will be:
The umbilical cord.
The not-I.
The pain.

The Age of Questions is the Age of Struggle, of
Movement, of Time, of Curiosity, of
Experience.

December 20, 2046, Valkyrie

"MARTIN, YOU SHOULD HURRY UP." Francesca sounded calm, but there was a vibrato in her voice that scared him.

"What is going on?" he asked.

"Just get on board."

Never had he tried to dock a suit and get out of it so quickly. He was still wearing his onesie when he hurried forward. At first sight, everything appeared to be normal.

"What happened?"

"We lost the laser," Francesca said.

"What did you say?" Frantically, Martin looked around. "Everything looks normal. Neumaier to commander, come in."

The loudspeakers remained silent.

The pilot explained, "I checked everything. Nothing is going out from here. But what is worse, nothing is coming in."

"But everything looks so ..." Martin said.

"I just turned off the searchlights when you came in. So we are barely using any energy right now," Francesca said in a low voice. He saw that she clenched her fist and put it in her pocket.

"Maybe it's just that the concentrator is out of alignment? Jiaying and Hayato are probably working on it already."

"Then we should at least be able to create a connection to them, because the signal is being fed in separately. Yet everything is dead…" Her last word was deliberately slow and harsh.

Martin thought of Jiaying. *How will she react to the fact that any contact with* Valkyrie *is lost?*

He asked, "Do you have an idea…"

Francesca stood in front of Martin and placed her right hand on his shoulder.

"Martin, you know I did not want to be here," she said insistently. "I really hope this is not the end. I hope you can get us out of here. You know the technology of *Valkyrie*. I am just the pilot."

I would prefer to hear some comforting news, but she is right. Back then, when they voted, he had not been on her side. He wanted to continue the mission. If one of them was responsible for the situation they were in now, he was the one. Martin turned around and started working on the computer.

"Okay, Francesca, I checked the signal transit time. We have about six kilometers of cable hanging from the stern. Three are missing."

"The cable must have some problem inside the ice layer. Maybe it's a kink?"

"That's impossible," Martin replied. "It's frozen solid in the ice. It would take a quake to bend it. But there are no tectonic forces here."

Francesca sat down on her chair, placed her arms on the console, and put her head on them.

"And now what?"

Martin could not answer that question. *At least not yet. First I have to check all options on the computer.* "Really, Francesca, we'll manage it, you'll see."

She heard him, but she didn't answer. Not a single muscle moved in her face. He had never seen the pilot act like this. He cast his eyes downward and looked at his display. *I will find a way out. If not...* he was feeling hot and cold at the same time. *I have to.*

"We can forget about the direct way back. The battery would never be enough for drilling. But you know that better than I do." Francesca now sat in front of her display, her hands in her lap. The light in the cockpit was dim. They were saving electrical energy whenever possible.

"We just have to find a different way." Martin tried to express confidence. *But I don't sound very convincing,* he himself noticed.

"Or we stay down here, explore the ocean as much as we can, and then we die. If we are frugal, we have eight or at most nine days before we run out of energy," Francesca said grimly.

"We should be able to do something with the battery. Can we somehow send signals?" he asked.

"Maybe. If we find the end of the cable, we could use it to send signals. But even if we get our fingers on it, could we patch it?" Francesca looked at him with raised eyebrows.

"A 5 MW cable? We could never fix it with on-board tools so that it would reach its full capacity, and we need that capacity. Unfortunately, it won't be enough just to wrap duct tape around it."

"So is it even worth looking for the cable?" she asked.

Martin shrugged his shoulders. "Good question. At least we could send a farewell message."

Then silence, Martin was thinking.

Finally, he asked, "Approximately how long would it take us to reach the Tiger Stripes, Francesca?"

"Probably two or three days."

"And if we go fast?"

"Then we get there earlier, but also die faster. The battery..."

Martin interrupted her, "Sure, we cannot outrun death."

He remembered a book written long ago. He had found this 'utopian novel,' as they used to call it, on his great-grandfather's bookshelf, *A Journey to the Center of the Earth.*

"Do you know Jules Verne?" he asked.

"I am sorry, never heard of him. Who was he?"

"A French author, from the 19th century."

"So he's been dead a long time," Francesca said. "How could he help us get out of here?"

Martin explained, "In one of his books, a team of scientists enters a volcano. They discover a subterranean world, just like we did."

Francesca looked at Martin in exasperation.

"Do you know how they finally leave the volcano?" he asked. "They go through a vent." Martin answered his own question.

"Really? That's rather unrealistic," the pilot said. "You should know that, after taking all those courses in geology."

"Yes, but we have a kind of cryovolcanism here. The Tiger Stripes connect the ocean with the surface. There must be a passage somewhere, otherwise *ELF* could not have discovered signs of life," he said.

"How do you know how wide the passage is?" Francesca's expression brightened a bit, but she was still not convinced.

"You've seen the root of one of the stripes. I don't know anything more, although with smaller obstacles we could still use the drill jets. In the end, it could only be ice that's in our way," Martin said.

"And what do we do once we are on the surface? The lander can't pick us up. We were supposed to come out in its immediate vicinity."

"I guess then we have to walk," he said.

"Almost 55 kilometers across a terrain full of crevasses, craters, and canyons? How long do you think that would take?" Francesca shook her head in dismay.

"I don't think we can cover more than three kilometers per hour. The suits provide air for six hours, less in case of physical exertion. So we have to come up with an idea."

"Then get started on having ideas." Francesca laughed anxiously. Martin did not dare to get his hopes up, but for the sake of the pilot he ventured a smile.

Age of Questions, Square

There is:
The I.
The not-I.
The all.
The thoughts.
The dreams.
The joy.

There no longer is:
The umbilical cord.
The pains.
There grows:
The curiosity.
A column in the Forest of Columns.
A wave in the all.
A thought in the ice.

There will be:
The...
This...

315

December 21, 2046, Valkyrie

MARTIN WOKE UP, but he knew he was dreaming. Somebody or something had taken him by the hand, invitingly, and Martin felt an irrepressible curiosity toward life. *Am I dreaming of myself as a little kid?* He did not recognize himself. When he looked in a mirror, he saw nothing, and there were many mirrors on the walls. He walked through a narrow corridor. The mirrors were facing each other so their images created an infinite sequence. The invisible thing that accompanied him stopped now. Martin felt this through his hand. He turned around. The mirror in front of him looked like an entrance. *Just do it,* he thought, and stepped through. He looked back, but there was nothing there. Everything lay in front of him. The invisible thing danced around him. *How do I know this?* He had no idea.

They went on, because the invisible thing wanted to show him something. He stepped through one mirror after the other, and each time the world behind him dissolved. It seemed to him their path took eons and they never would reach its end. Suddenly he stood in the center, which he recognized by the fact that there was a column here. *What should I do with it?* His question remained unanswered, since he was alone once more. Two words stuck in his mind, *I* and *not-I.*

He awoke drenched in sweat. Martin pinched himself to make sure he was awake. They had wondered last night whether or not there was another way back, though the path through the Tiger Stripes seemed to be the only one —unsafe as it was. Afterward, Martin had a hard time falling asleep. The columns had kept him awake. *It is impossible that they came into being naturally.* He wondered, *Who built them, and when? Was Enceladus ever visited by an unknown intelligence?* The sample he had taken was an incredible 1.6 billion years old. *I should have picked up material from the area closer to where I entered,* he regretfully concluded. *The columns are definitely in various stages of the aging process. However, without knowing how they actually came into existence, one cannot estimate how far apart they were created, whether the outermost ones are quite recent—and that, just maybe, their builders are somewhere nearby.*

And what do the symbols mean? Martin could not remember the details, but there were the recordings taken by his helmet camera, and the resolution should be sufficient to digitalize the contents so Watson could analyze them. Learning and classifying things was the favorite activity of the AI. *Creating a translation classifier for an unknown language should be a matter of hours using sufficiently capable hardware,* Martin thought. Unfortunately, he had no access to the computer on the mothership. The on-board computers here were sufficient as a runtime environment for Watson and Siri, but they could not handle a learning mode. *One step after the other,* he thought. First, he had to let Watson analyze the video material.

"Search camera recordings from yesterday's EVA for exotic symbols," Martin ordered.

"Confirmed. Definitely identified symbols: 1,434,266. Symbols identified with less than 95% certainty: 340,778," the AI reported.

"Classify definitely identified symbols."

"Confirmed. Analysis will be finished in t plus 144 hours."

"Cancel."

That will take too long, Martin assumed. He had to set priorities, as a complete structural and semantic analysis would be impossible under these circumstances. And he needed additional computer capacity. He explained the problem to Francesca. At first, the pilot had given him a quizzical look, but he also needed her for solving the problem.

"I understand," she said, "but where are you going to get the additional hardware? I'm afraid Amazon does not make deliveries here—yet."

"We have a lot of computing power in this vehicle," he said. "It's just used for other purposes. If we can release it..."

"What exactly do you have in mind?"

"There are the analyzers in the jets, the control modules, the measuring instruments. Even the light switches could help us. And then this here." He pointed at her head.

"Me?"

"Your little gray cells—and mine."

"I'm not very good at mental arithmetic," Francesca said.

"That's what you think. But there are the neural loops in our VR helmets. The technology might not be completely tested..."

Francesca's expression showed Martin that he spoke in riddles.

"How do you steer in VR mode?" he asked.

"I... think," she replied.

Martin explained. "This also works the other way around. The method is still new, particularly as there are ethical concerns—concerns which are understandable. Forcing a brain to do certain tasks by external means?"

"And you don't have those concerns?"

"I do. But I don't want to die here. Don't you want to be able to tell the others what we've seen?" Martin didn't mention that he also was thinking about Jiaying. *It cannot be true that all these years were wasted*, he thought.

Francesca asked, "So... 'might not be completely tested...' What is that supposed to mean?"

"It is not dangerous, that is obvious. The helmets are technically locked, so they only communicate in one direction, from your brain to the jets. I think I could change that through a firmware update. The helmets still run the old Kore OS, which has a known bug that gives me root access..."

Francesca interrupted him and shook her head. "You cannot do that. The Ethics Council banned that for good reasons. If supercomputers received write access to human consciousness..."

"And even if we—you and I—turn insane afterward, would that matter? Maybe only one of us goes crazy, and the other one will be saved? Isn't that worth a try?"

"No, Martin, I'm sorry, but I will not do it."

"Okay." He clenched his fists and pressed his lips together. Then he took three deep breaths. *Maybe I have gone too far. My fellow astronaut may be right. Some red lines should not be crossed. It still seems a waste not to use the gigantic computing capacity of the human brain.*

"We can use the computers in all those devices," Francesca said. Martin nodded.

"Watson, release access to all technical devices in *Valkyrie* except for life support," Francesca directed.

"Confirmed. Analysis will be finished in t plus 96 hours."

One third faster, but still too slow, he deduced. *Should I try to hack the neuro helmet after all? Just for myself, without Francesca noticing?*

No. He had to rephrase the question. The complete analysis of all symbols could wait. If they managed to escape the ocean, they would once again have access to all the computing power on Earth. *Right now, it's not important to be able to read the entire library. We just need to find something that helps us get out of here.* Martin thought about communication. *If the beings that created the columns are still present, they might be able to help us. I have no idea how these beings will do it, or if they will actually want to.* Yet, he clung to this straw.

"Watson, how does the required time change, if we limit the analysis to ten predetermined semantic units?"

"Analysis will be partially finished in t plus 3 hours."

Martin hit the armrest of his seat with his fist. *Yes! That is something we can work with.*

"We think of a short message, let Watson translate it, and then build a column ourselves," he explained to Francesca.

"And you think that will be useful?" She seemed doubtful.

"I hope so. If the purpose of the columns is to record information, and the symbols are more than decoration—which it looks to me like they are—then they must be legible to the beings that created them. I have no idea how, but that's not important. Maybe they see in the X-ray spectrum, or have radar sensors in their head, whatever. If we place a new column with our message, we might establish a channel of communication."

"And what do you want to say to them?"

"We visually show them how we are doing and what we are planning," Martin said.

"And then?"

"No idea. If we are very lucky, they will notice our message. Imagine that an invisible alien would like to communicate with us, but it does not know how. Then the creature realizes it could paint a cross on your forehead. That would be an obvious sign, and you would pay attention. That is what I'm hoping for. If we're even luckier, they will answer us somehow."

Francesca gave him a look of mixed disbelief and anger. "This is supposed to be your solution? You hope an alien will help us, although we don't even know if it exists?"

Martin shrugged. *Yes, this is what I hope for*, he thought, but did not say anything. *I can understand that Francesca is outraged. However, she has not had the same dreams I have experienced.*

THREE HOURS LATER, Watson had finished the message. Martin was already inside the suit at the SuitPort. He separated the suit and went to a storage compartment for an empty pressure tank. Then he used a special tool, a kind of can opener, to remove its top and bottom. This made the tank look like a miniature column. He wondered where he should place the column. *Maybe in front of the other columns, at the edge of the forest? There it will be clearly visible, but it might also be ignored. Or, maybe between two columns in the first row?*

He placed the copy directly at the forefront of the forest, where two columns had a large gap between them. Then he started to scratch the symbols determined by Watson into the steel. They were not raised like the original ones, but they still had a three-dimensional structure. This work took some time. Now and then he compared the symbols with the ones shown on his arm display.

He was almost done when Francesca spoke to him via helmet radio.

"Ahem, Martin," she said. "Take a look behind you. You notice something?"

He turned around, but did not notice anything besides the column that had already been there earlier.

"Below, look below."

The helmet had a limited field of view. He had to lower his head to look at the ground. Directly ahead of him, maybe twenty centimeters from his boots, a new column was growing.

"It wasn't there earlier, was it?" Martin started to sweat.

"I compared the area with yesterday's images," Francesca said. "Back then, the ground was completely smooth."

He bent down and touched the stump that reached the height of his ankles. There were raised structures, so the same process seemed to be responsible for both the growth and the inscriptions of the column. *Is this even possible through a natural process? What have we found here?* He licked his lips.

Francesca asked, "Could you take a sample when you are finished?"

"Okay. I will be back inside in ten minutes. Neumaier, out."

Ten minutes were not enough, and getting out of the suit took additional time. Francesca waited for him, picked up the sample container via a separate mini-port, and started the analysis.

"Take your time. I'll have the results waiting for you."

Martin felt like a kid at Christmas waiting for his presents. He was so excited his bladder hurt. What would the monitor show them? How soon? He noticed Francesca's cheeks were flushed.

"Watson, display analysis of sample," she commanded.

The main display revealed a landscape populated by two different kinds of single-cell organisms. This was at the bottom of the sample container under high magnification. The creatures moved through the water by rhythmically changing the shape of their cellular walls. When Martin took the sample, he must have also picked up some inorganic material. The single-celled organisms moved to the tiny clump and remained there. Then they approached the center, where they paused again. They emitted a minuscule quantity of some material, the composition of which Watson had not yet analyzed.

Martin noticed his hair stood on end. *We are watching the metabolism of an alien form of life*. Yet it was much more than that—the single-cell organisms, even though they were of different types, were working together, like ants. They all cooperated to build a miniature version of a column in the center of the sample container.

Age of Questions, Pentahedron

There is:
The I.
The not-I.
The not-I.
(Pause)
The not-I's.

The all.
The not-all.

A reader.
A reader of the I.
A story.
A story of the not-I.
The Mar-Tin.

The questions.
The intentions.
The feelings.
The discrepancy.

The curiosity.
The curiosity.
The curiosity.

There is not:
The I's.

There will be:
Dreams.
Change.
Adaptation.
Expansion.

December 22, 2046, Valkyrie

THEY HAD enough oxygen to last for another six or seven days. Martin tried not to imagine what problems still lay ahead of them. On paper, the plan looked like this: three or four days' journey to the Tiger Stripes, one day for surfacing, half a day's march to the lander, and one day in reserve. They would never again see the Forest of Columns. Martin hoped they had initiated something that would help them—*even if it is just an entry in the archive of a strange being.* They had watched these exo-creatures in the container until they died from lack of energy supply. *This is a perfect example of symbiosis, maybe of a symbiosis with a hidden goal. Ants also seamlessly work together in a colony, but they just fulfill a purpose, the survival of the colony—they don't have an intention. The task fulfilled by the single-celled organisms is not purposeful because it does not help them survive. Therefore,* Martin thought, *it must be intentional.* Francesca agreed on that point. It had an intention that somebody or something had formulated, had come up with.

How many such single-cell organisms might there be in the Enceladus Ocean? wondered Martin. The layer on the seabed was only a few millimeters thick, but it must contain at least 100 million single-celled creatures per square centimeter, according to their analysis. *If one assumed an area of 100 by 100 kilometers, this would mean 10 to the power of 22, or 10,000 billion billion cells. What did my old biology professor say? A human being consists of 100 trillion cells.* The Enceladus Ocean therefore contained as many cells as 100 million humans.

What if all these single-cell creatures cooperate in a giant organism? What if my idea of the aliens that created the Forest of Columns is totally wrong? What if—like in humans—only one in a thousand of these primitive cells are involved in thinking functions? This being would have the mental capacity of 100 million humans.

It would be a super-being of enormous intelligence. *What would it be like?* Martin tried to imagine it but failed. *Could the being he imagined not also be particularly cruel? An immensely smart creature limited to the area of the Enceladus Ocean and having no counterpart... What kind of morals would it develop? Would it even need morals, if it was all alone in its world, the undisputed ruler? Did it have values, was it curious, and how would it react if, in all its omnipotence, it suddenly met others?*

These ideas discouraged him. *Compared to this being, if it exists, we are nothing more than a fleeting disturbance. Maybe it does not even notice us. If it has existed for millions or billions of years, it will not think in terms of days. On the other hand, what is the new column but a form of reaction?*

He sighed. His musings contained too much speculation and imagination. He did not know anything about the physiology of such a super-being. *The signal exchange between cells will use chemical-electrical means, as in the animals on Earth, though few there are more than two meters long. This being, though, must synchronize cells that are up to a hundred kilometers apart. Even if it is as clever as ten million humans, it must be thinking correspondingly slower.*

And how can it act? Is it capable of influencing its environment? Is it to blame for the broken optical cable, which had lasted so long?

Martin shook his head again and again. *If we had an unlimited amount of time, we might be able to establish contact by means of the columns. If they can decipher the symbols, we will have a common language.*

Lots of 'ifs.' And Martin and Francesca did not have enough time. They would most probably suffocate in a few days. *Searching for a way out through the Stripes is probably a crazy idea.* There, the water was ejected with enormous velocity. Down here, though, hardly any current could be measured. This meant there must be a kind of nozzle in one location, or several that accelerated the water coming out. He should have Watson calculate just how wide the gap probably was. *Is it ten centimeters? Or even twenty? It definitely will not be enough for* Valkyrie *to fit through.* He had unnecessarily put a bug in Francesca's ear, even though he should have known better. *It would be better if we concentrated on how to make our farewells as dignified as possible.*

It was early afternoon. The jets were creating a deep hum. Francesca had aimed the bow of *Valkyrie* 20 degrees upward. The vehicle was on course for the Tiger Stripes. He yawned.

"Take a nap. I am still fit," Francesca said. *She is right. I can ask Watson later to develop a model of the geyser.*

ONCE AGAIN, Martin woke up shortly after lying down, even though he knew he was dreaming. He sat on his bed. The vehicle was empty, except for himself, his bed, and the control console, where Francesca sat looking forward. The walls were no longer covered in panels. All equipment was gone, including any technical apparatus. He was barefoot. He carefully climbed off his bed. His naked feet moved across bare steel panels.

"Francesca," he called, but the pilot did not react. He touched her shoulder and turned her seat around. Martin abruptly jerked back and gasped. He only saw Francesca's clothing. *Her body is... gone, no, it has been replaced by many small single-cell organisms, protozoa.* He recognized this living mass on her cheeks, her forehead, and her chin. She opened her eyes, but her eyeballs were also made up of a mass of tiny cells that were constantly changing. She held out her hand, but he did not shake it because he knew it consisted of protozoa.

"Phew," he said. There was no answer, not even an echo. He knew all of this was just a product of his imagination, yet he could not get out of it.

"I," said Francesca, who no longer was Francesca, pointing at herself.

"Not-I." She pointed at him.

"You," he corrected her.

"You," was the answer.

Francesca's eyes were big, much bigger than usual, as if she had to record everything she saw.

"Not-all." She started to walk around in the vehicle and randomly pointed at things. "Not-all."

"I," she said again. "All."

"How can I help you?" Martin asked. Francesca looked at him without comprehension.

"How can I help you?" she repeated.

"Yes, help. I help you, you help me." He had once heard that language was not easier to comprehend if you simplified it. He tried it nevertheless. "I help you. You help I."

He had not had such a lucid dream in a long time. *Can one go insane in a dream?* Francesca turned around again and bent over her console. She randomly touched letters, but without a plan.

"It doesn't work like this," he said, and first typed in Francesca's password, which was "Marchenko." *Well, if the administrator only knew. This is extremely careless,* Martin thought. Francesca gazed curiously at the screen. Martin displayed landscapes there, photos of Earth, of Mars, of Saturn. It was bizarre. He was in a dream, but fully conscious, and he was showing pictures, like family snap-shots, to a dream figure. He also pulled up the latest research, presented drawings of the two types of cells and their still mysterious organelles, diagrams of the ice moons, the geysers, and the ocean. Finally, he opened one of Francesca's hidden folders and found a poem from a collection by Rilke.

His gaze from passing metal bars
has grown so weary that it cannot hold.
To him there seem to be a thousand bars
and yet behind those bars no world.

This soft and supple step and sturdy pace,
that in a tiny circle turns,
is like a dance of strength around a place,
in which a mighty will is stunned.

Only at times the pupil's curtain slides
and opens quietly— An image enters it,
through the tense stillness of the limbs it
    glides—
and in the heart ceases to be.

The false Francesca moved her lips, as if she was reading each word aloud. She opened the next file, another poem. Her fingers moved downward on the cursor keys. One poem after the other briefly appeared on the monitor, and then was already overwritten by the next. Francesca smiled, and even in this smile he could see the protozoa that formed her lips.

MARTIN WOKE up startled and drenched in sweat. *That dream was so crazy, but also so realistic I have to tell Francesca about it right away.*

"Those terms..." she said afterward, "did you hear those for the first time?"

"Yes. No. Yesterday, in a different dream," he said.

"So? I often invent something in a dream."

"These are so... different. They do not belong to our world, and we do not belong in this one."

Francesca nodded. "And if they... want to communicate?"

"Not they. It." He explained to Francesca what he had concluded. "But telepathy, no, that doesn't exist. That's what you are alluding to, isn't it? That is New Age nonsense."

"No, not telepathy, this helmet here," she said, pointing at the neuro helmet, "this is no pseudo-scientific claptrap."

Martin nodded.

"And if this existed at some larger scale? What would be necessary for it?" she asked.

Martin was thinking, and then he approached the AI.

"Watson, I need a profile from the South Pole and 50 kilometers northward, up to a depth of 20 kilometers.

Temperature, pressure, all measured or probable phases. Where data is missing, try to measure again as well as you can."

It took the AI 42 minutes. A diagram of their surroundings with many colorfully shaded areas slowly appeared. After a quarter of an hour, Martin noticed something.

"Take a look at this." He pointed at the upper part of the ice layer. "Here we have normal ice. Ice Ih, with a Roman numeral one, and the 'h' stands for hexagonal. Each water molecule connects to four others. The result is a tetrahedron, like a shape made up of triangles. Most of the ice on Earth is frozen in this phase."

The middle part of the ice layer, which was relatively narrow, had different shading. "This is exciting," Martin said. "I didn't pay attention to that during our descent. Here we have a layer of Ice XI. It develops at low temperatures and high pressure. It's not that rare, and has been found while drilling in the Antarctic. Ice XI has one special feature—it is ferroelectrical."

Martin zoomed in on this area a bit.

"You can do a lot with ferroelectrical materials. You can think of them as permanent magnets, though they produce an electrical rather than a magnetic field. Or they amplify it."

He pointed at the neuro helmet.

"This material even possesses a memory. It is pyro- and piezo-electric. This means you can create an electrical field through heat or pressure, or use an electrical field to create heat or pressure, which means generating mechanical work. Imagine that you are superhumanly clever and you have had this tool right in front of you for millions of years. Would you have learned to use it?"

Francesca scratched her ear. "You can bet on it."

"Our fiber-optic cable ran directly through that area."

Martin zoomed closer, so that the position of the cable became visible.

"You see, even if the ice layer is moved only slightly sideways, our cable will break."

"A lot of evidence, I would say," Francesca commented.

"But no final proof, that's true. It doesn't matter, though. I think another question is much more important. What does it want from us? Maybe, more poems by Rilke?"

Francesca looked at him with flashing eyes. "Wrong," she said. "The crucial question is still, 'How do we get back home?'"

Age of Questions, Hexahedron

There is:
The knowing and the not-knowing, in continuous
*   increments.*
The not-I, a geometric representation of the I. A
*   translation and distortion in several dimensions,*
*   yet still related.*
The joy of exchange, of knowledge, new knowledge
*   that no age has brought forth until now.*
The hope of finding the meaning of the all.
The understanding. They call themselves human,
*   and they recognized the I.*
The I that watched the not-all.
The knowledge of solitude, which until now had
*   been impossible.*
Thousands of new words and concepts that fill
*   memory assumed to be empty, as it is highly*
*   compressed.*
The desire to take and to give.
There no longer is:

Standstill.
Solitude.
Boredom.
There no longer will be:
The wrong concepts.

December 23, 2046, Valkyrie

THIS WAS the first night he did not shut an eye. Normally, Martin always managed to sleep, even if he knew he might die the next day. Yet when they needed him to go to sleep, it did not work. He had tried last night, again and again. He had attempted to fall asleep by not trying to, but his mind could not be tricked that easily. *I have to talk to Francesca—maybe she has an idea. Will you still dream if you are knocked unconscious?* Martin did not really want to sleep. *I hope I can continue the conversation with the I. Of course, this could all be a trick played by my overwrought imagination, after all the stress. Watson had calculated a 20 percent probability for this explanation. Yet, I will at least have the feeling I can do something.*

Tomorrow they would reach the first Tiger Stripe. With some luck they would be in the spaceship by Christmas Eve, or close to it. True, their chances were extremely low. Martin had not even started to work out a solution for a forced march across the ice without enough oxygen. *Maybe I should start focusing on that, instead of waiting for a dream?*

He turned over on his left side, and then on his right,

trying to find the most comfortable position, but his mind was already wandering. *Why do we have to fail here, after all the stress and boredom of the last twelve months? We could have just surrendered to the coldness of space, back then when the DFDs wouldn't start up. On the other hand, Jiaying would not have survived then. This way, at least she will make it home.*

The others would wait for a while, even search for them, though he could not imagine how. Yet when it became obvious *Valkyrie* had run out of oxygen, they would have to accept the sad truth. Mission Control would order them to start the return journey. *Jiaying will protest—at least I hope so—but will have to give in. And she will get over it. She is young, and she will be much admired on Earth, even if the mission is not a total success.* Maybe NASA would build a monument for Martin, or somebody would set up a scientific award named after him. He was worried about his mother. *She has always insisted she would die before me.* Once his father, an American radio astronomer, had left her, she began thinking about death. *Will she forgive me for leaving before her? Or will she prefer to believe I am alive, as long as my corpse has not yet been found?*

That would never happen, though. The most important questions posed by the scientists back on Earth had been answered. There was primitive life on Enceladus, as everyone had assumed. It made no sense to spend a lot of money again in order to send a second mission, which would be just as risky. *Maybe in 200 years,* Martin thought, *when technology is much more advanced. After all, there are much more exciting destinations.* Enceladus is too inhospitable for humans. Titan, on the other hand, with its dense atmosphere and the extensive oceans of liquid methane, might at some time become a commercially viable target. Corporations could exploit its resources, while athletic tourists would be able to fly like birds through its dense atmosphere, using their own wings.

Valkyrie, with the corpses of Francesca Rossi and Martin Neumaier, would rest at the bottom of the dark ocean forever. Over time, the alkaline liquid would attack the steel hull, slowly, but surely—not in ten years, but in a thousand or ten thousand. *In a million years researchers will be surprised at the high content of vanadium and chromium in the water. Will the ocean floor still be alive then?* His thoughts faded.

"I. All. Eternally there," a voice said in his head. He had finally succeeded in falling asleep. Martin looked around. Everything looked like it had before. On Francesca's control panel, a blue light was blinking in a soothing rhythm.

"Understanding. Curiosity." There was no voice. He had been wrong. These were thoughts that inflated and deflated, and then once more formed an oval cloud. They were alien to his head, like Chinese characters, yet they were universal enough for him to understand them.

He closed his eyes so that he could concentrate on the concepts. Yet he could not grasp them, and the more he focused his own thoughts, the more quickly they evaded him. Then Martin understood. *I have to release them, give them space in my brain*. The neurons that embodied these concepts had been activated by an external field. If he tried to track them with his own thoughts, his electrical signals overwrote the external input.

Martin sank into himself. This gave the alien's thoughts the space they needed. They stabilized. They floated through the mindscape like *Valkyrie* through the Enceladus Ocean.

"Is that. Not-I. Question."

He imagined the drill vehicle larger, as if he was

creating a painting on an easel, and mentally went through the various sections and activated the jets.

"I. Not-I. Not-I. Two. Question."

Martin looked at his left hand, made a fist, and raised it. Then he first showed his thumb, very slowly, then his index finger, and then his middle finger.

"Three," he said, because he knew he could only pronounce what he had thought before.

"Three." The alien thought displayed a jumble of various dream images, of mirrors, columns, and cells. It counted three of each.

"Three. Three. Question."

Martin wondered, *What does this being want to know? How much is three times three? No, it probably knows that. It has just learned a concept that has been unknown to it during its entire existence. This must be a profound shock.* Mankind had reacted euphorically to the mere discovery of extraterrestrial life. This being had just discovered the Other.

Martin imagined strolling through the streets of his hometown. He met people he knew and greeted, while he simply walked past others. A bicyclist came toward him, riding on the wrong side.

"Three. Three. Three. Three." Numerous identical, turquoise-colored clouds drifted across the scenery.

"Many," Martin said. The four clouds expanded, became a fog covering everything, and then they burst. He felt the shockwave in his head.

A small child came running up to him. This was Martin himself. His prior self cried and called for his mom. The being had found one of his memories and brought it up. *Does it want to say something to it?* He felt the pain of the little boy who had skinned his knee.

"Pain. Sadness." The being was correct. *Who felt pain?*

The answer was the image of a cell. It seemed to have been taken in all wavelengths at once. None of their devices could do that. The cell walls dissolved. The entire cell died in front of his eyes.

We have caused this being pain by using our tools and measuring devices. Martin was shocked. He and Francesca could not have known that.

"*Sadness.*" There was no accusation in this word, only confirmation and a statement. The past was gone.

Suddenly Francesca stood next to him. Martin was confused, until he realized he was only looking at a memory. He explained the structure of the middle ice layer to her. Yet the image was not synchronized with the sound. Instead of zooming in, the ice changed and started to move. Two ice layers, each several meters thick, moved a short distance in opposite directions. The fiber-optic cable supplying energy to *Valkyrie* was cut quickly and efficiently. A repair was impossible, as this happened in the middle of the ice.

"*Sadness. Pain.*" Martin thought, *is this a kind of excuse? That would be impressive, as it suggests a kind of empathy. How could this being have learned empathy, if it has never had a chance to do so since its birth? It either is incredibly flexible—or empathy is inextricably linked with intelligence.* That was a beautiful thought, one that would make dying easier for Martin.

"*There is not. Not-always. Question.*" Yes, human existence was limited. *This must be terrifying to a being without a defined lifespan,* Martin theorized. *The 100 years a human might have, what is that in comparison to an eternity?*

"*There is not. Not-I. Two. Question*" Martin had been wrong. *It had not asked about the general human lifespan, but about my own. Does it suspect the answer?* Earlier on, he had imagined what their fate would be. Therefore, he did not have to recall the images of their impending death.

No new thought appeared, but the pressure in his head decreased. *Maybe the being now activates the larger part of my neural activity.* He imagined how electrical impulses raced across the ocean floor, how billions of cells turned into a cooperative, thinking organ that was much more powerful than any supercomputer on Earth. *How much could be achieved if mankind could cooperate with this being! Problems that baffle the smartest physicist might be solved in a short time by this being. Science would take an enormous leap forward.*

A Lot of 'if's. The fact was that nothing of this would or could ever happen. In his head he once again saw *Valkyrie* being slowly corroded by the ocean.

"Not-I. I. One."

The image of the vehicle changed without Martin doing anything. It was shiny again, even though it was in utter darkness. Starting at the ocean floor, a swirling layer of protozoa covered *Valkyrie*. The image was displayed in a strange scale. Martin could perceive the tiny cells, and he simultaneously saw a complete image of the vehicle. Its walls dissolved, the equipment disappeared, and the cell started to wrap the bodies of the two astronauts in a kind of cocoon.

Martin had to laugh. *This is a nice offer, which comforts me, but the biochemistry of my own cells is too different to be integrated into this being.* His neurons were inadequate. It took only three minutes for them to cease all their activities, and the residual voltage of his memories would fade soon after that. *Our thoughts, our knowledge—all that will turn into nothingness if we do not make it back to the surface,* he realized.

"There will be. Not-I."

Two HOURS LATER, Martin opened his eyes. His heart was racing, and he was scared. *I hope that was no dream*, he thought, and then he was relieved that he could remember every little detail. *Should I tell Francesca what I experienced? What had it actually been—a conversation, true communication? Or have I only misinterpreted it based on my own hopes?*

He was no good as a storyteller, as he could see from Francesca's face when he reported this to her. He had a hard time finding adequate words for the images appearing in his mind. Yet Francesca's skeptical, slightly bored look soon turned to definite fascination. She stopped drumming her fingers on the desk. She made him repeat what the being had said—and developed her own interpretations.

"That was an invitation for us," she finally said. "The being believes it can integrate our consciousness into its own. That is... overwhelming. Imagine if we could profit from millions of years of experience. Maybe this being has already figured out all the laws of nature? It certainly had the time and the capability for it. Consider how young humanity is compared to it."

"Do you think this is more than just an idea?" Martin asked. "This being does not know the chemistry of our brains at all. It has been alone for millions of years. What if it only wants us to stay?"

"Maybe we should give it a try," Francesca answered.

"I can't believe you are serious about this. Do you suddenly no longer want to go back home again?"

The pilot lowered her eyes. "I... know. This is probably not more than wishful thinking. It just seems to me our chance of making it through the ice is much lower than the probability of this dream becoming reality."

Age of Questions, Heptahedron

There is:
The I.
The not-I.
The fear.
The loss. The I must not let the not-I leave.
The worry.
The numbers. The existence of many.
The others.
The curiosity.
The limitless knowledge.
The exploration of the not-all.
There will be:
The not-I.

There must be:
The not-I.

December 24, 2046, Valkyrie

THE ABYSS YAWNED ABOVE THEM. Francesca had prepared
Valkyrie. They could have cruised below the ice for another
two days, pretending to be normal researchers for twice 24
hours, but that would have just delayed the decision. They
wanted to finish their ascent now.

*Today, on Christmas Eve, there are people who believe a savior
was born 2046 years ago.* Martin saw no one who would save
them, even if he hoped for it. *We will do what humans always
do when things get rough. We will try to survive, even though Watson
calculated our chance as below one in five.*

Francesca appeared calm, at least externally. During
the night he had heard her sob, but he had no idea how he
could comfort her. *I should try to reassure her, though I would
rather have someone else to tell me everything will be all right.*

THEY WERE BACK at a location where they had been several
days earlier. If *Valkyrie* aimed its searchlights upward they
would see a cathedral of ice with black sediments on the

347

inside of the cupola, as if made by centuries of rising incense.

The instruments registered a slight current. The water, having absorbed heat from the rocks at the ocean floor, moved upward. The path to the surface became narrower and narrower, increasing the pressure with which the water rushed toward the outside.

They had not yet reached that spot, though. They had a long discussion about what would follow. Martin concluded, *She is a good pilot, but she is not able to react as quickly as the AI can. Maybe she is better at evaluating tricky situations.* They finally agreed: Francesca would put *Valkyrie* in position, then Watson would steer it. The main task consisted of rising through a system of interconnected passages without crashing the vehicle into the ice, which was hard as steel, and without maneuvering it into a position with no way out.

Valkyrie was a drill that could swim, not a submarine that could drill. It was optimized for finding the direct path through the ice by using its hot water jets. A real submarine could be controlled more quickly and precisely.

Martin expected two kinds of obstacles. *For one thing, the path ahead of us might suddenly end, because ice masses have shifted. Then we will have to reverse and search for a different path. Much more likely, though, the passage may become too narrow for* Valkyrie. Water always found a way, but they would need at least three meters in all directions. *If the laser link still worked, this would have posed no problem.* However, they only had the remainder of their energy in the batteries. Even though they had used it frugally, it would only be enough to melt a few meters of ice. Exactly how many meters depended upon the temperature of the ice—which decreased toward the surface—among other things. The higher up they climbed, the more difficult it would get.

Francesca stood in front of her console and tried to concentrate. It seemed difficult for her to give the start command. If they got stuck in the ice, all hope was lost.

"It's no good, thinking too much," he said with a sigh. Francesca nodded.

"Watson, begin ascent."

The jets started up. The vehicle lifted its nose and aimed for the darkness. Watson used all of *Valkyrie's* sensors to find the right way. With radar and lidar the AI could see a bit into the future, and at least guess what awaited them beyond the next curves.

Martin watched the surroundings on the display. The channel in which they were ascending would have been wide enough for the mothership. Yet after about 450 meters it ended in a vent that looked like a chimney. The water rushed through it in a fast current. Watson agreed to this course. The vent was narrow, but not too tight. On the monitor, *Valkyrie* was moving at breakneck speed through the narrow passage in the ice, and the water current gave it more speed than the jets.

The vent ended after another 275 meters in a large cavity, a bubble in the ice. The vehicle slowed down.

"A short break?" Martin wondered.

"Why not," Francesca said. She deactivated the jets. *Valkyrie* now hovered in complete darkness.

Martin turned on the searchlights. Francesca cast him a questioning look.

"Doesn't really matter now," he said. "It will be over soon enough."

The screen showed the cave in true colors. Martin was amazed, as the floor glittered and sparkled as if they had found Aladdin's cave. *I cannot help but admire its beauty, even though I might not survive the day.* The suspended particles, which the water had quickly dissolved from the ice and carried along, had lost their impetus here and collected at the bottom. Due to the difference in concentration, they had crystallized. The crystals must have grown over millennia.

"It's like a fairy tale," Francesca called out. She pointed at several blue, shimmering structures that looked like starfish. "Look!" she said, "and back there. The rainbow colors on the wall—all of that was created only for us!"

She is right, Martin thought. *No one before us has ever seen this beauty. And it is very unlikely someone will ever come after us.*

"If a mining company on Earth only saw this," he said. "Those must be extremely pure substances. And this is probably not the only cavity here."

Francesca nodded. "Oh yes. Watson, delete the recording for the last three minutes. Authorization granted."

"Deletion not possible. Authorization level too low."

"We are offline. A higher authorization is not possible," she said.

"Deletion not possible. Authorization level too low," the AI repeated.

"Encode recordings made during the last three minutes with my personal password."

"Confirmed."

"Watson, continue ascent."

AFTER TWO HOURS they had covered at least half of the way. According to Watson, their chance of survival now reached 22 percent. *This is barely enough to be hopeful, but the trend is in the right direction*, Martin thought. In between, they had to turn back seven times, or rather, reverse out of a parking space. Going backward, *Valkyrie* moved much more slowly.

"Review required."

This is what Watson said when he needed them to make a decision. *If the AI does not know what to do, we have a problem*. Martin knew this was the moment he had been expecting. He stayed strangely calm, maybe because he had visualized the situation often enough.

They discovered the dilemma on the screen. Above them, the channel narrowed from about 90 meters to a diameter of only a meter. Then it widened again to about six meters, but between those spots there was about 45 meters of ice, which they could not overcome with their available reserves.

"Watson, alternatives?" Martin asked.

"Tiger Stripe about 15 kilometers from here."

On the way, the AI had already tried out all branchings, but they had often reached dead ends. The Tiger Stripe they had chosen now did not offer a way out. They could dive back down and try the next one. They had enough time, but once they reached the surface, they would be about twice as far away from the lander. They would never manage to walk for twelve hours in their suits.

"Should we try to get up there and then hope for a miracle?" Francesca looked at Martin. Her face made it obvious she did not believe in miracles. *I don't think much about them, either.* Nevertheless, he nodded.

"Watson, two jets for propulsion, all other ones for melting," Martin ordered.

He heard a rumbling sound. The jets had to turn 180

degrees. *Valkyrie* moved slowly upward. On the screen they did not see the work of the jets, only its result—the ice channel widened, just enough for the vehicle to fit through. It worked, but only for a few seconds.

"Battery at minimum level for ascent. Please recharge," Watson said.

"Great advice, you stupid AI." Francesca banged her fist against the desk. Soon afterward, a loud sound hit the vehicle like a gong. *Valkyrie* had hit the dome of the vent.

Martin said, "Watson, stabilize."

"Not enough energy."

The numbers were going haywire on the display. The flow rate of the water had tripled. The jets could not do anything about it. *What is going on?* Martin turned to the AI.

"Watson, explanation?"

"Insufficient data."

What they saw was literally impossible—except that it was happening. The activity of the geysers followed a certain rhythm. They decreased when Enceladus was far away from Saturn, and increased when the moon once again approached the planet. *Yet such a dramatic change in a short time cannot be related to the orbit, unless it is being affected by some cosmic force.* Martin could not believe it.

"Totally impossible," he said, shaking his head. He then thought about the being that inhabited the ocean. *Is it trying to help us this way? Does it have the power to do so? It is a fascinating idea, though it does not help us. Obviously, the being has misunderstood the concept behind* Valkyrie. *We cannot ram through the ice like in a tank. We need energy, not speed.*

Wait a moment. Speed is energy.

"Francesca, I have an idea," Martin said. He could no longer sit still. He heard a harsh noise, as the hull was obviously scraping against the ice.

"Watson, can we use the jets as generators?" he asked.

"Correct. During drilling mode the jets partially work that way."

"Will that work with cold water, too?"

"Correct."

"Calculate energy generation based on current flow rate."

"900 kilowatts."

Martin's idea was simple. *Instead of using battery energy to drive the rotors that move the water, we will use the high-pressure water to create electricity in the jets, like in a hydro-electric power plant.* Francesca was already at her console and had started to reconfigure the drill jets. They didn't even have to turn them for this purpose, but simply use the rotors in free-wheeling mode. The water that streamed through them from below made them move like millwheels in a river. That allowed them to recharge the main battery. And once it was charged, they could melt away a few meters of ice.

"Watson, calculate process cycle and duration," Martin said.

"Projection unreliable. Expecting twelve cycles. Bottle-neck can be traversed within seven hours," the AI reported.

"Wow!" Francesca jumped up and hugged Martin. "You... genius!"

He blushed. "No, this only works due to the elevated pressure. Otherwise recharging would take much too long."

"Then let's hope this won't change," she said.

"We better not wait too long."

Watson was responsible for implementing the cycle: collect energy, clear the passage; collect energy, clear the passage. They were moving ahead, though not quite as fast as expected. *Switching from generator to drill and motor takes some time. We did not consider the inertia of the moving parts.* Martin clenched his fists. He hoped the pressure would not fall back to normal. *From space Enceladus must now present an impressive spectacle—the geysers have never shot up into the sky below Saturn so forcefully.*

Martin sat down and then got up again. He could not bear to watch the events on the display. There, *Valkyrie* seemed so tiny, a blinking dot in the seemingly impermeable ice crust of Enceladus. The obstacle in front of them appeared to be so small. On the screen, it was only two or three millimeters wide, but these few pixels would mean the difference between life and death.

He had an idea as to why the water pressure had increased so much. It was not actually a speculation, but more of a wish. *Maybe the being uses the piezoelectric properties of the Ice XI layer to move it forcefully far below us, like pressing a pestle into a mortar. Should I ask Watson to look for signs of this? A brief look backward, like in the biblical story of Sodom and Gomorrah?* No, he would not do that. Knowing the cause did not change its effect. If there was a natural reason, the scientists on Earth would figure it out. And if Watson looked back instead of forward, even for a moment, they ran the risk of overlooking something important in their direction of travel.

The last cycle started, and the battery was already recharging. 85, 90, 95, 100 percent.

"Just a moment, Watson," Martin said thoughtfully. *Will we still have sufficient energy for the remaining ascent? We will not be able to 'fill up' again this way because the rising water will simply carry us along.*

"Remaining energy after drill activity?" Martin asked.

"40 percent. Sufficient for ascent."

"Ha, did you hear that?" Francesca's voice held a note of triumph.

He smiled at her. "Watson, continue."

For the last time, the jets changed from generator to a motor that shot heated water at the ice mass above them. *Valkyrie* moved ahead, meter by meter.

"Breakthrough," Francesca called out, beaming. Martin rejoiced, too, in his quiet way. Now Watson placed their survival chance at 45 percent.

A few hours later, the AI raised the value to 50 percent, though with a high uncertainty factor. On the way, the water pressure had normalized, and now was even slightly below normal.

They were 50 meters below the surface when they established contact with the mothership. Marchenko greeted them exuberantly and immediately woke the commander. A direct connection to the lander was not possible, so the mothership was needed as a relay station. Martin finally could talk to Jiaying again. When he saw her image she smiled, though he could tell she had been crying.

"It wasn't... a very good time," she said, "but even less so for the two of you. We will talk about everything once we're all on board."

On board, yes. Martin was glad Earth would not hear about their fate for several hours. He had almost used the term 'rescue,' but it was too early for that. They still had to march across treacherous terrain, and they did not have enough oxygen. Yet they had already cheated death once. Martin could not avoid a warm feeling of hope spreading in his mind. Francesca seemed to feel the same way, as she started to whistle a tune that sounded like a children's song.

Valkyrie was now bobbing up and down in a narrow,

deep black pond. The gap here was too wide to eject the water under pressure as a geyser. It would have frozen over long ago if the little vehicle was not constantly heating the water. It would be able to do that for another 40 minutes, Watson had calculated. In the background, the AI was transmitting all the data to the mothership. Mission Control would be amazed.

Before the 40 minutes ran out, Francesca and Martin would have to leave their vehicle. Then *Valkyrie* would freeze into the ice. A million years from now, a thick layer of snow would cover it so no one would be able to recognize it.

It was time for them to get into their suits. The panel on the arm of the suit would show them the way. On the mothership, the commander and Marchenko had calculated an optimal route. The spaceship no longer had to be located above the laser concentrator. In the meantime, they were told, it had created high-resolution maps of all of Enceladus in hopes of finding a trace of them. Position finding had shown they were exactly 48.7 kilometers away from the lander module.

Their path would avoid the most dangerous spots. Yet even if everything went perfectly, it would take longer than their oxygen supplies permitted. There were some extra tanks in the vehicle, but they could not put them inside their suits, and after exiting they would not be able to reach them anymore. *I feel like a condemned man who knows the message pardoning him will only arrive after his execution*, Martin thought.

Hayato had suggested the crew of the lander move toward them carrying fresh oxygen. *Ultimately, we have generated enough supplies for the entire trip back*, Martin calculated. *It's a nice gesture, but it will not save us. It will be at least eight hours before we can meet halfway. Too late—then Hayato and Jiaying will have to carry our corpses home.*

Martin shook his head. *It is true. Objectively, we stand no chance.* Yet he, and it seemed Francesca, too, had no doubt. They would try anyway.

Age of Questions, Octahedron

There is:
The I.
The not-I.
The joy.
The farewell.
The time. The small time. The big time.
The power to change the all.
The curiosity about the not-all.
The thinking.
The beauty of thoughts, of concepts, of terms, of
*   words.*
The desire to create a poem of thoughts.

There will be:
A poem that permeates existence and is permeated by
*   existence.*

December 25, 2046, Enceladus

FRANCESCA TURNED OFF THE LIGHT. She wanted to be the last person to leave the vehicle. Martin was already standing in front of the SuitPort when he remembered something.

"Just a moment, Francesca."

He rummaged through the drawers at the rear wall of the cabin. He found everything he needed—a pressure hose, and the injector filled with an anesthetic for emergency operations. Francesca looked at him but did not question him.

"Just in case," he said. Francesca nodded. *Does she see through my plan?* Then he slipped into the suit that might become his coffin. Martin examined his feelings, searched for the panic that should rise now, but all he felt was the coldness of the vacuum that had threatened him since the start of the mission. *I am probably so calm because I have allowed for such an ending for such a long time.*

He separated from the SuitPort and slid into the water. The stern of *Valkyrie* was only about two meters away from the icy shore. His heart was beating faster. *Why am I sinking so low? Shouldn't the buoyancy be much stronger than the limited weight of my suit? Nonsense.* He wanted to slap his hand against his forehead. *The weight of the displaced water is minimal. However, the spacesuit contains just enough air to make it float.* He paddled to the edge of the hole in the ice. The surface was about a meter above him. He had to pull himself up— *on Earth, this would be impossible in this heavy suit, but here it's child's play.*

Martin looked around. Saturn showed them the way. The planet hung over the eastern horizon, as if had been nailed there. Their way led them south-southeast. Martin discovered the first obstacle about 450 meters away. He checked the map on his arm display. *The distance is exactly 400 meters, less than half a kilometer.* The extreme curvature of the moon made it hard to estimate things like that.

He heard Francesca's breathing via his helmet radio. Martin turned toward her.

"Pilot disembarking," she said, saluting with her right hand. It was eerie. There was no sound when she jumped into the water. She paddled soundlessly through the black, salty pond. Then she stood next to him.

"Let's go," she said as she placed a hand on his shoulder. "We are going to make it." Martin nodded, even though he knew better, and he also knew she was aware of it. *I will only give up once my legs can no longer carry me.*

"Commander to ground team. Best of luck! We are keeping an eye on you."

Martin raised his head to the sky and tried to detect the spaceship that floated a few kilometers above them. He did not see anything. They were alone.

In front of the first major obstacle they linked their spacesuits with a safety line. The radar had detected several deep fissures. Climbing was surprisingly easy due to the low gravity. If the situation had not been so dire, it would have been great fun to be able to jump so far and so high. When the cliffs were higher than ten meters, though, they had no choice but to find a way around them. During mission planning, no one seemed to have considered mountaineering. These detours were not strenuous, but they took time.

After an hour, Martin first checked his oxygen supply and was shocked. *I have a capacity of four hours and forty minutes left.* They had used up a third more than planned. The display showed the distance to their goal as 44.1 kilometers. If they continued this way, their oxygen would be used up well before the half-way mark.

Martin stopped. "Francesca, can this be true?" He pointed at his display. Francesca checked the numbers and compared them to her own.

"This seems to be more exhausting than it feels," she said. "Maybe it's the adrenaline driving us."

"What should we do?" he asked.

Francesca shook her head. "Nothing. We can't change that."

"And if we carry each other?"

"What do you mean?"

"Imagine I was a piece of luggage," Martin explained. "You can easily carry those two kilograms. That way we alternate saving oxygen."

"Should I tuck you under my arm, or what?"

"No, we shorten the line and you would simply pull me after you."

363

Francesca laughed. "The ideas you come up with."

"Let's try it out," he urged.

The pilot nodded and tightened the safety line. Then she started walking. Martin fell down, but he did not fight it. *I am a piece of luggage. I need to relax and save breathable air.* The back of the spacesuit hit the ground, since this was the heaviest part. Each of Francesca's steps shook him. The numbers on his display went haywire because buttons were being pressed randomly.

This does not work. As a living piece of luggage I use up more air, not less.

"Thanks, Francesca, this has convinced me," Martin said. He got up and patted some snow from his suit. "I have a better idea, though." He pulled the injector from a side pocket. "When you are unconscious, you use a third less oxygen."

"Me, unconscious?" She looked at him. "Out of the question. And how would that help us anyway?"

"I would carry you. We are connecting our suits with the pressure hose. This increases our range by one-sixth."

"That won't be nearly enough, though, Martin."

"I know, but it will take us a bit closer to the goal."

"You are still hoping for a miracle, aren't you?" Francesca's voice sounded husky, as if she had been crying.

"Yes," Martin said, nodding.

The former fighter pilot sat down on a chunk of ice. She bent over.

"Then just do it. It might be better this way."

Martin did not hesitate for long. *Time is running very short, after all.* He placed the device on the thigh of Francesca's spacesuit. The hypodermic needle punched through the fabric and sealed it again. Francesca would not be conscious for the next few hours. *And what happens if we run out of oxygen?* The thought was painful. *I should have said farewell to her.*

Dragging Francesca did not make him faster, but oxygen consumption decreased. After two hours he had reached the six-kilometer mark, and the oxygen supply still stood at four hours and twenty minutes. The low gravity allowed for high jumps, but it made normal walking more difficult.

"Commander to ground team, how is it going?" *The question is useless.* Martin knew the others were aware of the statistics and projections. *I know the commander is just asking this to show she cares. But, it still feels good that she asked.*

"Well, it could be better. Though we are advancing according to plan," he answered. *Everyone knows what this means—death according to plan.* He could cover a maximum of 16 kilometers. Even in a best-case scenario, this would be considerably less than half the distance. *Hayato and Jiaying will arrive too late. I hope they have not started their march.* But he did not want to ask about that.

"This is Marchenko. Just a moment, I have an idea."

"Marchenko?" The commander's voice sounded surprised.

"I am currently in the airlock," he said.

"You said you were taking a nap," Amy said.

"I knew you were not going to give me permission."

"Permission for what?" the commander said in a flat, tight voice.

"I am getting the SAFER and two oxygen tanks from storage and I am flying down."

"Marchenko, you're crazy." Now Amy sounded really

upset. *She must realize, though, that she cannot stop the Russian*, Martin thought.

"No, I ran the calculations. The SAFER has enough fuel to get me down there."

"Impossible. It won't be enough for a clean landing. You cannot decelerate, and you are going to..."

"Maybe not. I am going to aim for a fissure that is not too deep. The oxygen tanks will certainly survive the impact."

"But you won't. Marchenko, don't be a fool. This is suicide," Amy pleaded.

"No, it is a pragmatic use of our resources. I am old. Francesca and Martin are more important to our mission."

There was silence on the radio channel. Everyone knew Marchenko would not budge from his plan. He would take the life-giving oxygen from the spaceship to the surface, and he would die in doing so. Martin heard a quiet sobbing. *Is that Jiaying?* Martin felt warm inside, but at the same time, a deep sense of sadness hit him. *I am not worth this sacrifice.* Yet if he protested, he would interfere with Francesca's life. He set her on the ground and looked at her. Her eyes were closed. Martin wondered what she would say if she were conscious. *Would she reject the doctor's sacrifice? Can I make the decision for Francesca?* Once, by voting to continue the mission, he had already decided her fate. *And yes, I would have done the same for Jiaying if I were in Marchenko's place.* He looked at the unconscious pilot in her spacesuit and felt guilty because he would profit from this sacrifice. *Would she accept the sacrifice? Probably not.* However, Marchenko left her no choice.

Martin took a deep breath, lifted the pilot's spacesuit and continued on his way.

AFTER AN HOUR, the commander spoke over the radio. "Marchenko is on his way." She added the target coordinates. "Touchdown in 14 minutes."

The target was a crevasse in the ice. According to radar it was eight meters deep. That was clever, as normally a SAFER and its passenger would simply bounce off the surface. The crevasse was supposed to prevent that and absorb the kinetic energy of the impact, which probably would have drastic consequences for the object touching down. On the other hand, it must not be too deep, so that Martin could reach the life-saving cargo. He hoped Marchenko had calculated everything correctly. *To lose both him and the cargo will turn a heroic act into a useless sacrifice.*

"Five minutes." Martin glanced at the black sky. There was no way he could detect a single astronaut. Marchenko would go down in history as the first human being to land on an extraterrestrial object without using a spaceship. The crevasse was about 100 meters ahead of them. He wanted to keep some distance, in case the landing did not occur at the precise spot.

Then it happened. A shadow raced across the sky, soundless as everything here, but faster than Martin had expected. The shadow disappeared quietly into the crevasse. There was a spray of snow, and Martin simply left Francesca behind and hurried forward in long leaps.

At the edge of the crevasse, he aimed his hand-held spotlight downward. At the very bottom, covered by a dusting of ice, was a human being in a spacesuit, twisted unnaturally. Marchenko did not move. Next to him were fragments of a SAFER, which must have impacted first.

Marchenko held something in his arms. Martin took a step sideways and recognized the gift. *Two gray oxygen tanks, our salvation.* They appeared to be undamaged.

"I am going down," Martin said into his helmet microphone. No answer. *Everybody seems to be waiting with bated breath.* It was about eight meters to the bottom. Martin jumped and landed next to Marchenko. He slowly bent down to look at him. The visor of his helmet was broken. A fine layer of snow covered his unshaven cheeks, and his eyes were wide open. *He looks as if he was curious about what was to come.*

Martin slumped. He had accepted that he himself might die, but the doctor's sacrifice was a heavy burden for Martin. *We have been saved, but a colleague, a friend is dead. And what will Francesca say when she wakes up?* Martin waited for a sense of relief now that his death was no longer imminent, but it did not come.

"COMMANDER TO NEUMAIER. Come in. I would recommend not waiting too long, as the two tanks won't last forever." Amy sounded very professional and calm. *She is a good commander*, Martin thought.

He got up and carried a metal tank with each hand. Due to the low gravity, they hardly bothered him. He jumped, hit the wall of the crevasse at half height, pushed off again, and landed back on the surface. He walked a few steps toward Francesca, who was still asleep. He put the tanks down next to her and turned around. He wanted to retrieve Marchenko's corpse from the crevasse, but then he saw a cloud of snow hovering above it. Martin was shocked. After three jumps he reached the place where the crevasse had been, but now it was only a shallow depression filled with pieces of ice. The crevasse must have been unstable for a long time. Now it had collapsed and buried Marchenko at the bottom.

Martin felt warm drops running down his cheeks. He could not wipe them away. He turned around and went back to Francesca's spacesuit. The pilot's eyes were closed, and she was breathing steadily.

"Let's fill up," he said to her, as if she was awake. Then he took the tank and connected the valve to her suit's life support system. The display showed the oxygen supply increasing. Afterward, he did this with his own spacesuit.

SEVEN HOURS after setting off from *Valkyrie*, they met the rescue team halfway to the lander. Hayato and Jiaying had brought enough oxygen for everybody. Martin was happy, like a little child, until he remembered Francesca and Marchenko. The Japanese engineer took the anesthetized pilot from Martin's arms. From here on, the terrain got easier. Only 13 hours after they had started walking they once more reached the place from where they had started their journey into the depths of the Enceladus Ocean not even ten days ago. *It seems like we have been gone a very long time, maybe half a year*, Martin thought.

They could not enter the lander as long as Francesca was still unconscious. Hayato woke her up with a small dose of adrenaline from the injector. After Martin made sure her eyes were open, he walked toward the lander module. He left it to Hayato to tell her what had happened. Francesca, who had just stood up, collapsed and sobbed inconsolably. Jiaying and Hayato tried to console the Italian woman. *I know nothing can console her.* Francesca lay on the ice, with Hayato and Jiaying crouched next to her.

After ten minutes, Francesca raised herself on her arms and got up. They all marched toward the lander in single file. It was not easy getting in. First Hayato and Francesca connected to the SuitPorts and went inside. Then the automatic system separated their suits so the SuitPorts were free again. Martin took the suits and carried them a bit away from the lander.

"Commander to ground team. We are waiting for you up here," came over the radio.

Martin thought of the laser concentrator Hayato had mentioned. Jiaying had already connected her suit to the SuitPort.

Martin replied, "Commander, there is something I've got to do here."

"Martin, what's going on?"

He did not listen to what Jiaying called after him via the helmet radio. *She is probably worried about me again. I am sorry about that, but I have an important task ahead. I will never have such an opportunity again.* He turned around, and no one tried to stop him.

He jumped in his suit to reach the laser concentrator with its large metal dish. The device was still connected to the optical cable that had been cut somewhere inside the ice. Martin knew the optical fiber core was surrounded by a conducting metal mesh. *Together with the dish on the surface, the cable can form an antenna that can amplify potential differences in the ice and transmit them into space—at least if I adapt the software a little bit.* He accessed the maintenance protocol and made his changes. Now the antenna would take variable electrical currents in the ice, amplify them, and broadcast them as a signal.

The rest is up to you, he thought. *I hope you make the most of it.*

Age of Questions, Nonahedron

There is:
The I.
So much more Not-I.
The confusion.
The curiosity.
The visitors, who are so different.
The exchange, which is not working.
8 billion not-I's who do not understand the
*   knowledge of the Twenty-Seven Ages.*
8 billion cells without an I.
The regret.
The wish to help.
The others.
The foam-born.
Different, yet still the same.
An address.
A giant without a ring, surrounded by rays.
There will be:
The ascent.

December 27, 2046, ILSE

GETTING UP, *taking a shower, working, exercise, free time, exercise, sleep—just two weeks ago, this routine had seemed terribly boring.* Now Martin wanted nothing else. They had already created schedules for the coming twelve months. Marchenko was no longer there, so the shift duties had to rotate more quickly. About three times every two weeks his work rhythm would overlap with that of Jiaying, so they could spend a night together in his cabin or hers.

The crew had quite a few plans. Most of all, they wanted to remodel the garden. Sol would start to crawl around a few months from now, so he should have a safe playground. Mission Control had given permission for this. The resource usage was back in the normal range. There-fore, they would not need the eco module for growing food or generating oxygen. Nevertheless, there ought to be a few plants there, so the child grew up with a little bit of green-ery. They would just have to make do without fresh food.

They had more time for their return trip than planned, as their stay on the surface had been shorter. This allowed for a bit of sightseeing in the solar system.

The planned course would lead through several fly-by maneuvers around other moons of Saturn and then initially into a wide orbit around Jupiter. Space probes rarely came by here, so the scientists would be happy about every scrap of data the crew could transmit back to Earth.

For the time being, Francesca had taken over Marchenko's cabin. She said she would manage and just needed some time.

Every day, the research community on Earth sent new questions the astronauts could not answer. The scientists would have liked them to have continued the mission. There appeared to be two factions among them. Some scientists could not believe what Martin and Francesca had reported from the depths of the ocean, and therefore they tried to find natural explanations in the dataset. The others were fascinated by the idea of communicating with an alien intelligence and pushed to build suitable devices for this, maybe giant antennas. Martin preferred the skeptics, for if they won out, the Enceladus Ocean would remain undisturbed for the foreseeable future. *If someone realizes what this could mean for developing theories of physics, the alien intelligence might become a slave of humanity.* After this intelligence had just accepted the idea of not being alone in the universe, it might not be able to withstand the arguing power of humans.

The media on Earth had turned all the astronauts into heroes, with Marchenko being far ahead. In his home country, he had even replaced Yuri Gagarin as the most famous space pioneer. One advantage of his being a dead hero was that he could not refuse when politicians of all stripes claimed him.

Jiaying had already been offered a high position in the

Communist Party. She had asked for some time to think about it. Martin feared their return to Earth.

Hayato Masukoshi took care of Sol whenever he had the time for it. Martin had never seen him this happy—even when Sol cried for hours, Hayato never became impatient. It was a quiet, shy happiness that deeply touched Martin.

He himself ignored journalists' requests for interviews. The PR department was very unhappy about that. *Sometime during the next few days I will have to change my mind,* he knew. Luckily, live interviews were impossible. That would give him sufficient time after each question to think about an answer.

Amy seemed quieter than she used to be. Martin suspected she felt that the events, particularly Marchenko's death, were partially her fault. *How could she have known what ideas he would come up with?* Per standard procedure, NASA was already investigating if someone had made mistakes.

AMY AND HAYATO had invited them to dinner. There were six places set, but one stayed empty. Hayato held the child in his arms. The boy was sleeping.

"Dear colleagues… forget that. Dear friends," she said. Hayato nodded.

"Today I would like to thank you for doing everything you could to support the mission, and, more importantly, to help each other. No one can take that away from us. Yet I would like to thank one person in particular."

She looked at the empty chair

"Marchenko, you cannot be with us today. But I hope you won't think it arrogant, but rather an expression of our sincere gratitude if we also name our son after you, by giving him a second name. Dimitri Sol. I think that sounds great. And I hope we will soon be able to tell him about you, Mitya."

Francesca sobbed, and Martin had a hard time suppressing his own tears.

Author's Note

Thank you for coming on this journey with me! I can't tell you how much it means to have your support and your company on this long expedition to the outer regions of the solar system. And now, let's sit down together and I'll tell you a bit about myself.

When I was a child, I always wanted to become an astronaut. I'm sure I shared this wish with many of you. I was only three years old in 1969, so I don't remember Neil Armstrong's first steps on the moon. However, I have a clear memory of the last ones in 1972. It was so cool seeing Eugene Cernan and Harrison Schmitt – admittedly I didn't recall their names and had to look them up – driving around on the moon in their Moon Buggy, even if it was on a black and white TV set. I really wanted to be next but unfortunately, theirs was the final mission of the Apollo program.

So I chose my second-favorite career path, to be a writer. After studying physics, I worked as a journalist for many years, writing about science and technology and, yes, space. The magazine I work for, not coincidentally, is called SPACE. I get to see contemporary space hardware, follow launches (my last one was from Vandenberg AFB in May 2018), and interview people involved with what has now become a viable industry.

But I want to write about more than today's reality. Even if I never become an astronaut, I can imagine adventurous spaceflights and write them down—I am still hoping for Blue Origin to offer affordable tickets to space, and yes, I have already registered my desire with them. In the meantime, my kind of fun is to make my fiction as realistic as possible, based on current science – a degree in physics certainly helps – but also based on viable technology. Prognoses are hard, especially concerning the future, but I have a bit of hope that someday you might say, *Wow, what's happening now is pretty similar to what I read in that book! I can't remember the name, but it was written by that Morris guy with the middle initial Q.*

Of course, I hope that you will continue to travel with me. The story of the ILSE expedition is not over. The first three chapters of the next book are included below (if you ordered the e-book). As the story develops, the crew must overcome a much greater threat than on Enceladus. Titan, another moon of the ringed planet Saturn, is most notable for its thick atmosphere. Did you ever try to fly? On Titan you could, and Francesca will even show you how to make your own wings. You can order *The Titan Probe*, the sequel to *The Enceladus Mission*, now for only $3.99 at Amazon by opening this link:

hard-sf.com/links/301759

See you back in space!

Or, you could get the full Ice Moon box set, consisting of four books, for just $ 9.99. Even if you already bought *The Enceladus Mission*, you still save $ 1.98. Click here:

hard-sf.com/links/780838

If you register at hard-sf.com/subscribe I will inform you about future publications of my science fiction titles.

As a bonus, I will send you the beautifully illustrated PDF version of *The Guided Tour of Enceladus* for free!

On my website at hard-sf.com you will also find interesting popular science news and articles about all those worlds afar that I'd love to have you visit with me.

I have to ask you one last thing, a big favor: If you liked this book, you would help me a lot if you could leave me a review so others can appreciate it as well. Just open this link:

hard-sf.com/links/302316

Thank you so much!

facebook.com/BrandonQMorris

amazon.com/author/brandonqmorris

bookbub.com/authors/brandon-q-morris

goodreads.com/brandonqmorris

Also by Brandon Q. Morris

The Enceladus Mission (Ice Moon 1)

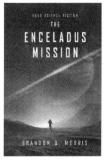

In the year 2031, a robot probe detects traces of biological activity on Enceladus, one of Saturn's moons. This sensational discovery shows that there is indeed evidence of extraterrestrial life. Fifteen years later, a hurriedly built spacecraft sets out on the long journey to the ringed planet and its moon.

The international crew is not just facing a difficult twenty-seven months: if the spacecraft manages to make it to Enceladus without incident it must use a drillship to penetrate the kilometer-thick sheet of ice that entombs the moon. If life does indeed exist on Enceladus, it could only be at the bottom of the salty, ice covered ocean, which formed billions of years ago.

However, shortly after takeoff disaster strikes the mission, and the chances of the crew making it to Enceladus, let alone back home, look grim.

2.99 $ – hard-sf.com/links/526999

The Titan Probe (Ice Moon 2)

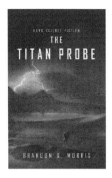

In 2005, the robotic probe "Huygens" lands on Saturn's moon Titan. 40 years later, a radio telescope receives signals from the far away moon that can only come from the long forgotten lander.

At the same time, an expedition returns from neighbouring moon Enceladus. The crew lands on Titan and finds a dangerous secret that risks their return to Earth. Meanwhile, on Enceladus a deathly race has started that nobody thought was possible. And its outcome can only be decided by the

astronauts that are stuck on Titan.

3.99 $ – hard-sf.com/links/527000

The Io Encounter (Ice Moon 3)

Jupiter's moon Io has an extremely hostile environment. There are hot lava streams, seas of boiling sulfur, and frequent volcanic eruptions straight from Dante's Inferno, in addition to constant radiation bombardment and a surface temperature hovering at minus 180 degrees Celsius.

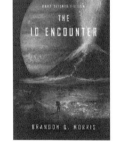

Is it really home to a great danger that threatens all of humanity? That's what a surprise message from the life form discovered on Enceladus seems to indicate.

The crew of ILSE, the International Life Search Expedition, finally on their longed-for return to Earth, reluctantly chooses to accept a diversion to Io, only to discover that an enemy from within is about to destroy all their hopes of ever going home.

3.99 $ – hard-sf.com/links/527008

Return to Enceladus (Ice Moon 4)

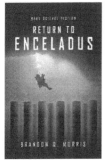

Russian billionaire Nikolai Shostakovitch makes an offer to the former crew of the spaceship ILSE. He will finance a return voyage to the icy moon Enceladus. The offer is too good to refuse—the expedition would give them the unique opportunity to recover the body of their doctor, Dimitri Marchenko.

Everyone on board knows that their benefactor acts out of purely personal motivations… but the true interests of the tycoon and the dangers that he conjures up are beyond anyone's imagination.

3.99 € – hard-sf.com/links/527011

Ice Moon - The Boxset

All four bestselling books of the Ice Moon series are now offered as a set, available only in e-book format.

The Enceladus Mission: Is there really life on Saturn's moon Enceladus? *ILSE*, the International Life Search Expedition, makes its way to the icy world where an underground ocean is suspected to be home to primitive life forms.

The Titan Probe: An old robotic NASA probe mysteriously

awakens on the methane moon of Titan. The *ILSE* crew tries to solve the riddle—and discovers a dangerous secret.

The Io Encounter: Finally bound for Earth, *ILSE* makes it as far as Jupiter when the crew receives a startling message. The volcanic moon Io may harbor a looming threat that could wipe out Earth as we know it.

Return to Enceladus: The crew gets an offer to go back to Enceladus. Their mission—to recover the body of Dr. Marchenko, left for dead on the original expedition. Not everyone is working toward the same goal. Could it be their unwanted crew member?

9.99 $ – hard-sf.com/links/780838

Proxima Rising

Late in the 21st century, Earth receives what looks like an urgent plea for help from planet Proxima Centauri b in the closest star system to the Sun. Astrophysicists suspect a massive solar flare is about to destroy this heretofore-unknown civilization. Earth's space programs are unequipped to help, but an unscrupulous Russian billionaire launches a secret and highly-specialized spaceship  to Proxima b, over four light-years away. The unusual crew faces a Herculean task—should they survive the journey. No one knows what to expect from this alien planet.

3.99 $ – hard-sf.com/links/610690

Proxima Dying

An intelligent robot and two young people explore Proxima Centauri b, the planet orbiting our nearest star, Proxima Centauri. Their ideas about the mission quickly prove grossly naive as they venture about on this planet of extremes.

Where are the senders of the call for help that lured them here? They find no one and no traces on the daylight side, so they place their hopes upon an expedition into the eternal ice on Proxima b's dark side. They not only face everlasting night, the team encounters grave dangers. A fateful decision will change the planet forever.

3.99 $ – hard-sf.com/links/652197

Proxima Dreaming

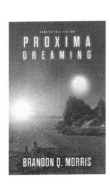

Alone and desperate, Eve sits in the control center of an alien structure. She has lost the other members of the team sent to explore exoplanet Proxima Centauri b. By mistake she has triggered a disastrous process that threatens to obliterate the planet. Just as Eve fears her best option may be a quick death, a nearby alien life form awakens from a very long sleep. It has only one task: to find and neutralize the destructive intruder from a faraway place.

3.99 $ – hard-sf.com/links/705470

The Hole

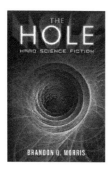

A mysterious object threatens to destroy our solar system. The survival of humankind is at risk, but nobody takes the warning of young astrophysicist Maribel Pedreira seriously. At the same time, an exiled crew of outcasts mines for rare minerals on a lone asteroid.

When other scientists finally acknowledge Pedreira's alarming discovery, it becomes clear that these outcasts are the only ones who may be able to save our world, knowing that *The Hole* hurtles inexorably toward the sun.

3.99 $ – hard-sf.com/links/527017

Silent Sun

Is our sun behaving differently from other stars? When an amateur astronomer discovers something strange on telescopic solar pictures, an explanation must be found. Is it merely artefact? Or has he found something totally unexpected?

An expert international crew is hastily assembled, a spaceship is speedily repurposed, and the foursome is sent on the ride of their lives. What challenges will they face on this spur-of-the-moment mission to our central star?

What awaits all of them is critical, not only for understanding the past, but even more so for the future of life on Earth.

3.99 $ – hard-sf.com/links/527020

The Rift

There is a huge, bold black streak in the sky. Branches appear out of nowhere over North America, Southern Europe, and Central Africa. People who live beneath The Rift can see it. But scientists worldwide are distressed—their equipment cannot pick up any type of signal from it.

The rift appears to consist of nothing. Literally. Nothing. Nada. Niente. Most people are curious but not overly concerned. The phenomenon seems to pose no danger. It is just there.

Then something jolts the most hardened naysayers, and surpasses the worst nightmares of the world's greatest scientists —and rocks their understanding of the universe.

3.99 $ – hard-sf.com/links/534368

Mars Nation 1

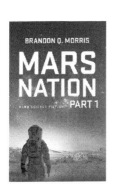

NASA finally made it. The very first human has just set foot on the surface of our neighbor planet. This is the start of a long research expedition that sent four scientists into space.

But the four astronauts of the NASA crew are not the only ones with this destination. The privately financed 'Mars for Everyone' initiative has also targeted the Red Planet. Twenty men and women have been selected to live there and establish the first extraterrestrial settlement.

Challenges arise even before they reach Mars orbit. The MfE spaceship Santa Maria is damaged along the way. Only the four NASA astronauts can intervene and try to save their lives.

No one anticipates the impending catastrophe that threatens their very existence—not to speak of the daily hurdles that an extended stay on an alien planet sets before them. On Mars, a struggle begins for limited resources, human cooperation, and just plain survival.

3.99 $ – hard-sf.com/links/762824

Mars Nation 2

A woman presumed dead fights her way through the hostile deserts of Mars. With her help, the NASA astronauts orphaned on the Red Planet hope to be able to solve their very worst problem. But their hopes are shattered when an unexpected menace arises and threatens to destroy everything the remnant of humanity has built on the planet. They need a miracle —or a ghost from the past whose true intentions are unknown.

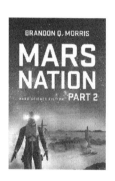

Mars Nation 2 continues the story of the last representatives of Earth, who have found asylum on our neighboring planet, hoping to build a future in this alien world.

3.99 $ – hard-sf.com/links/790047

Mars Nation 3

Does the secret of Mars lurk beneath the surface of its south pole? A lone astronaut searches for clues about the earlier inhabitants of the Red Planet. Meanwhile, Rick Summers,

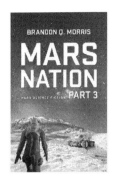

having assumed the office of Mars City's Administrator by deceit and manipulation, tries to unify the people on Mars with the weapons under his control. Then Summers stumbles upon so powerful an evil that even he has no means to overcome it.

3.99 $ – hard-sf.com/links/818245

The Death of the Universe

For many billions of years, humans—having conquered the curse of aging—spread throughout the entire Milky Way. They are able to live all their dreams, but to their great disappointment, no other intelligent species has ever been encountered. Now, humanity itself is on the brink of extinction because the universe is dying a protracted yet inevitable death.

They have only one hope: The 'Rescue Project' was designed to feed the black hole in the center of the galaxy until it becomes a quasar, delivering much-needed energy to humankind during its last breaths. But then something happens that no one ever expected—and humanity is forced to look at itself and its existence in an entirely new way.

3.99 $ – hard-sf.com/links/835415

The Guided Tour of Enceladus

Introduction

ASTRONOMERS NOTICED RELATIVELY late that Enceladus would make a fascinating travel destination. It had been discovered in 1789 by the German-British astronomer William Herschel as the sixth moon of the planet Saturn. At first sight, it acted as would be expected from a moon of its size. It was only the photos taken by the *Voyager* probes in the 1980s that changed this perception. During its fly-by on August 26th, 1982, *Voyager 2* sent spectacular images of the snow-covered surface, the network of craters and of deep fissures in the ice. These also showed that Enceladus was uncommonly bright, as it reflected 99 percent of the incoming sunlight.

The photos spurred imagination among astronomers in several ways. For one thing, the photos showed large plains without any craters, which indicated they must be relatively fresh. Therefore, there must be processes in the interior of the moon that renewed the surface. The high albedo (reflectivity), the highest of any known in our solar system, can also only be explained by a snow-covered surface that is refreshed at regular intervals. But if there was no atmosphere, where would the snow come from?

And then there was the mysterious E Ring of Saturn, which the Allegheny Observatory of the University of Pittsburgh first photographed in 1966. Spectroscopic analysis showed that it consisted mostly of small ice crystals —and there were other aspects of this ring that were exceptional. Enceladus moves around Saturn along the inner edge of the E Ring, exactly where the ring has its greatest density, which quickly made this moon the suspected cause for the unique properties of the E Ring.

On July 14, 2005, the *Cassini* probe sent by NASA and ESA caught it red-handed. It photographed clouds of frozen water vapor above the surface of Enceladus, which was covered by relatively warm fissures. Two years later, *Cassini* provided the first photos of the geysers near the South Pole shooting water from the interior of the moon into space. A portion of that water seemed to provide new material for the E Ring, while the rest fell back down on the moon and made it shine in the whitest of whites.

What other secrets does Enceladus hide? Follow me to an icy world, which might harbor unknown forms of life.

The Orbit of Enceladus around Saturn

ENCELADUS IS the sixth largest moon of the ringed planet Saturn, and it was also the sixth Saturn moon to be discovered. Today, a total of 62 Saturn moons are known. Counted from the center of the Saturn system, Enceladus is the fourteenth moon, though in the classical numbering system, it was the second. Therefore, it received the designation *Saturn II* by the International Astronomical Union. With an average diameter of 505 kilometers—about the distance from New York to Pittsburgh as the crow flies—Enceladus is considerably smaller than Earth's moon, which has a diameter of 3,475 kilometers, though among all the moons of the solar system, it still ranks as the seventeenth largest. It is the 'average' diameter, because the gravitational pull of Saturn flattens this moon slightly, by about three percent. This shape is called an ellipsoid.

Enceladus cannot be observed from Earth with the naked eye. Its apparent brightness is at 11.8 apparent magnitude, and the human eye can see an object—under ideal conditions—up to a value of 6.

Its orbit around the planet is an almost perfect circle.

The average orbital radius lies at about 238,000 kilometers. This puts Enceladus very close to its mother planet, which will be important for understanding the processes in its interior. The orbit of Earth's moon is about 50 percent larger. In addition, Saturn is huge compared to Earth. The distance from Enceladus to the 'surface' of the planet is only slightly below 180,000 kilometers, and Saturn has about 95 times the mass of Earth, and therefore 95 times the gravitational pull.

This strong gravity has several effects on Enceladus, including on its orbit. Over millions of years, it caused the moon to always face the planet with the same side, something called 'captured rotation.' If you land on the back side of Enceladus you will never see Saturn, while from the planet's perspective you could only see the 'front side' of Enceladus. This is also the relationship between Earth and its moon.

Like almost all of the moons of Saturn, as well as the rings, Enceladus orbits Saturn in a plane parallel to the equator of the planet. This is at an angle of about 27 degrees to the plane in which the planets move around the sun—the ecliptic plane. The orbit of Enceladus is also influenced by its siblings, which sometimes get very close to it. The orbit of Pallene, for example, the next moon closer to Saturn, is approximately 26,000 kilometers away, while the next moon further out, Tethys, has a distance of almost 57,000 kilometers. The tidal forces created by this interaction compel the moons into a kind of cosmic ballet. Dione, which is more than twice as large, is in a 2:1 orbital resonance with Enceladus. This means that for every two orbital periods Enceladus completes, Dione will finish one. With Mimas, which is further inward and a bit smaller, Enceladus is linked in a 3:2 resonance. And with the already mentioned moon Tethys, which is twice its size, Enceladus has agreed on a 4:3 orbital resonance.

For one orbit around Saturn, Enceladus needs one Earth day, plus an additional eight hours and 53 minutes. It orbits at a velocity of 12.64 kilometers per second. Therefore, Enceladus is twelve times as fast as our moon orbiting Mother Earth. The reason for this is not the laziness of Earth's moon, but rather the much stronger pull of Saturn on Enceladus. If Enceladus were as slow as our moon, it would have ceased to exist a long time ago. Our moon, on the other hand, would have quickly escaped the vicinity of Earth if it orbited as fast as Enceladus.

By now you know how slowly Enceladus rotates. As it always shows Saturn the same side, it finishes exactly one rotation during an orbital period. The axis around which Enceladus rotates is exactly perpendicular to its orbital plane. Therefore, Saturn can always be seen at the same location in the sky over Enceladus. The rotational axis of Earth, on the other hand, is tilted toward its orbital plane around the sun—otherwise, Earth would have no seasons.

White and Cold: The Surface

THERE IS a simple reason for the fact, as mentioned in the introduction, that Enceladus reflects light so well. The moon is completely covered with ice, perfectly normal ice as we all know it, i.e. water ice. This reflects light even better than freshly fallen snow on Earth. Enceladus is therefore often called an 'ice moon,' even though that is not literally true, as we will see in the next section.

This fact has some practical consequences for anyone traveling to Enceladus. You might know this from clear winter days—light reflected from the surface cannot warm the surface. Not only is this moon already at an enormous distance from the sun (more than 1.4 billion kilometers), but the high albedo (reflectivity) causes it to be even colder on Enceladus than the distance from the sun would make it. On the surface of its sibling, Dione, which has an albedo of 55 percent, i.e. much darker, the temperatures can reach minus 187 degrees Celsius, whereas on Enceladus the 'warmest' is only minus 200 degrees.

Even though the landscape on the surface is completely white, there are some variations. Plains (planitia, plural form planitiae) alternate with ridges 500 to 2,000 meters high (dorsum, plural dorsa), and both can contain trenches (sulcus, plural sulci), depressions (fossa, plural fossae) and cliffs (rupe, plural rupes), or be covered to some extent with craters.

If you try to find your way around Enceladus with a map, you might get the impression you are in the *Arabian Nights*. This is because the International Astronomical Union (IAU) decided to use geographical names from this famous work of world literature for this moon—except for the craters, which are named after protagonists from these stories.

Geologically speaking, the plains on Enceladus are very young. You can see that they—for example, the Sarandib Plain—contain far fewer craters than one would expect on a moon. It is estimated that many of its plains are less than a couple of hundred million years old. The impact craters, as the photos taken by the *Cassini* probe show, are in various stages of aging. While the climate on Earth makes craters wear away, and on Earth's moon they are destroyed by new impacts, on Enceladus shifting of the ice erodes the craters.

The trenches and canyons are witnesses to this activity, and they can be up to 200 kilometers long, 5 to 10 kilometers wide, and up to 1,000 meters deep. They often cut through other geological features, so one must assume that they are relatively new phenomena. On Earth, rocky continental plates collide, but on Enceladus it seems to be ice plates. This sometimes creates cliffs up to 1,000 meters high.

Chaos in the South

THE AREA around the South Pole of Enceladus plays a special role. Even in the pictures taken by *Voyager 2*, scientists discovered a chaotic terrain, a mixture of very different terrains. Since the *Cassini* probe sent its spectacular images, we know a lot more. The area reaching up to 60 degrees southern latitude (about the position of Tierra del Fuego on Earth) is characterized by fractures and cliffs, but it contains even fewer craters than the rest of the moon. The surface must therefore be far younger. Scientists estimate it to be an average of 500,000 years old. Geologically speaking, that is very young.

From above, the center of this region looks particularly chaotic. Besides the fractures and plates, there are also giant ice boulders measuring 10 to 100 meters. The area is dominated by four fractures with a depth of up to 300 meters, the so-called Tiger Stripes, each of which is several hundred kilometers long. Pictures show that the ice at their edges has a considerably different composition from the ice on the regular plains. Organic compounds have been found here.

The Tiger Stripes, which are up to 25 degrees Celsius warmer than their surroundings, form the source of the famous Enceladus Geysers. The entire world saw the photos of them taken by *Cassini*. Across almost the entire length of the stripes, large amounts of crystallizing water vapor are shot into space at high speeds, between 400 and 1250 meters per second (m/s). Part of it falls back on the moon as snow, part of it replenishes the material of the E Ring. As the escape velocity on Enceladus is below 240 m/s (860 km/h), an outgassing into space is perfectly possible.

The activity of the geysers changes periodically. It is suspected the Tiger Stripes are squeezed by the gravity of Saturn when the moon approaches the planet, which increases the pressure at which the material is ejected, and reduces its quantity.

The *Cassini* probe even managed to fly directly through a geyser plume. Therefore we know these consist primarily of rapidly freezing water vapor, but also include percentages of methane and carbon dioxide, as well as simple-to-more-complex organic molecules. The composition resembles that of a comet. How these compounds could have been created will be explained next.

A Great View

DUE TO ITS LOW GRAVITY, Enceladus does not possess a true atmosphere. The disadvantage of this fact is that a spaceship could not use the braking effect of the atmosphere during landing.

However, near the South Pole, enough of the geyser eruptions remain so that traces of an atmosphere have been detected, comprised of 91 percent water vapor, 4 percent nitrogen, 3.2 percent carbon dioxide, and 1.7 percent methane.

An astronaut who has just landed on Enceladus' surface might look up to the sky first. It would be completely black, as the moon has no atmosphere to speak of. No clouds will obscure the sun, which appears at 3.5 minutes of arc, just one ninth of the size we are used to on Earth.

Saturn can only be seen from the side of the moon that faces the planet. Here it appears in the sky at a height dependent on the geographical latitude of the observer's current position. Therefore, at the equator, Saturn shines vertically above you, but the closer you get to the poles, the lower the planet sits above the horizon. It is always impressive, though, as its disc with a diameter of 60 degrees is about 120 times the size of Earth's moon in our night sky.

Unfortunately, a space tourist would not get a good view of the rings of Saturn. After all, these surround Saturn in the same plane as the moon. Therefore, you are looking directly at their (very narrow) edge and will only see them as a line. Depending on the position of the sun, though, the shadows of the rings may be seen upon the planet.

If during your visit to Enceladus you experience a moonrise, don't worry. You are not confused—you just saw the inner moon Mimas, which moves past Saturn every 72 hours and has an apparent size in the sky like that of the Earth's moon. Tethys, on the other hand, appears to be twice as big, though you could only observe this outer moon from the side of Enceladus facing away from Saturn.

Other of Saturn's moons appear in the sky as star-like objects, or cannot even be detected with the naked eye.

Hiking on Enceladus

LET's say you are not satisfied with just looking at the
moonscape facing Saturn, but want to also explore the
other side of the moon. No problem. The low gravity lets
you almost float. If you weigh 86 kilograms, you would
weigh only 1 kilogram on Enceladus using a spring scale—
a beam balance would indicate 86 kilograms, as it
compares weights. Even with a heavy spacesuit, this would
not add up to more than 2 kilograms.

That does not mean you can jump 40 times higher
than on your home planet. For one thing, the space suit is
cumbersome. On Earth, no one can jump in a spacesuit.
On our moon, you could jump to a height of about two
meters in a spacesuit, though no human astronaut has
attempted so high a jump yet. On Enceladus you could
perform a 20-meter jump (even 40 meters without a spacesuit)—though that is not recommended. The issue is one
of safety. After all, you return to the ground with the speed
you jumped up with. A spacesuit ought to withstand that,
but the risk is simply too great.

A hike on Enceladus is rather like a spacewalk. Outside

there is a vacuum—almost. Therefore, the preparations should resemble those of an EVA in space. The fact that there is no atmosphere is actually rather fortunate. At minus 200 degrees Celsius your suit will cool off much faster in an environment filled with some kind of air than by just giving off heat as radiation.

Nevertheless, such a hike would be exhausting, and just because you weigh less does not mean you can quickly accelerate to a high speed. Your so-called inertial mass plays an important role in this, and that is not different from what you would have on Earth.

Realm of Water and Ice

RELATIVELY EARLY, astronomers realized Enceladus could not be a pure ice moon. Considering its size, it is too heavy for that. At a density of 1.61 grams per cubic centimeter—water weighs only one gram per cubic centimeter—it is third among the Saturn moons in this aspect. Inside it, there must be a dense rocky core. Earth's moon, for comparison, has a density of 3.3 grams per cubic centimeter, but water ice is relatively rare there.

Yet compared to the 'blue planet,' Earth, Enceladus has quite a bit of water. If all the water on Earth were formed into a ball, it would have a diameter of 1,384 kilometers (Earth's diameter: 12,740 kilometers). If all the ice on Enceladus were formed into a ball, it would be almost 400 kilometers in diameter (and the total diameter of Enceladus is 504 kilometers). To put it differently, billions of years ago, when Earth—which then was dry—received its water, several bodies the size of Enceladus must have crashed into it.

The rocky core of Enceladus probably accounts for half of its mass, with a diameter of 300 to 340 kilometers.

And it probably consists of materials rich in silicon (silicates), similar to the crust and mantle of Earth.

Scientists cannot agree on how high the percentage of short- and long-lived radioactive substances was and is. Their decay offers a mechanism that allows a celestial body to create heat long after coming into being. It was assumed earlier that on Earth this radioactivity was the precondition for all life. Actually, though, the heat of Earth's core is a remainder from the early period of the solar system. The core not only releases heat to the mantle, but additional energy is released when previously liquid material crystalizes—heat of crystallization. A compression of material sets in which releases additional energy as the gradually solidifying inner core slowly shrinks.

The rocky core of Enceladus does not play the same role, but heat rising from it may lead to a melting of ice.

Above the rocky core comes the realm of water and ice. Ice is not always the same, because it possesses various phases that differ in their physical properties. It is not exactly known which phases occur on Enceladus. The decisive factors are pressure and temperature, but the admixture of other substances can also change the properties of the ice. For instance, traces of ammonia would lower the freezing point—water in one place could be liquid even though elsewhere it would have frozen. However, such traces have yet to be found on Enceladus. It is likely that the majority of its ice layer consists of 'normal' ice as we know it from Earth; this is Ice I.

We also do not yet know how thick the ice layer is. Models resulted in a thickness of 50 to 80 kilometers. Somewhere in the ice or below it, as measurements of the orbital movements of Enceladus have indicated, there must be a liquid layer. Enceladus 'wobbles' a bit on its path, like a spinning raw egg. The moon therefore can be compared to a husked coconut with the addition of a large core—a sphere with a hard, thick shell and, below it, a more or less nutritious liquid, and within that liquid is an even harder, indigestible core.

The ocean under the ice may extend only below the South Pole (up to 50 or 60 degrees southern latitude), or around the entire moon. The first model seems to be the most likely one to most researchers. Then the ice crust would be 30 to 40 kilometers thick, but significantly thinner near the South Pole. French scientists have calculated that it might be only five kilometers thick at the pole.

The ocean itself might have a depth of about ten kilometers, and at the bottom the pressure would reach between 28 and 45 bars. That corresponds to the water pressure one would experience on Earth at a depth of 300 to 400 meters. Other models assume a water depth of 30 to 40 kilometers. For comparison, the average ocean depth on Earth is 3.7 kilometers.

Hot Stripes

THERE IS no doubt about the existence of the Tiger Stripes. In the roughly one kilometer deep by nine meters wide Baghdad Sulcus, the *Cassini* probe measured a temperature of minus 75 degrees Celsius. That is not actually warm enough for liquid water to exist. It is assumed, therefore, that the surface is covered by fresh, cold snow which lowers the measured temperature.

Water jets constantly shoot up out of the Tiger Stripes, and through this process Enceladus loses 150 to 200 kilograms of water per second. In its existence, it must have lost up to a fifth of its mass and at least three-quarters of its original water content.

Infrared measurements near the South Pole showed this area to be considerably warmer than its surroundings. At this distance from the sun, minus 200 degrees Celsius should be expected, but the average temperature is 15 degrees warmer. That does not sound like much, but it means a heat output of 4.7 gigawatts is emitted. That is twice the output of the power stations at the Hoover Dam.

Where does that heat come from? Currently, there is

no definitive explanation as to how the necessary heat is generated. It is probably a combination of several factors. First of all, Enceladus is under the influence of mighty Saturn. This moon is not completely homogenous (of a uniform structure), so that the gravitational pull of the planet acts with different force on different areas, strongly massaging Enceladus, as it were. This causes friction, and friction generates heat. However, this so-called tidal heat would not suffice to keep the ocean liquid, even considering that the ice crust acts as an insulating layer.

Besides physical forces, chemical ones could be another important factor. At the interface between ocean and rocky core, saltwater meets stone. This causes a reaction called serpentinization. The water reacts with the silicates, giving off energy. Per reaction quantity of 1 mol, enough heat is generated to melt 11 mol of water ice. During its history, this could have led to a chain reaction. It would have been enough if water reacted with silicates at one location. Then this reaction could have spread all over Enceladus. The composition of the water vapor jets from the cryovolcanoes on Enceladus suggests this must have happened at some time.

Finally, a certain percent of the heat could also come from the decay of long-lived radioactive substances in the core.

The Birth of the Moon

ENCELADUS WAS PROBABLY BORN at the same time as Saturn. At a distance of 9.5 astronomical units from the sun, the protoplanetary nebula cooled off more quickly than in the inner solar system, near the hot primal sun, where water more likely existed in liquid form or water vapor. Furthermore, the lighter elements predominated here—hence the creation of gas planets rather than rocky planets.

Once the temperature had fallen enough, first the firmer and then the more volatile compounds condensed down to water vapor, which froze into ice crystals. When particles met, they merged into larger clumps, which in turn combined into even bigger pieces. This finally created planetesimals, or minute planets, which were still undifferentiated. This means they had neither core nor crust, and that rock and ice were still randomly mixed.

At the very beginning, these pieces still contained a larger quantity of radioactive nuclides. These heated the interior of the future moon, which then had a diameter of 600 kilometers, instead of its present-day 500, and they baked the individual pieces more firmly together. The ice warmed up so that Enceladus could contract with the help of its own gravity, like pulling a coat more tightly around itself. Back then, the moon must have shrunk by about 20 kilometers. At some point, the interior temperature must have risen so much that the still widely-dispersed ice began to melt, and the hidden ocean came into being. The first serpentinization reactions started. This changed the properties of the silicates in such a way that the remaining water was pressed outward, where it froze again. When the core temperature finally reached 450 degrees, the reverse reaction to serpentinization set in.

This finally turned the core into what we know it to be now, an arid silicate core surrounded by a thick layer of ice. Between the two, the chemical reaction keeps a layer of liquid water. At the same time, Enceladus continually lost mass this way and shrank to its current diameter of 500 kilometers. The core has been gradually cooling and probably today is minimally warmer than the ocean, and possibly even cooler.

Other ice moons, by the way, have followed a different path. Mimas, for example, is quite large, but does not have a true core. It still resembles the dirty snowball that it was when it came into being. Scientists speculate that at the beginning, this moon contained less rocky material. Therefore, there were not enough radionuclides to heat the interior and to press the ice outward.

The Exploration of Enceladus

THE FIRST ONE to gaze on Enceladus was the British-German astronomer and musician Frederick William Herschel, who in 1789 focused what was then the largest telescope in the world (1.2 meters) on the ringed planet Saturn. The name of the moon was derived from the giant Enkelados (Latin: *Enceladus*) in Greek mythology. This was actually a mistake, because Enkelados, as one of the giants, never joined with the Titans in their war against the gods (whose leader was Kronos, called Saturn by the Romans). The giants, including Enkelados, rebelled later, after Zeus had locked away the Titans (the sons of the ancestral mother Gaia) in the underworld.

For almost 200 years Enceladus remained an unremarkable if unusually bright spot in the sky. Due to its closeness to Saturn and Saturn's rings, which were so much brighter, the moon was hard to observe. *Voyager 1* was the first object created by humans to pay it a visit. On November 12, 1980, this probe flew past it at a distance of 202,000 kilometers. The pictures taken then already showed that Enceladus had a very young face that showed no deep craters. On August 26, 1981, *Voyager 2* came even closer, as close as 87,010 kilometers, and thus provided images with considerably better resolution. These pictures excited scientists. How could such a cold, small moon have such differently formed areas, some of which could only be a few million years old?

The answer finally was provided in 2004 by the *Cassini* probe, which had been sent by NASA and ESA, and which had already placed a lander on the larger moon Titan. Afterward, *Cassini* followed an orbit around Saturn that often swung very close to Enceladus. Initially, fly-bys at distances down to 1,500 kilometers had been planned, but after it was discovered that water vapor shot into space from the region around the South Pole, planners decided to take an even closer look at this moon. *Cassini* sometimes came as close as 25 kilometers from the surface of Enceladus, and it was able to send spectacular photos. On October 28, 2015, it even managed to fly through a geyser eruption. During this, the probe analyzed the composition of the ejected material, which was so dense that it measurably slowed *Cassini's* rate of travel.

Currently, no space agency on Earth has specific plans for another visit to Enceladus. At the beginning of the 21st century, ESA discussed the concept of a Titan-Enceladus mission named TandEM. This was merged in 2009 with a similar concept at NASA and became the Titan Saturn System Mission (TSSM). For budgetary reasons, TSSM was canceled in favor of EJSM (Europa Jupiter System Mission, now often called *Europa Clipper),* which was proposed to explore the ice moon Europa orbiting Jupiter, scheduled to launch in the 2020s.

Time will tell whether that was a smart decision— Europa orbits within the radiation belt of Jupiter. While

Cassini was able to provide data from Saturn and Enceladus for a decade, the *Europa Clipper* probably won't even last a year.

Parallel to that, ESA is considering the mission *JUICE* (JUpiter ICy moons Explorer). The plan is to have a probe arrive near Jupiter in 2030 and explore the ice moons Ganymede, Callisto, and Europa for three years. They, at minimum, expect to discover an ocean on Europa similar to that on Enceladus, though the ice layer is considerably thicker there.

So far, *ELF* (Enceladus Life Finder) only exists as a proposal. It should be launched no sooner than 2021 and the goal is to hunt for traces of life, such as amino acids or fatty acids, in the water vapor of the geysers. For this purpose, the probe would make several flights through geyser eruptions. Parallel to that, NASA and JAXA are jointly developing *LIFE* (Life Investigation For Enceladus), a probe that could take samples from the geysers and bring them back to Earth. In 2015, both projects applied for one of five spots in NASA's Discovery Program (in which each mission cannot cost more than 450 million dollars). Yet when the decision was made in the summer of 2016, neither of the two missions was selected.

Yet there is some hope for the future. The lower-priced *Discovery* missions focus on using only proven technologies. *ELF* and *LIFE* would have used solar energy, which is rather optimistic at that distance from the sun. The *Europa* mission (which also uses solar energy) could now demonstrate that this technology has matured.

Furthermore, NASA announced in early 2016 that it would also accept proposals explicitly for expeditions to Titan and Enceladus for its New Frontiers program. This program (of which the New Horizons probe to Pluto was a part) accepts innovative technologies—and such proposed missions can be more expensive, in the two to three billion dollar range. In 2017, NASA selected a proposed mission to Enceladus as the recipient of technology funds in preparation for future mission competitions. Therefore, it is not improbable that *ELF* might be revived.

Flying to Enceladus with a Crew?

CURRENTLY, humanity lacks the technological capability of sending a manned spaceship to Saturn and its moons—at least if one looks at it realistically. A robot probe can take as much time as it needs and can do without many things humans absolutely need—life support (oxygen, water, food,) gravity, protection against radiation, a return ticket. While it might be possible in principle to build a spaceship for a Saturn mission with today's technology, it would be very, very expensive.

The *Juno* probe, which weighed almost four tons and entered an orbit around Jupiter in the fall of 2016, cost about a billion dollars. A manned spaceship would be at least ten times heavier and more complex. After all, it would have to accelerate for the return flight and then decelerate again. Therefore, it does not just need twice as much fuel, but several times as much. Considering all these requirements, it might cost 100 billion dollars or more. *Juno*, the fastest probe so far, took five years to reach Jupiter —and Saturn is twice as far from us. Therefore, the crew would spend 20 years on this mission.

However, there are already propulsion concepts that might offer alternatives ten or twenty years from now.

A magnetoplasmadynamic drive (MPD) uses very strong magnetic fields to accelerate a reaction mass (like the noble gas argon or the metal lithium) out of the thruster. This makes high exit-velocities of up to 40 km/s possible. A spaceship thus equipped could reach Saturn in one to two years. A current commercial variant is called VASIMR. Its manufacturer, Ad Astra, built a 100 kw prototype that, in a mid-2017 NASA test, worked for 100 continuous hours. One drawback of the MPD, though, is that it only works with an energy input of electricity. As solar energy is rather sparse in the environs of Saturn, one would need a small nuclear reactor, or Radioisotope Thermoelectric Generator (RTG). The latter creates electricity from the heat released by the decay of plutonium.

Another alternative would be a nuclear drive. The concept was already developed in the 1950s, 'Project Orion.' Back then, the plan was to ignite a nuclear bomb behind a spaceship (which was shielded by a large mirror) to propel it this way. Using about 1,000 such bomb ignitions in sequence, Saturn could be reached in one or two years. However, these days it would hardly be acceptable to send real atom bombs into space by rocket. The concept was further developed into Mini-Mag Orion. In that project, a small piece of fissile material would be compressed in a magnetic field until it ignited in a miniature explosion. Even that would not be possible without releasing damaging radiation, so the drive would have to be carefully shielded.

The most promising concept these days seems to be the Direct Fusion Drive (DFD). The idea of using nuclear fusion for powering a spaceship has been discussed since the 1990s. In contrast to nuclear fission, nuclear fusion does not create very much radioactive garbage. The only problem might be released neutrons, which then might be captured by stable atoms, turning them into unstable nuclides. Currently, the company Princeton Satellite Systems (PSS) is predominantly active in this field of research, and it also advised me on this book. In the DFD conceptualized by PSS, deuterium (heavy hydrogen) reacts with helium-3 (an isotope of helium) to form helium-4. It achieves an exit velocity of 70 km/s. Under these conditions, a spaceship would reach Mars in a month and Saturn in a year. The fusion reactor generates relatively few neutrons, so the spaceship would not require cumbersome shielding. At the same time, the DFD also generates electricity.

Neither deuterium nor helium-3 is radioactive. However, helium-3 is quite expensive, as it is very rare. There are only about 3,000 tons present in the entire atmosphere of Earth. The annual consumption on Earth is approximately eight kilograms, and one kilogram of the gas costs about 16 million dollars. PSS estimates a round-trip flight to Saturn would require about 20 kilograms of helium-3. Earth's moon might be a good source. In its upper rock formations, the content of helium-3 is up to 1,000 times higher than on Earth. A DFD could also serve as a source of energy for everything a human crew would want to do on Enceladus.

The final proof of the existence of life on Enceladus could, in all probability, only be found by an expedition directly exploring its ocean. The conditions on Enceladus are actually quite good for this, as at least parts of the ice crust are thinner than on other moons.

Humans have experience drilling through layers of ice.

Usually, conventional drill rigs are used for this, but it would be impractical to take them along to Enceladus.

The alternative would be a cryobot, an ice-drilling robot already developed by the German physicist Karl Philberth in the 1960s. In 1968, his 'Philberth Probe' reached a depth of 1,000 meters in the Greenland ice sheet.

The current leader in this area is the U.S. company Stone Aerospace with its '*Valkyrie.*' This 'Very deep Autonomous Laser-powered Kilowatt-class Yo-yoing Robotic Ice Explorer' is partially financed by NASA. It does not carry an energy source on board, but is supplied by a laser via a fiber-optic cable. Currently, Stone Aerospace is testing their *Valkyrie* with a power level of 5-kilowatts on Earth. The version for Enceladus would have to be considerably larger, but it would work according to the same principle. It would need from 250 kilowatts upwards to 1 megawatt of power. The more power, the faster the cryobot can drill, although "drill" is not really the correct term. The laser heats up the water, and the hot water is aimed at the ice, which then melts like butter. This works more quickly and requires less maintenance (which is very important) than a metal drill that would wear out. In addition, the hot water can also be used for generating energy. The fiber-optic cable, in turn, can be used for transmitting information.

However, the *Valkyrie* concept only works if you bring along a source of energy. One cannot simply generate 5 megawatts with an emergency generator. One would need a small nuclear power plant. Or one could use the dual function of the DFDs, each of which provides 10 megawatts of power. As Enceladus does not have an atmosphere, the energy could be beamed with negligible loss via laser from the orbiting vessel to the lander module, which then would feed it to *Valkyrie* through the fiber-optic cable.

Life on Enceladus?

IF THERE IS life on Enceladus, it would be located at the bottom of its ocean. Here, as already described, serpentinization reactions continually occur. These generate heat, hydrogen, and methane—each important for life. At the same time, other minerals that are important as nutrients for life might be dissolved in the water, along with the various salts it contains. The ocean probably has existed longer than there have been conditions on Earth suitable for life as we know it. Thus, there really was plenty of time.

Of course, these organisms would have to survive without photosynthesis, as no light reaches the bottom of the ocean. They also would have to go without oxygen. Yet even here on Earth, researchers have already identified three habitats with similar conditions. One of them found in the depths of a South African mine. It is based on radioactive decay energy and consists of bacteria-reducing sulfur. However, there is hardly any sulfur on Enceladus. The other two were found by scientists in volcanic rocks near hot springs deep below the ground. They are dominated by archaea. These organisms consume the hydrogen emerging here due to plate movements, and they burn it with carbon dioxide and generate the energy they need for living, as well as traceable byproduct amounts of methane and water. Together with bacteria and eukaryota, the archaea form the three domains of life, and they are the most ancient. Archaea are single-celled, and the DNA containing their genetic information is circular. They possess simple organs of movement (flagella) and sometimes build a kind of skeleton to stabilize their shape. They differ from bacteria in the structure of the ribosomal RNA, which is responsible for translating genetic information into proteins.

On Earth, archaea are often found under extreme conditions. Some varieties only flourish at temperatures above 80 degrees Celsius, while others prefer living in highly concentrated saline solutions, or very acidic or alkaline environments (pH value below 0 or above 10). Even the pressure at the bottom of the ocean, which measures between 2.8 and 4.5 MPa, should pose no problem. After all, there are microorganisms in the Mariana Trench which can withstand a pressure of 50 MPa. Even multi-celled organisms like *Pseudoliparis amblystomopsis*, a species of snailfish, can survive under these conditions.

Archaea can also perform amazing feats—they are among the fastest creatures on Earth, for instance. In the category 'body lengths per second' they achieve a value of 400 to 500. A cheetah only reaches 20, a human 11, and a horse 7. A sports car would have to drive at 6,000 km/h to rival the archaea. The reason archaea are so much faster than bacteria is that they have more flagella (50 versus 5 to 7), and they can also rotate these faster, as they possess a more efficient 'motor.' Humans use archaea, among other things, in biogas systems to generate methane.

On Earth, the archaea, which on average measure one micrometer, are much more common and more important for chemical cycles than was long suspected. After all, they don't absolutely need extreme environmental conditions. They are as common in fresh water as in the sea, where in some areas they represent up to 90 percent of living beings, and in the soil. They also exist as symbionts in the intestinal tract of animals and humans. Archaea have even been found in the human navel. The total number of archaea in the oceans is estimated to be more than 10 to the power of 28, that is, a 1 followed by 28 zeroes. The estimated number of all cells in a human multiplied by the number of human beings is about 10 to the power of 22 (the number 1 followed by 22 zeroes), which is six magnitudes smaller.

How Life Might Have Started

We do not know yet whether Enceladus harbors life—but if it does, it must have started at some point in time, with either the chicken or the egg. We are not sure about what happened afterward, even in the case of Earth. There are two theories about the origin of life that might also apply to Enceladus.

Theory 1: Origin in the Primordial Soup

The theory that inorganic molecules in a water-based 'primordial soup' randomly combine to form the first organic compounds, and then assemble the most primitive forms of cells, was proposed by Charles Darwin. In 1953, Stanley Miller and Harold Urey showed in a spectacular experiment how this might have happened on Earth. They had simulated lightning striking a mixture of methane, ammonia, water vapor, and hydrogen. Within two weeks, various amino acids had formed in the solution. These complex molecules are the basic building blocks of life.

Miller and Urey were wrong concerning the possible composition of the primordial soup, and they did not create life, but the experiment proved that under the right circumstances complex molecules can be formed from simple compounds. These basic materials and the necessary energy supply in the form of heat are also present on Enceladus, and they have been for billions of years.

THEORY 2: Origin from Hydrothermal Vents

At the bottom of Earth's oceans, hot water, in which various chemicals are dissolved, emerges from the crust of the planet. Some vents eject water with a temperature of almost 500 degrees. These might have been the places where life developed on Earth. In such places, chemical energy provided by the vents in the form of dissolved reduced gases meets with suitable reaction partners. If such vents exist at the bottom of the Enceladus Ocean, they could also form the starting point for life. After life developed at such hotspots, it could have gradually adapted to cooler environments and spread across the entire ocean.

THANKS FOR VISITING Enceladus with me! I hope you had a pleasurable ride. If you'd like to see all these places in their colorful glory, you can get the PDF version of the *Guided Tour of Enceladus* for free by leaving me your e-mail address at: hard-sf.com/subscribe

Glossary of Acronyms

AI – Artificial Intelligence
API –Application Program Interface; Acoustic Properties Instrument
ASCAN – AStronaut CANdidate
AU – Astronomical Unit (the distance from the Earth to the sun)
BIOS – Basic Input/Output System
C&DH – Command & Data Handling
CapCom – Capsule Communicator
Cas – CRISPR-associated system
CELSS – Closed Ecological Life Support System
CIA – (U.S.) Central Intelligence Agency
COAS – Crewman Optical Alignment Site
Comms – Communiques
CRISPR – Clustered Regularly Interspaced Short Palindromic Repeats
DEC PDP-11 – Digital Equipment Corporation Programmable Data Processor-11
DFD – Direct Fusion Drive
DISR – Descent Imager / Spectral Radiometer

DNA – DeoxriboNeucleic Acid

DoD – (U.S.) Department of Defense

DPS – Data Processing Systems specialist (known as Dipsy)

DSN – Deep Space Network

ECDA – Enhanced Cosmic Dust Analyzer

EECOM – Electrical, Environmental, COnsumables, and Mechanical

EGIL – Electrical, General Instrumentation, and Lighting

EJSM – Europa Jupiter System Mission

ELF – Enceladus Life Finder

EMU – Extravehicular Mobility Unit

ESA – European Space Agency

EVA – ExtraVehicular Activity

F1 – Function 1 (Help function on computer keyboards)

FAST – (Chinese) Five-hundred-meter Aperture Spherical Telescope

FAO – Flight Activities Office

FCR – Flight Control Room

FD – Flight Director

FIDO – FlIght Dynamics Officer

Fortran – FORmula TRANslation

g – g-force (gravitational force)

GBI – Green Bank Interferometer

GNC – Guidance, Navigation, and Control system

HAI – High-Altitude Indoctrination device

HASI – *Huygens* Atmospheric Structure Instrument

HP – HorsePower

HUT – Hard Upper Torso

IAU – International Astronomical Union

ILSE – International Life Search Expedition

INCO – INstrumentation and Communication Officer

IR – InfraRed

ISS-NG – International Space Station-Next Generation

IT – Information Technology
IVO – Io Volcano Explorer
JAXA – Japan Aerospace eXploration Agency
JET – Journey to Enceladus and Titan
JPL – Jet Propulsion Laboratory
JSC – Johnson Space Center
JUICE – JUpiter ICy moons Explorer
LCD – Liquid Crystal Display
LCVG – Liquid Cooling and Ventilation Garment
LEA – Launch, Entry, Abort spacesuit
LIFE – Life Investigation For Enceladus
LTA – Lower Torso Assembly
MAG – Maximum Absorbency Garment
MCC – Mission Control Center
MIT – Massachusetts Institute of Technology
MOM – Mission Operations Manager
MPa – MegaPascal
MPD – MagnetoPlasmadynamic Drive
MSDD – *Multi-station Spatial Disorientation Device*
NSA – National Security Agency
NASA – National Aeronautics and Space Administration
NEA – Near Earth Asteroids
PAO – Public Affairs Office
PC – Personal Computer
PE-UHMW – PolyEthylene-Ultra High Molecular Weight
PER – fluid PERmittivity sensor
PI – Principal Investigator
Prop – Propulsion
PSS – Princeton Satellite Systems
RCS – Reaction Control System
REF – REFractive index sensor
RNA – RiboNeucleic Acid
RTG – Radioisotope Thermoelectric Generator

SAFER – Simplified Aid For EVA Rescue
SIRI – Speech Interpretation and Recognition Interface
SFTP – SSH (Secure Socket sHell) File Transfer Protocol
SSP – Surface Science Package
SSR – Solid-State Recorder
TandEM – Titan and Enceladus Mission
TiME – TItan Mare Explorer
TNO – Trans-Neptunian Object
TSSM – Titan Saturn System Mission
UTC –Universal Time Coordinated
Valkyrie – Very deep Autonomous Laser-powered Kilo-
watt-class Yo-yoing Robotic Ice Explorer
VASIMR – VAriable Specific Impulse Magnetoplasma
Rocket
VR – Virtual Reality
WHC – Waste Hygiene Compartment

Metric to English Conversions

It is assumed that by the time the events of this novel take place, the United States will have joined the rest of the world and will be using the International System of Units, the modern form of the metric system.

Length:
centimeter = 0.39 inches
meter = 1.09 yards, or 3.28 feet
kilometer = 1093.61 yards, or 0.62 miles

Area:
square centimeter = 0.16 square inches
square meter = 1.20 square yards
square kilometer = 0.39 square miles

Weight:
gram = 0.04 ounces
kilogram = 35.27 ounces, or 2.20 pounds

Volume:

liter = 1.06 quarts, or 0.26 gallons
cubic meter = 35.31 cubic feet, or 1.31 cubic yards

Temperature:
To convert Celsius to Fahrenheit, multiply by 1.8 and then add 32

Copyright

Brandon Q. Morris

--

Web: hard-sf.com
E-Mail: brandon@hard-sf.com
Facebook: www.facebook.com/BrandonQMorris/
Translator: Frank Dietz, Ph.D. Editor: Pamela Bruce, B.S.
Final editing: Marcia Kwiecinski, A.A.S., and Stephen Kwiecinski, B.S.
Technical Advisors: Michael Paluszek (President, Princeton Satellite Systems), Dr. Ludwig Hellmann
Cover Design: BJ Coverbookdesigns.com
Brandon Q. Morris is a registered trademark of the author.

Printed in Great Britain
by Amazon